SARAH McCARTY

Luke's Cut

HQN™

If you purchased this book without a cover you should be aware that this book is stolen property. It was reported as "unsold and destroyed" to the publisher, and neither the author nor the publisher has received any payment for this "stripped book."

ISBN-13: 978-0-373-80423-8

Luke's Cut

Recycling programs for this product may not exist in your area.

Copyright © 2017 by Sarah McCarty

All rights reserved. Except for use in any review, the reproduction or utilization of this work in whole or in part in any form by any electronic, mechanical or other means, now known or hereinafter invented, including xerography, photocopying and recording, or in any information storage or retrieval system, is forbidden without the written permission of the publisher, HQN Books, 225 Duncan Mill Road, Don Mills, Ontario M3B 3K9, Canada.

This is a work of fiction. Names, characters, places and incidents are either the product of the author's imagination or are used fictitiously, and any resemblance to actual persons, living or dead, business establishments, events or locales is entirely coincidental.

This edition published by arrangement with Harlequin Books S.A.

For questions and comments about the quality of this book, please contact us at CustomerService@Harlequin.com.

® and TM are trademarks of Harlequin Enterprises Limited or its corporate affiliates. Trademarks indicated with ® are registered in the United States Patent and Trademark Office, the Canadian Intellectual Property Office and in other countries.

www.HQNBooks.com

Printed in U.S.A.

Read more about the daring heroes of Hell's Eight in these titles

Praise for Sarah McCarty's men of Hell's Eight

"McCarty is a sparse, minimalistic writer, with a great ear for dialogue. She's a passionate observer of history, and manages to deftly and accurately weave her spicy stories through with important facts and issues of the epoch she invokes. She's also good at capturing that intangible magnetism surrounding dangerous, rugged men… I'm hooked."

—USATODAY.com

"If you like your historicals packed with emotion, excitement and heat, you can never go wrong with a book by Sarah McCarty."

—Romance Junkies

"It's so great to see that Ms. McCarty is able to truly take these eight men and give them such vastly different stories and vastly different heroines, all of whom allow us to see different aspects of what life was really like for Western Frontier women, be it good, horrific, or simply unfortunate."

—Romance Books Forum

"Sarah McCarty's series is an exciting blend of raw masculinity, spunky, feisty heroines and the wild living in the Old West…with spicy, hot love scenes. Ms. McCarty gave us small peeks into each member of the Hell's Eight and I'm looking forward to reading the other men's stories."

—Erotica Romance Writers

"What really sets McCarty's stories apart from simple erotica is the complexity of her characters and conflicts… Definitely spicy, but a great love story, too."

—RT Book Reviews

"Readers who enjoy erotic romance but haven't found an author who can combine it with a historical setting may discover a new auto-buy author…I have."

—All About Romance

Dedicated to my wonderful editor, my fabulous agent and all my fantastic fans. It's been a great journey with the men of Hell's Eight. Thank you so much for being on this wild ride with me.

CHAPTER ONE

Simple, Texas, August 1861

Damn! He'd been outmaneuvered by a man twenty years his senior. Luke Bellen leaned against a post on the front porch and observed as the distinguished, blond-haired victor claimed the spoils. The normally smooth-running Hell's Eight Ranch was bursting at the seams with celebratory chaos. All because Hester MacFairlane had gone and married Jarl Wayfield. Right here at Hell's Eight, before God, the padre and half the town. No one could have seen that coming.

Luke had to admit though, during the past few weeks of upset, panic and last-minute wedding preparations, the women had managed to soften the ranch's rough edges. For sure he'd never seen the Hell's Eight looking so festive. Lazy breezes ruffled the ties on the smartly dressed men, the women's full skirts and the cheery, bright pink bows tied to every post within sight of the side yard. Everyone was wearing their biggest smile and their Sunday best. And Luke was no exception. But for some reason the whole day—the whole event—was aggravating the piss out of him.

It didn't matter that he hadn't seriously been in the game or that he was happy for the bride. Nor that he figured just enough of his father's teachings lingered in him that he didn't like to lose. Taking a sip of his lemonade, he grimaced as he swallowed the bitter reality. The truth was that he was jealous. If he could've made himself care the way he'd needed to, that could've been him standing up there with Hester, thanking the well-wishers and letting the stream of congratulations pour into his annoying internal demand for *more* and fill it up until it was too sated to nag him.

It might have been easier to accept the loss if Hester had chosen Jarl because the man had more money or more prestige than Luke, but money wasn't the spur to Hester's get along. The woman had more confidence than six liquored-up cowboys on a Saturday night. It was one of the things that had attracted him to her. No one could seize an opportunity like Hester, but she was also down-to-earth and perceptive, and she'd seen right through Luke's not-what-it-should-be interest, then turned to someone who could offer his heart along with his hand. He gave the lemonade a swirl, watching the light play hide-and-seek with the shadows. *Dammit.* Why the hell hadn't he been able to offer Hester what she needed?

The bottom step creaked in that familiar way he'd grown used to over the last nine months. He looked up.

"Looks like you could use something stronger," Ace said, advancing to join him. Sunlight glinted off the whiskey bottle he held up as he leaned a hip against the opposite porch rail.

Luke pushed his hat back. "How'd you know?"

Wry humor lurked in Ace's blue eyes as he uncorked the bottle. "You've never been one for losing gracefully."

Luke tossed the lemonade over the rail. "Age changes a man."

Ace snorted and filled Luke's glass. "You oughtta be six shots into the bottle before you start spitting nonsense like that."

"I'll be thirty-two next week." And beyond a couple dozen novels and his place in the Hell's Eight, he didn't have a damn thing to show for the time spent.

"You trying to tell me you can't still tear up the town?"

No. He just didn't enjoy it the way he used to. "The difference is, now it takes days to recover."

Ace filled his own glass. "Thirty-two or not, only a fool would bet against you in a fight."

Luke looked Ace up and down, from his scuffed boots to his serviceable pants and blue shirt, all the way up to his battered Stetson. The only concession to the formal occasion was a narrow tie around his neck. There was no sense pointing out gamblers were supposed to be sharp dressers. Ace went his own way. Always had. Always would. That didn't mean Luke couldn't prod him a bit. "Speaking of bets, after fleecing Jarl's pockets last week, couldn't you afford a new suit?"

Ace smiled. "You heard about that?"

"A twenty-six-hour poker game?" Luke swirled the amber liquid and watched a sunbeam make light of the potent beverage. "Do you think anyone in the territory hasn't?"

Ace's smile took on a feral edge. "Not if I have anything to say about it."

There would only be one reason for that. Ace was spreading the word. "Banking on a flood of hopefuls challenging you to a fifty-two-card duel?"

"Damn straight. Petunia's been harping about new furniture. Seems now the walls are painted, what we have is 'tired and sad.'" Ace took a drink and shook his head. "How the hell does furniture get 'sad'?"

Luke chuckled. "I haven't a clue. Did you ask?"

Ace cut him a look. "I might be still a newlywed, but I'm not stupid."

Ace had married Jarl's daughter, Petunia Wayfield, last winter. Funny how small the world got when a body stayed in one place too long.

"Well, Petunia is one opinionated woman."

Ace raised his glass in tacit agreement. "The word you're looking for is *stubborn*."

"Said the pot about the kettle." Ace and Petunia's courtship had been as much about love as about compromise. He'd never seen two people more determined to swing the deal to their point of view than those two. And enjoy it. He'd always doubted there'd be a woman who could go toe-to-toe with Ace, but Petunia had proven him wrong. She brought balance to Ace. And he to her.

"What makes you say that?"

Luke took in Ace's too-long brown hair, and well-worn clothes. Ace was a good-looking man, but he wasn't one for putting a polish on his shine. "The fact that you haven't taken me up on that appointment with my tailor."

"I'm a busy man."

A year ago, Ace had been a single gambler living above the saloon. Now he had a wife, a house and the responsibility of a school for unwanted children.

"Not only busy, you're living proof life can change on a gust of wind." He took a sip of the whiskey. He still wasn't sure how he felt about that.

"Not everything changes." Ace sobered. "We won't."

Luke touched his glass to Ace's, feeling the weight of the lie as he said it. "No, not us."

They'd been best friends from the moment they'd met outside the one-room building that served as church, school and town hall in the small border town with Mexico where his father had moved his family. They'd been so innocent then, insulated by their faith in their parents' dreams. They'd had no understanding of the tensions between the Mexican army and the Texan settlers. They'd just been friends enjoying the sunshine and the wild beauty of their new home. Their friendship had been tested by the onslaught of the war, but nothing had changed their commitment—not the massacre that occurred when the Mexican army had swarmed their town and taken their families, not the years of revenge upon which the eight surviving boys had embarked that had built their reputations as Hell's Eight, nor the struggle in the last few years to go from wild Texas Rangers to stable ranchers. But this becoming stable thing, it was taking Ace and the rest of the Eight to places Luke couldn't go. There was no way around it, he wasn't fitting in as easily with the rest of Hell's Eight as he used to.

"You could have at least polished your boots."

Ace held up the bottle. "Yours are polished enough for the both of us."

Luke held out his empty glass.

"Technically, it's your turn to be doing the tipping," Ace pointed out.

"I poured at your wedding."

"That doesn't count. Pouring at the wedding is the best man's job." Ace refilled each of their glasses and then set the bottle on the sanded planks of the porch. His expression sobered right along with his tone. With a jerk of his chin he indicated the wedding group. "Are you all right with this?"

Ace worried too much. "Why wouldn't I be?"

"Maybe because just a while back you were telling me how you'd give your eyeteeth to have a steady woman with whom to settle down, build a family…"

Damn Ace for his memory. "I think I was drinking at the time."

"Not that much."

"Uh-huh."

"Rumor was you were sweet on Hester."

Luke could feel the weight of Ace's concern. "She had potential."

Ace's gaze turned assessing. "It's not like you to underestimate a situation."

Luke switched his attention to the happy couple who were holding hands and sharing a smile warmer than the hot August sun. No doubt about it, they looked right together. Another pang of what-if hit. He shook it off. No bigger waste of a man's time than pondering what-ifs. "Truth is, I just wasn't any competition for your father-in-law."

"Uh-huh." Despite the skepticism in those two syllables, Ace changed the subject. "Our Hester's come a long way, hasn't she?"

"That she has."

Looking at Hester now, dressed in the beautiful pale pink gown that clashed somehow perfectly with her red, curly hair, it was hard to believe that she'd been abandoned by her husband and forced into prostitution to feed her children. It'd been a scandal around Simple when her new fiancé, Jarl, had filed a petition for divorce on Hester's behalf to formally sever her ties to her former husband, who'd already remarried. It'd been a bold move that had cost the mayor his position and his new family. Jarl Wayfield didn't fool around when it came to what was his. Luke had to respect him for that. "Dougall should have done right by Hester rather than trying to grind her into the dirt."

Ace lifted his drink toward the newlyweds in a silent toast. "Got to respect a man who knows how to dole out payback."

"Yeah, well, wherever his sorry ass is, I'm sure

Dougall wishes Jarl was a bit less proficient. That arrogance of Dougall's cost him everything."

Dougall had slipped out of town in the dead of night right after the scandal became public. Disgrace had lingered in his wake like a vindictive cloud. There'd be no getting that reputation back. Especially with Jarl funding explicit wanted posters all over the country. Jarl had no intention of giving the man peace.

Luke took another sip. This time without the grimace. Whiskey had always had a way of making things more palatable. "You know we're indebted to Jarl now. Hell's Eight owed Hester for protecting Petunia when that drunk Brian tried to kill her."

"Petunia only acted after she noticed he was beating his kid every time he tied one on. Which was nightly," Ace reminded him.

"You don't have to defend her actions to me," Luke soothed. "I went with you to fetch him, remember?" Recalling how the boy had looked when they'd rode up to that dilapidated shack Brian called a home, thin and bruised in clothes as tattered as his trust, Luke just gritted his teeth. Some men didn't deserve their sons. "Doesn't change the fact that in his eyes, she stole his son."

Ace's expression hardened. "He needed stealing."

Ace had a soft spot for kids and underdogs. "Yeah he did, but I still can't decide if your wife is one of the bravest women I know or the most foolish. A lot of men would be afraid to go up against Brian and his temper yet Petunia never hesitated."

Ace's expression softened around the edges the way it always did when he thought about his wife. "She's got a reckless side, for sure."

"To match yours." Luke smiled, waiting for the inevitable response. It wasn't long in coming,

Ace glanced at him out of the corner of his eye. "I prefer calculated risks to impulsive actions."

"Uh-huh." Luke suppressed a smile. "The fact remains, the kid's much happier living at the orphanage Petunia started."

"Don't let Petunia hear you call her school an orphanage. She'd likely spill that drink into the dirt."

Luke sighed. "The woman has no respect for good liquor."

"Not a lick." Ace swirled his drink with a certain satisfaction. "You realize that since Jarl paid our debt to Hester by taking care of Dougall, we now owe that hardheaded son of a bitch."

"Yup." And he wasn't upset with the reality. Texas wasn't a place for the weak. It was a hard land that demanded strong alliances to survive. Jarl might be an Easterner, but he'd proven himself.

Luke took another drink and let the liquor bite into his melancholy as happiness floated all around him, captured in the melodic trill of songbirds and the laughter of the guests. There, but somehow just out of reach. Damn, weddings were depressing.

A feminine voice rose above the cheer. Sweet and high, resonating with deeper notes that stroked along Luke's nerves like a silk glove. A tightening in his groin heralded recognition. The little photographer,

Josie Kinder. Like a homing pigeon, his gaze narrowed in on her. Jarl had brought the woman out from back East, his wedding gift to Hester—a photographic record of their union. All the guests were excited to have their image plastered flat on a piece of metal. And Josie was just as excited to do it.

Luke was unfathomably excited about the photographer. Unfathomably because, at first glance, she had no confidence, no fashion sense and no social skills. But that first impression didn't hold up once she brought out her camera. Once she picked up the camera, she changed in an indefinable way that was at once both mysterious and challenging. He was a sucker for a challenge.

He watched her direct people around, the feathers in her beribboned hat bobbing as she bustled about, putting people here and there and positioning them this way and that. She looked for all the world like a child bossing about her elders until she turned sideways and those curves of hers swelled into view. Damn, that woman was blessed with a fine figure.

Ace followed his gaze. He pushed back his hat and his eyebrows rose. "So that's how it is."

Luke ignored the twitch of Ace's lips. The problem with good friends was sometimes they knew you too well.

"Keep your nose out of my business, Ace," he muttered.

"Like you kept yours out of mine?"

"No."

Josie bustled about, waving folk back into place

as they shifted with impatience. Luke couldn't help but watch. Whatever it took to make a photograph, it wasn't quick. She tripped over her skirt. Half the people she'd just positioned—the male half—lunged to catch her. She was completely oblivious to their interest. He could almost hear the collective disappointment as she grabbed the hitching post and saved herself. There was no mistaking her exasperation though when she turned and saw what remained of her perfectly balanced group. "For the love of Pete. You moved!"

He smiled as she snapped her skirts straight and marched back, shooing her would-be rescuers back into position. It'd be a miracle if they got one picture done before the sun set. His cock stirred as he admired her. There was something completely charming about the woman when she went all martinet.

"I wouldn't have thought her your type," Ace mused.

Josie finally ducked beneath the little curtain attached to the camera. The position gave him a fine view of her admirable ass. Luke's cock twitched again.

"Fine women are always my type."

This time it was Ace who said, "Uh-huh." No little amount of skepticism in those syllables.

Luke reconsidered his initial decision not to dabble with the little Easterner. Even a night or two in her arms before she headed back East might be worth it. She wasn't a young girl. He'd place her age around twenty-five. The fact that she'd come out West to take pictures pointed to an independent nature. The two combined made for a chance she'd be open to a discreet encounter. Anticipation thrummed harder as he contemplated that possibility. It'd been a long time since a woman had been able to make him anticipate a glimpse of her.

Ace braced his foot on the bottom railing encompassing the porch and changed the subject. "Did I ever tell you I read your books?"

Shit. He hated for anyone to know he wrote fairy-tale novels about the Wild West for bored Easterners. Let alone read one. His writing was the one thing that connected him to the time before the massacre. The part that didn't fit the life he'd first been forced into and then, later, chosen. The novels were the only part of the dream his mother had had for him that he'd managed to keep alive. "No."

Ace just shook his head and sighed. "I don't know why you're so secretive about the damn things."

Luke just shrugged. There was no way to explain he was embarrassed.

"I've known you since we were three years old," Ace said exasperatedly. "Since before the damn Mexican army came into the village and wrecked our lives. I stood with you while we buried your parents. You stood with me while I cried over mine. Hell, you even dropped my bride into my lap when she got all stubborn."

"What'd you expect me to do? You were being inconveniently self-sacrificing and she wanted to talk my ear off about it."

"So you kidnapped her and plopped her in my bedroom?"

"Seemed the quickest way to bring back the peace."

Ace just shook his head and took a sip. "There's a get-it-done wild side to you. And the woman that'll match up with you, she's got to have that same drop-it-in-your-lap wildness."

Maybe Ace did know him too well. All of the Hell's Eight had been shifting from wild to leading more acceptable lives, from Caine to the wildest of them all—Shadow. All of them except Luke. "Wild doesn't match well with acceptable."

Ace snorted. "Shoot, Luke, there's about a thousand different ways people interpret acceptable. You just need someone who sees it the way you do. Hester's a good woman, but she wants a little house with a picket fence perched around it, lemonade on Sundays and a man who loves her. That's not you."

"I might have worked up to loving her." Luke didn't know why he was belaboring the point. Maybe because he just didn't want Ace to be right. Or maybe he wanted to be proven wrong.

Ace shrugged. "Maybe you could've loved her enough eventually, but for sure she couldn't ever love you like you need."

Luke swallowed the last of his drink. "What the hell makes you think that?"

"Because she just sent me over here."

"What the hell for? She's up there kissing her husband."

And she was. With all the enthusiasm that he wanted someone to feel for him. That he wanted to feel for someone, but never had. Sometimes, he wondered if he was dead inside, just a ghost of himself, haunting his own existence.

With a shake of his head, Ace reached into his pocket and drew out a note. "She asked me to give you this."

Luke took the carefully folded piece of paper. As he opened it, Ace added, "Just like it says there. You need someone who can love you from the inside out."

He cocked a brow at his friend. "You read it?"

Ace didn't look even a little bit embarrassed. "Of course."

Of course. Sometimes being wrapped so tightly in a knot with others was not a bonus. Luke glanced down at the slip of paper. "Then I guess I'd better catch up."

Luke read the note written in Hester's blunt, confident style.

Ace's tone softened as Luke refolded it. "She couldn't give you what you need, Luke."

Luke nodded, looking beyond the celebration, beyond the limits of the ranch to the mountains beyond. "I know."

Inside, the impatience he'd been fighting for months surged, anticipation rode double, prickling along his nerves. It'd been a long time since he'd had an adventure. With Ace married and Hester off the market, his reasons for staying in Simple were few. Almost nonexistent.

His gaze returned to Josie as she grabbed the tintype out of the camera and rushed to the wagon. She was such a mousy woman when not busy taking pictures. So shy he had yet to discern the color of her eyes, but once she brought out that wooden contraption of a camera, the real woman came front and center. Gone was the blushing, tongue-tied miss. And in her place was a woman who knew exactly how to get what she wanted.

It was an intriguing dichotomy. The glimpses of the woman beneath the crushing shyness were like catching a hint of a plot twist in a clever mystery novel. She intrigued and tempted. She was a challenge wrapped up in a self-deprecating package that was very intricately constructed; it just didn't fit the sense he had in his gut about her. He would love to have a conversation with her, to find out if her mind matched the impact of her body. He had a feeling it did.

He watched as she stumbled getting into the wagon. As he knew she would, she looked over her shoulder at him, eyes narrowed as if he were to blame for her clumsiness. And maybe he was. If she was as aware of him as he was of her, then she had to know he'd been staring. Just as he suspected she'd been staring at him a time or two. A pang of regret wove through the anticipation of a new adventure. Unfortunately, Josie was one bit of exploration he was going to miss. He didn't have the time or the patience for a fling. With a defiant toss of her head, she climbed into the wagon. And that fast, he reconsidered his decision. Some challenges just begged to be met.

HE WAS WATCHING HER. The well-dressed man with the broad shoulders and I-dare-you glare was watching her. Josie could feel his gaze like fingertips skimming her skin with sensual inquiry, looking for a reaction and getting it as her fingers trembled and her neck muscles tightened. If he were touching her, he'd feel the heat rise off her skin, see the pink flush of her cheeks. Oh darn, maybe he could see it from over there. She ducked her head just a little. Just enough for the shade of her bonnet to provide cover from potential revelation.

Look away. Look away.

The plea went unheard. More prickles of awareness flustered her composure. Even more flustering was the reality of who that man was. Luke Bellen. One of the infamous Hell's Eight. Men said to chew nails and spit bullets, eat danger for breakfast and gather women like wildflowers. Another shiver went down her spine at the thought. She didn't want to be gathered.

Liar.

The accusation came from within.

"Traitor," she whispered back. The last thing she needed right now was an ill-advised sense of temptation distracting her from the job for which she'd traveled so far. She was here to commemorate the wedding of her Uncle Jarl. Big and blustery, a handsome, hard-eyed businessman, Jarl Wayfield was very dear to her, and while not actually blood, he was as close to a real father as she'd ever had. From the day he'd come courting her mother, they'd had a bond. When his relationship with her mother had ended, he'd stuck around in the background of Josie's life. She'd long since stopped wishing he was her father and instead settled for the security he offered.

He was probably the only one who saw the sense of adventure that lurked beneath her persistent shyness. And he'd indulged it by summoning her away from the smothering small town in which she'd been born and the ever-stifling presence of her overly judgmental mother. Without him she wouldn't have this opportunity to see the West, to indulge her passion for taking pictures. She owed him so much. Too much to let six feet of wide-shouldered, lean-hipped, dark-haired pure temptation take her off task. Still feeling the weight of Luke Bellen's gaze, she hurried on, almost dropping the tintype in the rush to her wagon.

Darn it!

The wagon had been an off-the-cuff purchase, but she only had so long to develop her images and hard experience told her that in a household environment, no one respected her need for darkness to do her work. They were forever trying to shed light on her process. These images were too important to risk. Jarl giving her this opportunity to photograph his wedding meant the world. His faith in her ability to forever capture this precious time was a much-needed boost to her flagging confidence.

Being dumped like yesterday's garbage by the man
to whom she'd thought she'd been discreetly engaged
for the past five years had been a hard lesson in hu-
mility. And shame. She'd been a fool to let Jason convince her to keep their engagement a secret. She'd
been more than a fool. She'd been an accomplice in
her own humiliation when he'd announced his engagement to another. And worse, expected her to
understand.

She grimaced as she opened the back of the peddler's wagon and stepped up. She hadn't understood.
She'd wanted to kill him. Her foot slipped and her
knee scraped the metal edge. She bit back a cry and
the need to burst into tears. She hated being emotional. She hated being clumsy even more. And truth
was, she was only clumsy when she was under scru-
tiny. So it was really all Bellen's fault.

Holding the tintype securely, she glared over her
shoulder at the cause of her distress. He didn't even
have the decency to show remorse. Instead, he stood
up there on the porch with another of the Hell's Eight,
nonchalantly leaning against the rough-hewn support, looking for all the world like a lion surveying
his pride. She had the childish urge to stick out her
tongue.

As if he heard the thought, he smiled at her, a
slow, knowing smile. The full-on flush started in her
toes, crept up her thighs, heated her chest and burned
in her cheeks. It was sheer bravado that had her snub-
bing him with a lift of her chin before pure unadul-
terated cowardice sent her diving into the wagon.

Cowardice had often been the bane of her existence. And sometimes, her salvation.

The door banged shut behind her. Placing the undeveloped tintype on the plank counter, she braced herself, hands spread across the uneven wood as she took a steadying breath. She was twenty-six years old, for heaven's sake. Far too old to be undone by a man's glance. But there was something about Luke that just ferreted its way past the defenses she'd built up over the years and reduced her to the cripplingly shy child she'd been. She hated it. She wanted to blame him. And if he only would say or do something other than observe her from afar, she probably could. But he didn't.

He was probably doing it on purpose.

She reached for the developing chemicals only to notice her hand was shaking. She took another breath and waited. The chemicals that made the miracle of photography possible were highly flammable. Not to mention noxious smelling. She needed a steady hand when dealing with them.

She soon discovered that standing in the hot, humid interior of the darkened wagon was not conducive to relaxation. Alone in the dark, it was too easy for her mind to wander. And without anything else to distract her attention, her mind inevitably wandered to Luke Bellen. As she was sure hundreds of other women's minds had done before.

All the men of Hell's Eight were compelling but there was something about Luke that stood out. There was a symmetry to his broad-shouldered, narrow-hipped, well-muscled body that made her breath catch. A smoothness in the way he moved that made her fingertips tingle. And the way his utter masculinity prowled beneath the nonchalance of his expressions... She sighed. Well, *that* just made her want to sink to the ground at his feet and let nature take its course.

If she let him, he would take advantage. She was sure of that. Just as he would with any other woman who succumbed to his blatant sexuality, no doubt. She had only to look back at her own engagement to see the folly of her first line of thought. Her fiancé, Jason, had nowhere near the presence Luke had, but it had been enough for her to convince herself the words he'd whispered in her ear were real. That the emotions he professed were honest. And that the passion he'd made her feel was unique to them. All that only to find out at her own long-awaited engagement party that he'd whispered those same words to, invoked those same passions in so many others. And she'd been such a blind fool, building excuses on top of her ignorance because the little he'd given her had been easier to accept than venturing back into the tenuous social position of being unclaimed. Bastards could only be so bold.

She grabbed the bottle of developer from the wooden box. Thank goodness Uncle Jarl had offered her this escape. More than once he'd been her salvation, often stepping in to give her breathing room from her mother's constant expectations. As he had this time when he'd sent her the tickets to come out to Texas—Texas!—to memorialize his wedding with her tintypes. Even if she hadn't been wanting to escape her mother's newest press for her to choose a husband— she loved her, but in some ways she was absolutely relentless—she would have jumped at the chance to come out to the wild-and-wonderful West she'd read so much about. Texas was just Texas. Big, wild and full of potential. She couldn't take two steps without wanting to pull out her camera box and capture a moment.

Her mother was constantly seeking ways to regain the respectability she'd abandoned when she'd fallen for the wrong man and had a child—Josie—out of wedlock, and the subsequent pressure for Josie to accept any invitation dropped off at the house was becoming impossible to duck. One of the reasons Josie had been thrilled to take up Uncle Jarl's invite was to escape that sudden increase in invitations. She was long past marriageable age anyway. She'd been cast aside. By all measures, she should be a pariah, but in the wake of her mother's suddenly full social calendar, Josie had just as suddenly been receiving callers. As those callers had been of a certain age, she'd had the uncomfortable feeling her mother had found a new way to increase her value as a marriage prospect. It was too mortifying to contemplate. And too distasteful. She did not want to marry an old man, no matter how good their tailors made them look in their suits.

And that fast, her thoughts were back to Bellen and the way he looked in *his* suit. So many men looked awkward in more formal attire. But that man wore his clothes the way he wore his confidence, as if they were an extension of some deeper secret. She opened the bottle. She would love to photograph him in all his untamed elegance. To catch the way the sun highlighted the lighter streaks in his brown hair. To see with her lens the answer to the mystery he posed. To know *him*.

Darn it. She had to stop thinking of that man. He wasn't for her. She couldn't even manage syllables when he was around. Wiping the sweat from her brow with her sleeve, she took a deep breath and released it slowly, feeling the oppressive heat settle around her as she did. Even parking the wagon in the shade of the big oak and opening the windows was not much help against the brutal Texas humidity. For sure, she wouldn't last long in the closed wagon. She needed to focus or she was going to complete the most ladylike faint of her life before she found out if she'd truly underexposed those last photos as much as she feared. It'd taken so long for the group to get in position and maintain it, the clouds had moved in. She'd tried to compensate, but there was more art than science in this endeavor. Pictures came out best in bright light.

Putting Luke and his disconcerting smile out of her head, she let herself fall into that calm, competent place that surrounded her whenever she worked on her photography. Worry could wait a few minutes to torment her. Right now she had a picture to develop.

It wasn't the all-absorbing consolation it usually was.

Darn it again.

Luke sighed when Josie didn't come back out of the wagon, accepting the show was over for the day, but his interest lingered on past his acceptance. His curiosity was, as always, piqued by the contrast between the exotic depth of the woman's photographs and her downplayed appearance. And it had to be deliberate because any man who gave her a second glance couldn't miss the red hints in her hair or the porcelain clarity of her skin that made a body wonder if that same white smoothness extended beneath her clothes. Oh yes, there was something about Josie Kinder, something more than her self-effacing ways, her sexy, plumply curved body and her utter lack of awareness of her own appeal, that called to him. She might by all accountings look like a shy wren to be pitied, but he didn't want to pity her. He wanted to ravage her. And he'd be damned if he had a clue as to why.

"She's really not your usual type," Ace said from beside him, following his gaze as he took a sip from his whiskey.

Damn. Was he being that obvious? "I wasn't aware I had one."

"Oh, you have one." The whiskey in his glass caught the sun as he motioned toward the wagon. "But it doesn't lean toward shy innocents."

That shy innocent was watching him. Luke could feel it. "I'm leaving in a few days."

Ace nodded. "I figured. You've been restless since Hester announced her wedding."

And his tone again implied that Hester's choice was the reason. And it was, but not in the way Ace thought.

Luke shrugged and took a sip from his near-empty glass. The liquor slid down his throat in a smooth burn. Not like the days when rot-gut was the best they could buy. "Hell's Eight can't trust Tia's safety to just anyone."

Ace cut him a glance. "I wouldn't exactly call Zach Lopez 'just anyone.'"

The Montoya foreman was rattlesnake mean, coyote clever and generally a force to be reckoned with. "True, but I'm riding along."

Ace wasn't soothed. The man had always had a problem leaving things to others. "I don't like the thought of Tia out there at all. Especially after what happened to Pet…"

Petunia's kidnapping had been a near miss. Fortunately they'd gotten to her in time. "Nothing happened that couldn't be fixed."

Luke had to believe that, considering he'd been the one to put Petunia on that stage and straight into the arms of a Comanche raiding party. But it wasn't something he could just up and ask Ace.

"I'd feel better if Tia would wait until fall, when preparing for winter will keep the Comanche busy elsewhere," Ace muttered.

So would Luke, but as Sam's wife, Bella was Hell's Eight. Full of fire, courage and an unlimited amount of sass, she fit into the group as if made for them. He swirled the last swallow of whiskey in his glass. "There's no way Tia's going to miss delivering Bella and Sam's first child. Not after she promised to be there."

Ace frowned across the yard at Tia, who'd joined the group around the bride and groom. "She's not a young woman anymore."

Luke echoed his frown as the sun caught the gray in Tia's shiny black hair. When had Tia decided to get old? "She isn't in her grave, either. And that's what I think it would take to keep her away from this birth. Especially since Sam asked her to come." He attempted to change the subject. "You know, of all of the Eight, he's her favorite."

Ace snorted. "Tia isn't here to rile with that accusation, so you can just drop it and stop trying to change the subject." His frown deepened. "What the hell was Sam thinking?"

Luke didn't know, but it had to be serious. "That he needs her. He wouldn't have sent for her if he didn't. Sam isn't an alarmist. He knows the traveling risk right now and he loves Tia as much as all of us. Things have to be serious. To the point I'm thinking he left the Montoya ranch all but unprotected with all the men he sent to escort Tia."

That was a big thing for Sam. Sam was a wild card. A man who'd ride into a fray of bullets just for the challenge of surviving, but he took his responsibilities seriously. And that included the huge responsibility of the Montoya ranch he'd inherited when he'd married Bella. The ranch sat smack dab in the middle of Comanche country. Luke shook his head. It took a strong man to keep it in one piece. But Sam seemed to be flourishing under the challenge. The man no one thought would ever settle, just might have found his place.

Ace nodded. "So I heard."

"Did you hear when they're arriving?"

"Based on the telegram, they should be here any day."

"Good. We're going to need everyone. There's some rough territory between here and there."

Ace cocked an eyebrow. "And yet you're volunteering."

And looking forward to it. Being around so many settled people chafed. "It'll be a new adventure with which to thrill the readers."

"Uh-huh. Do your readers know how much truth is in your novels?"

It was Luke's turn to shrug. No one was more surprised than he at the success of his novels, written under the pen name of Dane Savage. More shocking than the money was the notoriety. According to his publisher, Easterners couldn't get enough of the rumored-to-be-autobiographical tales of the ever-so-honest, bigger-than-life Texas Ranger's high adventures in the West. As fast as Luke was writing them, they were selling. He adjusted his hat. "I get the feeling they're more interested in the fiction."

"Uh-huh."

A new voice entered the fray. "I wondered where the whiskey had gotten to."

Only one man of the Hell's Eight had such a deep voice. Tucker McCade. His tread was heavy on the stairs, his smile broad but tinged with concern.

Ace held up the nearly empty bottle. "You timed that close."

"Still can't get used to you wearing sleeves," Luke said, turning to greet Tucker. Nor to seeing him without his knives strapped to his thighs.

Tucker smiled and tossed his lemonade over the rail. The heavy muscles in his arms rippled under his shirt with the movement. His shoulder-length black hair fell over his face, casting his harsh features in shadow. "Me, neither." He held out his glass. "But having a wife who turns a jealous eye when other women ogle my manly attributes means I get tailor-made shirts."

Ace chuckled and poured. "I've heard it's good to keep a Quaker peaceful."

Tucker's smile reached his brown eyes and his teeth shone white against his dark skin, emphasizing the scar on his right cheek. "I do enjoy smoothing Sally Mae's feathers when they're ruffled."

"Pacifist or not, that woman has a way of getting what she wants."

"Not everything," Caine pointed out, coming up to join them, a fresh bottle in his hand. "She's not going to Rancho Montoya."

"You heard?"

"I think everyone within a mile heard you shouting last night," Caine said, pulling the cork from the fresh bottle with his teeth.

"That woman has a stubborn streak a mile deep," Tucker grumbled.

Luke smiled. Sally Mae was a tall, slim blonde and as cool as a spring day. She never raised her voice. The exact opposite of her dark, big, muscular husband. "Almost equal to yours."

"Yeah, but things, they're not good out there. You know that. I know that. With the cavalry pulled back East and bad blood, travel isn't safe. I know Sam sent his vaqueros, but I'd feel better if some of Hell's Eight were traveling with Tia."

Caine held up the bottle. Luke held out his glass alongside the others.

"I'm going," Luke offered. But he wasn't staying after he got there. The itch in his feet was too strong. The horizon too enticing.

Caine frowned and poured them each a measure. "I wish we could spare more."

"Sam handled that end."

"Yeah." Tucker took a drink of his whiskey and shook his head. "But I've got to tell you, I'm being plagued by a bad feeling."

Shit. There was nothing worse than Tucker having a bad feeling.

CHAPTER TWO

WITH DAWN JUST PAST, the ground wet with dew, the yard bustling with activity, the time to leave had arrived. Even with two cups of coffee in him, Luke was dragging. With the efficiency of long practice, he tightened the cinch on Chico's saddle. Thanks to a restless night, his mood was jagged.

Around him, the sounds of the group preparing for departure joined the sleepy chirps of rousing birds. Leather creaking, horses stomping their feet, people talking, items thudding into the buckboard—it was all familiar. The rightness of it had settled over his unease with a soothing balm. He gave the cinch a firm tug. It was time to go. A man who stayed in one place too long got stale.

Tia came out of the house, escorted by her husband, Ed. Her dark green traveling dress was impeccably tailored, and the gray-streaked black of her hair was pulled up into a distinguished bun. She was the perfect image of a refined lady, but if he wasn't mistaken, her dark brown eyes lit with excitement. It occurred to Luke that maybe he wasn't the only one who'd been feeling the weight of settling down. For Tia to have been out in the back of beyond as she had been when the boys of Hell's Eight found her, she had to have a spirit of adventure.

Funny how he'd never thought on that before. Tia had always just been Tia. The stability in their lives. The one they'd counted on. Behind her trailed Sally Mae. At six months pregnant, her belly led the way. It was her second pregnancy, the first having ended in miscarriage, and everyone was worried because, from the girth of her belly, this child was going to have Tucker's size.

"I should be going with you," Sally said and sighed, supporting her stomach with her hand. Behind Sally Mae came Tucker, carrying another suitcase. With a shake of his head he negated that idea. "Before you got two feet in that wagon, that baby would be bouncing out of your belly."

Despite the ease of his tone, there was no doubting the concern in his eyes. Sally brushed it aside with a flick of her hand. "Expecting women have been traveling since the beginning of time."

The suitcase landed on the pile in the back of the wagon. "Not my woman."

Before Sally Mae could counter, Tucker wrapped his arms around her and pulled her back against him, taking over the supporting of her stomach with his much-larger hands. Placing her hands over his, Sally leaned back and allowed him to support them both.

Her whispered "It'll be all right this time" carried.

Tucker ducked his head to respond. His hair fell forward to blend with hers. Light with dark. They were opposites that somehow formed a perfect whole. His "I know" reflected her conviction.

Luke didn't share their confidence. Sally miscarrying the first baby had sent a shock wave through their whole community. The Hell's Eight wasn't used to losing, but there'd been no fighting that. Tucker had been devastated. For a time Luke had thought there'd be no more, but Sally Mae, with that implacable quiet resolve of hers, had wanted to try again. Tucker had forbidden it. Clearly in this, Sally Mae had had the stronger resolve.

Watching them, remembering the devastation of that time, Luke wanted to swear. Never, since the days after the massacre that had stripped Hell's Eight of their families, had he felt so helpless and angry. Rubbing at the tension in his neck, he fought the feeling. Then and now, Tia was the key to the Hell's Eight unity. She always had been.

Then, they had been starving and consumed with anger when they'd stumbled upon the young widow's home. They'd tried to steal her pies, and she'd paid them back by taking them into her heart. Tia had given them discipline, education and a purpose. Now a mature woman, she gave them stability and love. Sam might need Tia, but Hell's Eight needed her, too. No matter how spread out they became, Tia was home. "We could just stay here."

He knew as he said it, it was a moot point.

Tia shook her head at him before smiling softly at Sally. "There is no need for worry. I will be back in time for this baby."

Sally nodded. "I know. Bella and Sam need you."

His "You're both crazy" went ignored.

"So do we," Tucker growled, placing his hand over Sally's.

Tia smiled in that knowing way only another woman found comforting. "Your wife is a healer. She knows this time it is good."

Tucker's clenched jaw made it clear he wasn't feeling any more soothed than Luke.

"I'd feel better with fact, not fiction," Tucker growled.

Sally Mae patted his hand. "You're going to just have to wait and see like the rest of us."

"I hate waiting."

Luke could put an *amen* on that. Fortunately, he didn't have to sit and wait.

Zach rode around the corner of the barn, controlling the prance of the powerful stallion with the same calm efficiency he used to manage the Montoya ranch with Sam. Behind, his men followed, all mounted on equally impressive horse flesh and all equally in control. Zach pulled the stallion to a halt at the edge of the yard. With a tip of his black hat, he acknowledged those gathered. In a slow yet somehow unified meander, his men flanked him. They were an impressive sight.

"We should not wait much longer," Zach called. "We must cover a lot of trail before dark."

Acknowledging the comment with a lift of her hand, Tia encompassed them all in a look. When they were growing up, that look had had the power to rein in their wildness. Now it had the power to convey conviction. "We're not losing another baby. Not here or at Rancho Montoya."

Ed took her hand and raised it to his lips. "We're not losing you, either."

"I'll be safe, my husband. I feel it." She stroked his cheek. "You and my boys should not worry. I am not so easily lost."

"I'd feel better if you'd wait so more of your 'boys' could be going with you," Caine grumbled.

"I know, but…"

"Ah, senora…" Zach came forward, spurs jangling, looking as cocky as always in his black pants, black shirt and black hat adorned with dark turquoise around the brim. "My men and I are not Hell's Eight, but we are of the Montoya and we have saved Hell's Eights' behinds before. You will arrive safely."

"One time," Caine muttered from where he was tying down the canvas on one side of the flatbed. "One time they save the day and we never hear the end of it."

Zach flashed a rare grin. "It is relevant."

"And we are very grateful," Tucker drawled with a sharp look at Caine.

That was the truth. Without the Montoya vaqueros, Sam would not have his Bella. Nor Tracker his Ari. And Desi's promise, which had started it all, to find her stolen twin and dance together once again in a field of daisies would have gone unfulfilled. He shook his head and stroked Chico's neck. From the day Hell's Eight had been hired to find the "runaway" Desi, all of their lives' paths had taken a pivot from wild to civilized. Caine said because it was time. Tia said because God had plans for them beyond an early demise. And Luke. Luke just didn't know who was making plans for whom. He only knew he wasn't fitting the mold.

"It is important you are reminded that not all that is good is Tejano," Zach added.

"Si," Tia said, patting Caine's hand this time. "This is true." She looked over at him. "So stop worrying, Luke. Bella needs me. Sam needs me. The baby needs me."

Luke tried one more time. "The baby isn't here yet."

She looked at him from under her brows. "For this reason, Sam sent for me."

Luke gave another tug at the cinch. Chico snorted his displeasure, emphasizing it with a stomp of his hoof. "Yeah, I know."

"That to the horse or Tia?" Tucker asked.

"Shut up, Tucker."

Luke dropped the stirrup back into place before addressing Tia. "I'm not exactly sure that Sam sent for you. That telegram could have been to keep you apprised."

Tia clucked her tongue and pulled her scarf up over her hair. "Do not be silly."

And that fast, Luke knew there was no point in talking further. He loved the small, plump woman from the tip of her bun to the soles of her pointy black boots. She was the anchor of Hell's Eight and now she was leaving the sanctuary. He didn't have to like it, but he would support her. "Then let's go."

"We can't yet."

"Why not?" he asked, preparing to mount.

Everyone went silent. The hairs on the back of his neck rose. From the barn came a rhythmic clanking. He knew that sound.

He looked around. No one would meet his gaze.

"Oh hell no."

A broken-down nag came through the doors, walking like an old man felt, as if every step dragged its past along with the gaudily painted peddler's wagon. Sitting in the seat, all delicious curves and annoying attitude, was Josie. She met his frown with a smile. The contents of the wagon clanked as it hit a rut.

Tia smiled. "We are ready."

"Why did no one tell me Josie was invited along?" Luke asked.

Tia looked at Ed. Ed looked at Ace. Ace shrugged. "Jarl made a promise."

And Hell's Eight owed Jarl.

"I, for one, will be glad to have another woman on the journey," Tia said.

"Well, I'm not."

Another woman might be one thing, but Josie wasn't just any woman. She was the thorn in his side. Trouble walking. A mass of contradictions. He ground his teeth to the rhythm of the wagon's rattle as she approached. Hell, even her hair was contrary. Neither blond nor brown nor red, it was an ever-changing mix of all three, depending on the light. Right now it was red. A warning to anyone who'd care to harken. He opened his mouth. Caine cut him off.

"I wouldn't even bother saying it."

Luke turned around to glare at Caine. In many ways, he was the same hard man Luke had grown up with. In others, he was different. Caine had been sent by an unscrupulous bastard to retrieve Desi, and in true Caine form, had ended up keeping her. In Desi, Caine had found everything he'd been searching for. And that hungry, restless wolf inside had settled down.

"What exactly do you think I'm going to say?"

There was a smile in Caine's gray eyes. "That if she goes, you won't."

The thought had crossed his mind. "It's a thought."

"It's a bad thought. I need to know you're there, Luke. Zach and his men, they're good but they're not Hell's Eight. I can't spare more than I have."

Yet another change of the last few years. Hell's Eight had once functioned as a unit. Almost as one man, one thought, but that had changed. Members had married. Settled down. It was as if each man had found the woman who completed him, anchored his restless ways.

"Hell's Eight is changing." Luke sighed.

"We're bigger," Caine countered.

"And more vulnerable," Luke added, looking at Tia. Hell's Eight had grown. More lives. More responsibilities.

Caine nodded. "I know the photographer irritates you."

"She does."

"Now, why is that?" Ace asked as the wagon came closer.

"She's too flighty. It's irritating." That got a raised brow from Ed and a snort from Tia.

"So irritating you can't take your eyes off her?" Ed asked.

Dammit. Luke yanked his gaze away. He was watching her.

"Where there's smoke, there's fire," Tia murmured.

"Better not be too much fire," Caine cut in. "Josie's under the protection of Hell's Eight."

Luke shook his head. He might be fascinated, but he wasn't suicidal. "No need to worry. As soon as that woman opens her mouth, any interest a man has dies."

"Oh?" Tia cocked her head. "I find her quite funny, and Sally Mae says she is a most interesting woman."

It was Luke's turn to snort. "All she talks about are those plates and chemicals she uses to make those tintypes."

"Have you even seen her work?" Caine asked.

"No." Ever since the woman had pushed him out of his place at the wedding to set up a picture and stolen his point of view with a smile and an elbow in his side, he'd been avoiding the temptation.

"You should."

"Uh-huh."

"She is my guest," Tia reminded him quietly. "And I promised her we did not mind her coming along."

He'd imagined Josie'd pushed herself into the trip. "You invited her?"

Tia shrugged. "Pictures of my grandson would be good to have in my parlor."

"There might be photographers out there."

Tucker snorted. "Now you're clutching at straws."

"Yes, he is," Zach cut in. "The Montoya ranch, it is big, but it's remote. There are no photographers."

There went that argument.

Tia smiled at Josie. Josie smiled back.

That smile had way too much impact on his libido, coming as it did from a woman holding the reins of a gaudily painted peddler's wagon drawn by a knock-kneed horse wearing a ridiculous bonnet sprouting a huge plume of weeds that bobbed with every plodding step. The right wheel hit a bump. The pans attached to the side clattered. Lounging on the porch, Desi's hound, Boone, lifted his head and moaned before sinking back onto the sun-warmed wood.

"Between that wagon and her…eccentricities, she'll get us all killed."

From the edge of the yard came an amused and far too appreciative "I think she will add some beautiful scenery to the journey."

The last thing he wanted was the too-handsome vaquero noticing Josie. "Shut up, Zach."

"What do you have against the woman, Luke?" Caine asked.

She was too flighty. Too pretty. Too aggravating. Too tempting. "She has no idea what she's riding into. Hell, she's probably got a picnic basket all packed for our little excursion," he growled under his breath.

Zach just chuckled. Luke had the overwhelming urge to knock him off his horse. As if to prove his point, Josie called over, "Good morning, everyone. I'm so sorry I'm late. I had the darnedest time getting Glory's hat to stay put."

Shit. Luke swung up into the saddle. She'd named the nag Glory. What more proof did his point need than that?

"Welcome, *hija*," Tia called, bringing the cacophony of horse and wagon closer.

Chico stomped his foot nervously. Luke patted his neck. "Easy, boy. Now is not the time to be temperamental."

Zach's horse started its own little dance. As if she didn't understand the disaster she was courting with that obnoxious wagon, Josie kept coming, shyly flashing those dimples that sent his imagination teetering into areas it had no business being.

"Thank you so much for inviting me. I can't tell you how excited I am by this opportunity."

Luke's cock perked right along with his aggravation. The wheel hit another bump. The pans clattered. A bucket swung, its contents grating around in its interior. Chico crow-hopped and flattened his ears. Zach's horse snapped its head up and reared. Zach's quick reflexes were the only thing that saved his ass from getting dumped in the dirt. "Stay back, senorita!"

"Josie," Luke ordered. "Stop right there."

Startled, Josie pulled back on the reins. He kneed Chico over. Josie watched him approach, her intriguing blue eyes big beneath her wide-brimmed satin, ruched hat. If he were honest with himself, he'd admit he liked her eyes on him. While there could be a certain haphazardness to her attention, when the woman focused on something, it was all out. He couldn't help but wonder if she brought that intensity between the sheets.

A shiver raced over his skin. He liked that image entirely too much. The corner of her lips twitched. Fear or humor? It annoyed the bejesus out of him that he wanted to know which. Seems he'd done nothing but watch the woman since the moment he'd damn near tripped over her, kneeling in the dirt taking a picture of a bee on a flower, the day before Hester's wedding. He'd known she was off-kilter from that second on, but it didn't seem to make any difference—then or now. He couldn't look away. Somewhere deep inside him, for some goddamn reason, it mattered if Josie was happy or sad. And that irritated the heck out of him.

Luke folded his arms over the saddle horn and stared right back at her. She cocked her head to the side and studied him.

"I'd like to take your picture like that someday."

"Why?"

Her eyes narrowed slightly. "The composition is perfect."

"Excuse me?"

She made a square of her hands, looking through them with the intensity of a hawk looking at a tasty mouse. "The way you're sitting, with the mountains behind. And the shadows…" She shifted slightly to the left and nodded. "It would be a good picture, a very good picture."

Glory stomped his foot. She frowned. "I don't suppose we have time now, do we?"

He had the insane urge to say yes. "Hell no."

She sighed. "I lose so many moments that way."

She was an odd one for sure.

Boone raised his head and gave a light woof. From around the corner of the barn came piling six of his offspring, barking and growling and carrying on. None of them seemed to share Boone's lazy porch hound ways. They charged in. One raced between his horse's legs. Chico jumped and snorted. Glory tossed his head and reared up in the traces.

With a scream as ugly as his hat, he threw his head back. Luke only caught a glimpse of Josie's terror before the horse took off with a surge of energy. The wagon went right along with it, banging and clanking in a cacophonous prelude to disaster.

Chico reared up. As soon as Luke got his hooves back on the ground, he started crow-hopping. Time slowed as Zach's horse joined in.

This time it was Caine's turn to say, "Shit."

He grabbed for Tia's team. Tucker lunged for Glory and missed. Luke pulled hard on the right rein, forcing Chico into a tight circle before sending him racing after the wagon, driving the gelding through his fear as Glory's hat sailed by. It only took a few strides for Chico to catch up with Glory. Grabbing his reins just below the bit, he pulled the bag of bones up short. The clanging lessened until the wagon came to a halt.

The whole rescue only took a minute, but at the end of that minute… Luke shook his head and glanced back over his shoulder. Chaos had been unleashed. The yard looked like a tornado had ripped through it, the ground chewed up by horses and wagons, pots and pans and other items strewn across the ground. And sitting on a rosebush was the nag's ridiculous hat.

The yard wasn't the only thing in disarray. Josie's bonnet was off to the side, and tendrils of hair framed her flushed cheeks.

"Why the he—" He caught himself just in time. "Why the heck don't you have your gear inside the wagon?"

Josie gathered her skirts and hopped down. Her hem caught on the edge of the footboard, flashing him a glimpse of pantaloons and ankle. She yanked at it. "It is in the wagon where it should be."

"Then what's all over the yard?"

On a last tug, her skirt came free. She turned and headed toward the mess. "The other stuff."

She said it as if it made total sense. Luke dismounted and followed. Shaking his head, he picked up a frying pan and handed it back to her. "You don't think we'll have cookware where we're going?"

Josie shrugged. Her hat listed a bit more. "It all came with the wagon. I had no idea what to expect, so I just kept it all."

"I see." He went to the back of the wagon and opened the door. It was easy to tell what was her stuff. It was tied down in sturdy boxes.

"We're going to have to cut back on some of this weight."

That brought her hurrying right over, two metal bowls and that silly hat in her hand. "You're not talking about my equipment, are you?"

"Would your equipment be in the large, thick wood box, weighing probably fifty pounds on its own?"

She came up beside him. The soft scent of lilac teased his nostrils. "The solutions I use to make my pictures need to be protected."

"Uh-huh. What about the rest of this? Are you married to it?"

She pointed to the trunk in the middle. "That has my clothes in it. I could let that go."

They could agree on one thing. Those ugly clothes she wore had to go. If she were his, he'd dress her in cool silk and simple designs to highlight her natural curves and beauty. Deep blue to match her eyes. Pink to contrast with her pale skin. "Do your clothes have to be in a trunk?"

Cocking her head to the side, she gave his question a second of consideration. "You know, I don't suppose they do."

"That horse of yours would probably appreciate a lighter load." For good measure he added, "And he could probably do without that hat. There's no dignity in that hat."

There was little left in her own for that matter. One more nod of her head and it was coming off.

She stuck her finger through the ear holes and wiggled them. "Actually, I've been informed that without this hat he's quite flighty."

Glancing around the yard, Luke shook his head. "It stuns the mind, imagining how much more he could be."

The puppies came up, tails wagging and tongues hanging out, completely unconcerned with the disaster they'd precipitated. Josie bent down and gave the one with the white front toe a scratch behind the ear. Her hat gave up and slid off. "Hello, Rascal."

"I wouldn't get too fond of them. Boone's pups are in high demand."

"I intend to get quite fond of this one. Tucker gave him to me."

"Tucker gave you one of the pups?"

"Yup." She snatched her bonnet out of his jaws. "I've never had a dog before, though."

"Why would you want one now?"

She looked up at him. "Because now just seems the right time."

Boone's pups had been in demand since the day Boone had fought to save Desi and then, shot and bleeding, tracked her, saving her life. Dogs with that kind of heart were rare. Boone was a legend. And everyone wanted part of a legend. Tucker was mighty particular about whom he gave a pup to.

Yet he'd given one to Josie. Luke's gut tightened, and not in a good way, at the implied intimacy. Was he actually jealous? "What are you going to do with him when you go back East?"

"They do travel, you know."

"Uh-huh."

The puppy made a jump for the hat. She held it above her head. "No, Rascal!"

Rascal kept jumping and she kept turning, uttering soft-voiced orders.

"You could help," Caine suggested, riding up.

So he could. Grabbing the pup by the scruff, Luke ordered, "Sit."

Startled, Rascal looked at him before slowly sinking down on his haunches. His face drooped into soulful despair as he realized his predicament.

Luke wasn't impressed.

Josie grabbed his arm. "Ooh, don't hurt him."

Holding the pup's gaze, Luke ordered, "Stay," before releasing him.

No one was more surprised than he when Rascal stayed put.

Josie blinked. "I confess, I'm impressed."

"Some things take a firm hand," he bluffed.

He'd be damned if that didn't send a little shiver down her spine, and he'd be damned if that shiver didn't send another bolt of lust through him.

"We don't have time to repack all this," Tucker noted, holding out a badly dented pot as he approached.

Rascal bounded up to Tucker the way all animals and children did. Women, however, were usually intimidated by his dark looks and the scar slashing across his right cheek that lent him a sinister air. Josie just gave him a big smile.

"I'm fine with leaving the cooking equipment and we can take my clothes out of the trunk."

Tucker turned the pot before tossing it to one of the hands. "That's good."

"Truth be told, I got this wagon off a peddler." She handed the bowls to Luke. "It was one price for everything." She said it as though it was pure luck the peddler had been selling everything lock, stock and barrel.

The bowls were almost rusted through in places. "I hope you didn't pay much."

"Oh no, I bargained." With a tug, she pulled her bonnet back up. The brim obscured her expression. She still held the horse's ridiculous hat. Bending down, she gave Rascal a pat. He wiggled and flopped over.

"You bargained?" he asked. She didn't look as if she could bargain her way out of a feed sack.

Tucker chuckled and started stripping the remaining items from the wagon. "The way I hear it, there was a man down in Parson's saloon whining about how he was fleeced by some good-looking filly."

Josie's smile widened to satisfaction. Luke noticed

she was more free with her expressions when she felt hidden in some way. "Why, thank you, Mr. McCade."

Tucker tipped his hat. "Always happy to pass on good news. And just call me Tucker."

Luke wanted to knock the bonnet from her head and expose that smile, that woman. "I didn't know you had such talents."

"Imagine that." Focusing on Glory's hat, she straightened the brim before heading to the front of the wagon.

Tucker snorted. Luke cut him a glare before following. He motioned to the weed-adorned monstrosity. "You know, it's darned undignified to make a horse wear that thing."

"Uh-huh."

The horse was too tall for her to position it properly. Luke folded his arms across his chest. If she asked nicely, he might help her.

She waved the hat. Instead of spooking, the horse lowered its head. She settled the hat over Glory's ears, carefully working the right, then the left through the holes. Looking over her shoulder, she smiled. "It seems, Mr. Bellen, there are some things about which you don't know everything."

Fifteen minutes later, excess trunks and cooking equipment were stacked by the house, the wagons were in line, the women were ready and there was nothing left to do but leave. Luke looked around, a mixture of unease and anticipation roiling in his gut. The anticipation was for him. The unease for the women. Here was safety. Ahead lay danger. And he was leading Tia and Josie right into it. He pulled his hat down over his eyes.

"I'm not happy about this," he muttered to Caine.

Caine nodded. "For the record, neither am I."

But it didn't make a difference. The trip was happening. Luke turned his horse and moved to the head of the small caravan. Zach's vaqueros fell into place, surrounding the wagons. Warriors who'd give their lives to protect the women. He had to believe it was going to be enough.

From the porch, Rascal barked. And then howled. Tucker hushed him with a tug on the impromptu rope leash. Behind him, he heard the goodbyes. Before he got too far, Caine stopped him with a sharp whistle.

"Don't forget where your home is."

Looking back at Caine, Luke saw all there had been, all there could be. And the reality of what was. He didn't know if he'd ever be coming back.

He touched his finger to the brim of his hat. "I won't."

Caine held up his hand. Right behind Caine was Ace. And behind him, Tucker. And then Ed. Solid men to the last. Dependable. His family. "If you do, we'll come looking for you."

And that was the beauty of Hell's Eight. Even when they were apart, they were never alone. He tipped his hat. "I'll hold it against you if you don't."

There was so much more he wanted to say, but all the words had been spoken and now it was only down to the doing, as it had been so many times before. But with this departure there wasn't a bounty or the need for revenge to drive him down the trail. There was only this aching need for…something. Just something.

And it was time to go find it.

With a wave of his hand, he put the caravan in motion.

The journey had begun.

CHAPTER THREE

FOUR HOURS LATER, Josie came to a conclusion. Luke might not be the only one who knew less than he thought he did. She'd awoken that morning, tingling with anticipation for this exciting adventure, but reality was beating her up. She sighed.

The wagon that had looked so perfectly suited to her needs was actually little more than an elaborate instrument of torture. The seat bruised her posterior. The reins chafed her hands even through the light gloves she'd put on, and the small overhang she'd thought would protect her from the sun did nothing but trap the heat. Worse even, the constant bouncing and swaying upset her stomach to the point where she was in danger of embarrassing herself by vomiting.

Gripping the reins, she took a deep breath. She refused to further embarrass herself. After the fiasco that morning, she couldn't afford to look more incompetent. Luke was just itching for a reason to send her back and they were still close enough to the Hell's Eight compound to make that feasible. Wagons, she'd discovered, had a more plodding pace than riding horseback. She tucked a stray hair under her bonnet. A trickle of perspiration slid down her back toward her already soaked corset. A glance at the sun showed it wasn't yet noon. How was she going to stand the full afternoon sun? How was everyone else able to stand it so easily?

The left wheels hit a rut. The wagon bounced over it, then swayed before settling. Her breakfast rose to her throat. Beside her one of the vaqueros asked, "You are well, senorita?"

Forcing a smile, she lied. "Fine, thank you."

The tip of his hat was as much an indication of skepticism as it was good manners, but he rode on without further comment. For that she was grateful. Being a bastard in a small town had made her a spectacle her entire life, her every move subject to conjecture. The experience had left her with a complete aversion to being the focus of anyone's attention. She much preferred being invisible.

She waited until the vaquero was out of earshot before groaning and fanning herself with her journal. How could she have been so foolish as to have underestimated the rigors of the journey? Driving a wagon over established roads was rough enough, but over open countryside? It was a nightmare.

She sighed and answered her own question. At the time, she'd just assumed all she'd have to do was sit in the seat, point Glory in the right direction, and follow everybody else. She hadn't given a thought to the pounding the wooden wheels rolling over rough terrain would deliver to her spine or how the raucous noise from her remaining hanging supplies would jar her nerves.

She also hadn't thought of how exposed to the elements she would be sitting on the hard seat or how much the wagon just…swayed. All the time. Back and forth. Lightly. Or more aggressively when the wheels hit a rock. Like now. Her teeth snapped together. She gave a fleeting thought to her equipment only to have it die under a wave of nausea. She swallowed hard. Her fingers twitched on the reins, but she knew they couldn't stop. Zach and Luke set a pace that was, in her mind, brutal, but in their minds undoubtedly not fast enough. She'd already had to stop twice to relieve herself. Which had earned her a sympathetic glance from Tia, a frown from Zach and a glare from Luke. What did the man expect, for heaven's sake? She was human, and a body could only take so much bouncing before something had to give. For her, it was her bladder.

"You pull that horse up and Zach's gonna leave you behind."

Josie didn't have to wonder who'd ridden up on her left. It was Luke. It was always Luke today. The man seemed to hover outside her view, just waiting for some infraction so he could swoop in with a comment to discomfit her.

"I wasn't going to—"

She looked up and that fast the thought left her head. How could the same sun that was wilting her seem to sink into his skin in a warm enticing glow? Or light his eyes from within so they looked as deep and full of possibilities as summer twilight. How could he look so incredibly, deliciously sexy leaning over with one arm propped on the saddle horn? A quirk of his lips drew her gaze down. He was laughing at her.

With a flick of his fingers, he said, "There's no sense in finishing that lie. You don't do it worth a damn."

"Is that so?" It had to be the heat that had that challenge just popping out, but darn it, she was tired of people amusing themselves at her expense.

"That's so."

He didn't have to sound so sure of it. She pretended there was a spot on her glove. With a little practice she was sure she could lie with the best of them. And darn it, there *was* a spot. With a sigh, she put her palm over it. And had no idea where to go from there. Silently, she willed him to ride on. Of course he didn't. The man was perversely dedicated to annoying her. The seconds stretched uncomfortably on.

Darn it again. He was still looking at her. She could feel it with that acute awareness that made her want to squirm. The squirming she resisted, but she couldn't resist looking back, albeit out of the corner of her eye. He was sitting on Chico with that lazy confidence that only added to his appeal. Beneath the brim of his hat, his eyes were a dark, smoldering blue. And yes, he was studying her with the intensity of a professor who'd just discovered a new bug and was about to stick a pin in it.

And that perverse part of her, the part her mother hated and she usually managed to subdue, came to life, running amok, poking at things best left sleeping until every one of her senses perked up with delight at being noticed. Stupid senses. The one thing she did not need was to be attracted to a cowboy. Especially this cowboy, who didn't approve of her horse, her equipment or her profession. As a matter of fact, she wasn't even sure he approved of her. More than likely, he saw her as a pain-in-the-butt distraction from whatever goal he'd set for himself. Aggravating man. She rubbed at the spot with her thumb.

"It's rude to stare," she blurted.

"I wasn't staring."

Did he think she was stupid? "Then what were you doing?"

"Thinking."

"About what?" She knew better but it just popped out again. Darn that perverse side.

"I'm thinking that horse of yours is not too far away from buzzard food."

"You leave Glory alone." The threat would have sounded much more intimidating if she could lift her gaze from the traces. Clearing her throat, she tried again. She got her eyes as high as Glory's ears, but at least her voice was steady, if a bit too soft. "Not everyone has to be beautiful to be worthy."

She'd been clinging to that belief her whole life. It had gotten her through the rejection and scorn of being a bastard and a misfit. She wasn't about to abandon it now, out here in the middle of nowhere with nothing but heat and annoyance to replace it.

"Uh-huh. Well, I'm not too concerned about beautiful, but sound would be good."

"What makes you think Glory isn't sound?"

"Honey, I looked at his teeth at the first halt you called."

That halt seemed like a lifetime ago. She checked the watch pinned to the lapel of her sensible brown dress. It'd actually only been two hours.

"So?"

"That gelding is on his last legs."

As if he understood the disparagement, Glory's head drooped. That was too much. Who did the man think he was?

Turning, she glared at him, sexy smile and all. The big bully. "They're darn good legs! No need to undermine them with your sarcasm."

She had the satisfaction of seeing him sit back in the saddle.

"Undermine? How the he…heck could I undermine anything. It's not like the horse can understand me."

"He most certainly can! He's sensitive and has feelings, too, and I'll thank you to remember that."

As if to emphasize that, Glory tossed his head, his jangling harness punctuating the sentiment.

"See?" she asked pointedly.

Luke looked anything but convinced. "He's not going to spook again, is he?"

"Not if you don't do something stupid and scare him."

"Given what happened earlier, it clearly doesn't take much."

"Anybody would be scared with those puppies snapping at their heels."

"They ran by!"

"They were rambunctious!"

"They were puppies!"

She sighed. "He's not used to them."

"My point exactly. He's not used to a lot of things."

"Mr. Caine said it was all right."

"*Mr.* Caine?"

She had to admit, it did sound silly. But she couldn't help it. Caine Allen was too imposing to use so informal an address even though he'd asked her repeatedly to call him by his first name. So she'd settled on adding a *mister*. It was a happy medium.

"He's an impressive man."

"And I'm not?"

She didn't have to look up to know his head was tilted in that arrogant gesture that doubted the veracity of the anticipated response. Tightening her grip on the reins, she shrugged. "I didn't say that."

"You don't call me mister."

"You're too aggravating to bother with a title." The truth just popped out. Again. She bit back a groan. His laugh, when she was expecting anger, yanked her gaze to his. Immediately she knew confusion and, just as fast, pleasure. Confusion because she'd been expecting his anger and she knew how to deal with that, and pleasure, well, the pleasure stemmed from his smile, his lips a line of amused indulgence and intrigue. The effect went right through her like sweet, warm honey spreading over her senses, soothing the agitation even as it brought out a bit of fire.

She wished she knew why he affected her so. He wasn't the most handsome man she'd ever seen. She'd met and photographed better-looking men. But there was something about Luke Bellen, something so elemental, something so overwhelmingly masculine, something so unique that just screamed "come hither" to everything female in her. But despite many thinking her fairly independent profession proclaimed her loose, she was still a virgin, and she intended to stay that way. And not just because of her mother's dire warnings, but from her own observations. To her knowledge, rampant procreation just complicated a woman's options. Not because a woman lost her reputation, but because of all the messy complicating factors, like feelings, entanglement and eventually babies. Pretty soon, a woman's life was bound to revolve around someone else. Josie had been doing that since the day she was born— paying for her mother's sin, her fiancé's selfishness, society's demands.

As a child, she'd thought her cousins were blessed with good fortune, but as they'd matured, she'd watched their dreams, one by one, be pushed to the back burner. And then she'd watched the fire under the burner go out. As they'd married, they'd settled down in little homes in little towns in little places

with little families and every one of their days con-
sisted of little things. Josie wasn't sure she wanted
to live just for herself, but she was certain she didn't
want her cousins' existence. She didn't want that any
more than she wanted Luke staring at her. "Don't you
have somewhere else to go?"

"Nope."

"Why not?"

"It appears that I've been assigned to you."

"Assigned by whom?"

He nodded toward the wagon ahead.

"Tia seems to think you need watching."

She was not a child. "Can't Zach or one of the
vaqueros do it?"

"Tia seems to think you need watching by me."

"Why?"

"Likely because no one else has the patience—"

"Patience? You?"

"—to deal with your procrastination and shilly-
shallying," he continued as if she hadn't interrupted.

"You don't know me well enough to make such
accusations." She couldn't lie about the procrastination. She did have a tendency to put off the un-
pleasant stuff for as long as possible. Of course he
picked up on that.

"I've got eyes and the fact that you're sidestep-
ping a flat-out denial cinches the deal."

"It most certainly does not." She didn't know
where all this opposition came from lately. She'd
argued more over the last couple of days than she

had in her entire life. She'd likely enjoy it more if she wasn't roasting from the inside out.

He brushed aside that denial with an arch of his brow. "People who don't like to lie usually aren't bold about dissembling."

She raised her own eyebrows at that. "*Dissembling* is a big word for a cowboy."

"Photography is a big hobby for a woman." He always had a comeback. She snapped her teeth together.

"And what's wrong with it?"

"I didn't say there was anything wrong with it. I just said it was a big one."

Now he had her off-kilter. She'd been ready to fight and he'd gone all reasonable. "Life is too short not to do things you enjoy."

"Uh-huh."

He was back to lounging in the saddle in that casual way that just screamed predator. He reminded her of a hawk perched on a branch, ready to swoop, except she wasn't sure what he was going to swoop on—her argument or more. It was the more that sent that little shiver through her. His eyes narrowed.

"Ghost walk over your grave?"

"That is the most nonsensical statement."

The corner of his mouth twitched. He knew she was avoiding answering the question. Some men were irritating like that. His horse, a beautiful roan, tossed his head again. A sharp whistle came down the line. Luke straightened in the saddle and scanned the horizon.

"What is it?" she asked.

"Nothing."

She didn't believe him. "I'd like to point out I'm not the one dodging questions now."

Good grief! She was getting positively belligerent. A thrill went through her. It was…exhilarating.

"Chico is uneasy."

"Glory is calm."

"I noticed."

Another short whistle came from ahead.

Reaching down, Luke untied something on the right side of the saddle. His rifle, she realized as he drew it out of the scabbard. The illusion of him as a predator suddenly snapped into reality. Her contrary enjoyment evaporated in a puff of fear.

"Can that horse run?" he asked, pulling out the weapon and resting the barrel across the saddle.

"Of course." Couldn't all horses?

"Will he?"

She didn't really know, but if she had to get down and push his behind along, she would. "Yes."

She might not have been as convincing as she'd hoped. For a moment Luke took his attention off the horizon to shake his head at her. "I can't believe Caine allowed that horse along."

Confession time. "He's the only one that wouldn't spook with all the banging."

"That will be remedied in the future."

He was making her very nervous.

"Mr. Caine said trouble wasn't likely."

"Unlikely doesn't mean nonexistent."

She couldn't argue that. Another burst of whistles cut across the distance. As if the message were spoken, Luke looked to the left. She did, too, but all she saw were rocks, grass and trees. Then again, she always had trouble seeing far without her spectacles.

"What is it?"

"Be ready."

For what? Thankfully, she had managed not to voice it. The last thing anyone needed was for Luke's attention to be diverted at a crucial moment. But it was getting harder to control this new, impetuous side of her nature now that he'd riled it up.

They rode on in silence. One minute passed. Then two. Three minutes passed without a single sound except the creaking of the harnesses and the bouncing of the wagon. Apprehension stretched her nerves. It took another few minutes for her to realize the birds weren't singing. A shiver shot down her spine. Something was definitely wrong. She just didn't know what.

Luke cut her a glance. "If I holler, you snap those reins on the nag's ass, but be sure to brace your feet. We don't need you pitching out of there and breaking your neck when he takes off."

A gruesome image of her body being tossed like a rag doll to the hard ground popped into her mind. She tightened her grip on her reins and braced her feet. No, they definitely didn't need that. But the slur to Glory—that she couldn't let pass. Glory and she had formed a friendship. Friendship demanded loyalty. Licking her lips, she tapped into her impetuous side. "Glory is not a nag."

The near whisper barely got her a look. Clearly her voice of authority needed work. For now, she clung to stubborn determination. "He's not."

With a grunt, Luke reiterated, "Just be ready."

That grunt could have gone either way. She chose to take it as agreement. Clutching the reins, she nodded. Ready she could handle. She hoped. A bead of sweat trickled down her temple. Another down her spine. More gathered between her breasts.

Apparently satisfied that she'd obey, Luke urged Chico into a trot, leaving Josie behind. She watched him go with a sinking stomach. In her wagon ahead, Tia had her husband. Back here there was just Josie and her growing fears. Wiping the sweat from her face with her sleeve, she looked around. The same countryside that had seemed so pretty yesterday, seemed ominously vast today. The wildflowers she'd viewed as serendipitous bits of whimsy now had a second potential use—as grave markers. At the front of the line, Luke and Zach conferred. She wished she were close enough to hear what they were saying.

Tia turned in her seat and waved. If Josie had her spectacles on she could have seen if she was smiling or frowning. Feeling even more in the dark, she waved back. First thing she was going to do when they stopped again would be to get her spectacles out of the wagon. Vanity be hanged.

As if reacting to some invisible cue, the formerly loosely strung line of men dropped into a tight for-

mation surrounding the wagons. A handsome man
dressed in brown, sporting ammunition belts across
his chest and wearing a large sombrero rode up beside Josie on a proud-stepping buckskin. He had
Zach's eyes and was about her age. Maybe younger. It
was hard to tell out here. Men seemed to mature earlier. He flashed her a grin full of Lopez confidence
before settling his rifle across the saddle. Strapped
to his thigh was a pistol. The wooden handle looked
worn from use. She found that comforting.

He tipped his hat. "Senorita."

If they were anywhere else, if she were anyone
else, she'd call his attention flirtatious, but this was
Texas Indian country and danger was all around.

She attempted a smile and a small wave. The tension hovered oppressively in the air. Her skin prick-
led. Even the horses were quiet.

A rabbit darted. She jumped. The wagons kept
moving. The tension mounted. She chewed her lip
What did they see that she didn't? Was it an actual
threat or just a worry?

She wanted somebody to do something already,
rather than passively plod along like prey waiting for
the pounce. But they just kept going.

An hour later, a rider cantered up. Luke and Zach
rode out to meet him. The group kept moving while
the men conferred to the side. They were too far
away to be heard over the creak of wood and metal.
Why did they have to be so far away?

Glancing at the well-armed man to her right, the

one whose flirtatious approach led her to believe he might be talkative, she asked, "What's happening?"

He didn't take his attention off Luke and Zach. "Nothing to worry about, senorita, I'm sure. Likely Lobo just spotted some Indians passing by."

"Indians!"

Terror flashed along her nerves. A shiver chased cold comprehension as every story she'd ever read in those lurid novels about the West—and she'd read more than her share—raced through her mind. Capture. Scalping. Unmentionable acts.

The wagon lurched through a rut. Her gorge rose. Heat, motion and now anxiety combining to make disaster imminent.

"Senorita?"

Clutching her stomach, she waved the vaquero's concern away. She wouldn't be sick. She wouldn't. "I'm fine."

He frowned at her, drawing his rifle from its scabbard. "You have nothing to worry about. Senor Luke would not allow you to be captured." He settled the rifle across his saddle. "And neither would I."

What could he do? He was just one man. So was Luke. And that rifle didn't look big enough to take on the hordes of Comanche that could even now be charging toward them. Unbidden, one passage from her favorite author's latest novel leaped to the forefront of her mind: "The Comanche came out of nowhere like a mist rising from the ground, enveloping everything in their path."

There was a whole lot of ground out there.

No. For him to say it was just some Indians did nothing to reassure her, even if he'd clearly been trying to. She took a breath to steady her nerves. Hot air filled her lungs. Cold sweat beaded her brow as the persistent nausea surged along with fear. She whispered soothing nothings to Glory as if the steady old horse was the one in danger of an attack of the vapors.

The man frowned at her.

"You do not need to be afraid of the Indians, senorita. You are well guarded."

She took another steadying breath, fighting dizziness. If they could just stop for a minute, her stomach might settle. Her request was met with a shake of his head. "I'm sorry, but we cannot stop."

Of course not.

"But you are safe, senorita." He gestured to his chest. "With me, Stefano." He broadened the gesture to include everyone. "And if I should fall, there are the men of Rancho Montoya and Hell's Eight." He tipped his hat. "You are very safe."

Was she? They had fifteen riders, plus Luke, Ed, Tia and herself. Hardly an army. And she didn't even have a gun. Good heavens. Why didn't she have a gun? The wagon hit a rut. The horizon tilted. Or was it the wagon? Her stomach lodged in her throat. She recognized the cold clammy feeling for what it was. Holding her hand over her mouth, she imagined Indians pouring over the little hill, swarming them, intent on driving them off their land. It was too easy to imagine their wild cries. Blast Dane Savage and his gift for description! She could see them as if they were real, dangerous men on horseback, armed with guns and bows, feral smiles on their painted faces… Intent on revenge.

Oh dear God.

"Senorita?"

The voice echoed around the periphery of her consciousness. The wagon bucked and swayed over a series of bumps. Her vision clouded. Nausea rose as hard as fear. In an obscure part of her consciousness, she realized she was about to faint. She reached out. Found nothing.

The last thing she heard was the shout of her name.

It sounded amazingly exasperated for a Comanche war cry.

CHAPTER FOUR

"SENORITA!"

Stefano's cry jerked Luke around in the saddle. Chico, bored with standing still, pranced right along with the shift in weight, which worked out just fine as what Luke saw chilled his blood. Glory was still plodding along, every step bordering on hipshot, but the wagon seat that should've been sporting the bane of his existence was empty. *What the hell had she done now?*

"Goddammit, Josie!"

Zach shook his head. "That woman is not made for this country."

Lobo nodded. "Then it is just as well the Comanche are intent on moving and not war."

Luke grunted and sent Chico trotting back to Josie's wagon.

Behind him he heard Zach order Lobo to keep an eye on the tribe.

Kicking Chico into a canter, he raced back down the line. Tia and Ed turned as he passed, and saw what he saw. Ed's curse and Tia's gasp trailed in his wake. By the time he got to Josie's wagon, Stefano was off his horse and climbing into the front seat.

Luke pulled back on the reins. Sitting back on his haunches, Chico slid to a stop just short of Stefano's buckskin. Momentum propelling him forward, Luke jumped off. His boots hit the dirt in time with Stefano's next curse.

"Back off, Stefano."

Stefano turned and stepped back, hands raised. "Whatever you say, Luke. You're the man with the gun."

Luke looked down. Shit, he was. *Damn.* Luke took his hand off his revolver. The wagon creaked and sagged as he stepped up. Josie didn't move from where she lay crumpled on the floorboards, her torso twisted to the left, one arm stretched out to the right. Toward him. "What happened?" he asked Stefano.

"She collapsed."

He could see that. "Why?"

"Do you want me to guess?"

"No." He wanted an answer. Josie was lying there so still, her breathing shallower than normal. Her face was pale but she was perspiring heavily. Reaching down, he slid his hand behind her. Her back was soaked.

"What is wrong with her, *mi hijo*?" Tia asked, coming alongside.

The hard bone of a stiff corset bruised his fingertips. Why the hell was she wearing a corset out here? Was she crazy?

"Might be the heat got to her."

Tia crossed herself. "That is not good."

No it wasn't.

Tia shook the water jug hanging on the side of the wagon. Liquid sloshed. She clucked her tongue. "The *pobrecita*. The water is untouched. She forgot to drink."

And he'd forgotten to remind her. "Damn."

"So we are back to heat," Stefano concluded.

Heat and carelessness. Luke checked the pulse in her throat. Her skin was smooth and hot under his fingers. Her pulse was steady but fast. This was his fault. He'd been too busy sparking her temper to pay attention to what Josie had been doing—or what she hadn't. Not drinking enough water was a typical tenderfoot mistake. He knew it as well as he knew his name. There was no excuse for his negligence. He touched her cheek, which was beginning to show a hint of sunburn. She deserved better.

Tia clucked her tongue. "I should have checked on her."

"Who would think she would not drink?" Stefano sighed.

Tia shook her head. "Apparently none of us."

For sure, it'd been a long time since an Easterner had landed at Hell's Eight. Josie's lashes fluttered.

"Josie," he called sharply. She didn't respond. He tried again, grabbing her by the shoulders, shaking her lightly. "Wake up, woman."

"Here, *mi hijo*." Tia handed him a wet handkerchief.

"Thank you." He wiped Josie's face carefully. Her skin was so pale, so delicate. As he wiped, a light dusting of freckles appeared.

How the hell had he missed that she had freckles? Looking down at the cloth, he got his answer. She'd put some kind of powder on them to cover up. He shook his head. There was no understanding women sometimes.

He shook her again. "Come on, Josie. Wake up."

"See if she will drink this," Tia said.

Taking the cup Tia passed him, he trickled a little water over her dry lips. The clear liquid pooled at the corners before sliding down over her cheeks and neck leaving a trail in the pale powder.

She groaned. He held the cup to her lips, tipping a little into her mouth. "Drink."

Half-conscious, she frowned.

"Don't fight me on this, woman. Drink."

Parting those sexy lips, she sipped.

"She'll be all right?" Stefano asked.

"Yes." He wouldn't allow otherwise. He smoothed the moisture over her cracked lips and tipped the cup again. "More."

"She needs to get out of the sun," Ed called, limping over.

He was right. The shadow he was casting over her merely darkened her expression, emphasizing her distress rather than providing any real relief.

"True enough."

Across the way, he saw the scout nod to Zach before heading out. He could tell from the slap of the reins against his boot Zach was worried. And rightly so. A Comanche sighting was never good news. They needed to keep moving.

Handing Ed the cup, Luke gathered Josie up. She struggled a little before settling into his arms as if she belonged there. The corset pressed into his forearm. He didn't know why she wore one. They were impractical as hell. A woman couldn't move in one, let alone breathe. While those restrictions might be fine and feminine back East, out here those restrictions could be a death sentence. The wagon creaked and dipped as he backed awkwardly down the steps. As his boots hit the grass, her petticoats caught on the brake lever, yanking him up short.

"Shit."

"Hold on." Ed reached over and tugged at them. There was a slight rip and then "There you go."

"Thanks."

Ed frowned as Luke carried Josie toward the back of the wagon. "I thought she'd handle the trip better."

"She is not used to our heat," Tia fussed, hurrying to get to the rear of the wagon before Luke. Her gait, he noted, was not as easy as it used to be. There was a stiffness in one hip. He shook his head, remembering his conversation with Ace. Damn.

She opened the back door, revealing the interior. Hot air rushed out.

At least the pallet on the floor was clear, he noted.

"Be careful," Tia cautioned as he propped Josie on the edge of the pallet, leaving her feet dangling over the side.

"Aren't I always?"

Tia clucked her tongue. "Hardly."

"Ed?" Luke called to the front.

"Yes?"

"Could you water the nag? We don't need him dropping from exhaustion, too." If they had to run for it, he needed the gelding ready.

"Stefano is already on it."

He wasn't surprised. Zach only kept on good men. "Thanks."

A tug on his shirt drew his gaze. Josie's lips moved.

"What?"

She said it again. He had to bend closer to hear.

"His name's Glory."

That again? "As in glory be to God?" he asked drily. "Or Glory be, will he make it through the day?"

She frowned up at him, a little of the fight coming back into her expression. "Neither."

At least her voice was getting stronger.

"Are you sure?" He hitched her up to move her back. Her nails dug into his arm. Her eyes opened wide. "Oh no!"

He'd been on the back end of too many benders not to know that look. He turned her just in time. She vomited. All over his boots.

"Son of a bitch!"

If her moan hadn't been so pitiful, Luke would have dropped her right there. Instead, he set her gently on the ground. She scrabbled to her hands and knees. He supported her with an arm around her waist as she vomited up all the water he'd just poured down her throat. Between heaves, she swatted at her bonnet. Since he hated the drab, ugly thing, too, Luke tugged it off and tossed it aside. His own stomach lurched, but he held it back, until finally, with a last retch, she slumped. With another sympathetic *"Pobrecita"* Tia handed him the cup. Water sloshed as he held it to Josie's lips. She shook her head.

"Rinse your mouth out."

She took a sip. "Don't swallow, spit," he ordered.

She did with an utter lack of self-consciousness that said more than anything about how horrible she felt.

"Good job."

When he was sure she was done, Luke pulled Josie back until she sat on his thighs. Her head flopped limply against his shoulder. Her breath shuddered out.

"I'm so hot," she whispered. "Just so hot."

"I know." He stood and turned to look into the wagon. It was dark and still, likely still stifling. "Stefano!"

"Yes?"

"Open the front panel, please."

The wagon slouched with the vaquero's weight. The panel rattled as it opened.

"It is done."

A little bit of light and air moved through the interior. Hopefully, more air would flow once the wagons were moving. Josie braced her hand on a trunk as he set her down on the thin mattress sandwiched between her belongings. Tremors vibrated from her to him. He started unbuttoning her dress. Her fingers wrapped weakly around his wrist. From behind him, Tia said, "I can do that."

"I've got it."

"You cannot undress a young, unmarried woman."

He didn't spare her a glance. "I can do whatever the hell I want."

Tia placed her hand on his arm. "No, *mi hijo*, you cannot."

Her resolution flicked at his determination. "Dammit. It's not the first time I've seen undergarments."

Tia's chin set. "You would mortify her."

"She should be mortified for being so stupid. Why the hell is she wearing so much?"

Tia elbowed him aside. "It is proper."

Dammit. There was no fighting with Tia when she got that set to her mouth. He stepped back. She didn't have to say it as if he were an idiot. "Proper will get her killed."

"Women are taught proper is what saves their lives." Tia glanced over her shoulder. "Turn your back."

Even more reluctantly, he did. "You're not wearing that much," he pointed out, tipping the cup and rinsing the vomit off his boots. It was going to take more than the cup he held to get the job done. Son of a bitch. His cobbler was going to be pissed.

"I should have talked to her," Tia fussed.

He could hear the sounds of clothing being removed. The slide of a sleeve down an arm. The rustle of petticoats being removed. His imagination pieced in the removal of the corset. At any other time his imagination would be running rampant. But right now, all he could think about was the Comanche, the delay and the risk to everyone every minute they were stopped here. A trunk opened and a minute later it closed.

He hated being forced to cool his heels. "Does she at least have something lighter to wear?"

Tia sighed. "Do you not have something else to do?"

"No."

"Then you can come make yourself useful."

"Uh-huh." Turning, he saw Josie drooped on the pallet, half sitting, half propped against a crate. Her eyes were closed. She looked pale and lethargic in the yellow dress. In need of support. "I could have been useful all along," he muttered, helping Tia down.

Tia just rolled her eyes as she stepped back.

Luke slid his hand between the rough wood and Josie's head. Her hair was silky against his palm. Her breath an airy caress as he tilted her face up. "You gave us a scare, my darling."

She blinked at him, whether at his endearment or his touch, he didn't know. Didn't care. She was still a little green around the gills.

"Sorry."

He smiled at the weak apology that could have covered anything. "You've got to be feeling pretty badly not to be taking a swing at me right now."

She licked her pale lips. "At least the darn wagon has stopped moving. All that back and forth…" She shuddered. "It's worse than being on a ship."

"You get motion sick?"

She nodded and swallowed hard.

He scooted back a bit. Just in case. His boots couldn't take another attack. "You feeling sick now?"

"Not yet."

That *yet* was ominous.

"Do you feel as if you could sip a little water?"

There was nothing lethargic about her "No."

"We have a problem with her dress, *hijo*. I cannot reach around to fasten it and she does not yet seem ready to stand," Tia interrupted.

"I can handle that."

"I thought you might be able to," she agreed drily.

He didn't have to look over his shoulder to know Tia was watching him with assumptions brewing. He'd never called anyone "my darling" before within her hearing. Hell, he hadn't done it within his own hearing, but what was done couldn't be undone. Tia would just have to speculate and he'd just have to deal.

"Turn for me just a bit, Josie."

Using his body as a brace, he turned her enough to see what he was up against. The dress had a little collar and buttoned down the back with over a dozen cloth-covered buttons. It was made of heavy cotton, and within the gape of the material, he could see red spots on her neck where the previous dress had chafed.

"She's got some prickly heat here. Do we have any ointment?"

"Of course." Tia called out instructions to Ed.

While he waited for the ointment, Luke began working from the bottom. Her camisole protected her modesty. He could see the deep creases in the fine material from her corset. He was equally sure that beneath it, her skin bore the same imprints. He traced a wrinkle with his fingertip. "No more corsets."

Her lack of argument settled a little of his annoyance. The satisfaction lasted a good five seconds, until she began to retch again.

"Son of a bitch!"

Letting gravity flip her forward, Luke barked a warning to Tia. Placing his hand against the wagon in front of her, he gave Josie something to brace against as she vomited. When she was done, Tia gingerly stepped closer and held out a fresh cup of water.

"You will feel better when you rinse your mouth, *hija*."

Luke took the cup and held it to Josie's pale lips. Cupping her hand around his, she attempted to take control. He circumvented the move through a simple application of muscle.

"I don't need help rinsing out my mouth," Josie muttered.

"Humor me."

"Maybe I don't want to."

"Why?"

She took a sip, rinsed and spat. Half her bun was straggling around her shoulders in a dark, sleek fall. "I'm trying not to be so obedient."

Interesting. "What have you got against obedience?"

"It's not part of my plan."

He humored her. "I see."

She seemed oblivious to the fact that she was half naked in his arms. He took advantage of the position to work on the buttons of her dress. The bottom seven were hopeless—the dress was cut to go over the corset, which held her in—but when he got to her rib cage they fastened.

"Here's the balm," Tia interrupted, handing him a small pottery jar.

"Thank you."

He pulled the cork out and set it on the mattress. He motioned with the jar. "You're going to have to lift your hair for this."

With one hand Josie held her dress against her chest, and with the other she lifted her hair. It was all very cooperative for someone dead set against obedience.

Dipping his fingers in the cool ointment, he smoothed the cream on her neck. She sighed and let him.

"What? No maidenly protests?" Luke asked.

"Always you are contrary," he heard Tia mutter.

Josie shook her head. "I'm saving them until I have the energy to scream them."

He chuckled. She suddenly clutched the side of the wagon.

"Are you going to be sick again?" he asked.

She swallowed twice before answering, "I haven't decided yet."

"If there's an option, my vote's for no."

"I'll bear it in mind," she muttered.

He smiled as he handed the jar and cork to Tia and went back to buttoning Josie's dress. The thin beige muslin of her camisole was transparent where it stuck to her skin, giving him peek-a-boo glimpses of soft skin everything male in him craved to explore. For sure she was a lush little thing.

He fastened the final button at her neck. "There. You're done."

He helped her down, avoiding the vomit. Her skirts hung limply without the support of the petticoats.

Standing, she reached behind her and clutched at the unbuttoned section at the small of her back. "Not quite."

"I've got a plan for that."

"You always have plans."

She didn't sound pleased about it. He shrugged. "I believe in being prepared."

From around the side of the wagon, Zach called, "If the photographer is better, we need to resume."

"Company coming?" Luke called back, keeping the concern out of his query. They were ill defended for a Comanche attack.

Josie stiffened.

"It does not seem so," Zach answered. "Lobo is keeping an eye on them."

"So we have time."

He heard the snap of leather against leather. Zach was impatient. "Not if we wish to avoid others who may be on the move. There is no cover here."

He knew that. "True enough."

"So if you could encourage the photographer…"

"I'll work on it."

"I have a name," Josie muttered.

"Tell him that." Luke waved in Zach's direction. "I can't."

He raised a brow. "Don't tell me Mrs. Not-So-Obedient is afraid…"

She shot him a look that spoke volumes.

He grinned. "Not as afraid of him as you are of getting back in that wagon, I bet."

"Heavens no."

He smiled again. She did amuse him. He plopped her bonnet on her head. "Don't worry. I've got a plan for that, too."

She looked at him and raised her brows. Beneath the misery in her expression, he caught a flicker of hope. "You might just be my hero."

"Hold on to that thought."

Tia rolled her eyes and snorted. "I will return to my wagon while you sort this out."

Josie watched her go. "I don't think I want to be sorted."

Luke whistled. "Too late to take a stand on that now. I'm married to the thought of being a hero."

"You don't strike me as the marrying kind," she muttered under her breath, straightening the ugly bonnet.

Chico came strolling around the wagon. Tossing his head, he nickered a greeting. Luke gathered up the reins and drew him up.

"Oh no." Josie plastered herself back against the wagon and shook her head as comprehension dawned. "I don't ride."

"Who said anything about riding?" Riding took effort. He wasn't planning on her working up to even a deep breath. Mounting, he turned the horse until he was perpendicular to where Josie stood watching with a mixture of horror and fascination. Any color she'd regained faded away as he scooted back behind the saddle. The sunburn stood out in garish streaks on her cheeks. Holding out his hand, he beckoned her closer.

"No."

He cocked his head to the side. "Chico doesn't sway like the wagon."

She pressed against the tailgate. "I don't like horses."

An idiot could see that. Tipping his hat back, he asked, "How much do you like Comanche?"

That did the trick. She looked around as if warriors lurked behind every anthill. He mentally shook his head. As if he'd permit any threat to get that close. Reluctantly, she placed her hand in his and allowed him to draw her onto the saddle. Her skirts tangled around her legs as she dangled awkwardly.

"Throw your leg over the saddle horn," he grunted as he strained to hold her high enough and keep Chico from prancing his displeasure with the unbalanced weight.

"We're too high."

"Hardly."

She grabbed the horn as Chico sidestepped. "Says you!"

"A horse is your best friend out here."

Clinging to the horn, she gasped. "Is he yours?"

"Yup."

"That explains a lot."

He chuckled. "You've got sass, I'll give you that. Now fix your skirts unless you want to ride with them cutting off your blood supply."

"I'd prefer not to ride at all."

"Duly noted."

Pulling her up and back against him, he waited for her to get the folds of material arranged to her liking before settling her back against him with improper closeness. She stiffened at the proximity, but he just grinned and urged Chico forward. Her hips rocked pleasingly against him as she clung to the horn.

"This isn't decent," she whispered.

At least her color was back. "But it is practical."

"I'm not a fan of practical."

He spread his fingers over her stomach, and clucked his tongue as Chico stopped to nose the grain bucket tied to Tia and Ed's wagon. "Not a fan of obedience or practical." He shook his head and smiled. "I knew you were going to be trouble."

IF SHE HADN'T felt so sick, Josie might have protested Luke's high-handedness. At the very least, been horrified at the enforced intimacy of her transport, but her sense of proper was otherwise distracted. She'd never ridden a horse before. It was not the liberating experience she'd attempted to convince herself it could be. In fact, it was terrifying.

On horseback she sat much higher than in the wagon and she couldn't get her mind off the fact it was a long way—maybe a neck-breakingly long way—to the ground. Combine that with the potential that Chico might object to her presence on his back and she had good reason to be nervous. If he reared or bucked she'd go flying. As if hearing her worry, Chico tossed his head and pranced. She grabbed the saddle horn.

Luke's arm tightened around her waist. "I've got you."

"Wonderful, but who's got him?"

"I've got him, too."

All he had when it came to the horse was the reins.

She bit her tongue on a retort. For her safety, she didn't need him distracted by an argument.

"Nothing to say to that?" he asked.

"What do you want me to say? You're holding two pieces of leather and calling it security. Clearly you're delusional."

She expected anything but his bark of laughter.

"I've been with Chico a long time. We understand each other."

"He doesn't like me up here. I can tell."

"He's not used to riding double."

"Which is what concerns me."

"He trusts me."

He said it as if it was the final word on the subject. "What if I don't trust you?"

"You will."

The confidence in that statement irked her. "What makes you so sure?"

"I'm very trustworthy. Ask Tia." He urged Chico forward until they were even with the front of Tia's wagon. Ed cocked an eyebrow at them. Josie cringed in embarrassment.

"Am I trustworthy, Tia?" Luke asked.

"Of course."

The chuckle Josie felt vibrating along her back was also present in Luke's voice. "There you go. Chico trusts me. Tia trusts me. All the confirmation you need."

"Some things a woman just likes to decide for herself."

He wasn't daunted. "And trusting me is one of them?"

"Absolutely."

"All right. I'll give you time."

She knew better than to leave such things open-ended. "How much?"

"We've got another two hours until lunch. I'll check with you then and see how you feel."

Two hours? She clutched the horn again. She didn't know if she could handle two hours. The nausea was settling and the light-headedness was fading, but all that did was make her more aware of the muscled forearm settled across her stomach and the strong chest cradling her back. The scents of leather, horse and Luke combined, filling her nostrils. She wanted to hate it, position it as something to resent, but the truth was he smelled and felt pretty darn good. Like the first exhilarating touch of fall after the draining heat of summer. Crisp, cool and inspiring.

It was easy to imagine him walking to the door at the end of a long day, bringing that certain excitement with him. She could imagine meeting him halfway, sliding her hands over his hard chest and around his neck, kissing him hello, breathing in his answer, letting his strength surround her. It was too easy to imagine him sitting down at the supper table, filling the room with his presence and masculine scent. Turning the house into a home.

As much as she loved the concept of happily-ever-after when she looked at Hester and Uncle Jarl and the happiness they embraced, when it came to marriage, her mother had always told her a woman had to be practical. Monotony and submission were a cheap price to pay for security.

She wasn't sure she wanted security all that much. She'd been trapped in monotony all her life, trying to be so good, so quiet, so obedient, that people wouldn't remember that she didn't have a father like everybody else. That her mother lived alone in a shame that Josie shared. That they wouldn't think about all the hours she spent on her knees in church repenting for sins she'd never committed. That they wouldn't see *her*.

"You've gone quiet on me." Luke interrupted her thoughts.

"I wasn't aware you wanted me to talk."

"It'd be nice. After all, we're sharing a horse."

"Not by my request."

"You didn't leave me many options, what with needing your modesty protected."

"I could have ridden with Stefano."

His "No" was terse and to the point.

She had to ask. "What's wrong with Stefano?"

"He's Zach's cousin. The Lopez men are good men, but womanizers to the last."

"And you're not?"

His chin rested on top of her head, squashing her bonnet flat. "I just got done proving I'm trustworthy."

She pushed the bonnet back off her face. "That's not an answer."

"You're mighty feisty for somebody who wouldn't say boo to a ghost a few hours ago."

She was, she realized. There was something liberating about not having to look at the person to whom she was speaking. She could just stare into space, say what was on her mind and not see their reaction. She kind of liked it.

"I'm sure Stefano is safe."

"He's not."

From the wagon, Ed snorted and Tia chuckled. Josie noticed Luke didn't tell her to be quiet. She supposed he wouldn't dare. From what she'd observed, the men of Hell's Eight revered Tia. A little part of her was jealous. She'd never known the sense of safety that came from somebody loving her like that. The love Tia and the men gave each other was an unconditional love. Well, maybe not uncon-

ditional, but they shared the same values, the same
strengths, the same code of honor, so the conditions
were easy to meet.

It was the opposite of her relationship with her
mother. She'd never done one thing to make her
mother think that she was a whore, but it was her
mother's overriding concern that she would become
one. Because she was born out of wedlock. Because
of that, Josie had to work harder, prove herself. If her
mother saw her right now, she'd point her finger and
yell, "Jezebel."

Josie couldn't help it. The thought amused her.
Despite all her mother's precautions and her own
efforts, here she was sitting on a man's lap in a state
of total dishabille.

Luke leaned over her shoulder and pulled the bonnet back. "You're smiling."

"I do that sometimes."

"I like it."

The way he said it in that deep drawl, the timbre
resonating with sexual meaning, so serious when
there was usually an edge of banter to his tone, made
her shiver. There was no hope he didn't feel it, either,
pressed up against her as he was.

"I like that, too."

And that fast her breath caught and her skin sen-
sitized. Through the gap in the back of her dress she
imagined she could feel the heat of his skin, a sensual connection through which his energy seeped,
flowing from him to her and back again. The urge
to squirm began deep inside.

Good grief. She clutched the horn for a whole different reason. She couldn't squirm, not for this man.

His hands covered hers. His palms were calloused and rough. They felt the way she'd always imagined a man's hands should feel. How would they feel against her body? Just thinking about it made her shiver.

"I was serious when I said you could trust me." His tone was softer without the banter. "I won't hurt you, Josie."

That wasn't a promise anyone could keep, but she went along with it. Maybe just to see how far he would take it. She glanced over her shoulder.

"A Hell's Eight promise?"

His head cocked to the side, casting half his face in shadow. Darkness and light. "What do you know about a Hell's Eight promise?"

"I've heard a body can take them to the bank."

"That's true, but that wasn't a Hell's Eight promise. That one was pure Luke Bellen."

Was that better or worse? She didn't know and he didn't offer clarification. One by one Luke's fingers pried hers from the horn. When her pinky released, she had nothing left to hold on to. Folding her fingers together, she placed them primly in her lap. She always lapsed back to proper when she was uncomfortable, and this was as proper as she could manage in her current circumstance.

Luke sighed. "I'll keep you safe, Josie."

She'd heard those words before. Believed them. And then had her world destroyed. "Am I?"

She felt his shrug against her back. "As safe as you want to be, at least."

"What does that even mean?"

"You don't know?"

Inside her, the hurt coiled into anger. He thought she was loose. It wasn't the first time she'd run into that assumption.

"I may be illegitimate, but I'm not a whore."

Almost imperceptibly, his muscles stiffened. If she hadn't been so focused on him, she probably wouldn't have noticed. He was very good at hiding his feelings.

"I don't remember asking you if you were."

"You implied it."

"No, I did not."

It wasn't the first time she'd seen a man backtrack once she'd confronted him, either. The only difference between this time and the others was the disappointment she was feeling.

"Do you think you're original? Don't you think I've heard it all by now? The insinuations? Men asking questions they wouldn't otherwise ask to see if I'm desperate enough to take them up on the lousy offer they're making me?"

"No, I actually didn't think that."

"Horse hockey!"

His finger caught her chin and turned her head up. He leaned forward so she had no choice but to see his expression. This close she could see the flecks of black in his irises, see the stubble on his jaw, the fullness of his lips and his ridiculously long lashes.

And the conviction behind his words as he stated, "I don't say what I don't mean."

She jerked her chin free and he let her. She went back to clutching the horn. Damn him for putting her in this position. Now she had to apologize. "Neither do I."

Usually.

"You shouldn't have had to face that alone. There should have been someone there to stand for you."

Yes. There should have been. "Uncle Jarl tried."

"But he's not really your uncle, is he, and he wasn't always around, was he?"

Luke was too astute by far. She shook her head. "No."

"And your mother?"

He knew the worst, so he might as well know the rest. "My mother, more than anyone else, believes I'm destined to be a whore—"

He cut her off. "That's twice you've used that word in regard to yourself. You won't use it again."

She hadn't meant to use it the first time. He had a way of making her reckless. "You have no say over me."

Another shrug and another tip of her face to his. "Say it again and see where it gets you."

His expression was as hard as his tone. Part of her didn't care. Part of her cared too much. The heat and the sickness had taken more than she thought out of her. She knew better than to confront a man like this.

She jerked her chin out of his hold and knotted her fingers together. "Please. I'm not feeling well."

It was, at best, a convenient excuse. She expected him to tear through it, but he neither agreed nor disagreed, just left her in a limbo of her own creation.

She could feel him staring at her, feel his impatience. His intention. He wasn't going to let it go.

"Please," she repeated.

She hated the whisper, but more than that, she hated the weakness it betrayed.

Luke's fingers splayed across her belly, the warmth of his palm soothing, the support even more so. His drawl eased across her nerves. "Rest, Josie. Let me handle things for a while."

With a whispered "Damn you" she leaned back against him, closed her eyes and accepted the comfort he offered.

CHAPTER FIVE

DAMN HIM INDEED.

The stop for lunch was going to be longer than Luke would have liked, but they didn't have a choice. The heat and humidity had taken their toll on everything and everyone. Luke couldn't remember a day in recent times when the weather had been so oppressive. The choice to stop at the waterhole made everyone nervous. It was too obvious a resting spot, too likely a spot for robbers and Indians to seek shelter, too, but there was shade. And water. And until the sun got a little lower in the sky, it was their only option.

Here the horses could cool off and rest. They could replenish the water that had evaporated from the water barrels and get a bite to eat. But he didn't have to like it. Especially since it'd meant he had to let Josie slip from his arms. No, he definitely hadn't been in favor of that.

There was something about holding her softness against him that created a sense of peace deep inside him. As if her presence filled a hole he hadn't noticed until now. Peace and Josie in the same sentence didn't make any sense. The woman was as contrary as they came and havoc followed her like a plague. Nonetheless, riding with her in front of him, he'd felt at peace, quite possibly for the first time in his life.

From where he stood beside Tia's wagon after watering the horses, he had a clear view of the campsite. Tia sat on a log by the water with Ed. They shared a tortilla while waiting for lunch. There were smiles and laughter aplenty despite the exhausting pace. Love might have come late to Tia's life but it'd come pure.

Luke watched as she handed the tortilla to Ed, whose smile was lost beneath his mustache. Tia flexed her hands. Her arthritis was probably acting up. It always did when it was going to rain. A glance at the sky didn't give him a warm glow. A storm was brewing. He wished they were on their way, but that wasn't possible. Traveling with women meant taking their needs into consideration, so here they all were, wagons tucked in among the trees as out of sight as possible, enjoying the shade.

The vaqueros not on guard duty were making lunch despite Tia's insistence she could do it. Zach's men treated Tia like a queen and when she and Ed stood and joined them around the campfire, they made a place for her to hold court. Conversation and laughter was muted—they were all aware of the potential threat—but Luke noted Tia was enjoying her adventure.

Luke wasn't surprised when Zach came up alongside a few minutes later. The Montoya foreman was a quiet man with an eagle eye and a quick hand with a gun. He also had a rather questionable sense of humor of which, at the moment, Luke didn't feel like being a victim.

"Keep on walking, Zach."

That could have been a slight twitch of the other man's lips as he leaned back against the wagon. It was hard to tell. Expressions came and went across Zach's face with the subtlety of a ghost crossing your path. He was a lethal poker player. "I would love to."

Luke could hear it coming. "But?"

"Tia asked me to come talk to you."

"Tia's not your boss."

"No," Zach said, pulling out a cigarillo. "But I like her."

"So?"

Zach shrugged and shook a sulfur out of the tin. "So it pleases me to make her happy."

"She has a husband to make her happy."

This time there was no mistaking the grin that came to his face. He clicked the tin closed. "I like him, too."

"Son of a bitch."

Zach struck the sulfur. The flame hissed a warning. He tilted his head as he lit the cigarillo, the tip glowing red when he took a drag. "Tia does not like that you make our guest unhappy."

"How am I making her unhappy? I haven't even spoken to her since we got here."

"This I believe is the problem." He blew out a steady stream of smoke. "Too much you frown at the woman. As a woman, Tia does not understand.

As a man, I understand even less. This one is an attractive woman. Single. Entertaining. Ripe for the plucking." He cocked a dark brow at him. "And she interests you."

"Throwing the little photographer at me is you 'fixing things'?"

Zach shrugged and offered him a cigarillo. "It is my start."

Luke declined. He was giving quitting another try. "Do you have an end?"

"That would depend on how amusing you intend to be on this journey."

"Not a damn bit. I'm here riding guard. I'm not here to entertain Josie Kinder."

"This would be a shame."

"And why is that?"

Zach grinned and Luke was suddenly reminded of how Sam had once grumbled about his foreman's too-attractive face and inherent charm. "Because she is pretty, alone and never have I seen a woman who requires a man more to help give her focus."

"Seriously? Lacking focus? Seems once the woman gets to taking a picture she just forgets everything else."

"Perhaps I should rephrase. She needs someone, a man like you, to help direct her focus to more worldly things."

"Tia wouldn't be trying to matchmake, would she?"

Zach shrugged. "I did not ask."

But they both knew Tia didn't want him to leave.

"Giving that woman direction is more work than I hanker for."

"Hmm." Zach took another drag and cocked his head to the side. "Have you seen her photographs?"

"No." It wasn't a total lie. He'd only allowed himself a glance at them.

"You should look at them sometime. There is beauty in her attention to detail."

Luke didn't want to know much more about the woman. She was already too tempting. No matter how lush her figure or how passionate her nature, she was an Easterner through and through. From her ridiculous hat to her impractical clothing with too many layers. Heaven forbid she ever had to run. She wouldn't make it two steps. And don't get him started on that damn horse she loved. It was as ill suited to this world as she was. But more important, she was heading back home when this lark was done. Why let himself get involved?

"Truth is, I'll be glad when we get to the Montoya ranch and my babysitting duties are over. Until then, I intend to keep a distance."

"As you did this morning?"

"Shut up, Zach."

Zach took a deep drag on his cigarillo and released it in a long plume of blue smoke before smiling a genuine smile that gave Luke pause.

"What?" Luke recognized that grin.

Zach glanced in Josie's direction, where she fussed with the box she'd had him drag out of her wagon and over to Tia's. "Like I said, Tia wants the little picture taker happy."

Luke had a feeling where this was going. "That has nothing to do with me."

"I'm afraid it does. Tia has decided you will watch over her."

"Then why isn't Tia telling me this herself?"

"She fears your reaction."

"Oh bullshit. Tia hasn't feared a thing in all the time I've known her."

Though admittedly, she might fear his reaction to her matchmaking. Tia had known him too long not to have noticed his interest.

"That's not true. She tells me she often feared for the Hell's Eights' lives when you were on your path of revenge."

"Yeah, well… There's a lot of things Tia didn't understand then."

Zach shrugged. "She is a woman. This is to be expected, but she wants softer things for you than the death you pursued."

That was true. The one thing that had kept the Hell's Eight civilized through all those wild years was the relentless pressure Tia had put on them to hold their honor sacred. And after that, to dream. She alone had encouraged his story writing. Especially in those times when he didn't want to write. He sometimes felt she'd pushed him the hardest then. Even when what he did write came out as black pictures of death and revenge, she'd told him his words were powerful. And he'd believed her because their impact was reflected in her expression.

He'd asked her about that once. Why she'd kept encouraging him when she'd so clearly been upset by what she was reading. She'd said a story had to run its course, and sometimes it had to come to the blackest part to find the light. He'd never found light, but he had found a neutral corner.

"You realize I don't believe you, right?"

"You realize I don't care." Zach took another drag on his nearly finished cigarillo before smiling around the thin dark smoke. "Oh, and one more thing."

Wonderful. "What?"

Zach straightened. "The picture taker? She would like to take some pictures of flowers down by the river before we leave."

Luke ran his hand over the back of his neck. Another delay. "I don't like that we've already had to stop so much."

"We cannot go any faster. The weather is bad and Tia and Ed are too old."

"And the wagons are heavy." Luke dropped his hand from his neck. "I don't understand why Tia had to pack so much."

Zach shrugged. "Tia doesn't travel anywhere without her necessities."

"I remember when her necessities used to fit in a knapsack."

Zach smiled. "It is a good life you have given her."

"Not good enough." He couldn't fight off death or the inevitable.

With a wave of his hand, Zach indicated the painted wagon and its occupant. "The photographer awaits you."

And so she did. Standing by the wagon with a box dangling from a strap over her shoulder, her lush figure clearly constrained once again by a corset, in direct contrast to his orders.

Son of a bitch. He slapped his hand against his thigh. Wasn't passing out once enough of a warning? Yet as soon as he'd turned his back, she'd gone in that damn wagon and strapped herself into that torture device.

She watched him approach, her gaze steady and her smile timid.

With a jerk of his chin, he indicated her dress. "You're wearing a corset."

The shy smile hovering on her lips died. A flush crept up her neck and over her cheeks. Her grip on the box strap tightened till it was white-knuckled. He'd noticed she did that when trying to control herself. No doubt she was stifling the urge to punch him.

"Not only is it improper for you to mention my attire, what I wear is none of your business."

What did he care for propriety? "It's definitely my business if you fall flat on your face again."

"I won't."

She sounded very sure of that. "Why?"

"Because I want this picture."

She was completely illogical. "Wanting a picture isn't going to keep heat exhaustion at bay."

She shifted the strap higher on her shoulder. "I want to get moving."

"Oh, now you want to get moving. Well, we're not going anywhere until you take off that corset."

"If I take off the corset, my dress won't fit."

"Then put a scarf around your shoulders or just let it gape."

She blinked at him as if he'd lost his mind. "I can't go around with my dress open. That would be indecent."

He folded his arms across his chest. "Indecent beats dead."

She had the gall to roll her eyes. "I'm not going to die."

"You're not walking around out here wearing that corset, either."

Her jaw set. So did his.

She tried again. "I don't have time to change."

"Why not?"

She waved her hand toward the sky. "Because the clouds will shift."

"They tend to do that."

"I've never seen clouds like these."

He had and it worried him. "A storm's brewing."

She stamped her foot. "The light is perfect. The clouds are going to make a perfect backdrop." She glanced over her shoulder. "And if I don't go now, I'm going to lose it."

Her grip on the camera mirrored her grip on the strap. She was clearly getting her stubborn all riled up, ready to pull it out and wave it in his face like a sword. He didn't have the patience for this.

"I'll make you a deal." He settled his rifle into the crook of his arm. "I'll escort you down to where you want to take a picture, but when the picture's done, the corset comes off. We can't be delayed again by your passing out."

She hitched the strap up again, a victorious smile twitching the corners of her mouth. "Done."

That smile was going to cost her. Bracing his rifle against the wagon, he reached for the camera box. "I'll carry that."

"I always carry my equipment."

"But I'm here now."

"This is unnecessary."

With a cock of his brow he used her own argument against her. "Do you really have the time to pitch a fit with me?"

She licked her lips, drawing his attention to their delectable softness. "No, but you need to understand I want to."

Somewhere to someone, that probably made sense.

He held out his hand. "But you won't."

Slowly, reluctantly, she slid the strap off her shoulder. "Please be careful."

"I already told you—you can trust me."

"But this is different."

He took the equipment. The box was surprisingly heavy. With his free hand, he tipped her gaze to his. "No, it's not."

Dropping his hand to her shoulder, he steered her around. "Now, lead on."

The look she gave him should have singed his short hairs. He smiled as she trudged off. Grabbing his rifle, he followed.

Not surprisingly, she led him to a patch of wild-flowers growing in the midst of a field, dotting the green expanse with pinks, yellows and whites. She stopped, made a square with her hands as if using them as a scope, and surveyed the scene. She moved all around the patch, standing, kneeling and twisting until she finally seemed to find a spot just shy of the middle that suited her. She looked pretty surrounded by the flowers. "This will do right here."

It didn't look like anything spectacular to him. "You sure?"

"Yes." She motioned impatiently. "Hand me the box, please."

"What's the hurry?" He slid the strap off his shoulder. "They aren't going anywhere."

"But the light will. Light changes on a whim. And those clouds…" She motioned again. "They're just perfect."

Shaking his head, he set the box down. Cradling his rifle in his arms, he watched as she efficiently put everything together, mounted the camera on its support, and meticulously lined up everything for the image she wanted. He might as well have been a bump on a log for all the attention she paid him. Which was fine with him. He enjoyed watching her.

She was so different when working with the

camera—competent and confident, her attention focused, a slight furl between her brows. There was no fumbling or bumbling, no tripping, no absent-mindedness. She knew what she was doing and it showed. She took her shots, exchanged the tins and reset the camera. He turned as she did, but try as he might, he couldn't see what she did. To his eyes they were just flowers, sky and clouds, but in her eyes they were clearly a vision. He wondered if it was a bit like when he stared at a blank page and the words started flowing and the story developed. It was an interesting concept.

Crouching down, she examined the scene again. Standing, she removed the camera from the tripod and brought it down to the ground. Her frown deepened. She looked up at the sky. Moved the camera a tiny fraction. Not enough to make a difference to bug dust. But it seemed critical to her. She changed the angle. Clearly wanting more of the sky. For someone in a hurry, it took forever for her to take the picture.

"So powerful," she whispered.

He followed her gaze and it was his turn to frown. The clouds were heavier, darker, forming a wall in the distance. On a hot, humid, oppressive day like today, tornadoes were known to sweep in. And this storm looked set to be the ornery type that would spring just such a surprise.

"Time to pack it up, Josie."

With a regretful sigh, she nodded, stood and arched her back. The pose stuck her breasts out in sharp relief. It was his turn to freeze.

With a satisfied "There" she picked up the camera.

With an inner shake, Luke found his voice. Josie was so wrapped up in her picture taking, he doubted she noticed the added roughness. Women weren't usually so oblivious to him. It was an…interesting experience. "Did you get what you wanted?"

The wind kicked up, blowing strands of hair across her face. She brushed them back. "Oh yes."

If he could've taken a picture of her right then, he would have. With the storm churning the sky in the distance, the wind whipping her skirts around her legs and pressing her dress to her lush figure, she was a confident siren. The smile on her face only added to the seductive tendrils she'd been wrapping around him since the day they'd met.

"What do you see through your camera?"

"Magic."

"Show me."

She made a square of her hands again. "Put your hands like this."

"Hold my rifle." She took it gingerly. He made a square as she'd shown him.

"Now get down here and look through that 'lens.'"

When he did, she moved him over. "Not there. Here." She tugged his hand down. "Now look."

Suddenly, he caught a glimpse of what she'd hoped to capture—the turbulence of the sky, the subtle peace of the flowers caught on the edge of the storm, the immenseness of the land—all of it encapsulated in one blink. And then wind blew, the cloud drifted and the moment was gone. He stood and retrieved his rifle, wondering if he'd even seen what he'd seen. He nodded to the tintype. "I want to see that when you're done."

"Of course." She frowned. "But I don't think I'll have time to develop it before we leave."

She sounded hopeful.

Another glance at the sky. "No, you won't."

"I was afraid of that." She loaded everything back into the case. The picture taking seemed to have re-energized her. "I don't want to wait too long in case the tins get damaged."

"I understand."

"Maybe when we stop for the night." She was still on the developing.

"Maybe." Taking the case, he waved her ahead of him. "It will be near dark by then."

"That's fine."

She hiked up her skirts and climbed up the slight hill. Not enough for him to get more than a glimpse of her serviceable shoes. More's the pity.

"I need dark to develop the image," she continued. "Too much light is bad."

Out of curiosity, he asked, "How do you know what you're doing if it has to be dark?"

"I use a tiny bit of indirect light."

"Do you ever make mistakes?"

"All the time. Developing is different with every picture." Looking back over her shoulder, she asked, "Do you think it's going to rain?"

"Probably." He cocked an eyebrow at her. "You

going to have room in that wagon for me when the skies open up?"

She stopped and turned before looking him up and down. "Do you think you'll fit?"

He had no doubt she meant that in the most innocent of terms. It didn't matter to his imagination. He could see himself lifting her onto the mattress, coming over her, forcing her back, easing himself down over her until they were chest to breast, breath to breath... He tipped his hat back.

"I will definitely make us fit."

That *us* caught her attention. She flushed a bright pink that just emphasized the color of her eyes. He was getting real partial to that particular shade of blue.

Clearly stuck in the moment, she licked her lips. "Um."

He waited but nothing followed.

"That's all you've got? Just 'um'?"

Her muttered "For the moment" floated behind her.

Luke smiled. He did like her sass. He checked the horizon again. The storm was moving fast. Camping in the open tonight was not going to be an option. There were some caves three miles west of their current course. They might be able to make it there ahead of the rain.

"If you hustle, you might not have to come up with a better retort."

Holding her hair back from her face, she asked,

"Do you think we can outrun the storm?" She seemed excited by the prospect.

He shook his head. "Do you honestly see that nag of yours outrunning anything?"

Frowning, she corrected, "His name is Glory."

"Uh-huh." He motioned her on. She didn't go any faster. "Woman, move."

With a sigh, she stepped up her pace. "Are you afraid of getting wet?"

It was a damn naive question. "I don't like to get caught in a wash or out in the open when a storm like that one brewing opens up. And a day as hot as today is usually goes out with a bang."

"Oh, I hope so. I love thunderstorms."

"Says the woman from Massachusetts."

She stopped and spun around. "Now, what do you have against Massachusetts?"

With a hand on her shoulder he kept her turning until she was back on course. With a nudge he got her moving again. "Not a damn thing, but you haven't seen storms like we have here. They spit out tornadoes as randomly as they spit out raindrops."

Another stop. Another turn. She blinked. "A tornado?"

"Yup."

She glanced at the storm with a little less enthusiasm. "Oh."

"Yeah, oh. One can't just ride out a tornado. You either avoid it or it picks up your butt and tosses it four states over."

Gathering up her skirts, she said, "Then we'd better hurry."

"I thought that's what I'd been saying."

"It's rude to boast."

Hitching the box over his shoulders, he caught her hand. "Even ruder to ignore sound advice."

She tugged at her hand. "I can walk, you know."

"You seem more inclined to stroll." He set a brisk pace. She was forced to skip a little to keep up.

"Do we have to run?"

"Yes." Mainly because it gave him an excuse to keep her hand in his.

When they got to the camp, everything was already packed up. Zach shot him a look. "Storm's coming in."

"I noticed."

Zach pushed his hat back. "Hopefully, it'll blow on by, but either way, we need to move."

Ed helped Tia up from where she sat. Driving this morning had taken a visible toll on her. She hobbled a bit on her way to her wagon, Ed hovering protectively, keeping his hand on the base of her spine, though he wasn't moving any easier.

Luke tugged Josie in the direction of Chico. "You come with me."

"As if I have a choice."

No, she didn't.

Josie shook her head and dug in her feet. "My wagon…"

It barely took any muscle at all to pop her along behind him. "I'll get one of the men to drive it."

"I thought you couldn't spare somebody in case there was a problem."

"You get sick."

"I'll drink plenty of water. And—" she sighed, shaking her head at him "—I'll take off my corset."

She might be learning. "A wise decision."

They'd arrived at the back of her wagon. She pulled her hand free as he opened the brightly painted doors. She clearly took exception to his tone.

Straightening her bonnet, she said with deliberate indifference, "A deal's a deal, after all. I got my pictures and now you get my corset."

He passed her the camera box. "I was wondering if we were going to have to fight on that."

"No, but I'm driving my wagon. No Comanche is going to wave my scalp around because you wasted a guard on something I can do myself," she stated firmly as she put the box in the back of the wagon.

So now she was giving orders? He pushed his hat back. "What do you know of Comanche?"

"I've done my research. I've read all about the West."

"You've read about it?"

She nodded. The brim of her bonnet cast her eyes in shadow. He didn't like it. "Extensively. The West and its traditions are quite fascinating."

"I see." He could just imagine what she'd read.

"Mr. Savage, my favorite author, has quite the descriptive flair," she informed him blithely. "To the point I feel as if I've already been here."

It was his turn to blink. That took care of the need

to imagine. Damn. He tugged his hat down over his brow. She was hot for his pseudonym? He didn't know how he felt about that. "You can't believe everything you read."

She was undeterred. "I believe enough to know I don't want to be scalped."

"No Comanche would snatch your scalp." They'd snatch her virginity and her future, but they'd leave that thick mane of hair.

Another roll of her eyes. "I appreciate your trying not to scare me, but I'm not beyond common sense, you know. I recognize danger when I see it."

As she ducked her head to climb in, her skirts stretched lovingly across her full hips. Lust that had been simmering all day rose hard and fast. Curling his fingers into fists to avoid the temptation to smack that ass, Luke gritted his teeth.

He wished he could say the same about himself.

CHAPTER SIX

THE STORM CHARGED across the open plain like buffalo of old, a stampede of violence, of churning clouds and lightning. Darkness swept before it, enveloping them all. Horses stomped and screamed in panic. Men yelled, "Take cover! Take cover!"

For once, Glory didn't plod. He took off. Holding the reins tightly, wrestling for control of the wildly careening wagon, Josie searched for anything that could be called cover. There was a copse of trees to the left. She steered for it. Behind her, she heard people shouting. She made out the word *cover* again. She slapped the reins on Glory's back, but he was already going as fast as he could. Looking over her shoulder, she didn't think it was fast enough. It was impossible to tell which way the storm was going. The clouds were odd, dense swirling demons, seething and spitting out lightning flashes. Even as she watched, a huge tube stretched down to the ground like a black tentacle reaching for hell. In the back of her mind she knew what she was looking at. She'd read about it in Dane Savage's books. Luke had mention it earlier…

Tornado!

The reality was more terrifying than the legend. Tornadoes were giant funnels of wind and death that wrenched up everything in their path—people, buildings and trees—and chucked them out, sometimes miles away as they relentlessly ripped across the land. Lightning flashed again. And again. The storm was delineated in the strobing light. Her stomach clenched and dropped. It was coming right for her.

Oh God, she prayed, *help me!*

In an answer to her prayer, Luke rode up alongside, looking as wild as the storm on his big horse with the wind tearing through his hair. He yelled something she couldn't hear. His hat flapped across his back. Leaning over, he slapped the reins on Glory's flank. Glory tossed his head. Luke waved her on, pointing forward. Slapping the reins down again on Glory's hindquarters, Josie whispered, "Hurry. Hurry!" Maybe she screamed it. Who could tell over the roaring wind? Inside, panic churned with the same violence.

The wagon clanked and bounced over the rutted ground, almost bucking her out of the seat. She no longer had control over the horse. Where they were headed, she didn't know. Just away. Away from the storm.

Luke shouted again. The wind tore away the words. Chico stretched out his strong legs and drew even with Glory's head. Luke reached down and grabbed the reins. He pulled to the right, away from the trees, toward barren land ahead. There was no cover there. They needed cover. Behind her, Josie could hear the tornado bearing down on them, sounding like a runaway train.

Releasing the reins, Luke dropped back until he was even with the far side of the wagon seat. Glory kept running. Josie watched as Luke held out his arm and beckoned with his fingers. For a wild moment she pretended not to know what he wanted. With a snap of his fingers, he pointed to the edge of the seat. The wagon bumped and careened. She inched over, expecting the wagon to tip or to be thrown out at any moment.

His lips shaped a word. *Jump.*

Was he crazy? Sane women didn't jump out of wagons. The wagon hit another rut. She pulled back on the reins. Glory was past caring what she did. He raced on. Another rut tipped the wagon dangerously. Luke shouted something. She was pretty sure it was a curse. He snapped his fingers again and held out his arm.

Digging her nails into the wood, she took a breath. Jump. She had to jump.

This was insane. Why did she ever leave home? This time, when the wagon tilted, it almost went over. She had to grab on to the frame to keep from being pitched out. In that split second, she saw the rocks waiting to cushion her fall. She'd never survive.

Holding her breath, she looked up, straight into Luke's eyes, seeing his confidence. This time his lips shaped the words *Trust me.* She didn't have a choice. Clinging to his gaze like a lifeline, she waited. On the next bump, she used the momentum to launch herself up and out, arms spread, screaming and grasping.

It wasn't a perfect job. And it wasn't a perfect catch, but Luke caught her. The point of his knee collided painfully with her side. She clung with everything she had, and so did he. He said something she couldn't hear. She couldn't focus, the relief was too overpowering. He hauled her up. And this time she heard the words.

"I've got you."

There were not three more beautiful words in the English language. Chico, whom she'd always thought of as a little flighty since he'd put on the display before they'd left, was as steady as a rock, pulling away from the wagon with rhythmic strides. She risked a glance back. The tornado stalked them like a devil gone wild.

Please God.

Luke's grip shifted and his body turned as he hefted her behind him. "Put your leg over."

Her skirts, sodden by the rain, wrapped around her calves, hampering her efforts, but he didn't drop her as she struggled.

I've got you.

Yes he did. Putting her faith in that promise, she let go of his arm and hauled her skirts out of the way. Weak with relief, straddling the horse, she collapsed against his back, wrapping her arms around his waist. As soon as she did, another order whipped past her ear. "Hold on."

She did, clinging for dear life, leaning over as he

and the horse became one, powering across the land. Behind them, the demon howled. She lost sight of Glory in the hell. She hoped he was all right. She prayed he'd be all right. *Please.*

Something slammed into her back like a small fist. Another something grazed her thigh. A white ball whizzed past her face. *Hail,* she realized. It was hail, but bigger than any hail she'd ever seen. It hit the ground and bounced. It hit them too and seemed to bite into their bones. They had to find cover. Burying her head in Luke's back, she clung to his waist. Why weren't they headed to the trees? The trees would protect them.

Trust me.

Right now she didn't have any choice. Luke was her only hope.

Lightning flashed. In the flash she saw the ravine.

"Watch out."

Luke pried her arms from around his waist. "Jump."

Was he crazy? "No!"

Without a word, Luke pivoted in the saddle, anchored her to his body, and threw them from the horse. There was a sensation of flying, a moment when up was down and then the illusion vanished. They hit the ground. Hard. Her teeth snapped together. Stars exploded behind her eyes. In the next instant, they rolled down the hill. Chico didn't follow them down the ravine.

Hail hit with bruising force and thundered against the ground. So many strikes she lost count.

She caught one brief glimpse of Glory silhouetted against lightning, still running, and then she saw the storm. It was a monster and it was almost upon them. "Luke!"

Grabbing her arm, Luke roughly shoved her up against the hollowed-out side of the ravine, forcing her flat on her stomach before throwing his body over hers, pressing so hard all she could breathe was dirt and him.

His hands came over hers, anchoring them into the ground. His lips brushed against her ear. "I've got you."

The promise came out as a whisper, but she was sure it was meant to be a roar. This was crazy. They were going to die. Because of a summer storm. She didn't even know what to do with that.

"I've got you," he said again, his body her protection, his determination her lifeline. Hail bounced off the ground. It had to be bouncing off him. Now and again, he'd grunt.

The wind yanked at them greedily. She could feel her skirts whipping up between and around his legs. Her hat was long gone. Everything was backward. With a voracious hunger, the storm tried to suck them in. She felt Luke's weight lift. Snaking her feet between his thighs, she hooked her feet over his calves and tensed her muscles.

No!

The demon couldn't have him. Wrapping her fingers through his, she clung with her legs and hands, using her body as anchor. It was her turn to yell, "I've got you!"

It felt like hell as she and the storm fought for possession. The battle seemed to last for hours. In reality it was probably only a couple minutes. Her muscles burned with the effort. Then, just as suddenly as the chaos began, it was over. With an abruptness that left her gasping the wind died, its roar silenced, and the first few rays of the sun kissed their locked hands. She could only stare uncomprehendingly. Beyond their hands, hailstones glistened in the mud as they melted. They looked almost pretty.

She took a breath and then another. It was over. The storm was over. Oh dear God. It was finally over. She wanted to laugh. She turned her head, not caring about the dirt that ground into her cheek.

"We made it," she whispered. They'd actually made it. Because of Luke. Through it all, he'd protected her. "Thank you."

Luke didn't respond. Her laughter faded. Something was wrong. The man never shut up. She pushed on his hands. Nothing. "So all it takes is a tornado to hush you up?"

Still no response. It took tremendous effort to unlock her fingers from his. She'd been holding on to him so tightly the muscles were cramped. Bracing her arms beneath her, she tried to come up on her knees but there was no moving him. This was not good.

Wiggling upward, inch by inch, she worked her way out from beneath him. The progress of his head down her back marked her success. She took her first break when his head settled between her shoulder blades, the second when it hit the middle of her back, the third when it hit the back of her thighs. By then she was sweating. She knew he was still unconscious when he didn't say something smart.

Her heart stuck in her throat. She swallowed it back. Now was not the time to panic. Struggling to her feet, she turned.

No, *now* was the time to panic. Luke lay on the ground against the side of the ravine. A large tree lay across his back, its roots sticking up like a monster's claw. He looked odd. She realized she'd never seen him without his hat. What an inane thing to notice. It was better, however, than looking at the bleeding gash on his forehead.

Kneeling beside him, she shook his shoulder. "Luke."

Still he didn't move. This close, she couldn't ignore the scope of the gash. It was about three inches long and just laid his skull bare. She hoped the bone wasn't crushed. Sliding her finger under his nose, she checked for breath. *Please.*

She'd done more praying today than she'd done in the last ten years. That probably wasn't a good sign. She felt his breath. He was alive. She stood. She could work with that.

Hands on hips, she surveyed the situation. First things first—the tree had to move. Grabbing one of the branches, she yanked. It didn't budge. She tried again, putting all her weight into it, but all she'd managed to do was work a couple branches deeper into the mud.

"Dammit!"

She had to think. Climbing out of the shallow ravine, she looked around. The copse of trees was gone. So was Glory and the wagon. She bit her lip. Maybe he'd survived. In the distance, she could see the tornado thundering on its way, clearly done with them. To the right, about thirty feet away, Chico stood, head up, ears flicking like another answer to a prayer. Chico could move that tree. Dusting off her hands, she headed for him. The closer she got, the more he tossed his head. When she got within six feet, he took a step back. She took another step. He took another one back. This wasn't working. She grabbed for his reins. He jerked his head, keeping them just out of her reach. His eyes were wild and rolling in his head. He was scared. So was she. Taking a minute, she paused to regroup. There had to be a better way. She decided to try sweet talk.

"Don't be scared," she crooned, holding out her hand. "Don't be scared. I'm not going to hurt you."

He wasn't appeased. With a toss of his head, he rejected her overture, and they were back to the game of cat and mouse until she wanted to throw up her hands in frustration. The stupid horse. Desperate, she whispered, "You can trust me, you know."

Chico flicked his ears at her.

Flicking was better than running. "I need your cooperation."

Chico just snorted and rolled his eyes, clearly prepared to run if she got ornery. She needed a new plan. "Fine. I'm just going to sit here until such time as you calm yourself, because obviously we're not getting anywhere like this."

And she did just that, sitting on the ground with her back to him. Reaching under her hip, she removed the stick that was poking at her. To her surprise, Chico didn't run. In fact, he seemed to calm down.

She heard him take a step. She didn't move. Didn't look up. He took another.

"I'm not talking to you," she told him. Another step, and air wafted by her shoulder.

"You're as contrary as your owner." His lips nibbled at her ear. She shrugged him away. "Nope, I'm mad at you."

His head drooped over her shoulder. He clearly expected affection. "Now? After running my butt all over this darn plain, now you want pets?"

His wuffle said *yes*. Very carefully, she reached up and rubbed his nose. He snorted and stayed put. "I know. I was scared, too. But your owner saved us and now we have to save him."

Very slowly, she eased her hand down his nose until she could grab the reins beneath his chin. She expected him to jerk and pull. He didn't. "Don't do anything crazy while I get to my feet." She smoothed out her dress. "You have no idea what it's like moving around in skirts."

He looked at her with soft brown eyes, as if to say he understood.

"So here's the deal," she told Chico as she led him back to Luke. "I'm going to take this rope and tie one end to your saddle and the other to that tree and you're going to walk that way." She pointed. "And using all the muscle we've got, we're going to pull this tree off Luke and then he will be okay because, because…"

She didn't know what she was going do if he wasn't. The catch to the matter was, she couldn't hold on to the horse and tie the rope at the same time. Thank goodness for Dane Savage's descriptions on how to ground tie Western trained horses. Wrapping the reins around a substantial branch, she walked back to Chico's side. "Stay now."

Chico just looked at her as if she were an idiot.

"Nobody asked your opinion," she muttered.

Taking the rope, she tied the free end around the trunk of the tree, as tightly as she could.

When the last knot was done, she glanced at Chico. Chico looked back at her. "This is it. Now it's up to you."

Giving his hindquarters a wide berth, she untied the reins. Chico tossed his head. She patted his neck. "All you've got to do is move that tree. Just a little. Just enough for me to drag him out from under it." She gave the reins a tug. Chico started walking, hit the resistance of the tree and stopped. She backed up, tugging on the reins. "Come on. You can do it."

He could have spooked, he could have refused, but as if he understood the importance of his job, Chico put his head down and his shoulders into the job. "God bless your muscles," she told him as the tree cracked and rolled. "Come on, big boy. We just need another foot."

The horse gave her that foot. "Thank you." Patting his neck, she wrapped the reins around a branch with a sigh of relief. "All right, stay here while I take care of things."

Looking down at Luke, she wasn't sure how she was going to live up to that statement. He was lying on his stomach, his head turned to the side. His legs looked straight, no odd angles. That had to be a good sign. The same for his arms. She didn't know about his back. Blood darkened his hair. That she did know how to address. Removing the knife from his boot, she hacked at her skirt and petticoats to make bandages. Thank goodness for Dane Savage's novels. Unlike other authors, he was willing to get into the gory details of life in the West. If he hadn't, it probably never would have occurred to her to take strips of her clothing to make a bandage.

Fetching the canteen from Chico's saddle, she moistened a strip of her petticoat before pouring water over the gash in his head. After cleaning the injury as best she could, she made a pad of another piece of petticoat and then tied a long strip from her dress around his head as a bandage. She sat back on her heels and wiped the sweat from her brow with her forearm. If it wasn't so hot, maybe she wouldn't feel like crying. Maybe she could think.

At least he was still breathing. Breathing was always a good sign. As she sat there, her own aches and bruises started making themselves known. Her right shoulder blade, where the hail had struck, twinged every time she moved. It'd be stiff before long. She couldn't imagine how much Luke was hurting.

He'd thrown his body over hers to protect her from the hail. She brushed the hair off his cheek, smoothed it back over his brow, then arranged it over the bandage to give him a rakish look, because, well, it just suited him. There was something very untamed about Luke Bellen. Beneath those fine clothes, beneath those proper manners, there lurked a mountain lion.

Cupping his cheek in her hand, emotion overwhelmed her. Feelings of gratitude, of awe, of more, flowed through her hand. Closing her fingers on the sensation, she drew her hand back to her lap. Touching Luke created the most powerful sensations.

"Please, wake up," she whispered.

"Why?" he rasped without opening his eyes, reaching for the bandage on his head. "You got a mean streak that needs indulging?"

She hadn't realized how worried she'd been until she heard his voice. "I imagine you have a headache."

He tried to sit up, groaned and flopped back down. "That's an understatement. What happened?"

"A tree landed on you."

He cracked his right eye opened. "Did anything major break?"

She bit her lip. "You might have broken your back or neck."

"If I broke my neck I wouldn't be breathing."

"I don't think that's necessarily true. Back home, there was a man in town that got thrown from his horse. He broke his neck but didn't know it. Nobody knew until that night at dinner. He turned his head, and then dropped. Dead," she added in case he didn't understand.

"Yeah, I get your point, but trust me. My neck's not broken."

She worried her lip with her teeth. She didn't trust him. "Then why aren't you moving?"

"Because I damn well hurt."

"Oh." That made perfect sense. A little of the tension left her shoulders. She really had to stop anticipating the worst when she started feeling happy. And she really should stop thinking there was no one she could trust when she started to feel free. Since coming to Hell's Eight, she'd begun to feel like she was finally free to live as she'd dreamed. That was scary.

She patted his shoulder. "Take all the time you need."

His thank-you was a bit sarcastic.

She didn't care. The tornado was gone. They were alive. He could take forever if he wanted to.

CHAPTER SEVEN

SHE'D LIED. LUKE didn't have forever. He had about
two minutes before she broke down and cried because looking at him lying there in the dirt, knowing
he was hurting, knowing she didn't know what to do
if he was hiding a bad injury was tearing her apart.
She was used to him commanding the space around
him, cracking jokes, being irritating, being *him*. He'd
told her he'd be all right, but the man wasn't one for
telling the whole truth. He spooned it out in bits and
pieces, based on what he thought a person could handle. But this time he couldn't hide what was happening. And that she really didn't know how to help.

His fingers twitched, digging deeper into the soil.
His moan was muted, but she heard it. *Darn it!* He
looked so alone, lying there, his silence masking
pain. It wasn't fair. It wasn't right. And she wasn't
tolerating it anymore. The man had been prepared to
die for her. She wasn't going to just sit over here and
watch him suffer in all his stoic splendor.

Scooting closer, she eyed her options. There
weren't many, so she went with her gut. Stretching
out beside him, using his upper arm as a pillow, she
put her arm over his back. It all felt rather awkward,

but she was here. She needed him to know he wasn't in this alone.

Her "Hi" was soft.

He cracked an eyelid at her. "What are you doing?"

She smiled. Why did touching him always make her feel better? "I'm keeping you company."

His lips twitched at the corners in that prelude to a smile she was coming to know so well. "Are you planning on staying long?"

"As long as you don't die, I'm staying."

"Not going to tolerate me stinking up the place?"

"No."

"Then if you're going to do this, do it right."

"I don't understand."

"Figures I'd be spooning in the dirt with an amateur."

"We're not spooning."

"Uh-huh." His muscles flexed. "Lift up."

She did. He groaned and pulled his arm out from under her before dropping it over her waist. She had a moment to appreciate the comforting weight before he growled, "Now, come here."

With a flex of muscle that should have been impossible in his current state, he turned and tucked her up tight against his side. Putting her hands beneath her cheek as a pillow, smiling into his eyes, she confessed, "That is better."

His eyes drifted closed. "Yeah, it is."

That panic she couldn't shake gripped her stomach in a cold fist. She clenched her fingers together to suppress the urge to touch his cheek. Even lying in the dirt, there was a limit to how forward she could be.

"No one should die alone."

"You're a rather morbid cuddler."

She'd be able to judge his mood better if his delivery weren't so deadpan. "I can't help it."

"Uh-huh." His eyes opened. They were blue and clear, and looking into them, she began to hope. "At least your instincts are sound."

She knew she probably shouldn't ask but the question just popped out. "Sound?"

His smile curved with irritating amusement. "You wiggled right into my arms like a homing pigeon. Shows you know who to trust."

It was surprisingly hard to fake outrage. "I thought you were dying!"

His smile let her know he was on to her ruse. "Well, I'm not."

Placing her palm against his chest, she felt for his heartbeat. "How do you know?"

"I hurt too damn much to be lucky enough to die."

She could feel his heart beating steadily. "I don't believe that's a true barometer."

Lifting up and twisting, he slid his other arm under her head. His shrug pressed against her cheek. "Trust me. It's damn accurate."

It was comfortable with her head resting on his arm, and his heart beating against her palm. More than that, it was safe. He made her feel very, very safe. And she'd almost gotten him killed.

She closed her eyes against the memory of his body jerking above hers as the hail pummeled him, the wind trying to tear him from her arms. "I'm sorry."

"For what?"

"That you got hurt because of me."

His thumb stroked over her arm. "I'll find a way for you to make it up to me."

That popped her eyes open. Her shock collided with his humor. "You're outrageous."

Grimacing, he shifted position. "You like it."

She did, but she wasn't going to admit it. With a huff, she refrained from answering.

The scents of dirt and blood filled her nostrils, adding to the chaos inside her. Beneath that was the scent of Luke. He was right. This was better. She shifted onto her back, because, well, just because it felt better. His hand came up and brushed her cheek. Startled, she turned her head.

"You've got a smudge."

"So do you. A whole lot of smudges." Smudges made of blood and dirt. She touched a spot beneath his eye. "Thank you."

"It was my pleasure."

"I doubt that."

His smile was a little crooked, a bit weak, but still wonderful to see. "Then you have no idea how good you feel beneath a man."

She blinked. She blushed and she brazened it out, because what was the point of being shy with a man who'd been willing to give his life for her? Maybe he would have done it for anybody, but he'd definitely done it for her. "I bet you say that to all the girls."

"Nope. Not the really skinny ones. All those bones hurt."

She chuckled. She couldn't help it. It was nonsense, but it was fun nonsense. And after the terror, that felt good. "Are you calling me fat?"

"Far from it. You, my darlin', are a beautiful, perfectly proportioned woman, and if you wear a corset again, I'm going to cut it off where you stand."

"I can't go around without a corset. It's unseemly."

"Uh-huh." The muscles under her cheek flexed as he shrugged. "You've been warned."

"Because you never say what you don't mean?"

"Unless I'm out of my head."

"Are you out of your head right now?"

"I might be."

She hid her smile against his shoulder at the teasing. There was silence for a bit. However, unlike most silences, this one didn't bother her. She finally broke it. "Chico is all right, too."

"So I see."

She heard the relief in his tone. "I couldn't have pulled that tree off you without him."

"I'll give him an extra ration of oats tonight." He shifted. "And Glory?"

And that fast her calm disappeared. The shivering started deep inside as she remembered the tornado's utterly relentless force. "I don't know. The last time I saw him he was heading for that bunch of trees."

"Relax. He's probably hiding in them."

She tried to contain the remnants of terror speculating about Glory's fate created but it was like a living breathing creature demanding to be free. She shook her head and bit her lip, but the tears came out of nowhere, seeping over her cheeks and dripping onto his arm. She was very afraid Glory was dead.

"He can't be." She shook her head. "The whole copse. It's…it's…just gone." She made a cutting motion with her hand. "Leveled. Like it was never there to begin with."

The finger he put over her lips was dirty and firm. She didn't care. There was comfort in the touch.

"Glory's been around long enough to have picked up some sense over the years. He's likely heading back to the river to get a drink after that run."

"Do you truly think so?"

"Trust me. I know ornery when I see it. And Glory is ornery enough to survive."

She managed a weak smile. "Glory is not ornery. He's sweet."

"So you keep telling me." The pad of his thumb was calloused, but his touch on her cheek infinitely gentle as he wiped away tears. "I do like to see you smile."

"Why?"

Running his finger down her nose, he tapped the end before he shrugged. "Because it makes me want to smile, too."

A simple straightforward answer when she'd expected evasion. Would she ever understand him?

His arm shifted beneath her shoulder. He tucked her a little closer. So close, he was all but lying on her.

"I'll have you know, I managed to wiggle out from almost this very position a little while ago."

His eyebrows arched and then he winced. "Now, why would you want to do that?"

Reaching up, she touched the makeshift bandage. A spot of blood was beginning to seep through. "I thought you were dead, and as exciting as Mr. Savage makes these events sound in his stories, it wasn't enjoyable at all in real life."

"You've got a real passion for that author."

"He's such a vivid writer."

"Uh-huh."

"You shouldn't mock him. Without the landslide scene in *Savage Storm*, I wouldn't have known how to tie off the tree and hitch it to Chico to lift it off you."

"Crap."

"What's wrong?"

He sighed. "Chico thinks he's too fine to be used as a plow horse. It's going to take a month of oats to soothe his ruffled dignity."

Luke might be complaining, but it was clear the man loved that horse. "How long have you two been together?"

"About eight years now. I've had him since he was a foal. His mom rejected him. I couldn't get another mare to take him on, so he became my responsibility."

"So you raised him from a baby?"

"Yes." He shook his head and immediately groaned and put his hand to the bandage. "Don't ever do that. They get to know you too well. It makes it hard for them to remember who's boss."

"Because you love him."

"Don't go fanciful on me. He's a horse."

"That you love."

He narrowed his eyes at her. "Is he standing nearby?"

"Yes. He's just on the other side of the ditch."

"Then I'm not answering that question."

"Why? Do you think if you don't say it, it doesn't make it true?"

"The truth has nothing to do with it."

She was beginning to understand his sense of humor. Another smile tugged at her mouth. "Oh?"

"The sad truth is, he's got a swelled head and he has a tendency to lord it over the other horses."

Humor after terror, she realized, was like the sun coming out after the storm. It was healing. And so was Luke with his calm acceptance of life's ups and downs. "You're feeling better."

"I wouldn't go whole hog on 'better.' I have a heck of a headache that's only getting worse."

She wasn't surprised. "You have quite a gash on your head. It should have stitches."

"But at least I've got the feeling back in my toes."

She struggled to get up, her wet skirts hampering the effort. The darn things were like octopi wrapping around her legs. "You didn't have feeling in your toes?" she asked, leaning over, yanking the twist of her skirt from under her knee.

With a tug, he pulled her back down. "Relax. It was a joke. I am feeling better."

She eyed him, not sure what to believe. "Is that the truth or are you feeding me bits and pieces again?"

He didn't pretend to misunderstand. "I started to feel better about three minutes after I woke up."

He'd been feeling better that long? "Why didn't you say something sooner?"

"Hey, if a pretty girl wants to lie in my arms, stroke my face and whisper sweet nothings in my ear, I'm not going to rush it to an end."

He made it sound so sordid, so why did she want to chuckle?

"Don't try to make it sound like such a rare thing. Tia told me how women love you."

He brushed the hair off her forehead. Her eye twitched as a strand dragged across the sensitive lashes. She was glad for the distraction.

"But just because women love me doesn't mean I love them back." He smiled and continued, "I'm a picky son of a bitch."

She believed that. In her experience, only the truly confident believed there was always another opportunity. And only those with plenty of opportunities were confident enough to be picky. Which didn't explain why Luke Bellen was here cuddling with her, but she wasn't questioning miracles today.

"Good."

Reaching up, she cupped his cheek in her hand,

tickling her palm with the light stubble, enjoying the novelty of the sensation. She knew she must have touched her former fiancé, Jason, like that, but for the life of her she couldn't remember when. Drawing her fingertips down Luke's beard-roughened cheek, she kept going until she found the remnants of his smile. His lips were soft yet firm against her touch. They pursed against the slight pressure in an equally light kiss that broke all the remaining rules of propriety. He was completely outrageous. And unique.

She sighed. "I do like you, Luke Bellen."

It was his turn to blink. "What brought that on?"

"Would you believe my nerves were overcome by the excitement of the moment?"

He snorted. "I might buy that from another woman, but not from you."

She chose to take that as a compliment. And as much as she was enjoying this moment, it had to end. Luke was a very seductive, very dangerous man. "We need to get up and find the others."

He didn't move. If anything, he pulled her closer to the seductive hardness of his big body. As if obeying a silent command, her curves melted into his planes. She was in so much trouble here.

"If they're out looking, they'll spot Chico and ride on over."

"But what if they're hurt?"

"There're more of them than us. If someone's hurt, they'll be able to handle it."

"All right, but what if there are bugs beneath where we're lying?"

He laughed outright. "What would your Mr. Savage say about your squeamish nature?"

"He'd likely say I'm a greenhorn."

"I'm thinking he'd say you're a beautiful lady too fine to be bug bait."

"You have an answer for everything."

"I'm an old man."

"You're not that old. Thirty, maybe?"

Sighing, he rubbed her arm. "Thirty-two, my darlin'. Thirty-two."

She steeled against reading anything into the endearment. "I'm twenty-six."

"That's a good age for a woman."

She looked at him askance. "Most call me a spinster."

"What's a thirty-two-year-old man going to do with an eighteen-year-old girl except listen to her giggle?"

"I don't giggle."

He didn't miss a beat. "Thank goodness."

The smile that was on her lips spread deeper. She really did like him. "I don't know what to do with you."

With a grunt and a smothered groan, he rose up over her. "I've got a couple ideas."

"Are they as scandalous as all your others?"

His finger traced her eyebrow, skimmed down over her temple and jaw before tantalizing the side of her neck in mesmerizing, butterfly-delicate strokes.

"Yes."

"Good." She hoped. It wasn't like her to court di-

saster. She was always the quiet one. The safe one.
The invisible one. But today, after everything they'd
been through—after almost dying—she wanted to
be seen.

His "Good" echoed hers.

He leaned in slowly, so slowly that she wondered
if he was giving her a chance to change her mind. He
didn't have to worry. She wanted this kiss. For once
in her life, she wanted all that was declared "forbidden." She wanted to be brazen and bold. She wanted
to actually be the scandal she'd always been accused
of being. He drew closer and closer, so close his features blurred and she had no choice but to close her
eyes and block out the distortion. She didn't want to
be distracted from this.

His breath touched her cheek first. Moist and
warm, it blended with the humid air, wafting over her
skin like a summer breeze. Every nerve ending came
to a fine point as his chest settled against hers, her
anticipation humming. The heat of his skin reached
out along with his scent, enveloping her in promise.
And then their lips touched in the briefest encounter. Once. Twice. A shiver took her from head to toe.

Oh yes. This.

That inner smile grew and then his lips were fully
on hers, testing, teasing, stealing that smile for himself. Chest to chest. Lip to lip. Heartbeat to heartbeat. Sweet, yes, this was sweet. And primal. And
inspirational. And all they'd done was touch lips.

The impact of that kiss went through her like a
lightning strike to her core. *Yes. This man. Just yes.*

His palm cupped the back of her head, tilting her up. She went willingly. A laugh followed his groan. "I'm trying to preserve your virtue, darlin'."

Damn. So much for their being in tune. "Don't."

Not now. Not when she wanted the full forbidden moment. Not when she wanted more. Digging her nails into his sleeves, she sought just that. More of his passion, more of his scent, more of the sensation he rained upon the parched landscape of her soul with such devastating ease.

"Please."

"Oh, I'll please you," he whispered. With a press of his fingers, he tilted her head a little farther. The firmness of his lips slid across hers, the brush of his beard providing a deliciously abrasive counterpoint. "I have a feeling we're going to please the hell out of each other."

"Yes."

He slid his tongue along the seam of her lips. "Then let me in."

Yes.

He did it again with a little more pressure. Her gasp gave him what he wanted. Entrance. He kissed her hard. He kissed her softly. He kissed her deeply. He kissed her as if she were his own personal nirvana. As if he'd searched his whole life for her and now that he'd found her, he was ready to devour her.

Moaning, she slid her hands up his arms, unable to bear a moment of separation, needing to be closer. So much closer. His hair, caked in mud, was stiff against her fingers. Cool when she wanted heat.

Needed heat. It took just a little effort to work her fingers under the collar of his shirt, to find his nape. Warm skin. Vital man.

He nibbled at her lip, taking it between his teeth, drawing it out slightly. Shivering, she dug her nails into the back of his neck, leaving her own mark. *Yes*.

No wonder women chased him. She'd never been kissed like this. Engaged for five years, the most she'd ever know was affection. Oh, that was a crime, because every woman should know this bliss, this pleasure, this joy, this anticipation. All of it feeding into desire, which fed into a craving that thrummed through her blood in a primitive beat.

She wanted him here. She wanted him now. She wanted him like hell on fire. She kissed him back, teasing his tongue with hers, tempting him and taunting him in an erotic duel, subtly daring him to take it further. They needed to go further. Groaning, he pressed her back into the ground. And she went, accepting his lead, his lust, his power. A nudge of his knee and her legs fell apart in natural invitation. Holding her face between his hands, holding her gaze, he settled between her thighs. In his eyes, she saw the pleasure. On her next breath, she breathed it in.

Luke groaned. "Sweet."

Yes. Yes, it was.

Against her inner thigh, he was hard. She wasn't so naive that she didn't know what that meant. She'd been warned about the evils of men's passions throughout her youth, so much so that she wondered if she'd ever truly been innocent. And now she didn't want to be. She wanted to be a siren for this man. A jezebel. A fallen woman. Just as long as it was Luke's arms into which she fell. She wanted to be free.

His hand on her hip drew her up. "Come closer."

Yes.

Closer. She needed to be closer. Arching up, she rubbed against him, finding pleasure in his guidance, in her power, relishing every groan she drew from his lips, teasing him just as he teased her. This was a kiss, but somehow more.

He pulled her closer still. It wasn't close enough. She kissed him deeper. It wasn't deep enough.

"Come here," he growled.

"I'm not going anywhere," she whispered back, her breath mingling with his.

His fingers fisted in her hair, anchoring her attention. Eyes dark with desire, he agreed, "No, you're not."

She didn't know if it was a threat or a promise, and in that moment, she didn't care. All that mattered was the passion arcing between them. She nodded.

He held her still for another moment, studying her with an intensity that made her shift, waiting on something she didn't know how to give. His eyes narrowed. Desire flickered.

"Luke?"

Immediately, his grip shifted to her cheek. "Right here, my darlin'."

And he was, this time his passion tempered with something else. Something powerful. Then his lips slid to torment the corner of her mouth, to nibble her cheek, her ear. Her ear! Who knew a man's lips on a woman's ear could start a wildfire? She moaned as her nipples peaked and ached. Arching up, she rubbed them against his chest, finding some relief, then gasped as he heightened the sensation, kissing his way down her neck, his lips finding the rapidly beating pulse in the hollow, his beard rasping over her skin as his teeth nipped lightly. He drew a long breath.

"How the hell do you smell so good after going through so much?"

"I'm a lady."

That backed him up.

"What the hell does that have to do with anything?"

She touched his cheek, amazed that humor could live within passion. *Yes*.

"Ladies don't sweat. We just get dewy."

Dropping his forehead to hers, he chuckled. "Dewy."

On her next breath, she took his laughter inside her. And discovered something else—intimacy within passion made it sweeter, hotter.

Looping her arms around his neck, she asked, "Do you have a problem with that?"

"Not a one."

"Good. Can we get back to kissing now?"

"Absolutely."

Yes.

CHAPTER EIGHT

THE OVERLY LOUD clearing of a throat broke through the passion.

Luke groaned and dropped his forehead to Josie's. *Shit.*

"To think we have been searching all over the plains for you two, and here you were just…relaxing in the ravine."

That accent was unmistakable. Shielding Josie with his body, giving her time to regain her composure, he called up to his tormentor, "Shut the hell up, Zach."

Zach, being Zach, didn't.

"I do not think this is what Tia had in mind when she asked you to watch over the little photographer."

Beneath him, Luke felt Josie start. *Dammit.* He hadn't meant for his flirting to get out of hand, but the woman was like Tucker's dynamite against his good intentions. With her, a peck on the cheek became a kiss. A kiss an embrace. And an embrace? Oh hell, that just exploded into pure fire. The thing was, he didn't mind. Which, for a man who prided himself on always keeping the upper hand, was a revelation.

"Just a heads-up—Tia's about twenty feet behind me."

Luke sighed. "Do me a favor and head her off, would you?"

"Of course," Zach said smoothly, "but you will owe me."

Beneath him, Josie squirmed. Of course he would. "Deal."

Zach wheeled his horse around. As the sound of hoofbeats faded, Josie pushed against Luke's chest. "For heaven's sakes," she muttered impatiently, "get off me."

That proved to be easier said than done. Lying in one position had given his body time to stiffen up. As soon as he got to his knees, all those abused muscles let him know what they thought of such nonsense. Josie seemed to have no problem. Galvanized by the prospect of being caught in a compromising position, she was on her feet and smoothing her hair and skirt before he even managed to straighten. Her cheeks were a brilliant red.

"How do I look?" she asked, slapping the mud off her skirt.

Like she'd been making hot, passionate love in the dirt.

"You look beautiful." And she did. From her kiss-swollen lips to the love bites sprinkled across her neck, she had the look of a woman well loved. There wasn't a man alive who'd miss those signs or misinterpret what they meant. There wasn't a man alive who wouldn't want to be in his boots. And if any son of a bitch dared to say one word to her, even look at her the wrong way, he'd gut the bastard.

Josie rolled her eyes. "Who cares about beautiful? I'm aiming for presentable."

"Well, if looking like you got dragged through a tornado backward is presentable, you've got it."

With the sleeve of her dress she rubbed at her face and neck, smearing dirt everywhere. At least the smudges disguised the red marks he'd left on her skin.

"I can't believe he saw us like that."

"Zach is a pain in the ass, but he's a good man. What he saw won't go any further than him."

"But he saw—"

"Yes."

"That's all you can say? Yes?"

He plucked a blade of grass from her hair. "It happened. Fussing isn't going to change that."

"But Tia—"

"Tia is not going to see anything except two people who survived a close call. Unless, of course, you blab about the rest."

She cut him a glare. "I'm not the blabbing sort."

Damn his head hurt. He rubbed his temple below the bandage. "Then just brazen it out. Nothing happened that you need be ashamed of. And nothing happened that anybody else needs to know about."

She licked her lips and rubbed a spot on her dress. Something he'd noticed she did when she was nervous. "I think I resent the fact that you've clearly done this a lot."

Did she think he was a virgin? "I'm thirty-two."

She rolled her sleeves down and began to gather her hair up. "I was referring to covering up your romantic activities."

Romantic activities? She was beginning to piss him off. "Well, that's a mouthful, and there you would be wrong." He gingerly felt under the bandage. His fingers came out bloody. "It's been a long time since I've worried about what others think."

She stood there for a moment, absorbing the information. Then, with a nod, she knotted her hair on top of her head.

"Josie."

She didn't look at him. "I understand."

No, he didn't think she did. Not worrying about what other people thought was only half the story. Truth was, no woman had ever made him lose his head to the point where he was rolling around in the dirt, making the sweetest love, when he should've been getting the woman to safety.

"Josie."

She just kept scrubbing that spot on her skirt, clearly uneasy.

A flurry of pebbles announced Tia's arrival at the edge of the ravine. Poised at the edge, she pushed her bonnet back and smiled. "Luke, Josie, I have been so worried about you."

He headed up the incline to meet her. "No need. You know the devil takes care of his own."

Ed limped his way down the hill, using a stick

to maintain his balance. "Hey, you two. Glad to see you made it."

"I could say the same." Holding his hand out for Tia's, Luke helped her down the rocky terrain. In comparison to their filthy appearance, her dress was only mildly wrinkled and every hair was in place. Leave it to Tia to come out of a tornado looking as if she was heading for a social. In her hand, she held Josie's ugly bonnet. Of course *that* had managed to survive.

"Got to say you gave us a few bad moments watching that tornado chase your tail," Ed called.

"You should have seen it from our side."

Ed clapped him on the back while Tia hugged him close.

"I'd have figured you were too busy running to waste time looking back."

Luke chuckled and patted Tia's shoulder, steadying her as she stepped back, her dark brown eyes studying his face while she touched the bandage at his temple. Tears she wouldn't let fall welled. How often had he seen her like that? Poised between tears and strength? From where she stood, Josie watched the exchange, her expression guarded. He'd give a week's pay to know what she was thinking.

"Do not scare me so again, *mi hijo*," Tia whispered.

Putting his arm around her, he held her close. She smelled of chilies and cinnamon. He closed his eyes. So familiar, but no longer home. "I won't."

Stepping back, she wiped at her eyes. "I would make you promise, but I know you cannot."

No, he couldn't. "How about this? I can promise not to do so again intentionally."

"I will be satisfied with this."

"At least we came through it all right," Luke said.

She looked at the crude bandage on his head. "Not completely all right."

"I'm sure it looks a lot worse than it is."

"If it is half as bad as the bandage makes it look, you need to go lie down."

"I did the best I could," Josie interjected.

Gone was the confident woman Luke had known the past day. In her place was the brown wren who'd stepped off the stage a little over two weeks ago. The transformation didn't sit well with him.

Tia looked between them. A frown pleated her brow. She glanced back at Luke. This time, he got a closer inspection. Her frown deepened and he knew she knew what he'd been doing. And disapproved.

"I am sure it is the best he deserves."

Damn. That hadn't taken long.

The next look Tia shot him was the we-will-talk look. If Josie had looked up quickly enough to see that, she'd probably stop rubbing at her skirt. There was no doubt who Tia held responsible for Josie's current state of disarray.

And he couldn't blame her. He'd been in enough tight situations to know how the aftermath left one searching for life. And there was nothing more life affirming than connecting with another person. He could have given Josie that connection with a hug. But he hadn't. He'd used his greater experience to secure a kiss. After that, he couldn't take responsibility for anything. Once his lips had touched hers, control had been wrenched beyond his reach by something that'd risen up like a tide, sweeping away his good intentions. There'd been no control. Within him or within her. If Zach hadn't interrupted when he did, Josie would've been his. He had to live with that shame. He wasn't a man who took advantage of innocents.

"I hate to break up the reunion," Zach called down, "but life has not gotten any less dangerous just because a tornado breezed through."

Tia nodded. "Yes, yes. We must go."

She handed the hat to Josie. For a moment, Tia stood there awkwardly, and then with a shrug and a smile, she said to Josie, "Forgive me."

Luke knew what was coming, but Josie didn't. The hug caught her by surprise. She stood there awkwardly with the hat dangling from her hand. After a moment, she patted Tia's back.

Ending the hug, Tia cupped Josie's shoulders between her hands. They were of a height. She kissed both her cheeks. "Thank you for taking care of my son. He can be reckless."

Over Tia's shoulder, Josie looked at him helplessly.

Ed chuckled and kissed the back of her hand. "Welcome to the family."

"But I'm…"

Ed didn't let her finish. "But now we've got to go." With the dexterity that had won him Tia's heart, Ed steered Josie back up the ravine, leaving Luke to escort Tia. From behind, Luke heard him say, "You'll get used to how fast things move out here."

Josie's response, if she made one, was lost amid the slide of dirt and stone as the group struggled up the soft side of the ravine.

When they cleared the top, it was Luke's turn to pause.

Josie had tried to warn him, but there weren't words to describe the devastation in the wake of the massive tornado. Devastation might even be the wrong word. Devastation implied debris. He looked around. Here, there simply just wasn't anything left. The tornado had picked up what was and moved it on down the way.

"Damn."

"Pretty impressive, eh?" Zach asked, pulling out a cigarillo. "Somewhere, someone got quite a mess dumped on their land."

"Yes." He walked over to Chico. The horse chuffed and rubbed his head against his chest. Looking around, Luke was amazed that any of them had survived. He'd never realized how much he relied upon the impermanent markers in the landscape to guide his way. Devil's Cut was still to the southwest and Hell's Pass to the east, but a whole lot of what was in between just wasn't there anymore. Those landmarks he'd used to judge distance, like that copse of trees, were gone. In time there'd be new ones, but for now, he was in unfamiliar territory.

Josie looked as stunned as he felt. Her hands were wrapped in her skirt. That god-awful hat was back on her head, hiding her expression more effectively than it protected her face from the sun. Releasing Ed's hand, she took a step forward. And then another. With a lick of her lips, she asked, "Will it come back?"

It was Tia who answered. "It doesn't work that way. New ones might come, but they do not return."

She nodded, then slowly turned a full revolution. Luke had a brief glimpse of her face. She looked... numb. He knew exactly how she felt.

"The sun's out," Ed comforted. "We've seen the last of them today."

Josie nodded. "I don't like tornadoes."

Ed patted her shoulder. "I don't know anyone who does."

Her torn skirts bunched in front as she clutched her hands together. "That sounded stupid."

"I'd call it more normal."

The smile she gave him was shaky. "Thank you."

Zach struck a sulfur and held it to his smoke. "You will be happy, senorita, to know we found your wagon."

Josie took a step closer to Zach, grabbing his stirrup. "And Glory?"

Zach took a few puffs and smiled around his cigarillo. "He is tired, but there was enough life in his old legs to dodge death."

Tia crossed herself. "Thank the good Lord."

They'd all been blessed.

"But now it is time to go." Zach held out his hand. "There is no need to risk further distress by riding in the wagon. You are welcome to ride with me back to the others."

Josie hesitated, looked back over her shoulder at him. She didn't have to worry. He had this.

Luke walked Chico closer. "Josie's riding with me."

Josie didn't look any happier with that option, but he didn't care.

Zach straightened and, tipping his hat back, observed, "I offered first."

"And I offered last. What's your point?"

Flashing that too-charming smile at Josie, Zach bowed gallantly. "It is your choice, senorita."

Luke had the urge to push him off his horse. "No, it's not."

Josie's attention bounced between them, following the war of words, looking for all the world like a wren caught between two feuding cats, but it was Tia who broke the standoff.

"That is enough. You are both being childish, presenting yourselves before a decent woman like two dogs fighting over a bone." With a wave of her hands, she shooed them off. "There is no flattery in this."

Ed helped Tia up into the wagon. "I'm afraid I'm gonna have to agree with my wife here. You're both acting like a couple of jackasses."

"Stay out of this, Ed," Luke warned.

"You might be out of short pants, Luke, but you don't tell me what to do. And you damn well don't show my wife disrespect." He handed Tia his walking stick before awkwardly getting up beside her.

No, he didn't. Rubbing his hand over the back of his neck, Luke apologized. "I'm sorry, Tia. It's been a rough day."

"For everyone," Ed said pointedly.

"Where would you like to ride, Josie?" Tia asked. "You need to make a decision. Luke's wounds must be tended properly and I cannot do that here."

Luke knew what Josie was going to do before she did it. The indicator was in the way she fussed with her skirt. When trapped between a rock and a hard place, the woman had a tendency to run. Without so much as a glance in his direction, she chose to squeeze alongside Tia on the far side of the seat.

Zach shook his head regretfully. "Another time, perhaps."

The glance he cut Luke from under the broad brim of his sombrero let him know that last was for his benefit.

"You're pushing it, Zach," Luke growled, checking Chico's cinch.

The other man didn't look repentant. "I am told it is a bad habit."

The cinch was tight. Luke eased the stirrup down. "One you might want to break."

"Why?" He arched a brow. "It amuses me."

"Uh-huh." Luke swung up into the saddle and immediately groaned as every muscle protested the action. At least it got easier the more he moved. Gritting his teeth, he shielded his eyes. The sun was blinding without his hat. "While you're having your laugh, keep an eye open for my hat."

With a chuckle, Zach spun his black around and took point. Spicy smoke from his cigarillo drifted in his wake. Luke breathed it deep, savoring the remembered pleasure. His fingers twitched and his mind whispered, *Just once.* But once led to twice and twice led to constantly. He knew this, but on days like today, he regretted his promise to give up cigarettes.

With a curse and a press of his knees, Luke sent Chico cantering to catch up. There was a price to pay for everything. His interest in Josie was no exception. And after what Zach had witnessed, it was going to be open season on his pride until Josie moved on or moved in. As he passed the wagon, Luke touched his fingers to his brow in a silent salute. The anxious glance Josie shot him before ducking her head followed him down the trail.

If he had any decency remaining, he'd swear off her, too, but in his mind that little voice that wouldn't be silenced sat up and whispered in his ear, *Just once.*

"You CANNOT ALLOW such behavior, *mi hija*," Tia advised as soon as Luke caught up with Zach.

Josie'd known this conversation was coming from the minute Tia had intervened. She was close to both men and Josie had never met a mother who didn't want to protect her sons from the taint of Josie's birth. Women of all ages always felt compelled to remind her of her place as a bastard. She held on to her anger with a tight grip. Yelling and fighting never got her anywhere. Neither did reason, but she gave it a try anyway. "It isn't as if I'm encouraging them, or like I can stop them. In case you haven't noticed, they each outweigh me by about a hundred pounds."

"This I understand, but it is up to a woman to set standards for the men who wish to court her."

And for men to break them. "All I asked was if Glory was all right."

"You are a beautiful woman. With beauty comes great responsibility."

The wagon hit a bump. Josie grabbed the edge of the seat to keep her balance. "Responsibility?"

"Yes."

Ed leaned around Tia. "What Tia is trying to say is that men out here aren't like the men you are used to dealing with back East. They have a tendency to go after what they want, no holds barred."

"So I've noticed." Her lips were still tingling from Luke's kisses, her convictions still shaking from their encounter. She'd never met anyone like Luke before. She didn't recognize herself when she was with him.

"A woman who shows favor toward too many men at one time can get one of them killed," Tia elaborated.

"I don't see where I've shown an excess of…favor. To anyone."

Ed shrugged. "Probably not, but competition for women is high out here. Not a lot of good women to go around. You've seen today how life and death can be decided in the blink of an eye?"

"Yes." She dug her nails into the side of the seat, holding on to her composure with all she had. She hated this. The judgment. The blame. All she wanted was to be free to be herself, to be seen for herself, to be valued for herself without dragging her mother's mistake with her wherever she went like a stinking lunch sack gone bad. She wanted to be loved without a *but*. She just wanted someone who understood the restless need to see the world that so often took her. She wanted to be loved. And free, she acknowledged. Two things that did not go hand in hand.

"Then you understand why men are quick to stake their claim," Ed finished.

Maybe it was the day. Maybe it was surviving the tornado. Maybe it was the fact that she was just damn sick and tired of everybody putting the responsibilities of the rest of the world on her shoulders.

"No, I don't believe I do. I'm trying to survive just like everybody else. I didn't ask for anybody to fight over me for any reason. I have dreams of my own, you know."

Tia nodded. "Then you need to choose a man with whom you can build your dreams. As he needs to choose a woman who can build his."

She made it sound like a cooperative effort. As if marriage was a give-and-take. "We both know marriage doesn't work that way."

Ed clucked his tongue. "Someone handed you the

wrong end of the stick when it came to marriage, little lady."

"I'm twenty-six. Nobody had to hand me anything. I can see quite plainly for myself."

Support came from an unexpected place. Placing her hand on Ed's thigh, Tia gave it a pat. "I know of what she speaks, *mi amado*." Keeping the connection with Ed, Tia scooted around to face Josie. "For a long time in my home country, I lived the life my husband wanted me to live. I cooked what he liked, I sewed what he wanted and I moved where he wished. It was what my mother had done and her mother before her. Life was very structured and I knew my place within it." With a wry grin, she confessed, "I was very bored."

A bystander could have knocked Josie over with a feather to hear her own fears put in so many words. "And yet you married again."

Ed chuckled and took Tia's small, strong hand in his. Both were worn with age. Both bore witness to hard work. Both looked as though they belonged together. "Took me a few years of fast-talking to convince her to stroll to the altar with me, but I pulled it off."

Tia leaned against his shoulder. There was a wealth of respect and love in the gesture. "I was afraid," she confessed to Josie.

It was hard to see the ever-competent Tia afraid of anything, let alone of a man. "Why?"

"It was hard after my husband died, lonely until the boys came, scary after they did. They had so much anger but they also had so much need. It was like *Dios* dropped them into my lap to give me purpose. It's good to have a purpose."

Josie nodded. "Yes."

Tia waved her hand descriptively. "You have your photography. I had the boys. Through both, we find our strength."

Ed snorted and lightly flicked the reins on the horses' hindquarters. "If I'd known the fool woman was afraid I wanted to change her by marrying her, I could've claimed her before three months passed." He sighed. "We wasted a lot of years."

Tia shrugged. "I would like to say that isn't true, but…" Another shrug. "The fear of what was can too easily blind us to what could be."

"I don't understand."

Tia swept her hand wide, encompassing all the devastated landscape. "It is like this land. In the wake of the tornado you look, and all you see is the destruction."

"There's nothing left."

Tia nodded. "What once was is now gone, this is true. But nature, when she looks at this land, she does not see the end, instead, for her there is a new beginning. A chance to start over. Not as things have always been, but as things need to be now so they can work."

Josie was beginning to understand.

Tia continued. "We will come back this way next year. And maybe, that copse of trees will be starting to grow right back there where it used to be. And we once again will know that we have reached the halfway point to Devil's Cut by its existence. But maybe it won't and we will find a new something to mark the halfway point. Both could work, but one will work better than the other and that's the one we will live with." She took a breath and released it as she opened her hands wide.

"The people of this land are like nature. We have to be flexible to survive. So we keep what works from before and throw out what does not, and when we come together we create what works best for us because there are no rules here, not like you are used to. Here it's about survival and dreams and how to build a path to both."

It was an interesting concept. A relationship not built on societal expectations, but on the dreams and hopes of the people who were trying to carve an existence out of a hard land.

"You're telling me that the rules are different here."

"I'm telling you that you can be anything you want here."

That was an exciting prospect.

"What if I want to be a spinster?"

Ed pushed his hat back. "Why would anybody want to be a spinster?"

The wagon hit another bump. Keeping from being pitched off the edge gave her a moment to think on that. *Because it was easier.* "It has its appeal."

Tia clucked her tongue. "There is a fairness to this land, but do not mistake it for easy. Nobody, neither man nor woman, will succeed without the other. It takes cooperation to thrive. You will build here or you will die here."

"Or I can leave."

There was always the option of going back to the stifling existence of her hometown.

"Yes," she agreed. "You have that option."

She didn't want to go back. She suspected Tia knew that.

The wagon climbed a hill. As they crested the top, everything changed, debris littered the ground, making the wagon rock about. Josie's stomach lurched right along with it.

"Guess we know where that tornado started dumping its load," Ed said.

Tia clucked her tongue. "*Si*, but I would have preferred it hold on to it for much longer."

"Me, too," Josie gritted out. Steadying her stomach with one hand while gripping the side of the seat with the other, she asked, "How much longer before we get to the campsite?"

Tia turned. She took in Josie's grip on her belly. "Your stomach is bad?"

Licking her lips, Josie swallowed back a surge of nausea. "Wagon rides do not tend to agree with me."

"Damn." Standing in the seat, Ed let out a piercing whistle. The horses kept moving. The wagon rocked.

"Oh no." Josie held up her hand but it was too late. Zach and Luke turned at the sound. Her "That's not necessary" trailed off as Luke wheeled Chico around.

Horse and man moved as one. Backlit by the late afternoon sun, they cut a fine, powerful silhouette. For a heartbeat, it was the cover of one of her favorite books. She licked her lips again. She did love those books. As he came closer, the alignment changed and now it was Luke who was highlighted. She licked her lips again as her toes curled in delight. Luke was a fine figure of a man. Better than any book cover. And she'd dared to kiss him. Sometimes she just amazed herself.

Chico trotted up and kept pace with the wagon. Luke took in the situation with one glance. With a shake of his head, he held out his hand, "Come here, my darlin'."

Ed and Tia exchanged a glance. *Wonderful.* As if they didn't have enough speculation perking in their heads. She stood carefully and pulled her skirts away from her thighs. "Stop calling me that."

He cocked an eyebrow at her. "Is that an order?"

"I prefer to think of it as a strongly worded request."

He crooked his fingers at her. "That's just a fancy way of saying order."

She shrugged. She wasn't going to argue the obvious.

"Ride with him, *hija,*" Tia urged, putting a steadying hand on her thigh. "This trip is too long to willfully suffer."

"C'mon, Josie," Luke taunted. "What are you trying to prove?"

Nothing that would make sense to anyone but her.

And nothing that couldn't wait until they arrived at the Montoya ranch. Taking his hand, she grumbled, "You are entirely too used to getting your way."

He merely smiled and wrapped his calloused fingers around hers.

"Jump."

With the tug, he pulled her off the wagon and up against him. Instinct had her arms wrapping around his shoulders. And then, she dangled.

Ed chuckled. "Not the best mount I've ever seen."

Luke just shook his head. "This will work better if you throw your leg over the horse."

Tia laughed. "He's got a point."

It was easier said than done. Chico danced and pranced, not liking her skirts flapping around his legs, hindering her efforts. "Couldn't we just stop and do this right?"

"Mounting from a wagon is a necessary skill out here," Luke grunted.

She had no way to verify if that was true or not. "Clearly it's not one of mine."

He held her steady while controlling Chico. "Keep trying."

Hitching her up with a little toss, Luke gave her the leverage she needed to get her knee over Chico's flank. Wiggling and squirming, she managed to haul herself up, from then it was just a matter of sliding over. Of course, it didn't go that cleanly. A goodly amount of calf was showing on one side.

Of course he noticed that. "You want to cover up?"

The skirt was bunched painfully up between her

thighs. She now understood why everybody said the first thing that was sacrificed when one moved West was modesty. "Not particularly."

Mainly because she was either going to fall or vomit if she tried.

He looked at her over his shoulder. "And if Zach and his men go wild with lust at seeing that gorgeous leg?"

Wrapping her arms around his waist and leaning her cheek against his back, Josie smiled, closed her eyes and let the peace drive out the sick. "That's what I've got you for."

CHAPTER NINE

AFTER TWO MORE days of grueling travel, an ungodly climb up a mountain and a spooky trip through a cave that everyone misleadingly called a "cut," the end was near. Josie was finally coming into the light. Stefano, leading Glory so he wouldn't spook in that suffocatingly dark cave—he'd been a little jumpy since losing his hat—pulled the horse to a halt. Without a word, he walked to the rear of the wagon where his own mount was tied.

"What's happening?" Her question echoed in the cavern.

Stefano led the pretty mare up alongside. He smiled at her.

"Nothing. I am needed elsewhere. You can handle it from here."

She could? Unwrapping the reins from where they were tied, she stretched her back. If she never had to ride in a wagon again, it would be too soon. The last three days had been grueling. "Thank you."

He touched his hat. *"De nada, señorita."*

"Do we have much farther to go?" she called as he mounted.

"Not so far now. Half a day at most, if we don't run into trouble."

"Could you elaborate on 'trouble'?"

"You do not have to worry."

"And yet I will, so you might as well tell me."

"The wagons could break down—we could run into Indians or bandits. The horses could get snake bit. The path could fall away. The—"

He'd been too quick to whip that out. She held up her hand, stopping the litany. "I'm sorry I asked."

He smiled a weary smile. "As you wish."

If the trip had been rough on her, it'd been rougher on the vaqueros. They had to do double duty as guards at night. She didn't know when they slept.

Rubbing the back of her hand against her forehead, she sighed. She didn't need any more excitement. The tornado had filled that need for the foreseeable future. "Thank you, again."

"It was my pleasure." With a tip of his sombrero, he turned his horse. "Just follow the wagon ahead and you should be fine."

A touch of his heels to the mare's side and he was off. Her thank-you trailed in his wake.

She sighed. And then she was left alone with her thoughts. That was never a good thing. She had a habit of worrying a notion to death. Right now, topping the list was the kiss she'd shared with Luke. She'd tried blaming it on the storm, gratitude and too much spinsterhood, but no matter the excuse, the memory wouldn't go away. It pestered her like a hungry mosquito. Always buzzing around her thoughts, irritating her, making her crazy with the thought of doing it again. No matter that she'd avoided Luke for the last two days. Out of sight was not putting him out of her mind.

No matter what she tried, she could not erase that memory nor diminish its impact on her senses. She went to sleep with the feel of Luke's lips on hers. She slept with an echo of his weight upon her and awoke with the anticipation of feeling it again. He was like a drug in her blood. A daydream that wouldn't quit. She didn't know how to get rid of it. Worse, she really wasn't sure she wanted to. The man had been willing to die for her. In short, Luke Bellen was a hero straight out of her dime novels.

The now familiar signal cut through the quiet. With a creak and a groan, Tia's wagon jerked forward, its plain gray exterior monotonously lurching along. Josie had spent hours mentally framing pictures she wanted to take, then imagined hanging them on the back of that boring surface.

With a sigh, she clucked her tongue and urged Glory to follow. Before she got fully into the sunlight, she retrieved the ointment Tia had given her from her pocket. Pulling the cork, she dipped her fingers into the little pot and spread the cream on her nose and cheeks. Her bonnet just didn't have what it took to prevent sunburn. Wrinkling her nose at the smell, she resigned herself to another long ride.

At least her motion sickness had diminished. Sealing the jar and putting it away, she sighed. Just a half a day more, she consoled herself. Then this excruciating journey in this horrible wagon would be over. She couldn't wait. God help any Indians or bandits that might delay them, because if they did... Well, she might just go crazy and kill them herself.

She shook her head at the wild thought. Before she'd come out here, she'd never had so much as a violent inkling. All of her energy went into disappearing into the crowd. The West was certainly changing her. Whether it was for the better or not, that remained to be seen, but she was definitely changing.

At three o'clock, just as they were coming up on a steep-sided canyon opening, another sharp whistle came down the line. Ahead of her, Tia's wagon pulled up. But this time, the vaqueros fell in around the wagons in a protective barrier. Fear stirred in the pit of Josie's stomach. Glory tossed his head. The harness jangled.

Please don't let it be Indians.

She wished she had a gun.

"Is there trouble?" she asked the vaquero on her left.

"We are at the Montoya ranch."

This was the ranch? All she could see was a wall of mountains with a narrow pass between. "Then why are we stopping?"

"There are bandits in these hills. And Indians. We must wait to be allowed through."

She didn't want to wait. She was tired, queasy, thirsty and, quite frankly, dying to take pictures of this fascinating countryside. "I don't suppose we could just ride through and get approved later? After all, this is your home."

"El Montoya does not take chances with his family."

The waiting chafed. "So we have to wait."

"Yes."

"For whom?"

"The sentries." This man was older than Stefano and Zach. She didn't see a family resemblance until he smiled. He pointed to the peaks on either side of the valley opening. "If you look hard, you may see the glint of a gun barrel."

Shading her eyes with her hand, she peered off into the distance. She spotted what might have been the reflection of light or she could've just blinked. It was a long way up. "Can they hit anything from there?"

"The proof is under your feet."

He couldn't mean what she thought... Everything inside her cringed in horror. She glanced down. "You're not saying..."

The man laughed. "I only tease. We bury the dead over the hill."

She thought he might be teasing still. "Lovely."

"He's not joking on that," Stefano called back.

Even lovelier.

The sun beat down. Time crept by like a tortoise on a lazy day. Glory dozed in his traces. Josie chomped at the bit. She wanted to get there already. She wanted a real bath. She wanted a good meal. She wanted to develop the tintypes she'd already taken. She wanted to break out her equipment and take more. She wanted to do anything but sit in this wagon in the hot sun. This grand adventure was turning out to be little more than a bruise on her behind.

When there was a flurry of activity at the front, she perked up. When the call came to move, she could have cheered. After arranging her skirts more decorously and putting on her gloves, she picked up the reins and released the brake. Finally!

Before the wheels could make a full revolution, the wagon dipped to the left. Startled, she turned just as Luke settled into the seat beside her, his recovered hat sitting low on his brow. A glitter she didn't trust shone in his eyes. Beyond him, Chico kept pace with the wagon. Looping Chico's reins around a post, Luke pushed his hat back and gave her that smile that sent her imagination skipping along paths she kept trying to avoid.

"I told you mounting a horse from a wagon was a useful skill."

All she could think of was how she'd experienced that smile firsthand, felt it brush her skin, tasted it on her lips. She still had a mark on her neck from his kiss. Without thinking, she touched it.

"You neglected to mention it also works in reverse."

"A man likes to have some secrets."

She bet he did. "What are you doing here, Luke?"

He took the reins from her hand. "The path down to the Montoya ranch is steep."

"Then I'll get out and walk."

Suiting action to word, she got as far as one step down before he spoke.

"Watch out for rattlers."

She pulled her foot back in. "Are you saying that just to upset me?"

"No, I'm saying that because you need to watch out for them. This terrain is prime rattler territory."

"I hate snakes."

"I see. It's the spiders that get to me. They're so big you hate to stomp them because their guts squirt all over."

That was just too disgusting. She checked the overhang above her head. It was, thankfully, spider free. With as much dignity as she could muster, she sat back down on the seat.

Luke cut her a glance. "Staying?"

She glared at him and flopped back against the backboard, then considered what might lurk there and sat up straight again. "You know darned well I am."

His lips twitched. "I appreciate the company."

Ed and Tia's wagon started down the path. The vaqueros who'd been riding beside were nowhere close. With a flick of his reins, Luke woke Glory up. With a long slow breath, Glory expressed his displeasure. But on the next cluck of the tongue, the horse grudgingly put his weight into the harness. The wagon jerked into motion.

"Is the path really steep or did you just say that to scare me?"

"It's steep."

"Then thank you—".

He cut her off. "You're welcome."

She finished as if he hadn't interrupted. "But I'm sure Stefano could have driven me."

She had the satisfaction of seeing his jaw tighten.

"You and Stefano have spent a lot of time together lately."

"He's been a wealth of information on potential places to take pictures. Did you know there's a waterfall on the Montoya ranch?"

"No, I didn't."

"I've never photographed water before. I don't even know if it's possible."

"I'll take you."

"Stefano already volunteered, but thank you."

His hands tightened on the reins.

"You've been a bit busy of late."

The change of subject made her blink. She'd been entertaining the idea he might be jealous. Disappointment prompted the unvarnished truth. "I've been avoiding you."

He nodded. "I know."

He said that so casually. Didn't he care? This time she did sit back. It was hard letting illusions go. "You're better at this than I am."

He raised his eyebrow at her, not pretending to misunderstand. "I've had more practice."

"No doubt."

"Or it could be my ammo is bigger."

She blinked.

The corner of his mouth kicked up. "It's hard to top spiders and snakes."

"They are a hard act to follow."

"Are you ready to talk yet about what happened?"

"Between us?"

"Well, I sure don't want to talk about what happened between Ed and Tia last night."

The blush started at her toes. Another discovery she'd made. There was just no privacy on the trail. By the time it got to her cheeks, they were on fire. "It's good to know people can enjoy each other at any age."

"I don't know about you, but I could go another twenty years without revisiting that lesson."

"Me, too."

For a couple minutes, silence carried. Then Luke broke it with "You didn't answer my question."

"I know."

"I've been patient."

That had her turning in the seat. "Patient about what?"

"Ed and Tia said you needed some time."

There was no hiding her gasp. "You discussed what happened with Ed and Tia?" If a hole opened up in the ground in front of them right then, she would've jumped in.

"Hardly."

Now she felt foolish. "Then what exactly did you discuss?"

"The fact that you're not in much of a hurry to

chase down a husband." With a calm she had to admire, he added, "I'm aiming to get around that."

"Is that threat?"

"No, I just figure maybe you had reason in the past to be suspicious of men, but, my darlin', I'm not them."

"Stop calling me that."

"Why?"

"People will get ideas."

"What kind of ideas? Like that I'm interested in you? That you're under my protection? That I'll kill anyone who tries to hurt you? Darlin', there isn't a soul here that doesn't already know that."

She blinked. Except her, apparently. "Why are you telling me this?"

"Because we're almost at Rancho Montoya."

"And?"

"You're going to be a very popular woman once we get there."

The blush drained away in a rush. "I told you I'm not a whore."

"And I told you that's a filthy word."

"I don't understand."

She had to wait for his explanation as the path dipped suddenly. With a competence she'd never have managed, he worked the brake down the incline.

His jaw bunched. "Men are going to come courting."

He had such a warped view of how men saw her. "I don't—"

He cut her off. "They'll come. Most with good intentions."

She couldn't conceive of such a thing. "And?"

"And I'm writing my name at the top of your dance card."

It was finally dawning on her what he was saying. She glanced around in a minor panic. None of the vaqueros were within earshot, which could only mean he'd orchestrated that, too. At least that was something of which she approved. "You want to court me."

She couldn't blame him for the incredulous breath. She had been a little dense. They hit another downward section. He worked the brake and the reins in a coordinated effort, his arm muscles bulging with the effort. He'd handled her with the same efficiency. Still was, she realized as she caught him assessing her reaction out of the corner of his eyes. Grabbing the edge of the seat, she held on for dear life. She hadn't expected this. "Why?"

"Why do I want you?"

She shook her head. Below them, the ranch came into view. Rancho Montoya was a huge enterprise with multiple barns and corrals spread out over a large portion of verdant valley. A river threaded through the picturesque setting, guaranteeing the occupants ample water. Whoever had started the ranch had planned on leaving a mark, and whoever was maintaining it was building on that. She could feel Luke watching her, waiting for an explanation.

Why did no one understand that her dreams were just as big?

"Why what, then?" he prompted in that low drawl that made her goose bumps compete with her shivers. The man could probably talk a woman into his bed without ever laying a finger on her.

Looking at the ranch, she sighed. "Why is the choice always lover or husband? Why is it never friend?"

THE SMALL CARAVAN pulled into the yard. From the corral a colt nickered a greeting just as Bella waddled from the house. Her long dark hair was pulled back in a chignon. Luke could see the lines of strain hovering around her big brown eyes, but her smile was as beautiful as ever. Behind her hurried her mother, Bettina. She was an older, more reserved version of Bella.

"You know the doctor told you you're not supposed to be out of bed, Bella," she fussed.

With her hands on the small of her back, Bella dismissed the concern. "I have been waiting forever for Tia to get here. A few minutes will not harm."

From the look on her mother's face, she didn't agree.

Tia's expression mirrored Bettina's. Very carefully she hugged Bella, before putting her hand on her belly.

From where he was unhitching the team, Ed waved. Bella waved back, her face alight with joy.

"I am so glad you are here but, Ed, what has happened to you?"

"I lost the argument."

"He will be fine, Bella," Tia soothed.

Luke pulled Glory to a halt. He set the brake and wrapped the reins around the holder. "*Hola*, Bella."

"Luke!"

In typical Bella fashion, she started to rush over. He stopped her with an upraised hand. "Stay there. I'll come to you."

She laughed. "I am not so delicate that I cannot greet family."

"Humor me." He hopped down. "Sam would kill me if you dropped his son here in the courtyard."

"Sons," she corrected, beaming with pride.

"Whoa!" That put a hitch in his step. No wonder Sam was worried. "Twins?"

"Yes. Can you believe it? We wondered when I was so big, but then we could feel each move." She rubbed her belly. "After so much time and worry we might not be able to have babies, now we will have two."

Luke hugged her even more carefully than Tia had. Against his stomach, he felt a kick. "What the heck?"

"Do not be silly, they, too, say hello."

He really didn't know how he felt about that. Before he recovered, she was looking over his shoulder. "And who is this you brought with you?"

"This is Josie Kinder," Tia explained. "She is a

wonderful photographer. She has agreed to take pictures of our babies."

Bella clapped her hands. "I have heard of such things. I cannot wait to see how it is done."

Following his lead, Josie held up her hand. "Just wait—I'll come to you."

Bella had to wait a little longer for Josie to come, her skirts getting stuck on the brake handle. Then it was Luke's turn to say, "Hold on." She freed her skirts just as he reached the wagon. She looked beautiful standing there with the sun shining on her hair, an embarrassed flush on her cheeks and a sparkle in her eyes. She was so cute when she was flustered.

"Come here."

Catching her by the waist, he lifted her down. She immediately started fussing with her clothing. Catching her chin on the side of his finger he lifted her gaze to his. The softness of her lips begged his touch. The anxiety in her gaze demanded his comfort.

Why is it never friend?

He didn't have an answer. Touching his thumb to her lips, he told her, "You've got nothing to worry about."

Her breath was moist against the pad of his thumb. He wanted that heat against his lips, his neck, his chest, his cock. Why was it never friends? Because he wanted so much more than that.

"Are you sure?" she asked, her fingers fussing with her skirt. "I'm not usually welcomed by people like this."

"Like this?"

"You know." She glanced at the house.

She was intimidated by the Montoya wealth.

Because he couldn't do anything else, because he had to do something, he pressed the pad of his thumb against her lower lip in a subtle kiss, reminding her of what had gone before, of what he'd said before. "I promise."

She visibly relaxed. When he stepped back, he could feel Bella's curiosity. He could only hope she didn't blurt out something damaging. Things with Josie were tenuous right now. He thought that time after the tornado had been a beginning, opened a door to more, but in many ways, it'd closed the only one he cared about. He needed to come up with a new plan.

"It's nice to meet you, Mrs. Montoya," Josie said, crossing the dusty yard with her head held high.

Bella smiled. "It's MacGregor, actually, but I understand your confusion. The men call me La Montoya." With a grimace she confessed, "I am sort of named after the ranch. It would be embarrassing if it did not make me feel so grand." She caught Josie's hand in hers. "You, however, must call me Bella." Turning, she indicated Bettina. "And this is my mother, Bettina Montoya."

"It is my pleasure to meet you, Mrs. Montoya."

Bettina was much more reserved. "The pleasure is mine." She turned to her daughter. "And now that the pleasantries are over, you, *mi hija*, need to be back in bed."

Bella rolled her eyes. "I am sick of this bed."

"Your boredom is of no matter."

Bella nodded. "I know, I must do for my children if I would give my Sam strong sons."

"And you will," Tia interrupted, "but to do that you must rest."

Standing where he was, Luke intercepted the look Tia shared with Ed. She was worried.

"Not too much," Bella countered. "I have had a feast prepared. If you do not mind the informality, we can have a picnic in my room and you can join me. We will eat and talk of your journey and I will discover how this picture taking is done."

The look Josie cast him was equally as concerned as Tia's but for entirely different reasons. Luke shrugged and motioned her in.

The women escorted Bella into the house, hovering around her in a protective cloud. When the door closed behind them, Luke headed back to unharness Glory. Ed shook his head from where he was taking care of his own team. "Sam must be out of his mind with worry. Twins are a dangerous prospect."

"Yeah. I don't know what Sam would do without his Bella."

All of Hell's Eight had been worried about Sam that year before he'd met Bella. He'd always been the wild card in any fight, always willing to take a risk, but that last year the risks had gotten too frequent and too big. It was as if something had been eating him from the inside out. Bella seemed to not only understand that wildness, but she stabilized it and reshaped it into purpose. Watching them together was like watching a perfectly choreographed dance. They were deeply in love. And it showed.

"Let's hope we never have to find out."

Unhitching Glory from the wagon, Luke walked him to the water trough. Both the trough and the water were clean. He wasn't surprised. Sam was meticulous about everything he cared about. Ed brought over the gray. The two horses drank companionably.

Luke leaned against the corral fence and rubbed at the stitches Tia had put in his gash. They'd reached the itching stage. Ed leaned opposite where he stood.

"You're not coming back to Hell's Eight after this, are you?"

Ed was always direct. Luke admired that quality. "Things have changed."

"Evasion is as good as a no."

He supposed it was. "It doesn't feel like there's anything there for me anymore."

"There's your family."

"They're settled."

"And you want more."

"I don't know if *more* is the right word."

Ed pulled his pipe out of his pocket. "What would be the right one then?"

"I don't know."

Packing his tobacco into the pipe, he struck a sulfur on his boot. Putting it to the bowl, he took a few puffs. "Is that an evasion?"

"No."

For a few minutes silence reigned. Ed was the first to break it.

"It makes sense, you know."

"It does?" It sure as hell didn't make sense to him.

"You've been giving Hell's Eight everything you've had since you were a child. They've been your world, but now everyone is settling down, splintering off into families of their own."

Smoke drifted between them, filling the space with the sweet earth scent. Luke cocked an eyebrow at Ed. "Are you telling me I need to grow up?"

Ed took another puff before pointing the stem at him.

"I'm telling you you've delayed finding your place long enough, so when this is over—" his hand swept the horizon "—go out there and find it."

"Are you kicking me out?"

"Without a lick of guilt."

Well, damn.

CHAPTER TEN

SHE FELT LIKE an intruder beside the big four-poster bed where Bella sat propped on a mound of pillows looking like a queenly sprite who'd inadvertently swallowed a watermelon. It wasn't that anyone did anything to make her feel uncomfortable. Quite the opposite. They tried painfully hard to make her feel included, but that was easier said than done. Years of making oneself invisible, especially to those who lived in houses like this, had cultivated all the wrong skills for proper social interaction.

Instead of feeling included in the happy camaraderie, Josie was vividly conscious of how drab her brown dress was, how plain her bun looked compared to Bella's chignon, how completely boring and inappropriate most of her life stories were. Hearing how Bella had stood her ground against bandits and saved Sam's wolf dog, Kel, made her realize how odd her upbringing had been. She knew which fork to use when and how to use the proper address no matter what a person's station. She could even hold a proper conversation while pouring tea. The difficulty there was that the only compelling story she had was about how her fiancé had played her for a fool and essentially stood her up at the alter for another woman. Which, of course, violated another one of society's rules.

One never aired one's dirty laundry in public, which lowered her conversational participation to a one sentence gambit of "We came to realize we were not suited." After five years, no one believed it was that simple or clean. Especially not her.

Ugh. This had to change. She couldn't be this pathetic and continue to look at herself in the mirror. In her imagination, she was so much more daring and exciting, a heroine worth innumerable pages in one of Dane Savage's novels. In reality, she was the woman sitting in a borrowed dining room chair, unobtrusively inching her way to the door.

Looking at Bella, who from what she'd overheard might very well lose these babies along with her life, she felt ashamed. Bella wasn't cowering or bemoaning her situation. She was laughing and smiling, enjoying whatever time she had. Was she happy to be confined to the bed? Of course not, but she didn't cave to her circumstances or complain. Instead she was holding court, inspiring laughter and lighting up the room with her spirit. Josie had yet to meet her husband, Sam, but she would bet he was a very happy man. It was no wonder he protected his treasure so thoroughly. Bella was sunshine brought to life. Josie didn't necessarily want to be sunshine, but she'd like to at least be a flicker of light.

I'm putting my name at the top of your dance card. The memory came unbidden as all of her mem-

ories of Luke seemed to, sneaking past her guard.
Playing with a loose thread on her sleeve, she cut a
glance at him from the corner of her eye. He sat in
a chair much closer to the bed, the remnants of his
meal on a plate in his lap. In his own way, he was as
vibrant as Bella. Josie had no idea what he saw in her
unless it was an easy conquest. It hurt her pride to
remember just how easy she'd been for him. It hurt
her heart to know it would never happen again. She
had her pride. Not to mention a strong, if belated,
sense of self-preservation. She scooted her chair back
another inch. It was probably the tenth time in the
last forty-five minutes.

Of course Luke chose that moment to turn her
way. Getting caught staring always sent panic flashing through her. Getting caught staring like a love-
sick cow was just humiliating. Oh yes, her mother
had taught her well. Don't look. Don't draw attention.
Don't hope. Don't be the person that makes them remember. Don't be you.

As no convenient hole opened in the floor, she
had no choice but to brazen it out. Full panic didn't
lead to her best thinking. With an arrogance she'd
seen him use, she arched her brows and tilted up her
chin, doing her best to provoke. She didn't need anyone's pity. She expected anger. Instead, he smiled.
A soft intimate smile that hinted at understanding
and support. He approved of her bravado, she realized. This time when she inched her chair back it
was because of shock.

And she promptly froze as the perspective came

into focus. There it was. Right there. The picture she'd been looking for. A perfect tableau of hope and love. Bella, sitting on the bed, looked like a Madonna. Sunbeams dancing and playing with her expression, flirting with her smile, hinting at the shadow. The sun played the same game with her family, highlighting the hopes of some while dropping others into somber shadow. And there was love. So much love. This was the picture she'd come here to take. This was the moment she needed to capture. With a soft "Excuse me" she got up.

It was easy to make her escape. They were in the middle of a story about Boone stealing Sunday dinner and Sam's Kel catching him in the act. It was one that left them all howling with laughter as she slipped away. Out of the room, she breathed deeply. Free of social expectation, she could let her mind sink into the coming photo. She'd need the special plates she'd prepared for low-light settings. And the lower tripod. She didn't want the shot straight on. She wanted Bella centered and elevated. Lost in her thoughts, she took a wrong turn. Instead of the foyer, she ended up in what looked to be a library.

"Well, shoot."

"Want some help?" The deep drawl came from behind her.

Luke. She hadn't even noticed he'd followed her.

"What are you doing here?"

"I thought you might need a hand."

"With what?"

"The picture you're about to take." His brow

cocked. "That is why you got that intense expression before jumping up and rushing out of the room, isn't it?"

"I rushed?"

His smile was gentle. "Like a scalded cat."

So much for her discreet exit. "Oh."

"Don't worry, I made your excuses."

She gathered a fold of her skirt in her hand. "What did you tell them?"

He took her hand. His thumb rubbed the back the way she'd been rubbing the skirt. "That you're about to make magic."

"That might have been an exaggeration. I'm not even sure there's enough light in the room. All I might get is a blank tintype."

"Josie?"

She sighed. There was a world of patience packed into her name. "I'm babbling, aren't I?"

"No, but you are wasting time. As you told me before, light and clouds wait for no one."

"There are no clouds."

He steered her down the hallway. "I was being creative. It sounded better than light and people."

"Oh."

In under a minute he had her through the front door and outside her wagon. Opening the back doors, he asked, "Do you need help?"

"No."

"Good, because I'm not sure I'd fit in there."

She eyed him absentmindedly, focused instead on the upcoming shoot. "Not standing up at least."

It just popped out. His bark of laughter as he grasped her waist and set her on the mattress made her realize how her comment could be taken.

The impression of his touch lingered after he took his hands away. So did the gleam of his smile. "I meant—"

"I know what you meant." With a wave of his hand he indicated the trunks. "Get what you need. We can talk about my much more interesting version of your proposal later."

"But…"

"The light's changing as we speak."

Darn it, he was right. She didn't have time to waste. Ignoring the smothering heat, she opened the trunk lids with trepidation. The journey up here had been rough. There was no telling if her tintypes or the camera itself had survived. As quickly as she could, she unpacked the box that held her supplies. Sawdust fell to the floor as she laid out her necessities on the mattress. A quick check showed everything was in good shape. She quickly added the specially treated tintypes to her box. Checking the camera lens and mirror for dust, she wiped them with the special brush she kept handy. Closing the box carefully, she stood.

"All set?" Luke asked.

She nodded.

"Then pass that over and let's get moving."

The box was heavy with the extra tintypes. She levered more than lifted it to the edge of the mattress. As if it weighed nothing, he set it on the ground.

Grabbing the tripod, she prepared to hop down. He was there before her. Catching her by the waist, he swung her away from the edge of the wagon. Bracing her hand on his broad shoulders, she caught her balance. Beneath her palm his muscles flexed as he slowly lowered her down his body. And that fast, the wild feminine side of her made itself known in an eager gasp that ended on a moan as her hips dragged across his. He was hard.

She bit her lip when her feet hit the ground. His smile was knowing. She was torn between wanting to hit him and wanting to sink into a puddle of willing mush at his feet. Neither was a good choice. Somehow, she found her voice to ask, "What are you doing?"

His answer stole the resentment right out from under her feet. "Being your friend."

She didn't know how to respond to that. Fortunately, he didn't seem to expect it. Without further ado, he gathered up her equipment, took her hand and led her back to the house. His stride was longer than hers, causing her to skip every other step. Sweat broke out on her brow. It was only slightly cooler outside than in the wagon, and now that she thought about it, neither was ideal. She cast a nervous glance over her shoulder. Had she closed the box? "Don't worry. No one will bother your equipment."

"It's not that."

He opened the door for her. "Then what is it?"

"I can't remember if I closed the box. The chemicals I use to develop my pictures are volatile."

"You did."

"Still, it's hotter here. They don't do well in the heat. I think we'll need to move the wagon to the shade."

"Not a problem."

Nothing ever was for him. She envied that.

Even if Luke hadn't been holding her hand, she wouldn't have had any trouble finding her way back to Bella's bedroom. Happy laughter floated down the hall like an audible road map.

"I like your friends," she told him as he ushered her into the foyer.

That got her a considering glance. "Good. So do I."

She chewed her lip. "I hope I can capture the emotion that flows between you all when you're together."

"You want to take a picture of an emotion?"

"Oh yes. Definitely."

"Then let's get to it." Still holding her hand, he led her down the hall.

The house was built of adobe. The thick walls acted as insulation, keeping the heat out. The arched, wood-framed doorways provided a nice architectural contrast to the smooth walls dotted with family portraits and delicate watercolors. Lace doilies covered heavy wooden tables sitting in front of ornately carved wood and leather chairs.

The frilly curtains in the parlor wouldn't have

been her taste, but they worked somehow in the odd blend of overt masculinity combined with pervasive femininity. The house reflected the best of its owners' abilities to negotiate to a happy compromise. It was warm and happy and welcoming. And a photographer's dream. Everywhere she looked there was a contrast demanding to be captured, but it would never happen. The heavy walls that kept out the heat also kept out the light. She sighed as the parlor fell out of view.

"What was that about?"

"I would love to take pictures in here."

"You can later. It's not as if the house is going anywhere."

"There's not enough light."

He glanced around. "Damn."

"Exactly. Maybe someday, though. They're making advances all the time."

"Is there going to be enough light in the bedroom?"

Some of her confidence slipped at being put on the spot. Successful photography, she'd discovered, was half luck and half experimentation. "I hope so. I've created a new prep for the tins that I'm hoping will make up the difference when combined with the special lens I created, but…"

"You created it?"

Again she found herself wishing for a hole to open up. "Yes."

"I'm impressed."

"Don't be. I don't know if it will work."

He opened the door. "There's only one way to find out."

Yes, there was. Taking a breath, she walked through the door.

As soon as she stepped into the room, conversation ceased and all eyes locked on her, but it wasn't the people she was concerned with. The light had shifted, but not to her disadvantage. With the sun lower in the sky, there was more intensity in the room. A glow. A surge of excitement shot through her. This was good. She held out her hands for her equipment and Luke handed it to her.

"What do you want us to do?" Bella asked from the bed.

Loosening the screws that secured the legs, she stood the tripod up. "Nothing right now. Go back to talking. It takes a while to get everything ready."

"But you will let us know when it is time?"

There was no such thing as surprise photography. The whole process was laborious. But so rewarding.

"Absolutely." She wouldn't have a choice. The lighting wasn't going to be the only problem. As marginal as it was, the cooperation of her subjects was likely to be even more marginal. She wanted a natural picture, but any movement blurred the image. She hadn't quite figured out how she was going to avoid that, but right now the most important step was to get her equipment set up so she could take advantage of whatever opportunity came her way.

"What can I do?" Luke asked.

Hug me. Kiss me. Make love to me. "You can go back to your seat."

A flicker of something chased across his face. Hurt? Placing her hand on his arm, she explained, "You're part of the picture. Without you in it, it's incomplete."

He eyed her hand for a second and then, with a nod, took his seat. She moved the tripod around the room, looking for the right angle. At first everybody watched her as if at any moment she was going to yell, "Ready!" She could only dream it would be that easy. One of these days, though, somebody was going to build a camera that snapped a picture as fast as a photographer could press a button and all she'd have to do to get a natural picture would be to sneak up on people. She was much better at sneaking than she was at socializing.

Which was a shame, she finally admitted to herself. The way she'd lived her life until now had been a waste of her youth—hiding in the shadows, hoping not to be noticed. Her mother might have had good intentions, but it'd been a disservice. With a sigh, she set the camera on the tripod.

"What is it?" Bella asked.

"Just trying to get the right perspective." Making a square of her hands, she framed her options. After that, everyone studied every move she made, clearly fascinated by the process. Being the center of attention in any other circumstance, she would have deteriorated to all thumbs, but once she was behind the camera, she never felt awkward. She never felt foolish. In this, she knew what she was doing. In this, she was confident because from behind the lens, she could make magic happen. Some people were orators, some were schemers. She captured moments.

"Please, just continue your storytelling. It gives me something to enjoy while I do the tedious setup."

The conversation was awkward at first, but she concentrated on being invisible and eventually they seemed to forget she was there—all except Luke. It might've been wishful thinking, but he seemed to be as aware of her as she was of him. Gradually, the conversation became more animated. More natural. She slid the tintype into the camera.

Luke cocked an eyebrow at her. She didn't mind if his attention wasn't centered on Bella. If just for this photograph, she wanted to be the center of his world.

All right, she corrected. Maybe for two photographs. She desperately wanted an image of him sitting up on Chico, arms crossed over the saddle horn with that deceptive indolence that was so much a part of him. A king surveying his world. A wildly regal, solidly dependable force that begged to be reckoned with. That's what she'd put as his caption, she decided—A Force to Be Reckoned With. With a last adjustment, she had her shot lined up.

In a low voice not meant to intrude, she ordered, "I'm all set, so here is what I want you to do. Keep talking as if I'm not working over here. When I get the angle I want, I'm going to say 'freeze.' When I do, I want you to hold perfectly still, keeping whatever expression you have in that moment."

"Just freeze?" Tia asked.

"Yes. Don't worry about how it's going to look. In truth, you can never tell how it's going to look."

"But you can see how it will come out, eh, Josie?"

"Yes, Bella, I can see and when it's perfect, that's when I'm going to tell you to freeze because I have the magic of the camera."

And a lot of optimism.

"I like this thought of magic."

"Me, too." Smiling at Bella, she went over it one more time. It was crucial they held absolutely still. "So just remember, when I say 'freeze,' you need to stay in your position. No talking. No turning. No scratching." She couldn't count how many times people developed itches they couldn't resist during the exposure period and ruined her image.

"Got it."

"Good." Excitement surged through her. "So let's get a picture made."

The silence in the room was deafening.

Bella laughed. "A second ago we were laughing and giggling and carrying on, and now I can't think of a single word to say."

She'd have told them that happened a lot, but this was the first time she'd ever tried capturing a natural-looking shot. Still photography was fine, but every time she looked at one of those stiff portraits, the artist in her whispered that there had to be a way to do it better. A way *she* could do it better.

"I know it's hard." That's why she dreamed of a camera that took pictures in an instant. Just the thought of being able to sneak in, capture the moment and then move on to the next with no one being the wiser gave her artistic chills. But until it became a reality, she had to deal with the process as it was.

"Did they tell you about the tornado that almost swallowed Luke and me whole? One minute I was grouching along in that godforsaken wagon and the next, I was running for my life. It was monstrous!"

"As you are standing here, I know you survived, but I wish to hear. It sounds as if it was a grand adventure. I do love adventures," Bella said.

Luke shook his head at Bella. "I thought Sam cured you of those grand-adventure moments."

With a wave of her hand, Bella dismissed the silliness. "My Sam is my grand adventure, yes."

"And keeping you out of trouble is his grand adventure," Ed teased.

Tia laughed. Bettina nodded her head. "This is true. Bella is most impulsive."

"Happy," Bella corrected without missing a beat. "I am not impulsive, I am happy. And, Luke…" She reached over—no simple feat in her condition—and patted his hand. "My Sam's love for me and mine for him… Our love is the grandest adventure of all. Someday, I hope you find this out for yourself." She looked over at Josie, and in that split second she had the perfect shot.

"Freeze."

As one they all turned to look at her. The perfect shot was lost.

"Darn it."

"We weren't supposed to move," Ed pointed out unnecessarily.

"That's all right." Josie sighed. "We can try again."

"We will not move this time," Tia promised.

"Thank you."

Bella was the only one not thrown off her stride by the failure. As if her conversation had not been interrupted, she hitched herself higher on the pillows. "Do not believe them, Josie, when they say these things. I do not look for danger."

"But danger always seems to find you." Bettina sighed. Clearly her vivacious daughter was a source of both pride and consternation to the older woman.

Bella inclined her head gracefully. "I admit there was a period in my life when it seemed that way, but now I am a respectable married woman about to have twins." She folded the sheet in a precise layer over the top of the blanket. "My adventures will be different from here on out."

"I hope so," Tia interjected. "It was a close call when Tejala kidnapped you."

"But my Sam saved me. That was all good."

"And then we almost lost him," Tia added.

Bella's face clouded over. "That was a dark time, but it is behind us now. There is no more trouble."

Another perfect shot. Before she could say "Freeze" Luke had to add his own sardonic spice to the conversational mix. "Unless you count Indians and bandits."

Under the camera curtain, Josie gritted her teeth

as another perfect shot died an ignoble death. She might be biting off more than she could chew with this endeavor. She didn't have much more time to get the shot. The sun was moving out of position. If she had any sense, she'd just line them all up like cadavers at a funeral home and take the picture. But she didn't have sense, she had ambition, so she crouched behind the camera and she waited.

As one, they started arguing back and forth about whether trouble looked for Bella or whether she strolled up to the door and invited it in. As she watched, Josie marveled at how, even amid the fighting, there was still so much love between these people. It lurked behind how they phrased their arguments, in the way they touched an arm or shoulder to soften a point, in the way they smiled when a particularly witty point found its mark.

The first time she'd thought she had the perfect shot, it wasn't a success, the second not much more. Fifteen minutes later the food was gone, the coffee drunk and they'd stopped anticipating that moment, which meant they finally gave her what she wanted—the liveliness she could only hope to capture on film, the intensity of love in the tilt of a head, the softening of an expression. When they paused for a breath, laughter lingering in their eyes and exasperation tingeing their smiles, she had her moment.

"Freeze."

And they did. She held her breath through the exposure, mentally counting off the minutes. When the last second passed she closed the shutter. She couldn't wait to get the tintype back to her wagon. It had to have worked. It just had to. The third time had to be the charm.

Fingers trembling, she came out from under the curtain. "You can relax now."

"Thank goodness. I was getting a charley horse."

She apologized to Ed, and to all of them for having to hold still for so long.

"You did it?" Bella asked.

"It's impossible to know without developing, but I think I got what I was looking for."

"What exactly did you hope to find?" Bettina asked.

She opened her mouth to respond, but it was Luke who answered for her. "Love."

CHAPTER ELEVEN

SHE HAD TO wait to develop the tintype. Complications came about when they had to figure out a safe place to put the wagon. The first suggestion had been the barn. To the outsider it was a perfectly logical solution. There was shade, water and some privacy. At least during the day. It would be hard to find a better space except for one thing. The chemicals she worked with were highly flammable. She'd been keeping that quiet. For a very good reason. People tended to react the way Luke was right now.

"What the hell do you mean they could explode?"

"In the right environment, if the proper precautions aren't taken, ether can become…unstable." So could collodion, but it only burned.

He slapped his Stetson against his thigh, a habit she was beginning to understand meant he was furious. "You mean it can damn well blow up."

"Or catch fire." She shrugged. "It's not an all or nothing kind of thing. But fire would be more likely."

The minuscule hope that downplaying the risks would soothe Luke's reaction died when he narrowed his eyes.

"And you've been working with this for how long?"

"For a couple years, but let's not get sidetracked. We were figuring out where to park the wagon." She had no idea where the courage to face down a grown man was coming from, but she liked it.

"I'm not sidetracked. I'm just looking at the much bigger problem in front of me."

He said that while looking directly at her. "I'm not a problem and neither is my profession. There are just certain precautions that need to be taken."

He raked his hand through his hair, sending it spiking in different directions. "I thought Tucker was bad with his dynamite, but you've got him beat six ways to Sunday."

"You're getting emotional."

"I passed emotional about five minutes ago when I found out you've been riding around in a bomb."

"It is not a bomb."

"That's your opinion."

"And it's the only one that matters at the moment since this is my wagon, my endeavor and my problem."

"If you park that wagon in the barn, it'll be everybody's problem."

Taking a deep breath she rubbed her fingertips against her temple. He was giving her a headache. "This whole discussion started because I told you I didn't want to park the wagon in the barn."

"But you didn't have any intention of telling me why."

"Contrary to popular opinion, I am not stupid."

"In accordance with current opinion, current being mine, you are out of your ever-loving mind."

For heaven's sake, he was impossible.

"Is this a private argument, or can anybody join in?"

Josie turned. A handsome blond-haired man with green eyes and a rakish hank of hair falling over his right brow stood beside the paddock, holding the reins of a beautiful pinto. At his other side stood a very mean-looking, very large dog, one that could easily pass for a wolf. Both man and beast had a wildness about them that made her uneasy.

"That depends on how you feel about flammable substances."

As she watched, the wolf lifted its lip. She took a step closer to Luke.

"Quiet, Kel." With a cock of his brow, the blond man asked, "I take it this one belongs to you, Luke?"

"I could wish." He cut her another glare. "Because if she did, she'd be over my knee right now."

"I certainly would not!"

The stranger laughed. "So now you've got two arguments going."

Luke growled in his throat. "Welcome home, Sam. Good to see you. Now shut the heck up."

Sam laughed. "Good to see you, too, Luke."

Josie stared. This deadly-looking man wearing more guns and knives than she'd seen in one place before was *Sam*? *Bella's Sam?* The man she described as the sweetest thing in the world?

"You're nothing like I imagined."

He took his hat off and hung it on the saddle horn. "Bella's been spinning tales again, I see. Mind if I ask what you were imagining?"

"I was expecting somebody more—" she waved her hands "—more...Lancelot-like."

"Ouch." With a snap of his fingers he directed Kel to sit. "Did she go on about how I'm an angel come to earth?"

"That might have been mentioned."

"I was afraid of that. The woman's hard on my pride with her descriptions, but since whatever I am makes me the man of her dreams, I just study on clearing up the confusion later." He held out his hand. "Sam MacGregor."

She took it gingerly, keeping her eye on the dog. "Josie Kinder."

With a different snap of his finger, he told the dog, "Say hi to Josie, Kel."

With a cock of his head, the dog held up his front paw. Behind her, Luke sighed. "You might as well take it. Kel knows he won't get a treat until you shake, so he's not going to give up."

She leaned forward, stopped and looked between the two men. "He doesn't bite, does he?"

"He does, but not pretty little women who are friends with my wife."

That wasn't the complete comfort Sam clearly intended it to be. "Who decides if she's pretty?"

With another sigh, a softer one this time, Luke put his hand on the small of her back. The gesture was encouraging and protective at the same time. "Go ahead and shake his paw. You're safe."

She did and she swore the creature smiled at her. Just in case, she smiled back. She didn't want to offend him.

"There. Now you're friends."

Of course they were. Josie rolled her eyes. "And to think I spent years doing it the old-fashioned way with pieces of chicken and long intimate conversations."

Sam laughed. "I like her."

"Well, with that recommendation, I guess I'll keep her."

"Even with her penchant for—" Sam tilted his head and looked in the wagon "—ether, collodion and alcohol?"

Luke stepped around to check for himself. "She didn't say anything about alcohol."

"Can't develop a tintype without it," Sam said.

It was Josie's turn to be surprised. "You're a photographer?"

"No, but I once chased down a bounty that was. Made the mistake of letting him talk me into keeping the wagon with us."

"Oh no."

"Yup. He damn near burned the entire town down trying to escape."

"I bet you never made that mistake again."

"No, I didn't, which is precisely why we will not be storing your wagon in my barn."

Putting her hands on her hips, she turned to face

Luke. "See, I told you storing it in the barn was a bad idea."

"I never said it wasn't."

It was Sam's turn to roll his eyes. "While I don't have much of a solution for the whole spanking dilemma, I could suggest parking the wagon under the oak tree in the backyard. It's far enough away from the house that even if it blows up, there won't be a problem, but close enough you won't be in any danger."

She only allowed a hint of sarcasm in her voice as she agreed, "There. I told you there'd be a reasonable solution, Luke."

"Then we'll let Sam handle the wagon and you can come with me."

"In case you're missing the subtext," Sam told her, "you're going to be the next thing *he* handles."

That probably wasn't meant to send a thrill down her spine, but it did. "What if I don't want to be handled?"

"Then you tell me, and I deal with the problem. You're a guest here in my home. That gives you certain rights to my protection."

Sam and Luke were best friends. She'd be a very small person if she used good manners to pit them against each other. "Thank you, but I'm not afraid of Luke."

It might have been her imagination, but a little of that inner tension left Luke with her declaration.

Sam cocked his head to the side. "I believe you're the first woman I've ever heard say that."

Luke just shook his head. "Go see your wife, Sam."

"Gladly."

As if on cue, a vaquero came strolling across the yard to take the reins from Sam. "Welcome home, *patron.*"

Sam grabbed his brown Stetson off the saddle. *"Gracias, Guillermo."*

"De nada."

"And, Guillermo, when you're done with Breeze, could you get some men and move this wagon under the big oak in the backyard?"

"Sí, patron. With pleasure."

Josie frowned at the man. Obviously he'd been eavesdropping on their discussion. How much had he overheard?

"It's nice to meet you, Josie." Sam settled his hat on his head. The image of a desperado was complete. "And, Luke?"

"Yeah?"

"There's a garden shed to the left of the barn if you want a little privacy."

Josie didn't like Sam's smile one bit. Watching him go, she muttered, "I take back every nice thing I ever thought about that man."

Luke's smile didn't do much to calm her. Cupping her elbow in his palm, he guided her across the yard. "Why?"

She gave an experimental tug on her arm. His grip tightened. The message was clear. She was going where he wanted. "He just gave you indirect permission to abuse me!"

"He offered us some privacy."

"So you could spank me."

"You keep harping on that. Are you trying to convince me it's a must?" She could have smacked him right there for his sardonic quirk of the brow. "Because I've got to tell you, I'm not averse."

To the left of the barn was a small, whitewashed building. They were heading straight for it.

"You know darned well I'm not convincing you of *that*!"

"Then I'd suggest not giving me ideas."

"I wasn't the one who brought it up in the first place!"

"And yet, we're still beating that dead horse."

"If it were dead, we wouldn't be talking about it."

"My point exactly."

She wanted to scream.

The shed wasn't a very prepossessing structure, nor was it ramshackle. Like everything on the Montoya ranch, it was well cared for and sturdy. The door hinge didn't even creak when Luke opened it. It was one of those scream now or forever hold her peace moments. With subtle pressure on her elbow, he guided her inside. He didn't push. She didn't scream. Luke closed the door behind them.

The interior wasn't completely dark. A small window on the opposite wall let in enough light for her to see his expression. Her brows rose. Violence was not what was on the man's mind. A smile started inside. "Is this where you spank me?"

His hand slid across her cheek, curved around her skull, wove through the tight strands swept up into her bun. The delicate tension flicked along her nerve endings.

"I'm mad as hell at you."

The growling timbre in his voice shivered down her awareness. She'd never thought she was a woman who was attracted to danger, but there was no denying Luke was a very dangerous man. And there was no denying she found him compelling. A slight curl of his fingers pulled her up on her toes. She went without resisting because of what she saw in his eyes—lust, caring and determination. The emotional mix was as tempting as all get out. Goose bumps raced up her arms. She remembered how good it felt before, and those circumstances had been less than ideal. How much better could it feel now without terror clouding her response?

"Why?"

"You have no right risking your life like that."

She hadn't risked anything. She understood how to handle the chemicals. But that really wasn't what was important here. "Why?"

His eyes narrowed. "Be careful what you ask for, Josie."

"It's a simple question."

"Nothing is simple between you and me."

Curling her fingers around his wrist, she held his gaze and asked again, "Why?"

It happened so fast, she didn't realize what he'd done until it was over. In the blink of an eye, she was pressed up against the shed wall, her hands pinned beside her head and he was smiling down at her with the expression of a predator well satisfied with his prey.

So much for being in control.

"You, my darlin', keep judging me by Eastern standards."

Leaning his body into hers, giving her a bit of his weight, pinning and teasing her at the same time, he drawled, "But when you push a Western man..."

"He pushes back?"

Was that low husky voice her own?

The kiss on her forehead was very soft. The whisper in her ear, very deep. "No, sweetheart. A Western man gives you what you want."

A shiver shook her from head to toe. "And you think I want this?"

The question came out in a breathy gasp.

He kissed the sensitive skin beneath her ear. "If you don't, all you have to do is say no."

Her nails bit into her palms as lightning streaked under her skin. He was so close, she could do nothing but feel him, not just with her skin but with her senses. His scent teased her memory, his voice her anticipation, his eyes, oh his eyes—they teased her most of all. Soft with emotion, dark with passion, lit with amusement, there was so much life within his eyes. So much...adventure. Maybe too much.

She took a breath. And then another. Releasing it

slowly, she strove for balance. All she had to say was no. Just no. That was it. One syllable. No big deal.

Slowly, deliberately, she unclenched her fists. "Yes." The word slipped out on a blissful sigh.

His resulting smile was slow-growing. Mesmerizing. He had a wonderful mouth. Lips neither too big nor too small, the lower lip was slightly fuller than the upper. How had she never noticed that before? She wanted to nibble on it. Run her tongue over it. Suck on it. She needed a picture of his mouth.

"That's my girl."

She should have protested the possession in that statement. Common sense said it was a must. Desire said, "Why bother?" She wanted this. She wanted him. "I thought you were going to give me what I wanted?"

"In my time, not yours."

"Why can't it just be our time? Why does it have to be one or the other?"

Keeping hold of her hands, he guided them over his shoulders. "No reason, whatsoever. Put your arms around my neck."

She did, relishing the cool silk of his hair between her fingers. She had to stretch up on her toes. The tips of her breasts brushed his shirtfront. Her nipples hardened. Her breath caught as they tingled with sensation. He slid his arms between her shoulder blades and the wall, protecting her from the hardness.

"Now what?" she asked.

"Now, hold on."

She would've asked what for, but he was already

showing her. Pulling her closer, letting her feel proof of his passion, proof of his intent. His lips ghosted over hers. She couldn't move. She couldn't breathe. All she could do was cling to his shoulders and open her mouth and welcome the tumult.

Mouth to mouth, breath colliding, they flowed together. Close but not yet close enough. His left hand cradled her head, his right her back, their lips barely touching. Close. So close. She was surrounded by him, supported by him, suspended before him in a heated moment of anticipation. Heavens, she wanted done with this teasing parody. She wanted his kiss.

And still he didn't deliver. And with every second that passed, her need increased. It was a test. It was a challenge. And she didn't care whether he won and she lost. He was keeping her from the one thing she'd wanted her entire life… Completion.

Digging her nails into the back of his neck, she stood higher on her tiptoes, moaning when he leaned back, keeping the distance between them. "Darn you. Kiss me."

His chuckle was just another added dimension. "I thought you'd never ask."

She frowned at him. "Darn it, you made me ask."

He smiled back. "But I won't make you regret it."

No he wouldn't. Whatever it was between them was powerful. She might not know much, but she knew that. Keeping the connection soft at first, he backed her up against the wall and claimed her mouth with a bold thrust. Giving her the weight of his body, the depth of his passion, he kissed her like she was the only woman on earth for him. Oh, that was a gift she appreciated. To feel like she mattered. She never wanted it to end.

His tongue teased the corner of her mouth. It tickled. He chuckled when she flinched. "Not your favorite?"

She shook her head. "There are things you do much better."

"Like what?"

He was making her think. She didn't want to think. This was about feeling. This was about all those experiences she'd never gotten to have. This was about finally getting to be the woman that she'd always known she had the potential to be. This was about being wild. Uninhibited. This was about living. "I don't know. Surprise me."

His eyes narrowed. "That's an awfully big invitation."

Did he think she didn't understand? "If I'm going to hell anyway, I might as well go all in."

"That's a tall order."

"Consider it a challenge."

"I hope like hell you don't regret this." His hand closed over her right breast. Even through all the layers of material, she could feel the heat. Her eyes closed on the sublime.

Yes.

He rubbed the tip with his thumb, flicked it with his nail, teased a response in random patterns. Moaning, she squirmed against the wall. He was watching her, and she didn't care. Or maybe she did. It was hard to tell with pleasure streaking from her breast to her pussy in one impossibly long building ache.

"That's right, Josie. Moan for me. Cry out. Show me what you want."

What she wanted… She wanted to be loved. She wanted to be possessed. She wanted to be swept off her feet by a passion that was epic in nature. The kind of passion they wrote stories about. The kind men fought wars over.

Opening her eyes, she saw him looking down at her with the same lust that was burning in her. And she knew what the answer to the question was—she wanted him.

But she didn't want him like this, like a puppeteer pulling the strings. She didn't want him dispassionate and disengaged. She wanted him wild, tearing at her clothes, as hungry for her as she was for him. Reaching deep, she found the old her, the one who'd once defied convention. She found a strong woman who'd survived being the only bastard in a town of very proper people. She found her, and she set her loose.

Placing her hand over his, she wove her fingers between his, anchoring them. Luke's breath hissed when she reached for the collar of her dress with the other. One by one, ever so slowly, never taking her gaze from his, she undid the buttons.

"Damn."

His respirations came faster. His eyes narrowed. By the time she got to the fourth button, she knew she had his full attention. His fingers clenched under hers, squeezing her breast. It was her turn to moan. Her nipple ached. Her pussy right along with it.

"Do you know what you're doing, woman?"

"I'm imagining how good your hand will feel against my skin," she whispered, rubbing against his hand. "What are you doing?"

His head cocked to the side and his eyes narrowed. "Seeing how far your courage is going to carry you."

Her instinct was to say "as far as we can go," but she'd never played this game with a man before. This was wildly exciting. She'd never known her breasts had so much feeling. Never known what was felt there would go lower. The temptation to find out just how connected they were was impossible to resist. "Probably way over my head."

His expression softened. "I won't let you go that far."

There were only a few buttons left. Her dress was open to just above her belly button. Her plain muslin camisole peeped out from between the open placket. In a moment of regret, she realized she wasn't wearing her best. When she'd gotten up this morning, she hadn't thought she'd wind up in the garden tempting a man to touch her flesh. Lesson learned. Seducing a man took more preplanning than she'd invested. And more fortitude. When it came to buttons and revelations, she'd gone as far as she could.

Ducking his gaze, she confessed, "I might have run out of courage."

The look he gave her was assessing. "Are you ready for me to take over now?"

"Yes."

"Thank God."

She was finally letting go. It'd taken every bit of patience Luke had to wait Josie out. But rushing her now would've been the worst thing he could do. He used to think of her as a brown little wren, but in reality she was a butterfly trapped in her chrysalis, and watching her come alive under his touch was beauty in its purest form. She stood before him scared and eager, trembling. That fourth button on her dress was in danger of being twisted off. Catching her hands in his, he lifted them to his mouth and pressed a kiss on the back of each one. "I don't want you to think anymore. Tonight, between us, there's no holding back. If you want to squirm, squirm. If you want to scream, scream. This is about feelings, not fear. You can trust me. I won't take you over your head."

"All right."

She was a hot little thing. "Good. Now, do you think you could release that death grip on your dress and put those pretty hands back up on my shoulders?"

"I'm not sure." She looked up to the side, a wry, embarrassed smile on her lips. "It was so much easier before I decided to be audacious."

He could've told her that was because she'd been in familiar territory, but now she was stepping off the ledge and into his arms. But to do that would just get her thinking and worrying. Was she good enough?

Was he satisfied? Was it proper? He didn't want any of those thoughts spinning in her head. He'd told her exactly what he wanted. He wanted her to feel.

"I like audacious."

She placed her hands on his chest. The right one moved over until it covered his heart. He noticed she liked to do that. Truth be told, he liked it, too. There was something intimately possessive about your woman measuring your heartbeat in her palm.

With a slow steady glide her hands traveled the rest of the way to his shoulders. Her gaze locked somewhere around his chin. Her breath came in small, nervous pants. He made short work of the last few buttons. As the last one came undone, she stiffened.

What did she think he was going to do? Go insane with lust? Throw her to the floor and rape her? He shook his head. For a woman who'd been engaged, she was pretty green.

"Easy now." Very lightly, he drew his fingers up beneath both edges of her blouse, widening the gap as he went, distracting her from reality with sensation. She shivered and clutched at his shoulders when he reached the underside of her breasts. Her nipples drew tight, making little tents in the front of her dress. Continuing the steady glide he dragged the back of his fingers over those hard tips, catching the sensitive nubs between his ring and middle finger for a slow steady pinch.

"Oh my God." She fell back, bracing herself with her hands flat against the wall down by her hips. Her breasts beneath the thin muslin of her camisole jiggled with her erratic breaths.

"Perfect." Just perfect.

In a coordinated move, he slid the sleeves off her shoulders, leaving them halfway down her arms, binding her lightly with the material, knowing the implication was more powerful than the reality.

"Oh God." A flush climbed up her chest to her cheeks.

She reached for a sleeve.

"No. Stay like that."

With a nervous glance at his groin and then another at his expression, she lowered her eyes and stood there as he'd asked, exposed and vulnerable to his pleasure.

She had no idea what her trust did to him. It was like an aphrodisiac to his soul. He took a step closer, towering over her as he hooked a finger under the square neck of the camisole. She shifted uncomfortably as he ran his fingers along the upper edge.

"What's wrong?"

Her hands clutched at her skirts. "I didn't think we'd be doing this today."

It took a second to figure out what she meant. "You're dressed perfectly."

And she was. The thin undergarment was semitransparent across the front, giving him a tantalizing glimpse of large pink aureoles topped by equally large nipples. A lush bounty for his lips and tongue. He wanted to rip the camisole from her voluptuous little body. He settled for untying the drawstring.

Keeping his movements slow and deliberate, he placed his hands over her breasts, centering each one of those hard peaks in the middle of his palm, spreading his fingers over the full curves. He left them there, letting her get used to the feel. When she bit her lip and shifted, he eased his hands under the garment. Squeezing gently, he drew his fingers up in concert, elongating her breasts as he did until he reached the tips. Not every woman enjoyed this, but he could hope.

Capturing her sensitive nipples in a firm grip, he drew her breast out farther, suspending the heavy weight from the plump tip, gauging the pleasure from her expression, seeing the wonder at the glide of his fingers, the confusion as he held them out, the pleasure as the nipple took the weight, the utter shock as he gave them a jiggle. Goddamn, he liked to watch them jiggle.

Her head fell back. "Dear heavens."

Dear heavens indeed. The shock of the connection shot through him like a lightning bolt, shaking his conviction. He'd promised not to take her too far, but she hadn't made the same promise back. His hands clenched around her breasts, shaping the mounds, lifting them, preparing them. He wanted to rip the camisole apart and bare her to his mouth. He wanted to taste her.

"Did you like that?" he asked as she squirmed, his voice a hoarse husk of sound.

She didn't answer. He didn't push, just milked her breasts in slow steady strokes that stopped short of the puckered aureole. Drawing a little harder each time, stretching a tiny bit farther, reminding while denying.

"Did you like that?" he asked again. This time he let his pinky graze the tip. Her whole body jerked. So did his cock.

"Yes. Yes! Dammit, yes!"

"That's my darling."

This time he finished the milking motion with a steady pinch, increasing the tension until her lips parted and her lids dropped. "Right there?"

She nodded. He shook his head.

"Don't hold back. Let me hear it. Tell me what you like."

She licked her lips, leaving them moist and shining. "Yes. Like that."

He did it again. And again. Relishing in her response. Her pleasure fed his. Her desire spiked his. God damn, she was a dream come true, intelligent, curious, passionate, adventurous, with a body that could bring a man to his knees. Was on the verge of bringing him to his knees. She moaned and arched up. He reached for his belt.

Why is it never friend?

Damn. Damn. Damn. Grinding his teeth, he reluctantly removed his hands from temptation. They were in a shed. Anyone could walk in. She deserved better than this. Pulling her into his arms, he righted her dress.

She pushed it right back off. "Luke."

Did she have to say his name like that? As if he were the ache in her soul?

"Right here."

Burning up in the same fire consuming her, clinging to decency by a toehold while she cut the ledge out from under his feet.

"What's wrong?"

"Nothing."

"Then why did you stop?" Another blush and then a whispered "I told you I liked it."

"I know you did. So did I."

She licked her lips, tempting him. He could kiss her. He could control a kiss. Maybe. Sinking his fingers into her hair, he growled, "Come here."

The joy with which she welcomed his kiss undid his good intentions. In minutes he had her squirming and moaning his name. When her hand brushed his aching cock, the shock jerked him out of the haze.

"Son of a bitch."

"What?" she asked, leaning back in his arms, hair tumbling around her face in complete disarray. Her dress gaped, revealing a seductive amount of cleavage. His hands shook as he tugged the edges back together. His cock ached at the insanity. She was ripe for the plucking and he was covering her up. He should be nominated for sainthood after this.

"That shouldn't have happened."

Clutching the front of her dress together, she whispered, "I don't understand."

But she did. He could see the understanding

creeping past the passion. Her chin came up. "You don't want me."

It wasn't the question it should have been.

He drew the back of his fingers down her cheek. "I want you like hell on fire."

She blinked rapidly. "Then why?"

Dammit. Were those tears? He couldn't take tears. Tears tore him up and if he had to comfort her, he'd take her, and that wasn't what she wanted. "It's not right."

On an "I'm a big girl, Luke," she pushed her dress and camisole off her right shoulder, exposing her full white breast to his hungry eyes. She had beautiful breasts with big nipples that begged to be teased and suckled. He'd like to make her come that way, to feel her pussy convulse around his fingers as he drove her over the edge with his lips and teeth. He ached to rub his cock over her tits, to sprinkle them with love bites before he fucked them. He wanted to brand them with his touch and his come until she couldn't see him without remembering the pleasure and wanting more.

"Luke?"

Lust drove him a step forward before he caught himself. He was losing the battle. "Fuck."

She blinked at the expletive.

He clenched his fists. "Cover up." It came out harsher than he intended.

A tear slipped down her cheek as she yanked her dress up and haphazardly buttoned it. Catching her chin on the ledge of his hand, he tilted her face to his. Wiping the tear away, he swore.

"Goddammit, Josie, I'm trying to be your friend."

Swatting his hand aside, she glared at him. "Well, who the heck asked you to do that?"

CHAPTER TWELVE

IT WAS TOO much to hope he'd be able to enjoy some peace and quiet. The front door opened. Light spilled onto the porch. Sitting in a shadowed corner, watching the stars populate the sky, Luke silently willed whomever it was to move on. Luck was not with him.

Sam paused in the doorway, a bottle and glasses in his hand. He looked left and then right. There was no hope he wouldn't spot him. The man was like a bloodhound. Sure enough, Sam headed straight for him.

"That's an awfully long face for someone who was sparking out behind the barn earlier."

Luke stroked the cigarette he'd pulled from his pocket. It would taste damn good right about now. "A little quiet seemed right."

Sam set the whiskey decanter and glasses down on the floor. Grabbing one of the wooden chairs, he tugged it around and sat down. Stretching his arms above his head and yawning, he asked, "You going to smoke that?"

"I'm thinking about it."

Sam leaned over and snatched it out of his hand. "Hey."

"I didn't promise to quit."

Pulling a sulfur out of his pocket, Sam struck it on the side of the table. Before he could set it to the smoke, Luke snatched it back.

At Sam's inquiring look, Luke pointed out the obvious. "Doesn't make it any less mine."

"You always were a possessive son of a bitch."

"Said the pot to the kettle."

Sam smiled. "Only about a few things."

That was true. There never really was any telling what Sam would care about, but when he cared, God help the one who threatened it.

"So what has you sitting out here rather than sparking with your lady? Besides a bad case of frustration."

Luke grunted and put the unlit cigarette between his lips. "The fact that women have no idea what they want."

Sam picked up the glasses and passed one over. "Have a drink."

A drink didn't sound bad, but a smoke sounded better. "Why?"

Picking up the decanter, he motioned to the cigarette. "I can't sit by and watch you break a promise for the first time in your life."

With a cock of his brow, Luke held out his glass. Sam filled it. "So we're drinking to preserve my honor?"

Sam leaned back in the chair and took a sip and closed his eyes. "It's as good a reason as any."

He had him there. Sighing, Luke tucked the cigarette back into his pocket. "It was probably too stale to enjoy anyway."

Without opening his eyes, Sam asked, "How old is it?"

"Three months, two weeks, four days and about six hours."

That got a crack of an eyelid and a sideways glance. "Not that you're counting."

"Nope." The first sip of whiskey burned in a good way. He remembered back to the first time he'd tasted it. That had been with Sam, too. But then he'd coughed and choked and, in effort to pretend it wasn't burning a hole in his throat, taken another sip, only that one went down the wrong hole. The man they'd bought the whiskey from had had a good laugh. Until Sam knocked his teeth down his throat. Luke remembered the all-out brawl that ensued afterward and took another sip. That had been a good evening.

"Now what are you smiling at?"

"I was just remembering that night you introduced me to the joys of whiskey."

Sam smiled. "That was a fun night." He finished his whiskey in one swallow. "Right now, I'm missing those days. A good fight takes the edge off."

Luke touched his glass to Sam's. "Bella will be fine. Tia will take care of her."

"That's what they say."

But Sam didn't fully believe it. Luke understood that. He probably wouldn't, either, if he had so much on the line. He also understood that Sam needed something else to think about right now. "Now, if Tia and Bella can just poke some sense into Josie."

Sitting up, Sam poured another drink. "What's the problem?"

"Either the woman doesn't know what she wants, or I don't know fiddly-squat about women."

Sam shrugged. "I've found if you pretend they're horses, they're not quite so confusing."

Horses? "Somehow I don't think you've shared this theory with Bella."

"I phrase it differently with her."

"I bet."

Settling back into the chair, Sam cradled the glass in his hands. "It's like that smoke you're saving. Sometimes what you want just isn't good for you."

"Josie's good for me."

"There's always the possibility that you're not good for her."

It was Luke's turn to toss back his drink and let it burn. "The damn woman doesn't know what she wants."

"Yeah, that's what Bella said."

"You've been talking about this with Bella?" He didn't know how he felt about that.

"I talk about everything with Bella."

"Everything?"

Tapping his fingers on his glass, he confessed, "No, not everything. Not lately. I don't want her to worry."

"What's going on?"

"You remember Tejala."

It wasn't really a question. Who could forget? The bandit had ruthlessly ruled this area for years. Somewhere along the line he'd decided the crowning feather in his cap would be to own Rancho Montoya. To do that, he needed Bella as his wife, something he figured he'd accomplish by kidnapping her.

But no one took what was Sam's or Zach's. Hell's Eight and the Lopez men had ridden to get her back. The battle had been vicious and ugly, but in the end, Bella returned to her home. And Sam stopped resisting the best thing in his life and married the woman.

There'd been relative peace for the last year or so, but from Sam's expression, the peace was over. "I know damn well Tejala hasn't come back. When you kill a man, he stays dead."

"Yeah, he's dead, but killing him created a hole and now someone new has come to fill his place."

"That's usually the way it goes. Does this one want Bella, too?"

Sam shook his head. "No. He doesn't think he needs Bella to take Rancho Montoya."

That sounded ominous. "Is that a relief?"

"Not in the least. Bella is safer when she has value."

He had a point. "So what is it about this new bandito that's got you worried?"

Picking up the decanter, Sam refilled Luke's glass. His chair creaked as he sat back. "He's organized, Luke. Tejala, to put it bluntly, was loonier than a rabid coyote, so I could almost count on him going crazy now and then, but this one?" Sam shook his head. "This one is methodical. He plans everything out and sticks to his plan. His band is loyal. And while he's not a sadistic asshole like Tejala, he's ruthless in going after what he wants. He's even picked off a couple of my vaqueros."

Luke knew Sam well enough to know what that meant. "So now it's personal."

"It's always personal when somebody touches what's mine."

Kel came from around the house, strolled up the steps to sit before Sam. They looked at each other as if they spoke a language only they could comprehend before Kel lay down by the chair.

"I swear that dog can read minds."

"Bella says so."

A second later, Luke became aware of another scent blending with the aroma of his whiskey. He sniffed. Cedar mixed with…lavender? It didn't take a genius to find the culprit. "Did that dog get a bath?"

Sam nodded. "Yup."

"Who the hell is brave enough to do that?"

"Surprisingly enough, Bettina. She's very meticulous about what comes into her house. A couple months after she realized he wasn't going anywhere, she relented, under the condition he be brought up to her standards. And that meant flea baths."

Luke looked at Kel. "Poor bastard." Kel licked his paw and flopped on his side. Luke swirled the liquor in his glass. He really didn't want any more, but wasting good whiskey was a crime. "Was Kel agreeable?"

Sam chuckled. "Not at first. I wasn't sure whether Bettina was going to lose an arm or Kel was going lose a leg, but in the end, they worked it out."

The scent was building. He waved his hand in front of his face to dispel it. "Is that camphor?"

"I don't know what she puts in the shampoo, but it does the job. He doesn't scratch and Bettina doesn't gripe."

There could be beauty in compromise, but Luke wasn't sure he could handle any more of Hell's Eight changing. His world was already tilting on its axis.

"Is that what you're going to do with the bandits? Find a compromise?"

Sam set his glass of whiskey on the floor. Kel lifted his head, snorted to clear his nostrils after getting a whiff of the spirits and flopped back down. "I'm going to find them. And then I'm going to kill them and their damn leader. What else you do with that kind of folk?"

It was a relief to hear. Sam was still Sam. "Not a damn thing."

Sam sighed. Luke could feel his frustration. "But it's going to have to wait until Bella has the babies. I can't risk leaving them here alone."

"Do you honestly think a few bandits are going to be able to defeat the great Sam MacGregor?"

Sam snorted. "You might've made me out to be real fancy in those books of yours, but I'm human like anyone else. There's always a chance the bad guy will win. You know that. I know that."

Yes, he did, but it was shocking to hear Sam

"Wildcard" MacGregor say it. "Since when did you start admitting it?"

"I always knew it to be true. I just didn't care. But now I have Bella."

"And you care."

"More than is healthy."

"I'm not sure about that." Luke had always thought Sam needed a healthier sense of self-preservation, and if Bella was what it took to for him to finally get it, Luke was all for it. That wasn't change. That was common sense. "Well—" he set his glass on the floor, too "—we're glad you're still around."

Sam chuckled and propped his feet up on the railing. "Thank you, I think. Time for a change of subject. How are the Eight doing?"

How best to answer that? "They're…stabilizing. The Comanche have been pushed West. San Antonio is growing like a weed and life has become more…settled."

"That must be driving you crazy."

How had he known? "What makes you say that?"

"You've always been there, Luke. For every one of us, you've been there. But I've noticed where you really like to be is where the excitement is."

"True. There isn't a lot of excitement around Hell's Eight anymore. We're chasing horses instead of bandits, exploring our options in cattle rather than exploring new frontiers…"

"You ought to join me at Rancho Montoya. Plenty of excitement for a man out here."

The front door opened. Ed paused on the threshold before spotting them. "Is this a private party or can anybody have a drink?"

"There's nothing private on the Rancho Montoya," Sam said. "That's the first thing I learned. I learned it the hard way, too."

"What exactly constitutes the hard way?" Ed asked.

"I went to make love to my wife in what I thought was a private location. Turns out, a lot of the vaqueros had to look the other way."

Luke couldn't stop laughing until he thought of the garden shed. "Damn, I'll keep that in mind."

"There's been a time or two you all almost caught me and Tia," Ed volunteered.

"No. No. No." Luke held up his hand. That was an image he *didn't want* in his head. "This is a conversation we don't ever have."

Ed laughed and picked up the decanter. "Tia's not in her grave, you know. She's a fine-looking woman with a youthful mind."

Sam took the whiskey bottle away from Ed. "If you're going to drink my whiskey, we don't talk about that stuff."

"Fair enough. While I go get a glass, why don't you two change the subject?" The door opened and closed behind him.

Sam looked at Luke. "I'm never getting that image out of my head."

"A scrub with lye soap might help."

"Nothing will help."

Ed came back, took one look at their expressions

and shook his head. "Don't be such wimps." Holding out his glass for Sam to fill, he continued. "You're going to be a father, Sam. Eventually your children will grow up and leave, but until then, are you not going to touch your wife?"

"Oh hell no."

"Then don't be a hypocrite."

Damn. That reality hadn't ever crossed Luke's mind. Nor Sam's from his expression. Luke shook his head. "Making love to your wife is going to get a lot more complicated, Sam."

"I'll manage."

"That's the spirit," Ed said. "The one thing we men are good at is managing that sort of thing."

He cut Luke a glance. "Though some of us need more practice."

There was no doubt to what he was referring. His tryst with Josie had been found out. "Dammit. Does everybody know?"

"Well, some of us are guessing," Ed said. "But from the way Josie came running in here, her hair in disarray, her dress all buttoned wrong, it can't be too far off the mark."

"For your information," he informed them, "I was a goddamn gentleman."

Ed shared a conspiratorial look with Sam. "In his way, I'm sure."

"Uh-huh." Sam didn't bother to hide his grin. "By the way, Bella wants me to remind you that Josie is a guest in her home."

Here they go. "You can tell Bella the reminder is unnecessary."

"She disagrees."

Maybe he'd put that whiskey down too soon. Bella was like a dog with a bone when she found something irritating.

"Then I'm grateful she's bedridden and isn't at liberty to follow me around expressing her disagreement at will."

Sam chuckled. "That Bella is a damn good judge of character."

"I don't need a judge right now, thank you very much."

"On that she agrees. What she says you need is to find your cojones."

"I can back him on that," Ed interjected.

"It's Bella's opinion that when it comes to romance, a man can't let a woman lead."

They were ganging up on him. Luke glared at Sam, who had the gall to look innocently concerned. "How much can she know about women if she says that? After all, she led you on a merry chase."

"In some ways, yes, and others, no."

"In which way was it no?"

"Bella is much younger than me. She was innocent, sheltered—"

"And hell on wheels," Luke added.

"Yes, that, too. When it came to personal things between us, physical things, I was definitely in charge. But when it came to making me see that she was a woman who knew her own mind, she was in charge."

"And there's your problem," Ed put in. "Josie doesn't know her own mind. From what I heard from Jarl, her mother made life tough for her growing up. She either spent her time in church repenting for the fact that she was born a bastard—"

"That was her mother's sin," Luke countered.

"Or avoiding reminding the town she existed. It was a public shame to her mother to have a child out of wedlock. I don't think she ever forgave Josie's father for that humiliation."

"So she took it out on Josie?"

Ed shrugged. "I don't think she's a bad person. According to Jarl, Josie's family had some status in the community before her mother humiliated the family with her pregnancy. And she's been trying to regain ground ever since."

Which explained why Josie walked around looking like she wanted to apologize for her existence. "Damn."

Sam shook his head. "How much shame can they foist on a child?"

Ed swatted a fly away from his face. "You've been back East, Sam. You know how it is. Rules laid upon rules laid upon rules, and everybody jockeying for position based on how well they follow them."

He nodded. "I much prefer it out here."

"Yes, well, we have our rules, too, but they're more flexible."

"And by the way, Luke, Bella says if you get Josie

pregnant, she will waddle out of bed and hunt you down." Sam paused for effect and then added, "She's got a brand-new shotgun."

Luke did not fear Bella, but his impulses when it came to Josie? Those could lead him right past his best intentions. He threw back his drink. He was beginning to understand how a good woman could change a man. "I'm only going to say this because I'm drunk and y'all are wasting a whole lot of effort beating a dead horse—"

"Fire away," Ed interrupted.

"Josie wants a friend."

Ed's "Ouch" coincided with Sam's "Nothing wrong with that. Bella is my best friend."

Luke looked at Sam. "Her exact words were, 'Why did it have to be a husband or lover? Why couldn't it be friend?'"

Ed nodded. "That makes sense. I imagine to somebody who grew up the way Josie grew up, feeling isolated and unwanted without anybody having her back, friendship would be very important."

Damn. The picture Ed painted was not the cheery happy childhood he wanted to imagine Josie'd had.

"Jarl told you this?"

"He spent time with Josie's mother for a bit. He grew fond of her."

"He couldn't help her?"

"There was only so much he could do. You know those stuck-up bitches back East don't even let their children play with bastards in case the taint is contagious."

Luke hadn't known. Unlike Caine and Sam, who went back East every couple years, he never did. He liked his wide-open sky and the freedom of adventure too much to leave them. Even for a short time.

"Society back there can be unbending," Sam agreed. "To the point it's possible Josie doesn't know what love looks like."

Luke sighed. "There is that."

And where he was supposed to go with that was something he hadn't figured out yet. Sam poured them all another round. Luke accepted it, but didn't drink. His world was pleasantly fuzzy around the edges. For a moment, silence reigned. An owl hooted in the distance. A breeze ruffled the shrubs in front of the porch. As if reading his mind, Sam sighed.

"Bella loves it out here."

Luke did not envy Sam in having to deal with Bella's forced confinement. "What did the doctor say about her condition?"

Sam grunted. "That she's pregnant."

Luke snorted. "I was looking for a delicate way to ask how things are actually going."

"Since when did you get delicate?"

"Since I got surrounded by women."

Sam forced a laugh. The harsh edge hurt Luke to hear. He'd never seen Sam like this. He usually charged toward problems. Leaped over barriers. It spoke to the severity of the issue that this one had him sweating.

"They're worried they might come breech. There's been some bleeding. And they're big babies."

"You're a big man." Luke wanted the words back as soon as he said them. This wasn't anybody's fault.

"Yeah." Raking his hands though his hair, Sam confessed in a hoarse whisper, "I could lose her."

"Damn, Sam." Luke didn't know what else to say. No wonder Sam had sent for Tia.

Ed slapped Sam's knee. "You won't. You've got Tia here. Add in the doctor and Bettina and that's a whole lot of experience at one birth."

"How can Tia help?" Luke asked.

Sam rubbed his jaw. "There's an operation that can be done if things go bad. The doctor has never seen it done, but Tia has."

"An operation?"

Sam didn't mince words. "Apparently, they can cut the babies out of her."

Luke's stomach heaved. "Son of a bitch."

"If it's safer than giving birth, I'm going to demand he do it."

Luke would, too. "Where is the doctor?"

Considering how meticulous Sam was when it came to Bella, Luke was surprised the man wasn't parked and waiting in Bella's room already.

With another rake of his hand through his hair, Sam sighed. "He's on his way. I couldn't spare the men to fetch him earlier. It would leave the ranch vulnerable, but as soon as Zach got back, I sent Guillermo out with a fresh guard."

"And he'll stay here?"

"You can bet your bottom dollar his ass isn't leaving until Bella delivers. I've just got to get him here before she goes into labor."

"Doesn't she have a couple months?"

Ed sighed and topped off the glasses with the last of the whiskey. Luke's too-full glass spilled over his hand. "Twins often come early."

Sam nodded. "Tia says the twins are restless. Bella says they want to meet their father."

Luke doubted Bella knew how much that prospect terrified his friend. He wasn't sure Sam could go back to a life without Bella.

"Tell her to cross her legs and keep them put."

"How many men did you send for the doctor?" Ed asked.

"Twenty good men."

"How many do you still have here?"

"Thirty."

"The last time I was here, you only had thirty total."

Sam shrugged. "Civilization's been pushing into the West, taking up the land. Indians and whites alike have been fighting over the scraps."

"Has there been trouble?"

"One of the things I like about living out here is there's always trouble. It keeps a man on his toes." Sam finished off his whiskey in three quick swallows.

Luke took a more cautious sip of his.

Ed raised his glass at him. "You might want to ease up on that liquor, son."

He cocked a brow at his friend. "It's been a long

time since anyone's been able to tell me how much to drink."

Ed shrugged. "I heard Josie wants to get out and take some pictures."

"Josie can just cool her heels until I'm ready to take her."

Ed looked at Sam. Sam looked at Ed. The hairs on the nape of his neck lifted. Reaching over, Sam relieved Luke of his glass. "Josie might cool her heels waiting for you, but Zach isn't likely to abide it."

"What in hell does Zach have to do with anything?"

"He volunteered to take her out at first light. He said something about watching the flowers greet the sun."

"Josie offered to cook him breakfast in payment," Ed added helpfully.

The depth of his anger caught Luke by surprise. "Fuck that."

Sam smiled that taunting smile of his and took a sip of *Luke's* whiskey. "I feel obliged to mention, I'm going to be damn annoyed if you try to kill my foreman because he wants to spark a pretty woman."

Damn. Sam and Ed were enjoying this entirely too much. "Then prepare to be annoyed, because if he touches Josie, he's dead."

"Josie is a free woman," Ed pointed out.

"Only in her mind." Luke recognized the emotion churning in his gut. Jealousy. He was jealous.

"If you're aiming to be her friend, it's not your

place to get in the way of her happiness," Sam pointed out.

Luke yanked his Stetson down over his eyes, shielding his expression. "Then consider me a piss-poor friend."

CHAPTER THIRTEEN

IF IT WEREN'T for the promise of seeing flowers open to the sun, Josie would not be up before the crack of dawn, frying eggs and bacon, baking home fries and flipping pancakes. She'd still be lying in bed justifiably moping over Luke's rejection. The man had a horrible sense of timing. He had no business ravaging her senses to the point she'd begged—begged!—him to take her. The memory made her cringe. And then to reject her under the guise of looking out for her best interests… Who did he think he was? He wasn't her father or her guardian. He was the man she'd chosen to liberate her. And he'd rejected her.

She'd cried last night, but this morning? Oh, this morning she was furious. The man had no right to manipulate her that way. She was a grown woman. She knew her own mind. She didn't need some Western lothario playing with her emotions. She'd had enough of that her whole life.

Opening the oven, she checked the home fries. Moist heat redolent with the scent of onions and garlic heated her cheeks. She slammed the door closed. Straightening, she wiped her hands on her apron.

Truth be told, she couldn't figure out Luke's game.

She'd seen men play the love 'em and leave 'em game before. Jason had played a rather chaste version of it, stretching it out over five years, but in her admittedly observational experience the leaving part usually happened after they obtained the loving. Not in the middle of it. Damn him. She wasn't sure what made her madder—his rejecting her in general, or the fact that he'd left her dangling from that sensual precipice.

"The home fries have offended you this morning?" Zach asked from where he sat at the table, enjoying a cup of coffee. It really should be illegal for a man to look that rakishly handsome at this hour of the morning. It should be more illegal for her not to be affected by it.

Her mother was right. A woman could not control whom she lusted after. And Dane Savage was right. A woman had to choose her own destiny.

Picking up her own coffee from the wooden counter, she took a sip. It was lukewarm. "I'm afraid I've got the oven too hot. I almost burned them."

"It will not be a problem. Burnt offerings from a woman as beautiful as yourself will still be a delectable treat."

She blinked. "Oh dear heavens." Setting her coffee down, she asked, "Do women really fall for that?"

He cocked an eyebrow at her, smiling around his cup, and suddenly the nice safe man seemed not so safe. Her stomach did a flip-flop.

His eyes narrowed. "Other women are not a concern."

"Oh." She put the last pancake on a plate and brought it over to the table. He stood. She'd never realized how tall he was. "Are you flirting with me?"

Standing, he held out her chair for her. "Apparently not successfully."

Oh, he was being successful. She just didn't know what to do with it. She caught his scent as he tucked the chair in. He smelled of clean soap and expensive tobacco. It was a pleasant aroma. "You took me by surprise."

Zach reclaimed his seat. "I am thinking I should have used my other line."

Curiosity demanded she ask "What was that?"

He didn't miss a beat. "Your beauty will sweeten any meal until a man would only know the delectable taste of ambrosia."

She choked on a bite of pancake.

Pushing her coffee closer to her, he asked with a too-innocent expression, "No?"

She shook her head, and cleared her throat, laughter bubbling. "Definitely no."

Replacing his napkin on his lap, he sighed. "Ah well, I will have to work on it."

"Please don't. At least, not on my account."

The amusement disappeared from his expression as fast as it had appeared. "But I insist."

"On what?"

"On seeing your smile. You have a beautiful smile."

Feeling very daring, she placed her hand over his. His hand was warm under hers, but the tingles she felt with Luke? They were markedly absent. "Thank you for making me laugh this morning."

All pretense left his expression. His gaze met hers—intense, focused, dangerous…a trickle of awareness slipped over her senses.

"It was my pleasure."

She slowly pulled her hand back. He returned to his meal, and she to hers, though more slowly now, as her mind caught up with reality. She had another suitor.

AT FIVE THIRTY that morning, Luke opened the back door to the kitchen, his hangover dragging along his mood like a ball and chain. The scent of pancakes and bacon swirled out to smack him in the face. His stomach lurched as he stepped into the room. His temper growled louder than his headache at the scene before him. Sitting at the table was Zach, looking content as a cat curled up in front of fire. But he wasn't sitting in front of a fire, he was sitting at the table, the expression on his darkly handsome face intense as he watched Josie bustling around the kitchen. That inner growl rose again. If Josie was going to cook breakfast for anyone, it should be him. Today, she was dressed in a dull gray suit dress with a light bustle and she looked as pretty as the morning with her fresh scrubbed face and wisps of hair escaping from her braid at the temples. The red hue accented the creaminess of her skin and highlighted the blue of her eyes.

As she turned to grab a towel, he gritted his teeth.

He was going to have to reconsider his no-corset de-
cree. Without the corset the camisole didn't support
her breasts as well. With every move, they swayed
enticingly.

"Morning."

Josie jumped and dropped the towel. "Good morning."

"Morning, Luke," Zach drawled as if he wasn't sitting at the head of the table, coveting Luke's woman.

Luke knew exactly what Zach was thinking when
Josie bent over to retrieve the towel and her full
breasts swelled against her bodice. He knew exactly
what Zach was imagining when her breasts jiggled
softly as she shook out the towel. Remembering how
they'd felt in his hand, his fingers curled into a fist.

Luke took a seat across from where Josie had been
sitting. Her breakfast looked barely touched. "Any
of that coffee left?"

"Of course."

She brought over a cup along with the pot. Leaning back, he let her pour. "Thank you."

"Would you like some breakfast?"

"No, thanks." After last night, just the smell was
nauseating. "Coffee's fine."

She poured his cup and then just stood there awkwardly. "So what are you doing up this early?" he
asked.

Josie cut Zach a nervous glance. The gentle smile
he sent her in response gave Luke the urge to punch
him in his freshly shaved face.

"I wanted to take some pictures," she finally said.

"And I have agreed to escort her to where the wildflowers greet the sun."

"I'm hoping to catch them as they open."

Luke took a couple swallows of coffee and winced as the hot coffee set his head pounding. Ed was right. He was regretting the drinking of the night before. "Do you think the flowers are going to hold still for you?"

She shrugged and her breasts bobbed ever so slightly. His mouth watered. He should have tasted them when he'd had the chance.

"I have no idea. I hope so."

"And you asked Zach to take you?" It came out in a growl.

She had the grace to look guilty. For all of two seconds. Then she just looked mad. Obviously, she was still annoyed about last night. That was understandable. So was he.

Zach, on the other hand, was remarkably unconcerned with the undercurrents. "It is my pleasure to accompany such a beautiful senorita on this journey."

He just bet. "If you don't mind, I think I'll tag along."

Josie took the pot back to the stove. The set of her shoulders said she wasn't happy. Glancing back, she muttered, "I suppose. If Zach is all right with that."

Zach smiled over his cup at Luke. "I do not mind, senorita, if Luke tags along."

He didn't mind? Luke's mood went further south. It'd be a cold day in hell before he'd need Zach's permission to go anywhere. He rubbed his forehead. Damn, his head hurt.

Josie's expression softened and gave Zach the smile she refused him. "Oh please, call me Josie."

Zach inclined his head. "I am honored."

Josie blushed.

Another man might've been uncomfortable in the situation sitting between two lovers, but Zach wasn't for the simple reason Zach wasn't just any man. He was a good man with a strong sense of loyalty, a fighter who went after what he wanted. A man of standards. And women loved him. If Zach wanted Josie, he was serious competition. With a lift of his own cup, Luke acknowledged the challenge. Catching Josie's eye, Luke motioned to her plate. "You didn't finish your breakfast."

"Oh. I got distracted packing lunch." She dismissed the food with a wave of her hand. "I'll eat later."

"You'll eat now."

"It's cold."

"No problem." Getting up, Luke walked over to the stove and put a pan and a griddle on the burners. "Have a seat and drink your coffee."

She stood there, fussing with her apron. She was clearly uncomfortable with him cooking for her. The woman was too independent by far. "Sit, Josie."

She sat. The obedience was a good indication of her stress level.

He poured some batter into one pan and with his free hand, took an egg out of the bowl and cracked it into the center of the griddle. The pancake cooked and the egg sizzled.

From the table came a request. "No pancakes for me please."

"Why?"

"A woman has to be careful of her figure."

It was clearly an oft-repeated statement. Had that no-account fiancé of hers put that thought in her head? The bastard. Luke put another small pancake onto the griddle. Fuck him.

"How about this? You handle the eating, and I'll handle your figure."

She gasped. "You will not!"

He flipped the first pancake. "In case you haven't noticed, I pretty much do as I please."

Zach shook his head. "It would be my pleasure, Josie, to take him out back for you and remind him of his manners."

Her "No" came out choked.

Zach was undeterred. "The offer is sincere."

The foreman was getting on his nerves. "Shut up, Zach."

Josie's gaze bounced between them with the hunted expression of a rabbit caught between two predators. Transferring the egg to a plate, adding the still-warm home fries and flipping the second pancake, Luke figured she was probably right to feel hunted. As he'd told her before, they'd entered Montoya territory. Many men would be pursuing her. He just intended to be at the head of the line.

He wasn't worried about the vaqueros, but Zach?

He was going to be a complication. Luke was reasonably sure Zach hadn't kissed her yet. She didn't react to the man like a woman comfortable with his touch, which meant Luke had an edge. One he fully intended to exploit. He placed the food in front of Josie. Meeting Zach's gaze over her head, he answered the other man's challenge with a calm smile.

Zach was just wasting his time.

LUKE WASN'T SURPRISED to see that it wasn't only Stefano, Zach and himself accompanying Josie. Six additional guards were lined up by the wagon. Men and horses drooped in a sleepy expectation. As one they perked up when Josie came out of the house. They greeted her with smiles and questions. Josie perked up, enjoying the attention.

Zach led Chico over.

"Thanks." Luke took the reins, watching the interaction.

"She is finding her feet," Zach observed.

"Yes."

"You are not mad."

It was a statement not a question. "I'm not an ass."

"Not a total one anyway."

Swinging up into the saddle, Luke asked, "Is there something you want to get off your chest, Zach?"

"I have an interest in the little photographer."

"Too bad."

"Until she declares a preference, she is fair game for pursuit."

"Uh-huh." Sensing his tension, Chico pranced and

tossed his head. Luke reined him in. "I don't have a problem with that as long as you don't have a problem with the consequence."

"You think I fear a threat?"

The cigarette in his pocket whispered Luke's name. His fingers twitched. "Nope."

He squinted against the sun as Stefano called Josie's attention to the pose the vaqueros were striking, claiming it would make a good picture. Josie laughed and smiled and teased them back. She was finally getting to feel what it was like to be a beautiful woman in the company of men. As much as Luke wanted to wrap her up in the soft sweet comfort of cotton wool and take her away to a place where she couldn't be hurt, he couldn't bring himself to end her pleasure. Every woman should get to feel desirable.

THE CLIMB OUT of the valley was rough. The wagon bumped and swayed along. Luke watched Josie carefully, noting Zach did, as well. Her banter faded first. Then her smile. The next casualty of the constant motion was the pink in her cheeks. When her color went ghastly, he moved Chico up alongside. "Is your stomach bothering you?"

"A little."

Zach rode up on the other side. Raising his hand, he called for a halt. "I think more than a little."

With a flick of his hand, Zach summoned Stefano. When the young vaquero reached them, he indicated where she sat. "Switch places with the senorita."

"I'm fine."

Luke rolled his eyes. "No, she's not."

"This I can see. My horse is yours, senorita."

With a hunch of her shoulders Josie confessed, "I don't know how to ride."

"Then now would be a bad time to learn." Zach's smile was pure wolf. He held out his hand. "You may ride with me."

Startled, she glanced over at Luke. The question in her big blue eyes smoothed the edge off his temper.

"She'll ride with me," Luke countered.

"Is that your preference, Josie?" Zach asked.

There was a long pause before she nodded.

"Then come here." Luke held out his hand. It was a long second before she took it. But when she did, it was with confidence.

She made the transfer from the wagon to the horse like an old hand. Swinging her leg over in one easy movement. "You're getting better at that."

Excitement laced her agreement. Her arms slipped around his waist. "I am, and on my second try, too!"

He shifted her hands up for no other reason than it was an excuse to touch her. "Practice makes perfect at most things."

"So it does."

He could feel her smile against his back. Even better, Zach could see it.

"Enjoy your ride, senorita." With a tip of his sombrero, Zach wheeled his horse around, and waved the group on.

Stefano clucked encouragement to Glory, who

now sported a brand-new hat. Glory tossed his head, but then ambled forward.

"Do you think I hurt his feelings?" she asked quietly.

"No. Zach is tough."

"Oh."

He couldn't tell if she was disappointed or relieved. And for the moment, he didn't care. He had Josie's arms wrapped around his waist, those gorgeous breasts pressed up against his back. It felt like a new beginning.

"Are you feeling better?"

"Do you mind if we don't talk?"

Normally that wasn't a problem, but right now he had a couple questions he wanted to ask her. Some points he wanted to make. Out of the corner of his eye, he noticed the vaqueros easing closer. Sam was right. There was no privacy on Rancho Montoya.

"No, I don't mind."

There was always later.

DESPITE HIS DOUBTS, Luke had to give Zach credit. The spot he'd chosen was perfect. He'd expected Zach to bring them to a big field where wildflowers waved in the breezes, but instead Zach had chosen a spot halfway up a small mountain where wildflowers clung to rocks in little bursts of beauty contrasted against an otherwise harsh environment. It was that dissonance that had Josie leaping off Chico as soon as Luke pulled him to a halt. It actually wasn't so much a leap as it was a tumble, but she hit the ground animated. All signs of nausea clearly gone. Lifting her skirts, she all but ran to her wagon. Along the way, she found Zach. Grabbing his boot, she smiled up at him. Her happiness shone as bright as the sun.

"I don't have to ask if you approve."

"This is just perfect. Thank you so much."

Zach's smile softened his face. "It is my pleasure, Josie."

As fast as she'd landed, Josie was off again. The door of the wagon clanked as she threw it open.

Sitting in the calm of her wake, Luke realized he'd never seen Zach smile such a natural smile. The kind that started on the inside and worked its way out. It was definitely a different side of the man, and seeing it, he couldn't resent his infatuation. When Josie let her defenses down, she had a genuine appreciation for the moment that brought happiness to those around her. It was a rare quality anywhere, but more so out here in the West, which took quite a toll on women, often resulting in more sadness than smiles. With a nudge of his heels, he directed Chico over to Zach.

"Luke."

Luke pushed his hat back and motioned to the flowers. "Thank you for this."

"I did not do it for you."

"I know, but thank you."

Zach smiled. "I like your woman."

"Now you're wandering into dangerous territory."

Zach shrugged, unconcerned. "But it is clear she

is your woman. Whether she acknowledges it or not, she has made her preference known."

The knowledge settled deeply. "Yes, she has."

Zach sighed. "There is, of course, no accounting for taste."

"Uh-huh." Leaning on the saddle horn, Luke asked. "So how did you find this place?"

"I could say I know exactly what a photographer would like…"

"But?"

"I found it when I was scouting for new sentry posts. I chose it because I can see anyone approaching for miles."

"And it's safer." He would have done the same thing. "So it would appear I have another thing for which to thank you."

"It is my job to protect all those who come to Rancho Montoya. No thanks are necessary."

"Just out of curiosity, what would you have done if Josie hadn't liked it?"

"I would have then pretended ignorance, but if she liked it, ah—" he smiled "—I would then be a hero and maybe she would take a picture of my brothers and me in gratitude."

That was probably a given. "So this was a means to an end?"

Another of those laconic shrugs. "I prefer to think of it as an opportunity."

Luke could buy into that. "Be careful, Lopez. I might just end up liking you."

"Do not do me any favors."

Luke chuckled.

A series of crashes came from the wagon.

"It sounds like she's emptying the whole wagon."

"It is best we help. She can be careless when she rushes."

Luke thought of the ether. "I'll handle it."

"Good. You deal with her and I will deal with the men."

Dismounting, Luke led Chico over to the back of the wagon. Josie was balanced on the edge, wrestling with a large wooden box. In a second, she and it would both end up in the dirt. Dropping Chico's reins, he hurried over.

"Slow down a minute and I'll help you with that."

He reached up. She spun around, her elbow hitting him in the face. He grunted. "I have it."

Catching her by the waist, he lifted her off the wagon. Her start shivered up his arms. "You, my darlin', need to understand something."

"What?"

"I'm no longer being your friend."

As she hesitated, he took the box from her hands.

"Where do you want it?"

She pointed to a spot on the ground. "Right there is fine for now. Just be careful, that's got the ether."

Wonderful. He was carrying the bomb.

"It's not going to blow up on you."

"How do you know?"

"It needs air for that."

"Seems to be a whole lot of air around here."

With a wave of her hand, she dismissed his concern. "It's more complicated than that."

Before he set the box down she was back in the
wagon tugging at a folding table. Again he caught
her by the waist and plucked her off the wagon bed,
before taking the table. "Where do you want this?"

"Right beside the box."

She followed him over. It was simple to set up.
When he was done, she was still standing there looking at him. It was his turn to ask, "What?"

"What are you being?"

"Huh?"

"If you're no longer being my friend, what are
you being?"

That she needed to figure out for herself.

"Apparently, the beast of burden."

The uncertainty of her smile brought back what
Ed and Sam had said last night—Josie didn't have a
clue what a relationship between a man and woman
looked like. And until she determined what she
wanted out of one, he couldn't be anything to her.
Certainly not anything of the depth he desired.

"So what's next?" he asked.

She stared at him uncomprehendingly.

"From the wagon. What else do you need?"

She pointed to a couple more trunks. He set them
with the others.

As soon as she had her supplies laid out, she
became all business. Watching her work was like
watching a well-choreographed dance. The differ-

ence between Josie the photographer and Josie the shy wren never failed to fascinate him.

Leaning against the wagon, he watched her line up the tin plates. "What are you doing now?"

Without looking up, she said, "The plates have to be prepped."

"And then?"

"And then I take the pictures."

"For which you need light."

She nodded.

"But you don't need light when you develop them."

"No. That would ruin everything."

"How long does it take to develop them?"

"It depends on the effect I want and how long they're exposed."

"It sounds more like art than science."

That brought her head up. "Thank you. So many don't appreciate that."

He wasn't sure he did, either, but the amount of equipment she needed was impressive. "All this…it must be expensive."

She nodded as she slathered a solution on the individual tins. "It is, but I've managed to make some money off it."

"Doing what specifically? Portraits and such?"

She wrinkled her nose. "You really don't want to know."

Yes, he did. He wanted to know everything about her. "I asked, didn't I?"

"The undertaker sends me a lot of work."

"What?"

"A lot of people want a last picture of their loved one, so I take it. Of course, they don't know it's a woman doing it. They'd never hire me if they did, but it's turned out to be good money."

He couldn't be hearing her correctly. "Are you telling me—"

"I take pictures of dead bodies."

"I see."

She laid the tins out. "At least they don't move."

"No, I don't suppose they would." He paused and considered what she'd told him. "I think I'm impressed."

"And appalled, I bet."

"That, too."

She shrugged. "The money's surprisingly good and it allows me to do the work I really love."

"Do you do a lot of portraits, too? Of the living, that is?"

"I would like to but people don't trust a female photographer. I have started a new line taking pictures of hunter's trophies." She cut him a glance. "They don't tend to move as much as people."

The laughter caught him by surprise.

"I'm adding innovative to the list of adjectives I've mentally jotted by your name."

"Do I want to see this list?"

"It's not all so flattering."

"Then I'll pass."

Folding his arms across his chest, he watched as she mixed her solutions. Gone was the shy disorganized woman. He loved the sight of her in her element. "You've changed a lot since you came here."

"I know." She looked up. "I like the West."

"Most women find it intimidating."

"Oh, it is that. And big and scary, but it's wide-open with possibilities in a way back home can't be. You could fall flat on your face, of course. And something could squash you when you're down there, but at the same time, you can be anything you want to be and for someone like me, that's pretty exciting."

He felt the same way when he looked at the horizon. He'd just never heard someone put it so succinctly, before. Picking up her camera case and hitching it over his shoulder, he cupped her elbow in his hand. "You know what, Miss Kinder?"

"What?"

He steadied her over some loose rock. "We might just make a Texan of you yet."

CHAPTER FOURTEEN

THE MORNING WAS going beautifully. The sun was hot on her back, the breeze refreshing on her face. The flowers were opening up and Josie was sure the images she was capturing were going to set a new standard. So much so, the photographic society would have to sit up and take notice regardless of the fact that she was a woman. She'd been waiting a long time for this opportunity. Being recognized by the society would guarantee her status. And that status would lead to her income and financial freedom. She'd been working a long time for her freedom.

She sighed as she lined up the last shot, biting her lip as she squinted through the lens. If there was a fly in the ointment of her day, her feelings for Luke were it. The man was a confusing mix of gallantry, sexuality and compromise. The latter being the confusion in the mix. Gallantry wasn't that vital. Sexuality was as common as fleas on the ground, but a man who saw the value in compromise with a woman? That was like finding a unicorn prancing across the meadow. She didn't know what to do with it. What to do with him. Dammit. Why did Luke have to make things so complicated?

Slipping the last of her tintypes into the exposure slot, she ducked back under the curtain, centering on the single pink wild rose in perfect bloom nestled between two jagged rocks. The way the shadow cut across the flower with subtle distortion was pure visual poetry. And if she could capture it, she would have a piece of art that would clear her path to recognition. Which was much more important to her future right now than the confusing nature of one Luke Bellen.

The one thing she'd promised herself as a child was that she'd never be caught in the same traps that imprisoned her mother. She would never search for herself or for security within a union with a man. That was folly because once a woman took her vows, she used up the last of her options. But then again, without marriage, a woman fought for any options she had and the struggle to keep them was ongoing and difficult. Which explained, at least to her, the popularity of marriage.

The shadow shifted with the changing light. Darn it. She pulled the hood off. Now she had to move the camera again. More focus and less daydreaming, that's what was required here. She was too close to her goal to mess up this opportunity.

Picking the camera up, she moved it to the left, checked again and then nudged it forward. The light was changing fast. As she worked, she could hear the men in the background talking in a quiet hum. Now and then a horse would nicker or wuffle. It was a peaceful rhythm to work to.

A dull sound reverberated around the outskirts of her focus. Frowning, she blocked it from her awareness, mentally counting off the seconds to the proper exposure time. Then the first was followed by a second. A gunshot? She bit her lip, told herself it could just be a hunter and kept counting. This picture was going to be perfect. Just perfect.

"Josie," Luke called softly.

As long as no one interrupted her before the exposure was finished. She ignored the summons. Low and urgent, it came again. Couldn't Luke see she was ignoring him?

"Goddammit, Josie."

Five seconds. That was all she needed. Five more seconds.

There was no pretending the next explosion wasn't a gunshot. No telling herself it wasn't closer.

"We've got to go."

All around them were miles and miles of open country. Where did he think they could "go"? Surely, one more second wasn't going to matter.

Footsteps pounded closer. Darn it!

She had a second to close the lens, protecting the image before Luke grabbed her by the upper arm and yanked her out from under the hood.

"My camera!"

"Leave it!"

No way in heck was she leaving her camera. Digging in her heels, Josie yanked her arm out of his grip. In a mad dash, she scooped up her camera. Hugging it against her chest, the tripod banging on her legs, she ran toward her wagon. Thank goodness she no longer worked with glass plates.

"Forget the wagon."

"I am not leaving my wagon." Every tintype she'd taken was on that wagon. Her developer was on that wagon. Her future was there.

Luke caught her arm. His fingers bit deep into the muscle. "Goddammit, Josie."

She spun around, her hopes and dreams clutched in her arms. "I'm not leaving my camera. I'm not leaving my wagon. Not unless it's absolutely necessary."

And maybe not even then.

"We've spotted riders, senorita." Zach's impatience was barely concealed from where he sat mounted, rifle across his saddle.

"Where?" She looked around. Nothing was untoward here, if you discounted Zach and his men's hard-eyed expressions and drawn rifles.

The vaquero over at the ledge called something out in Spanish before heading back to his horse.

Zach cursed. "Montoya vaqueros are under attack."

Oh crap. "Where?"

"Is it the Doc?" Luke asked.

"Si."

"I don't understand—"

Zach interrupted, "She will be safer here away from the fighting."

Her brain finally caught up. "Bella's doctor? The one they're waiting on? He's under attack?"

"Yes."

Josie plucked at Luke's fingers. He didn't even sway. "You've got to go."

"I can't leave you here."

"What am I going to do in battle besides get in the way?" Switching the camera to her left side, she swept her free arm wide. "Who's going to look for me up here? I'll be fine, but Bella needs that doctor."

"You know she is right," Zach agreed.

Luke was torn, she could see it in his face. She was touched, but time was wasting. She opened the back door of the wagon. "Go." Setting the camera down, she scrambled up onto the bed. Kneeling and holding the door, she promised. "I'll lock myself in my wagon. I won't make a sound. No one will even know I'm here."

"Fuck."

She blinked. No one had ever said that word in her presence. It was a measure of Luke's stress that he had.

"Who's got a spare revolver?" Luke snapped.

"What's wrong with yours?"

"Hair trigger."

Stefano rode forward and handed Luke a gun.

"Thanks." He handed the revolver to Josie. She took it gingerly.

"Do you know how to fire that?"

She nodded. He didn't look convinced but also didn't argue.

"Luke…" Zach said.

"Go ahead. I'll catch up."

The vaqueros rode out.

"You've got six bullets," Luke explained.

Six didn't seem like much.

"The first two you're going to use to signal for help if there's trouble." He held up a finger. "One shot. Count to three slowly and then fire again. Someone will come running."

Swinging up onto Chico, he paused. "If I don't come back—"

"You'll come back."

"If I don't come back in three hours, ditch the wagon, hop on Glory and give him his head. He'll find his way back down to the Rancho Montoya."

"I can't ride."

"Then you'll have to learn fast. The wagon's too visible and too slow."

More gunshots reverberated off the hills. Chico pranced. Luke's jaw tensed.

Urging the horse closer, he hooked a hand behind her neck and pulled her forward. They were of a height with him on the horse and her kneeling in the wagon. His eyes searched hers as she balanced there. "Promise me you'll do as I say."

"I promise."

His kiss was hard, quick and possessive. Her lips tingled. "If you don't, I'll hunt you down."

"If you don't come back," she whispered against his lips, gripping his wrist, the conviction coming from someplace deep inside, "I'll hunt *you* down."

He shook his head. "No, you won't. You'll get your ass to safety."

She wouldn't promise that. He was too busy ensconcing her in the wagon to notice. The left door closed, then the right, and she was back in the familiar dark of her workspace.

His "I mean it, Josie" came through the door.

She placed her palm on the warm wood. "I know."

But she wasn't going to promise.

Chico galloped away. As his hoofbeats faded, she realized she was truly alone for the first time since coming out West. The vastness of the land surrounded her. The wagon was just a spec on its face. Gunshots reverberated. Birds tweeted. She could add her screams to the mix and no one would hear.

She was, utterly and completely, alone. Panic started to build. She wanted to get on Glory right now but not to ride back to Rancho Montoya. She wanted to be where Luke was. To know what he faced. To stand with him. But that wasn't an option.

Still, she had to do something or she'd go crazy. The camera box whispered her name. She couldn't lose that picture. And she was trapped here anyway...

Cracking the window to let in the teeniest amount of light, she took out the latest tintype. Her hands shook in a mixture of excitement and dread. It was bittersweet to be developing the photograph of her lifetime during the most dangerous time of her life. But maybe that's what life was all about. Balancing your risk against the possible reward.

Developing the tintype was no less stressful than waiting on Luke. Wondering if he was all right. Wondering if he and the men were saving the doctor. They had to save him. Just as she had to save this picture. Assuming they didn't die today, she still had a future to worry about. She couldn't hide out in the West forever.

Despite her shaking hands and strained nerves, the developing went smoothly. When the process was complete, and the image was dry, she opened the window. Sunlight streamed in.

And she smiled.

The flower bloomed on the plate in endless gradients of gray. The shadow cast by the sun highlighted hidden depths of the wild rose, the slight blurring of the captured breeze added to the complexity. Letting her breath out, she placed it very carefully beside the picture of her puppy, Rascal, caught in the midst of stalking a grasshopper. Just as carefully, she layered a cotton cloth over both and closed the lid of the box.

Sitting down on the trunk, she took a breath. She'd done it. No one had ever taken the unpredictably of movement to create something more. Something new. This was art. *Her* art. And it was groundbreaking in a way that wouldn't be ignored. Maybe others would even want to study her technique. There might be lectures and talks, a demand for work. Probably not forever, but it would be enough to give her a start. Clasping her hands in front of her, she tried to contain her excitement. She'd actually done it.

Outside the wagon, the familiar jangle of a bridle brought her to her feet. Luke was back! Full of excitement, she threw open the door. She expected to see Luke and Zach standing there flanked by the vaqueros. Instead, she tripped out into the arms of a smelly bear of a man with long hair, a tangled, bushy beard and breath that smelled like a rotten garlic clove was stuck in his teeth.

"*Hola, señora.* We were just about to knock."

"It's senorita." Pushing away from his chest, Josie wiggled out of his arms. She didn't fool herself that she was successful because of any weakness on his part. She'd felt the muscle under her hands. He'd wanted her out of the wagon.

"My apologies." His tone made a mockery of the words.

With feigned calm, she closed the door to the wagon behind her and turned back around to face them, dropping into the shyness that used to consume her life. Hiding in the illusion, she took stock of her situation. There were four men in all. She didn't need to be told they were bandits. Their filthy attire spoke volumes. Men who had no respect for hygiene had no respect for anything else.

"Thank you." It was a stupid thing to say, but manners were all she had to work with right now. She spared a brief thought for the revolver sitting in a box in the wagon. Six bullets would be very welcome right now.

"You are here alone, senorita?"

Was there a right answer? She didn't look up. "Yes."

"I find it strange that a beautiful woman such as yourself would be left unchaperoned."

"These are modern times," she whispered. "I don't require a man's escort to go where I need."

He looked at her like she'd sprouted a second head. Clearly, her suffragette speech was better saved for back East where it was no more appreciated but at least politely tolerated.

"Do you think me a fool, senorita?"

She kept her head down, buying time with meekness. "I don't know you well enough to think anything."

His eyes narrowed and that false friendliness disappeared from his tone. "I asked you a question."

He likely wasn't going to believe the truth any more than a lie. She waved her hand to the hill. "I'm taking pictures of the flowers."

"You drove a wagon all the way up here to take pictures of the flowers?"

"Yes."

"I think you are perhaps a little *loco en la cabeza*."

That did not sound flattering. "I don't understand."

He made a circular motion by his temple.

Would being crazy help or hurt? "I wouldn't say so."

"The crazy never see themselves as such."

She whispered, "Now you're just being insulting."

Looking over his shoulder, he said something in Spanish. The men laughed. "You are the one who takes pictures of flowers when you could just pick them."

"It's not the same."

"I would see your pictures."

She crossed her fingers behind her back. "I haven't developed them yet."

"I think you are lying, senorita."

Oh no.

"I think you came up here in your fancy wagon to this place where no one ever comes to meet your *novio*, eh?"

"My what?"

"The man you meet."

He thought she'd come up here to spark with a man? That meant he didn't know about Luke and the others. That had to be an advantage. He was waiting on an answer. She shrugged.

"Which of the Montoya men do you wait upon?"

Wracking her brain, she tried to remember the name of one of the more obscure vaqueros. She came up blank.

"You are ashamed, perhaps?"

Shame she could work. One of his men chuckled, the sound making her skin crawl.

"It is a shameful thing for a woman to be out meeting a man without a chaperone."

She peeked out from under her lashes and whispered, "We're going to be married."

At that, they laughed outright. She would laugh, too, if anybody told that tale to her, but she'd seen her mother go through the same self-delusion too many times. She knew how to make this believable. It was time for indignation.

"You don't know him like I do. He loves me!"

"And yet he is not here, and we are."

"He will be, and when he arrives, you'll be sorry."

"For what? A man cannot be blamed for speaking to a beautiful woman."

The wind shifted and his body odor surrounded her. She ducked her head again and itched her nose, pretending to sneeze. She didn't know if bandits would be offended by someone vomiting on their boots, but she might be about to find out. Why hadn't she paid more attention? Why had she been so sure she was safe? Texas wasn't bucolic Massachusetts. It was wild and untamed and dangerous. She wouldn't forget again—assuming she even got the chance.

She didn't like the way the men were looking at her, as if she was a prime slice of beef ready to grill.

"I think you should come with us, senorita."

"My fiancé will be coming for me."

She was beginning to resent how just saying the word *fiancé* sent the men into guffaws. It wasn't so inconceivable that someone would want to marry her.

"I am afraid we must insist."

He took her by the arm, his grip only tightening at her resistance.

Darn.

"It would not be gallant of us to leave you here."

One man with a pointy face and an aura that made her think of vermin, sidled closer.

"I would not mind relieving this one's disappointment."

She would. It took everything she had to keep her head down. Her fingers clenched into a fist. The revolver was just five feet away behind the thin wood walls of the wagon. She had to get to it. She hadn't saved her virginity to lose it this way. That was so unfair, she wouldn't accept it.

Renewed gunshots echoed out from below. One of the bandits strode over to the ledge and then came back. He said something in a rapid spate of Spanish.

"It looks like my friends have found some strangers roaming our land."

"This is Montoya land."

"It is no longer."

Sam would have something to say about that.

"It might be your *novio*."

Luke!

He let her go. She ran over to the ledge and looked down. It was pointless without her spectacles. Pulling them out of her pocket, she settled them on her nose and gasped. There was Luke being pushed along before a group of men. She would recognize that arrogant swagger anywhere. His hands were tied behind his back. With a hard shove he stumbled into the middle of the circle. One man stepped forward. She assumed he must be in charge. Words appeared to be exchanged.

Don't be aggravating, please.

It was a vain hope. The man struck Luke down. He fell to his knees.

Stay down. Stay down.

But she knew he wouldn't. Luke wasn't a quitter. He was more the type to stand up and spit in his enemy's eyes with his last ounce of energy. Reality settled in with grim clarity. They'd been captured.

She turned back and squared her shoulders. "I'm not leaving without my wagon."

She'd managed to sound calm when in fact she was terrified. She'd never done anything like what she was planning before. Up until now, the biggest deceit she'd ever pulled off was pretending she wasn't resentful while kneeling in church, and honestly, no one ever truly believed they were fooling God.

"You will have to."

"I can't. It's too valuable."

"The wagon stays."

"I can't possibly fit all those boxes on a horse. And they're far too valuable to leave here." She put extra emphasis on the word *valuable*.

He stilled. "What is in the boxes?"

"Gifts." That wasn't a lie. Some she was planning to give away as presents.

"Wedding gifts?"

"Yes."

"I would see."

No!

"*Jefe*, we have delayed too long."

Saved by impatience. She folded her arms across her chest. "I'm not leaving my wagon."

He bit off a curse. With a snap of his fingers he summoned the pointy faced man. "Jorge, check the wagon."

He got halfway in and grabbed a box. Fortunately,

it was the heavy one with the iron tintypes. "It's heavy. Too heavy for the horses."

"*Basta*. We will bring the wagon back to camp and sort it out there."

With a jerk of his thumb, Jorge asked, "What about her?"

"She can drive the wagon."

They highly overrated her skills. She had to back up three times during which she angled the wagon the wrong way twice. Then she did it a fourth time just because she could. Their exasperation was palpable.

"You!" Jefe barked to a heavyset man. "Take over."

The man leaped from the horse onto the wagon seat. She blinked. Luke was right. It apparently was a useful skill to have. She scooted over as he took the reins.

"Thank you."

All she got in response was a grunt.

She made it a mile down the road before her stomach started rolling. She didn't fight it. Putting her hand over her mouth, she groaned. "I'm going to be sick."

Fat Man swore. Opening the window behind the cab, she scrambled into the back so fast she kicked the driver in the head. He swore again and lashed out. She didn't even care about the glancing blow to her hip. Diving for the bucket, she grabbed her puke pot and heaved into it so loudly no one asked what she was doing. Between heaves, she could see the

box where she'd put the gun. Just six short inches to
her left. Her fingers tingled with the need to open
that lid and lift it out. Did she dare?

Before she could decide, *Jefe* snapped at her to
come out. She curled her fingers into a fist. Darn.

She didn't need to fake unsteadiness as she
climbed out the front window and sat on the seat.
Leaning her head back against the rough wood, she
took slow steady breaths.

"You do not ride well in wagons."

That was the understatement of the year. Eyes
closed, she shook her head. "No."

"I like this."

Cracking a lid, she glared at him. "I could ride
with one of you." It was a gamble that they wouldn't
take her up on it, but she didn't want them suspicious. The beginning of a plan was forming. But for
it to work, she would need her gun. And she would
need them to continue to see her as weak and harm-
less. She never thought she'd be grateful for a weak
stomach.

"I believe I will keep you where you are," Jefe
said. "The sickness will keep you quiet."

She let her moan convey the proper response.
Leaning to the side, she fumbled for the ladle in the
water bucket. She almost toppled off the seat.

Falling back against the seat, she took a sip. No
sooner did the water hit her stomach than it started
rebelling. Jefe motioned with his hand. He couldn't
want what she thought he wanted.

"What?"

"Stand up."

"I can't when the wagon's moving."

Fat Man pulled on the reins. Glory came to a stop. Grabbing the metal rein wrap post, she stood. Jefe nudged his horse up close to the wagon. Before she realized what he intended, his hands were all over her, feeling her breasts, between her legs, down her thighs. The men laughed and offered encouragement. Clenching her fist, she gritted her teeth and strove for meek. When he was done, he grunted and sat back in the saddle.

"You may sit back down."

Dear heavens, he'd been checking her for weapons. Her knees gave out and she sat. Thank goodness she hadn't picked up the gun.

Fat Man shook his head. "You are a weak woman. Too weak for this land."

She might be too weak for the wagon rides, but the rest? He was wrong. So very wrong. Like a heroine in one of Savage's novels, she had hidden grit. And as soon as she discovered it, they were going to regret kidnapping her.

Another half mile and her stomach revolted again. This time Fat Man scooted clear when she dove for the back. When she was done and returned to the front, they went through the same procedure. Jefe patted her down. And Fat Man made comments.

"You should stay back there."

"It's too hot."

He grunted.

She got another sip of water. The warm liquid felt good against her raw throat.

Jefe took the ladle back from her. Instead of hanging it on the hook, he dropped it in the bucket.

"What're you looking for when you search me?" she asked him.

"To see you don't bring a gun out of there."

She looked at him. "I can't ride a horse, what makes you think I can shoot a gun?"

He spat to the side. "You really are useless."

Her stomach heaved. This time she retched over the side, aiming for his leg. Swearing, Jefe yanked his horse away just in time. The spasm was over quickly. There wasn't much left in her stomach.

"No more water for you."

"I'm thirsty."

"You only throw it up."

She nodded. The next time she came back out of the wagon he didn't search her. She could tell from the tension they were getting closer to their destination. Covering her mouth, she moaned, "How much farther?"

Fat Man cast her a wary glance. "Five minutes."

It was now or never. This time when she headed for the back, he practically threw her through the opening. She almost puked for real when she landed. The revolting stench of vomit overpowered everything. Feigning retching noises, she opened the box where she'd hidden the gun. Unbuttoning her dress, she took the gun out of the box and gingerly tucked it into her camisole between her breasts, tying it there with the strings. Thankfully she wasn't wearing a corset. It would have been too tight to fit. She wasn't going to ever tell Luke that. He'd never let her hear the end of it. She then tucked a small knife in her garter and then there was only one thing left to do before going up front. Her knees quaked.

Please don't let him search me.

Feigning more retching, she opened the trunk containing her chemicals and paused. Was she doing the right thing? She wasn't even sure how long these things took. With no other option, she opened the jars, letting the air in. She looked at her tintypes one last time. So much work. So much beauty. Her future in layers of tin. She could only save one. Regretfully setting Rascal's image aside, she studied the remaining two options. This was so hard.

"What are you doing back there, woman?"

Heart pounding in her chest, Josie made retching noises again before moaning, "Yes."

She was taking too long. They were getting suspicious. Making a decision, she slid the tintype up under the back of her skirt. Working it beneath the waist band, she tucked it into the waistband of her pantaloons. As the sharp image bit into her skin, panic set in. This was never going to work. The gun was too obvious. The tintype poked out. She should put everything back before it was too late. Taking a breath, she summoned Luke's face. Then Bella's. Then Tia's. She didn't have the luxury of fear. She was the only hope they had. Very slowly she arranged the chemicals one last time and closed the box from which she'd retrieved the gun.

Crawling back to the front, the clunk of the gun against the side was shatteringly loud to her ears. The tintype cut into her back. They had to notice it tucked there. How could they not notice? Her heartbeat thundered in her ears. Fear cut into her breathing. It was crazy. She was crazy. This was never going to work.

Fat Man cut her a disgusted glance. She hunched over as if her stomach hurt, folding her body over the gun so they wouldn't notice the bulge, hoping her hair, which had long since fallen out of her bun, would cover the points of the tintype. She moaned again. How long did she have?

Jefe looked at her and shook his head, but he didn't ask her to stand and he didn't search her. So far, so good. The wagon continued to bounce and sway. Sickening fear blended with bitter nausea until she couldn't tell the difference.

"How much farther?" she asked Fat Man again, licking her dry lips.

"We'd be there already except for this nag."

She hoped he suffered for that disrespect. "Glory is a good horse."

"He is nothing."

There was a clearing ahead. From that direction came the sound of men's voices. They were almost there. Oh God. She wrung her hands together. Oh God.

Please don't let Luke be dead.

Please don't let me be wrong about the timing.

The wagon hit a bump. Terror swept under her skin in millions of tiny pin pricks. She wanted to scream, to jump, to run. She sat there and moaned again.

Please don't let me die.

Please, please, please.

Please let this work.

The group entered the clearing. Men immediately surrounded them. Ahead, against the rocks sat the Montoya men. Luke swore. Zach shook his head. Only Stefano smiled.

Behind her the chemicals fermented.

Please. Please. Please.

CHAPTER FIFTEEN

THE FAMILIAR JANGLE and rattle coming closer and closer pulled Luke's head up. It couldn't be. He'd told her...

But it was. From out of the stand of scrub brush Glory emerged, hat bobbing, ears twitching, plodding along like his owner was in her right mind.

"I thought you told her to stay put?" Zach asked, the words slightly slurred by his bloody lip.

"I did." And once he settled this, he was going to paddle that delectable ass of hers for not paying attention. As the wagon entered the yard, the men stood and surrounded it, funneling the occupants to the center of the small area. "I might have to bring up that whole obedience thing again."

Josie was looking a bit green around the gills. Her hair hung in a straggle around her wan face. As he watched, she leaned over the side and retched.

"Perhaps you should wait until she's feeling better," Zach said.

She must have been puking for a while because she was down to dry heaves. The bastard driving the wagon didn't even help her back up. Sick or not, however, her presence was causing the desperados to perk up. Shit.

"Do you know the young lady?" Doc Shane asked. Though he was bound like the rest of them, the only thing damaged on him was his hat. Dented with the crown listing at an odd angle, the jaunty bowler had definitely taken a beating, but the rest of him was relatively unruffled. Either the bandits had a respect for doctors or the bandits needed him. Luke was betting on the latter.

He forced the "Yes" out between gritted teeth.

Josie was upright again. Sort of. Luke didn't like the way she stayed mostly hunched over. Had the bastards punched her? Broken her ribs? He renewed his work on his bonds. The rope was thick and strong. He wasn't making much headway.

"I thought you gave her a pistol?" Zach asked again in that dry way he had.

"Apparently, my instructions weren't clear enough."

"She appears injured."

"I noticed that."

Doc Shane cocked his head to the side. Luke realized he was probably just a few years younger than himself.

"Do you suppose they hurt her?"

"For their sake, they'd best hope not."

Doc nodded. "I understand. I don't approve of gentlemen laying hands upon women."

What good was his disapproval? Shane was an average-sized man with soft Eastern ways and a calm, understated manner that suited his profession. He'd moved into the area six months ago. According to Bella, people had talked for days about his hair. Luke could see why. It was so deep a red it resembled the banked embers of a fire. Bella's letters had been littered with tales of young ladies trying to get the new and very eligible doctor's attention. Tia had looked forward to those letters. So had he. Bella had a way with words.

Luke wasn't expecting much help from him in a fight.

"Neither do I. Especially my woman."

"Speaking of injuries—" Doc nodded toward Zach "—that lip needs stitching."

"No offense, Doctor, but no one gets near my face with a needle and thread."

Doc sighed. "We don't actually use thread, you know."

Zach just looked at him. With a shake of his head, he repeated, "No."

With a shrug, Doc let it drop. "So, since we're not the center of attention right now, are we going to attempt a rescue?"

The men were closing in on the wagon. Josie inched her way to the edge.

"Dammit, Josie. Don't get down," Luke ordered quietly, willing her to hear. "You'll be too vulnerable."

Josie half slid, half hopped to the ground.

"She really doesn't listen well," Zach observed.

"No, she doesn't."

Josie was standing now. Still hunched over. The big boss who'd introduced himself as Santino walked over to the little group. He started talking with the newcomers' leader. Clearly they knew each other. There were a few gestures toward the wagon. Raised voices. A note of incredulity carried.

Santino probably wanted to know why the other man was bringing a hat-wearing horse pulling a ped-dler's wagon and a sick woman into their midst. More words. The exchange got heated. Luke caught the word for gold. Maybe it was riches. For whatever reason, they thought the wagon was valuable.

Oh, Josie, what have you done?

Luke had no doubt she'd done what she'd had to in order to save herself, but in the long run, promising bandits wealth and not delivering was a risky option.

"Shit."

At this point, her only way out was to wait for the right opportunity and then to run like hell. No hero-ics. No looking back.

As if she heard him, Josie looked up. She was a mess, pale and wan, her dress hanging oddly, her hair dragging down her back. But she was somehow still the most beautiful thing he'd ever seen.

Unbelievably, she gave him a little smile. If he hadn't been attracted before, he was now. She blinked. Once. Twice. A couple times in succession. Damn. Was she about to pass out?

He mouthed the words *Hold on.*

He worked harder at his bonds. His wrists ached. His shoulders burned. His ribs throbbed. They weren't getting any looser. Frowning at him, she braced her hand on Glory's hip, leaning against the horse. No one paid her any mind. They were too busy arguing among themselves.

"It looks like there might be a challenge for leadership," the doctor offered.

Maybe. Now they just needed a way to take advantage of it.

"How are you doing over there, Zach?" Luke asked.

"Not so good. The ropes are not giving."

Josie started fiddling with Glory's harness.

"What is your woman doing?" Stefano asked.

"It appears to me that she's unhitching that odd-looking horse. Do you know why it's wearing a hat?"

"It keeps him calm."

Doc raised his eyebrows. "Any calmer, and he'd be dead."

She moved around to the other side.

"Now, what is she doing?" Luke muttered.

"I think Doc's right. She's unhitching Glory," Zach said, his muscles bunched as he strained to loosen his bonds.

"Glory is the horse?"

"Yes."

"A very impressive name for a very unimpressive animal."

"Don't let Josie hear you say that. She sets a store by that horse."

"Are we rescuing her yet?"

Luke had to admire his pluck.

There were twenty bandits all told. And four of them if he counted Josie. Even if they weren't bound like hogs waiting for the slaughter, it would be an impressive feat to pull off a rescue. "Yup. Just as soon as I get my hands free."

"Would you like help?"

He'd like his guns, the Hell's Eight and five minutes with the bastard who'd killed their men and hurt Josie, but right now he'd settle for his hands being untied. "If you're so inclined."

It was a rhetorical statement.

To his shock, he felt the unmistakable saw of a blade against his bonds.

"I've been waiting for our opportunity," Doc explained.

"Where the hell…?"

Doc grinned. "I am a surgeon, you know. Knives are my stock and trade." One strand of the thick rope broke. "It's amazing how many people forget that when they see a stylish bowler hat."

"I will never again underestimate a bowler hat." Zach angled his body to disguise what Doc was doing. It was a small hope. If anyone truly looked, they'd be suspicious immediately. But at the moment they had a distraction, and sometimes the difference between life and death lay in one distraction.

Stretching his wrists as far apart as possible, keeping tension on the rope, Luke grunted. "Now, if only Ace could learn the value of style."

Zach abruptly ordered, "Stop."

All three men stilled. A tense minute passed. "All right. They're back to arguing."

Doc went back to sawing. "Ace the gambler?"

"You've heard of him?" Luke asked.

"Who hasn't? I look forward to meeting him across the table one day."

"You know, Doc…" Luke felt a bit more give. "I think I'm looking forward to seeing that, too." Considering how Doc Shane had managed to keep a knife on his person after being taken captive… "I bet you've got one hell of a poker face."

Doc chuckled. "So I've been told."

"What's your lady friend doing?"

"Still working those traces."

"I have to wonder why."

So did he. "She's damn fond of that horse."

"Women do have a fondness for the ugly and un-wanted."

"That explains her attraction to Luke," Zach joked before suddenly hissing, "Stop."

Luke froze. Why was she surreptitiously getting Glory out of his traces? Why had she told them the wagon was valuable?

Doc leaned in and warned, "This last cut will do it. Don't jerk when the tension releases."

Luke nodded. "Go."

The bonds gave. Luke held perfectly still. Watching. Waiting. He sent a mental message to Josie. *Just a little longer, my darlin'. Just stay strong a little longer.*

The men were walking around toward the back

of the wagon. One of the guards noticed what Josie was up to and barked out an order. She ignored it. Instead, she grabbed Glory's bridle and started walking him out of the traces.

Another shouted order and once more it was ignored. Clearly displeased, Santino signaled for four of his men to go after her while he followed the other man toward the back of the wagon. Luke watched in horror as the four men closed in. In another few steps, they'd have her.

Run!

Instead of running, Josie lifted her skirt and grabbed something from beneath. There was flash of sun on metal and then Glory screamed and bolted. She had a knife and she'd used it on Glory. A cold sick feeling filled his gut.

"Hurry it up, Doc."

With a glance, Doc took in the situation, swore and abandoned all subterfuge. He sawed aggressively at Zach's bonds.

Uncaring if the bandits saw that he was free— hell, *preferring it*—Luke jumped to his feet and yelled, "Run, Josie. Now!"

With another nervous glance over her shoulder, she did, bolting through the men like a rabbit in front of hounds, heading straight for him. A heavyset bandit caught her skirt as she flew past, hauling her up short. She spun around, knife raised. The bandit laughed and reeled her in. Hand over hand. She slashed frantically at her skirts, hacking through the material. The wagon door squealed open.

Zach and Doc jumped to their feet.

Men hollered and swarmed. Josie cut herself free, spun again and ran straight for Luke, waving her arms, eighteen bandits in pursuit.

She'd never make it. He ran toward her. Hell, *he'd* never make it.

They were going to need a goddamn miracle.

THE MIRACLE CAME in the next second. It came in the form of a violent, sensory bombardment of light and sound that unfolded so fast the world seemed too slow to accommodate it. A fireball exploded upward and outward followed by an ever-expanding cloud of smoke. The sound came next. A deafening roar that ruptured his ears. And after that, the devastation of an invisible wave that picked up everything in its path, before pitching it violently aside.

First, the bandits. The percussion ripped them apart, tossing them in pieces in a prelude. Next it caught Josie, lifting her off the ground and chucking her toward him. He had a quick glimpse of her face, the shock, the terror, before he caught her. The force of the blast threw them both to the ground. Clutching Josie tightly, spinning as they fell, he took the brunt of the impact. Searing pain shot through his already hurting ribs. His vision blurred, sound distorted. He turned his head. Where the wagon once sat was a roaring bonfire. In front of it, four sinister shadows separated from the ground.

"Josie!" She wasn't moving. *Goddamn, Josie.* Rolling her beneath him, he tapped her cheek. She wasn't conscious but she was breathing. Fuck. He shook her again.

Sound grew louder. Took shape. Time sped up bit by bit until it kept pace with reality. They were lying on the ground like sitting ducks for Santino's men to pick off. He had to get up. He had to protect her. He made it as far as his hands and knees. The ringing in his ears wouldn't stop.

"Don't." The cock of a hammer by his temple punctuated the order.

"Shit." He was temporarily out of options.

The muzzle prodded his temple. "Now move."

And leave Josie in the line of fire? "Not a chance."

"Then die."

Josie moaned and twisted beneath him. Something cold and hard pressed against his stomach. He'd recognize that shape in his sleep. A gun, she'd given him a goddamn gun. Now he had an option.

Taking it, he dove to the side, took aim, palmed the hammer and fired. The victorious expression on the bandit's face switched to shock and slow-dawning comprehension. First his face went slack, then his hands. His gun dropped to the ground. He stared blankly at it as his knees buckled and he sank slowly to the ground, his arm dropping over Josie in a sick parody of a lover's embrace. Screaming, she shoved the body off and scrambled backward.

"Stay down." The threat wasn't over. The other bandits were out there somewhere. Kneeling beside her, he covered her as much as he could, using his body as a shield.

"Zach, you got the others?"

"I can't see them."

Doc pointed to the left of the wagon. "They rolled out of sight over there."

Luke exchanged a glance with Zach. "The riverbed."

"Cover me." Luke crept carefully to the edge. Before he got there he heard the hoofbeats. Peering over the edge, he looked down and saw what he expected. Riderless horses—some of theirs and some of the bandits—were scattering like the wind down the dry riverbed. In front of them rode the missing bandits. Damn.

Holding his ribs, he spotted a familiar horse. Taking a breath, he whistled for Chico. The horse tossed his head and kept running. Nothing Chico liked better than a good run. Luke whistled again. With another toss of his head, Chico swung around. Confused, his companions slowed, and dropped to a trot.

The cautious tweet of a bird joined the slowing sound of hoofbeats. Life was getting back to normal.

The bandits slowed, too. Wheeling their horses, they looked back. Luke took aim. Zach put his hand over the barrel and pushed it down. "Don't waste the bullet. They're too far away."

Shit. They were. Luke lowered the revolver. "I want to kill something."

"You already did."

"I want to kill more."

"I'm sure we'll get another chance."

He watched the riders, memorizing every nuance of their posture. "No doubt."

"At least they left us our horses."

"Yeah."

Luke's fingers twitched on the trigger. He kept seeing Josie hunched over, sick and hurting. Flying through the air as the inferno reached for her. He should never have left her.

Holstering the revolver, he turned on his heel and headed back. Doc was sitting with Josie. She was propped against a rock and he was running his fingers through her hair at the temples. Luke reached for his gun again. Zach caught his arm.

"He is examining her, *m'amigo.*"

So he was. Luke raked his hand through his hair, winced and clutched his ribs. "Where the hell's my hat?"

Zach ran a hand through his own hair. "With mine, making a fancy home for some mice out there on the plain."

"Damn." That was his favorite hat.

He whistled again for Chico. The horse ambled over.

Zach squinted against the setting sun. "Do you think the others made it back to Rancho Montoya?"

Luke shrugged. "We bought them enough time." He looked at the burning wagon. "Leastwise, they won't have much trouble finding us."

"Yeah. And, Luke, the little photographer…"

"Yeah?"

"I would not make her angry, my friend."

Looking around at the carnage, he couldn't argue. "I'll keep it in mind."

"But you will have to replace her wagon."

Among other things. "Yeah." He stumbled.

Zach groaned. "I'd hold you up, but I need to sit down."

"Me, too."

The bandits had been mean-assed fighters.

Zach slowly sat down where he stood. Luke managed the ten steps to Josie's side. As soon as he got there, he sank down. That inner shaking didn't stop until he gathered her in his arms.

Doc cocked his head at him. "I am not done examining her."

Luke shifted his position until the rock supported him, wincing as his ribs protested. "No one's stopping you."

He just needed to hold her.

Doc opened his mouth and then closed it.

Josie leaned her cheek against his chest. Her hand came up and covered his heart. "I saved you."

"We need to talk about that."

"I didn't think I could."

"I shouldn't have left you."

"You had to save the doctor. Bella needs him."

And Luke needed her in a way he couldn't define.

"I shouldn't have left you."

"But I saved you."

"And I you."

"It's not a competition."

"She's a little disoriented from the blast," Doc explained, "but I think she'll be all right."

She wasn't disoriented. She was her contrary self. "I need better than a 'think.' *Is* she going to be all right or not?"

"Time usually determines these things."

Josie patted his chest. "I'm fine."

Doc stood. "She needs to be kept quiet. Rest for at least a week. I'm not sure if she has a concussion."

Luke overrode her "No" with a "Yes."

Doc squinted at him. "I don't suppose you'll let me take a look at you now?"

"Later."

He sighed. "You know, back East, people flock to me for my opinion."

"Then head back East."

"Right now, west is my direction. Mrs. Mac-Gregor needs me and from the messages I've been getting, there isn't any time to waste."

That was true. Even now it could be too late. Luke waved to the smoldering wagon. "The Montoyas that got away will bring help. They'll be here soon."

"Then there's time enough for me to look at those ribs."

It wasn't happening. He'd have to put Josie down for that. "I've cracked my ribs before."

"But now I'm here with all this medical training—"

"No, thank you."

Chico entered the clearing, snorted at the stench of death and stopped.

Doc sighed. "I see I'm getting nowhere here so I'll

go waste time with your friend Zach instead. See if I can convince him to let me stitch his lip."

"Good luck with that."

"Yeah. Hopefully, they left my bag on my horse."

"You stay the hell away," Zach called from where he sat. "I'm resting over here."

They couldn't rest for long, but for this moment? Luke rested his cheek on Josie's head. Yeah, he could do that.

Doc shook his head and headed toward the horses. "You are some distinctly odd sorts."

When he was out of earshot, Josie said, "I'm not staying quiet for two weeks."

"I don't think he meant mute."

She smelled of smoke and vomit and horse. He'd never thought he'd associate those scents with bliss.

"I'll go crazy being in bed for a week."

"I don't care."

"You have to care. I saved your life." She sighed with satisfaction. "Dane Savage would be proud of me."

"The hell I would."

She didn't catch the slip.

"Luke?"

"What?" She still had her hand over his heart. Looking up at him, she asked, "Why didn't you run away?"

"When?"

"When I told you to."

"When you were waving your arms? That was a little late, my darlin'."

"No, before that."

"I have no idea what you're talking about."

"When I was blinking at you."

Leaning back, he glanced down at her. "You're going to have to elaborate."

"Haven't you ever heard of Morse code?"

"Morse code?"

Bracing her hand on his shoulder, she moved her fingers in code. "You know, the tap-tap-tappity-tap that makes telegraphs possible."

"I know what it is, but I sure wasn't looking for it in your blink."

"Well, why not? Didn't it at least strike you as odd that I was doing that?"

"I thought you were about to pass out."

"So I'd blink out b-o-m-b because I was woozy?" Zach laughed.

Luke growled. He didn't find it funny at all. "Shut up, Zach. Bomb? That's what you were trying to say?"

"Of course."

There was no "of course" about it. "What the hell were you doing making a bomb?"

"I couldn't think of anything else to do. And it wasn't exactly like I made it. I merely created the right conditions."

"You could have run when I told you to."

"I couldn't. I wasn't sure about the timing."

A cold chill went through Luke. He'd worked with Tucker, who was a big fan of dynamite, who knew everything about it. He could tell by looking at the fuse exactly how long it would take for a stick to blow. But the one thing Tucker always said was you could never underestimate the unpredictability of an explosion. That was why you should never ignorantly proceed with an explosive. "Would you care to explain that?"

"I saw you from up on the cliff. They made sure that I saw you. They wanted me to know there was no hope anybody was going to come save me, that I wasn't going to escape. And I remembered what you told me. That I had to be strong, that I had to use my brain."

"I believe I told you to pay attention and set off a warning shot if you needed help."

"You didn't send off a warning shot when you needed help."

"A warning shot would've been lost amid all the other gunfire."

"Well, so would mine."

With a groan, Zach got to his feet. "I'm going to help Doc find his bag."

With a flick of his finger, Luke waved him off. "We're getting off track. You were explaining this insane plan of yours." With a finger under her chin, he tipped her face up to his. "What happened after I left, Josie?"

"I stayed in the wagon just like I promised."

"But?"

"But I got caught up developing the tintype I'd just taken." Her whole face lit up. Her fingers wrapped around his wrist, binding him to her excitement. "It's beautiful, Luke. Gorgeous. Perfect. A completely new technique. That technique will get me recognition from the photographic society. Recommendations lead to introductions that lead to paying opportunities."

"Where does a husband fit into your plans?"

"I'm not sure one does." With a wave of her hand she dismissed the whole concept. "A husband is no guarantee of anything. A husband is more a gamble than security. But if I have a position in which I can make enough money, then I'll be free."

She meant every word. The truth was written in her expression. In her eyes. "Does love fit anywhere in this grand plan of yours?"

She tried to duck her head. He didn't let her. "No more hiding, Josie."

With a sigh, she let him go. Her fingers clenched in a fist on her lap. How the hell could she let him go?

"I don't believe in love, not for a life plan. It's too unstable. It comes and goes on some invisible whim."

"No, it doesn't."

"Oh please." She rolled her eyes.

"Infatuations come and go, I agree. Lust definitely does. But love?" Rubbing his thumb across her parted lips, Luke shook his head at her. "If you think that about love, my darlin', you don't know what love is."

"And I suppose you do?"

"Oh yes, I do. I've seen firsthand the kind of love people die for. The kind of love that gives people hope. The kind of love that creates the foundation futures are built on. The kind of love that creates a space rather than closes doors."

"When?"

"I saw it in my parents, I saw it between Caine and Desi. I see it every time that Tracker reaches for Ari. Whenever Bella smiles at Sam. Look at any of the Hell's Eight. Look at Tia and Ed." He pressed his thumb lightly against her mouth, parting her lips. Feeling her breath flow past as she inhaled deeply. "I feel it every time I look at you."

"No…"

"Yes."

"This isn't the place."

"I know."

"I don't think…"

Replacing his thumb with his index finger, he silenced the impending ramble. "I know you just lost everything. More than I expected."

"I saved one."

"One what?"

"One tintype. I couldn't let it go."

He should have known. "So your dreams aren't over?"

She shook her head. "No, I don't think they are."

Curiosity wouldn't let it rest. "How did you save it?"

"Before I opened the ether, I tucked it up under my dress."

"You managed to get a lot under that dress."

"That reminds me, thank you for forbidding me to wear a corset."

With the softness of her breasts against him, he didn't have to lie. "That was my pleasure."

He felt along her back. "So where is it?"

"Doc took it for me." She wrinkled her nose. "It's not the most comfortable to lie on."

"I want to see it."

"I'm not ready."

"Why?"

She scooted out of his lap. "Stop asking so many questions."

He caught her wrist. "Stop giving me orders."

"Is this a private argument or can anyone join in?"

Josie pushed to her feet. The tatters of her dress hung about her stockinged legs. Luke had a choice to force her to stay or to let her go. He let her go.

"No, we're done," he said, then slowly got to his feet. Running his fingers through his hair, he watched Josie all but dive into the circle of horses surrounding Sam. Reinforcements had arrived. Dammit he felt naked without his Stetson. "Anyone ever tell you your timing sucks, Sam?"

"Nope. Can't say they have."

"Well, let me be the first."

CHAPTER SIXTEEN

SEVEN HOURS LATER, the story had been retold repeatedly, and with each new telling came a new twist and a new perspective. Thankfully, Bella hadn't gone into labor while they were gone, and the doc had time to settle in. The excitement was behind them for now, and yet Josie couldn't relax, still unsure of what she wanted to do about Luke.

Standing on the porch and looking out into the velvety darkness, temptation slid beneath her weariness. The night sky, spotted with stars and a sliver of moon, gave off very little light, offering the perfect cover if a woman was foolish enough to pay a night visit to a man. If she were so inclined, she could sneak across the yard to the barn and find that room in the back that Luke called his...

Everyone was either asleep or busy with their own agendas. There'd be no one to stop her. No one to see. No one to shove it in her face come morning.

She'd thrown everything—*everything*—away today. Her dreams. Her hope. Her pride. Even though she liked to say there was no choice to make, the minute she'd looked over that cliff and seen Luke in trouble, she'd made one. In the intervening hours, the question hadn't become whether it was right, but more what was she going to do about it now?

God had thrown a gift right in front of her, A big man. A strong man. A man with a heart of gold. A man who'd been prepared to give his life for her more than once. A man who did it without question. Who saw it as his duty. So why couldn't she take that step off the porch?

She was scared. Luke wasn't in her life plan. There'd be no freedom with him, but almost dying had a way of making a woman reevaluate her short-term goals. And one thing was clear, to her at least, and had become clearer with every mile she'd clung to Luke on the ride back to the ranch—she didn't want to die without knowing what loving Luke was like.

Gathering the lightweight shawl around her shoulders, she stepped off the porch. The barn was a good thirty feet away, plenty of space for something—a sign she was making a mistake—to stop her. Her heart beat loudly in her ears. Her respirations came in short pants. She licked her dry lips, waiting, waiting, waiting for any omen to stop her from this foolishness, but nothing happened and she arrived at the barn, her presence unchallenged.

She walked around the side. The shadows were deeper here, forcing her to trail her fingers along the side. The thought of spiders made her cringe but she couldn't take her fingers off the side. The man damn well better be worth it. Just when she began to think the spider potential was the omen she'd been hoping for, the side door opened and a familiar silhouette stepped into the light pouring into the yard.

"Josie?"

Luke's deep drawl only heightened her anticipation. She froze, breathless, unable to take those last few steps.

"Hi."

A smile she couldn't see was clear in his voice as he held out his hand. "Come here, my darlin'."

She did love it when he said that in just that way. It sent all the butterflies deep in her stomach fleeing for cover. She took another breath and measured the distance. Three steps. Just three steps to take his hand. Three steps to be in his arms. Three steps to have what she wanted. "I can't."

A cock of his head prefaced his "Why not?"

"I don't know."

"You were coming here to see me."

It wasn't a question and somehow that made it easier. "Yes."

"And now that you've seen me, you've gotten your fill?"

Neither one of them believed that.

"I think I'm scared."

"Scared of what?"

She liked that he didn't drop his hand, just kept the offer open while she talked her way through this. "Of where this can go."

The words came out in more of a breathless rush than she intended.

"Why?"

She shrugged. "It's not part of my plan."

"Have I ever mentioned that I really don't like your plan?"

She nodded. "You're not alone. It's a common reaction."

"And yet you continue to present it as a good idea?"

"I know. I can get stuck on the logic—"

He cut her off. "And this is all about feeling."

And that scared her to death. "Yes."

In the end, he was the one who bridged the gap. What would have taken her three steps only took him two. He towered over her in the dark, blocking the light, absorbing her into his shadow so completely she could no longer see, but she could smell, and he smelled of soap and that unique essence that was only him

"What do you want, Josie?"

"I want you."

"For how long?"

"I don't know?"

"How?"

"I don't know?"

"Why?"

That she could answer. "Because without you, I don't think I can breathe."

His clothing rustled as he moved. The back of his fingers touched her cheek, slid across. His hand turned, and those fingers wove though her hair, curving around her skull, pulling her up and into the softness of his kiss.

How could such a strong, hard man kiss so softly?

"Good answer," he whispered into her mouth.

Was it? It seemed like the worst answer possible. A woman who acted on emotion was a woman who ended up with nothing. Or so she'd thought, but this wasn't nothing. The warmth of Luke's embrace. The tenderness in his kiss, the security of his presence. When she was here, surrounded by *this*, it was everything, and all the pieces that she worried about, all the questions she had, they fell into place with an answer that made complete sense.

"Yes." The answer was always yes with Luke.

Yes to the passion. Yes to the joy. Yes to the potential, but mostly yes to the completion, because here in Luke's arms she was complete in a way she couldn't define, in a way she'd never dreamed possible. Complete maybe even in the way her mother had always searched for. It was illusion and strength at once, and she needed it. She needed him. For how long, that she didn't know, but right now she needed him. Above her he froze, just for a heartbeat, but as close as they were, so entwined that his breath was hers, she couldn't miss the reality. This was truth. This was them together.

"Say it again," he growled.

"I need you."

She could feel the disappointment in him. Had he wanted more? She didn't have any more to give right now. Her world was in turmoil. The entire foundation of everything in which she believed was up in the air. Her carefully crafted plans for the future were all but gone. This was new territory, but she was venturing forth willingly.

He took a step backward. She followed. She hadn't lied when she said she trusted him. She didn't need to know what was under her feet, because he would never let her fall. She knew that, too.

"I'm not going to ask you if you're sure."

It was her turn to say "Good."

His lips brushed the top of her head. "You're not even going to ask me why?"

"Does it matter?"

She felt his smile. "No."

"I can tell you where we're going right now."

"Where?" She had a good idea.

"My bed."

A little thrill of forbidden lust went through her, but then she smiled because it didn't have to be forbidden. She was committing the sin of her mother, and she didn't even care.

The door closed softly behind them. And then it was him and her in the candlelit bedroom.

"Were you expecting me?"

His lips twitched at the corner. "Will you slap me if I say yes?"

Would she? Poking and prodding that little feeling, she came to a realization. "No. I'm comfortable with your understanding me."

"No defenses?"

"Not between us."

His arm around her back pulled her close. "Good." But he had defenses against her. She could feel

it. There were walls in place that she couldn't cross,
but she couldn't blame him because what was she offering him? Even she didn't know, but he was going
take whatever it was and he was going to make it
good. Because that was who he was and that was the
man she wanted to make happy. The man who was
always there for everyone else. The man who'd been
there for her. Since the day she'd met him, he'd been
putting himself between her and danger, prepared to
give his life for hers, willing to give his everything.
No, that wasn't right. Happiness. He was willing to
give her happiness, and she was willing to take it.
She leaned back.

He frowned down at her. "What is it?"

She should say she couldn't do it. She wanted to
be as good as him, but she didn't because something
inside kept saying yes. Yes to being selfish. Yes to
taking what he was giving. Yes to following where he
led. Yes to this path for which she'd been searching.

"I want to say the words."

"Are you telling me to stop?"

"For a moment."

"Damn."

As was his habit, his hand cupped her cheek,
guiding her through the commitment she was afraid
to make even if it wasn't forever. Even if it was just
for now, she had to say the words. "Make love to
me, Luke. Please."

She expected his sense of humor to kick in, for
that knowing smile to spread across his face and
that tone to invade his voice, but he didn't say any-

thing at all. As if he knew about the chaos fluttering about her insides, he opened his hand across the small of her back. Without a word, he left it there. The warmth permeated her skin, anchoring her in that moment, in that place. She released the breath she hadn't known she'd been holding. His thumb slid across her cheek and settled over her lips. She loved it when he did that. The possessiveness fed her emotions on a deeply primitive level.

"I've got you."

Yes. "I know."

"Good."

Holding his gaze, she tasted him in a quick flick. He tasted of man and salt. It was a hint of what was to come. His eyebrows rose and his mouth softened.

"I like that."

"Me, too."

"Good. There's just one thing about tonight, my darlin'."

Holding his gaze, she bit his thumb. His eyes darkened and narrowed.

"A condition?"

"Yes."

"What?"

"You don't get to speak."

"But I want to."

Slipping his thumb between her lips, he corrected, "You want me."

"Words make it easier." The protest came out muffled. It was hard to speak around his thumb.

He smoothed the moisture over her lips, prepar-

ing her. With a shake of his head he negated her protest. "This isn't about words. This is about emotion.
Strong, powerful, unpredictable emotion."

"That's not my strong suit."

"But it is mine." The calloused pads of his fingers
caressed the nape of her neck. Goose bumps jumped
across her skin, sending a shiver down her spine.

"Tell me you want this."

"I thought we weren't using words?"

He waltzed her two steps back toward the bed.
The mattress hit the back of her thighs. She teetered.
He smiled. Slipping his fingers under the edge of
her shawl, he gave it a tug. It tumbled to the floor,
leaving her standing before him in nothing but her
robe and nightgown. Fingering the soft cotton tie just
above her breast, he drawled, "Take down your hair."

As she started pulling the pins that held her bun
in place, he started pulling at the bows that held her
robe together. One by one, the pins hit the floor. One
by one the bows unraveled. Her hair fell past her
shoulders as her robe pooled at her feet. Only her
sheer nightgown covered her nakedness.

"Beautiful."

She felt beautiful, and vulnerable, and that only
increased the desire unfurling deep within. This man
really did know what he was doing.

With a slight push on her shoulders, he toppled her
onto the softness of the featherbed. He came down
over her, bracing himself on his elbows, surrounding
her with warmth, pinning her with his weight. Softness below and hardness above. Heaven no matter

which way she turned. His fingers threaded between hers, anchoring her hands beside her head.

Oh how she loved that smile. She loved his kiss even more. The mating of his lips to hers, the shifting of pressure, the thrusting possession… The passion. Dear heavens, the passion.

Clinging to his hands, she rolled with the need, letting it toss her this way and that, learning it, nurturing it. Catching her lower lip between his teeth, he bit gently. He took her moan as his, giving it back when she arched up. Pinned she was, she couldn't do anything but take what he gave…and that was everything. That was a lifeline. That was her security. That was her goal. To have him. Complete him. As much as she wanted. As much as she could take.

Twisting beneath him, she gasped as he kissed the side of her neck, set his teeth on the taut cord and bit ever so gently. Lightning stroked through her body, jerking her up against him. His laugh blended with the fire before settling with a pulsing throb in her clit. The throb spread up and out, peaking in her breasts, lingering in her pussy. And she couldn't do anything except take and take and take, all that he gave her in such abundance, but it wasn't enough.

"More," she whispered as he kissed his way to the hollow of her throat. She held her breath as he tasted her with his tongue, released it as he worked his way back up the other side, holding it again as he drew the sensitive skin between his lips and sucked, holding it until goose bumps chased shivers.

As she arched, he growled. "Yes."

His teeth found her earlobe. The tiny sensual pain ripped through her, tearing at defenses she didn't know that she had. She wanted him to take her, to teach her, to lay her bare. Emotionally, figuratively and, yes, in actuality, too.

"That's right," he encouraged against her cheek as she arched against him. "Show me what you want. Give me your passion."

Turning her head, she bit at his lips. He laughed and gave her more. Opening his mouth against hers, kissing her so deeply her breath chased away. Digging her fingernails into the back of his hand, she leaned into the press of his cock against her thigh. So close, but she needed more.

Bringing her hand to his mouth, he kissed the back. "You're wearing too many clothes, my darlin'."

He wanted her naked. Oh, that was a big step. She'd never been naked in front of anyone before.

"This might be the part where I go screaming into the night."

The confession hung between them. So did his "Why?"

"What if you don't like what you see?"

"I love what I see."

He kept using that word.

Taking the hand he'd just kissed, he brought it to the front of her dress. "Show me."

It was the most erotic thing anyone had ever said to her. It was also the most terrifying.

A series of dainty buttons was all that was stood between him and her modesty. The first button was the hardest. Try as she might, she couldn't make herself slide it through the hole. The longer it took, the more unsure she became, while he just leaned back on his elbow watching her, his eyes dark blue in the flickering light. Not for the first time was she reminded of a lion surveying his prey.

"Do you want help?"

"No." She could do this. "Just don't look."

"Oh. I'm looking." And he was. Quietly. Intently.

She got three buttons undone before her courage ran dry.

His "Good girl" curled her toes but did nothing to replenish the well.

As if he knew, he asked, "Mind if I take over from here?"

"Please."

With light skimming touches, he parted the material, revealing the upper curves of her breasts. She remembered how he'd touched them before. Made them ache. More buttons gave. His hand slipped beneath. She squeaked.

"Beautiful."

The warm air felt cool on her overheated flesh as he pushed the material aside. "Very beautiful."

He was looking at her. Air seemed to still in her lungs. He trailed his index finger between her breasts. "Breathe, Josie."

She'd forgotten how.

His finger under her chin turned her face to his. Emotions she couldn't read darkened his eyes and softened his lips. "I've got you."

"Are you sure?"

That got her a smile. "And I won't let go."

It was all too easy to remember the terror of the tornado. The threat of the bandits. He'd held her then.

"Promise?"

Cupping her breast in his hand, he nodded. "Always."

With a sigh, she relaxed. More buttons gave as he traced their lead, following the path down over her collarbone, between her breasts, over her stomach and then lower. Her breath caught as his fingers tangled in the tight curls he found. With a tug, he centered the jumble of unfocused sensation within. The ache blossomed.

His voice deepened as his middle finger slipped between the slick folds. "I'm going to taste you here."

She blinked.

"No complaints?"

"I trust you."

Emotion flared in his eyes. "Shit." His hand clenched.

"Oh!"

"I want you to see what I see. Sit up."

She did. She looked like a pagan offering with her full breasts quivering with every breath, legs splayed wide, his big hand nestled between them. She was beautiful and enticing, earthy and primal. And all for him.

He wiggled his fingers. Ghosts of sensations trickled out. She tried to catch them, but they trailed away. When his hand left her, she moaned.

"Now, think how much better that's going to feel when it's my tongue."

"Oh my God."

The rest of her gown came off in a tear. It was hard to lie still under the heat of his admiration. Harder still to not writhe with frustration.

"What do you want me to do?"

"What do you feel like doing?"

"I'm stuck between running and wiggling."

"I've done enough chasing."

It wasn't exactly a preference.

Cupping her cheek in his hand, he kissed her softly. "I'm sorry. It's been a long time since I've been with innocence." Another light kiss and then a more lingering one. "There's nothing more arousing to a man than watching his woman give in to the pleasure he brings her, so wiggle, squirm, bite, scratch, scream. It's all good."

Catching his hand, she turned her head, holding his gaze as she kissed his palm. "Thank you."

"My pleasure."

Unsure of what to do, she lay back and waited, her legs falling apart naturally.

"Oh yes, very nice."

His big hand cupped her breast. Heat. So much heat.

"Look."

She did, seeing how the contrast of his dark skin against her white, his strength plumping her softness. His heat stoking her fire.

"I love your breasts."

"I love your hands on them."

Shadows flitted across his expression, playing with the passion and desire, creating something deeper, something more powerful. Something that everything inside her responded to. Oh, she would love to take his picture now, right now, like this. She wanted to see him with his soul laid bare.

"I want to see you, too."

"You will."

"When?"

"You come for me like I want, and you can have all the naked me you can stand."

She didn't even know what that meant. She told him so.

With a shake of his head, he came over, his shadow swallowing the light. His hands on her breasts became more demanding. She loved how he worked them, shaping them to his pleasure, milking sensation from every inch, drawing it as he built on that fire within. He made her burn. The stronger that fire grew, the stronger their connection. There was nothing brutal or painful in anything he did, but there was an imperative that wouldn't be denied. And she gave. Her moans, her surrender, everything. The tightness within her spread to an ache as his thumb brushed her nipple, drawing it taut, prepping it for his attention. The ache gave birth to a moan as his head lowered.

He took her nipple into the wet heat of his mouth, rolling it across his tongue, teasing it in little flutters, rewarding it with tiny bites, every move designed to fulfill... But still it wasn't enough.

"More."

He turned his attention to the other breast, giving it the same loving kiss, the same tickle, the same tease, the same bite, the same nibble. Everything she wanted he was giving to her, and it wasn't enough. Her thighs were wet with passion. Her heart full of anticipation. The rough material of his pants abraded the inside of her thighs as he slid down. His shirt scraped across the ultrasensitive tips of her breasts. Grabbing his hair, she tugged him to her. Taking her hands in his, he pinned them back to the bed.

"Easy now, we're getting there."

Who cared about there? She wanted this, here and now. "Luke."

Kissing and nibbling his way down her stomach, he parted her with two fingers, and blew gently.

It was an odd feeling. A hold-the-moment sensation.

Before she could figure it out, his mouth was there. Slowly and delicately, he eased her into the sensation, seeming to understand how shock had taken her down from where she wanted to be. He built her back up one lick at a time, keeping it light until light wasn't enough, giving her more until more wasn't enough. Pushing her thighs back against her chest, he opened her to his ravishment. And it still wasn't enough.

"More."

She held him to her and he laughed. She pulled

his hair, and he growled. The pleasure changed and became intense, following his lead until it was no longer a feeling but a demand.

"More." She needed more. "Harder." She needed harder.

And he gave it to her. Sucking her clit between his lips, laving it with his tongue, pinching it between his lips, drawing it out from its hiding place, shaking it, stretching it, he zeroed in on that hard little point where her world manifested.

He gave her no choice. Taking the demand and making it his, he drove her higher, sending her to a place where she was afraid to go. But this was Luke and he wanted it, so she trusted him and let go. The explosion came hard and hot, ripping his name from her throat. Her body convulsed and jackknifed, the storm buffeting her.

And still he didn't let her go. He just took her down to a softer place where the storm was a memory that lived in delicate kisses.

"Oh my God. Luke!"

She felt his smile. "Right here."

His tone was yet another stroke along her lust.

"I didn't know."

"You do now." She couldn't even begrudge him the smugness in those three words.

"Yes." She stroked his hair contentedly. "You promised me naked."

"You promised to come."

"Didn't I just?"

"Not enough. The second time is always better. Trust me."

The magic words again for him and for her.

And she did trust him, riding that wave again, this time her fingers tearing at the bedsheets, she came screaming his name. Inside and out. Just "Luke."

"Hold on." She didn't hold as much as float. The aftermath of so much storm needed calm. She heard his boots hit the floor. He was undressing. She forced open an eyelid. She didn't want to miss this.

The pants came off, then the long johns and last the shirt. He was beautiful. All broad shoulders, tight muscle and tanned skin except for *there*, but even there he was beautiful. His cock stood out from his body, hard and hungry. She should have been embarrassed, but maidenly modesty had no part between them. That little voice inside whispered, *more*.

"Can I touch you?"

"A little."

"You touch me a lot."

"I'll explain how it's different later."

Yes. Explanations could wait. He stepped forward. She reached out, and all that maleness was in her hand, throbbing and hard.

She glanced up. "I don't see how it's going to fit."

Taking her hand again, he pressed a kiss in the center of her palm before placing it back upon him. "Trust me."

And, of course, she did because it was him and because logic said people did this every day so it had to fit. They had to fit. She couldn't bear it if they didn't.

Stroking her finger over the tip, she discovered a silky moisture. Bringing it to her mouth, she touched it to her tongue. He moaned and caught her hand.

Rolling the flavor across her tongue, she smiled. "Salty."

Chuckling, he shook his head. "Come here."

Crooking her finger back at him, she scooted back and spread her legs wide. "You come here."

"Witch."

"Lover."

With a groan he settled between her thighs. It was natural to arch her back and sigh as his mouth claimed her breast. She held his head as he took from her what he needed, giving her what she desired.

It was all in balance and still not enough. His cock settled into the well of her pussy and she thought this was it. Her body tensed. Her mind braced, but nothing happened.

Opening her eyes, she saw he was looking down at her with a wry twist to his lips. "This isn't where I turn into a raving lunatic and attack you."

"I never thought you would."

"You stiffened."

"I'm nervous."

"Why? It's me."

Why indeed. "I'm sorry."

"Don't apologize, just close your eyes and feel me from head to toe. From the outside in. All of me."

With a nod, she did just that. Taking in his heat, his scent, his presence, breath to breath, heart to heart in an intimate hug. Her tension eased. This was

Luke. He'd die for her. Wrapping her arms around his neck, she clung. When that point came when she knew that this was as it was supposed to be, that this was who she was supposed to be, she whispered, "I trust you."

"Good." He hugged her back, keeping her close until he was her world. Slowly the fire began to build. Little prickles of awareness spread again. Where his skin touched hers, fires ignited.

The ache she thought sated beyond recall pulsed between her legs. And her nipples… Oh her nipples. They burned for his touch.

And he knew. They were so in tune she didn't even question how she knew he knew. It just was. Slipping her hands down his back, she pulled him closer. Sliding one hand behind her back, he arched her higher.

She kissed him then. The first kiss she'd ever initiated. She'd been starving for him for so long and now he was giving her free rein. Like a wildfire whipped by the winds of need, passion took over, burning through her good intentions, leaving her no choice but to run in front of it or get burned in the heat. Sweet, hot, consuming, she couldn't get enough of his taste, of his touch. Of him.

Somewhere along the way, Luke took control.

With his hands under her knees, he spread her open. His thumb settled with delicate precision on her clit. Anticipation froze her in place. His gaze meshed with hers as tightly as their fingers. "Now."

He took her one slow rock at a time, little by little,

whispering words of encouragement, taking her past her fear until inside something gave and she was taking him, his passion, his lust, his desire. His heart. He forged deep and the shock went through her, but so did the pleasure. Intimate muscles stretched to accommodate. His thumb on her clit never stopped. The fire burned.

"Easy. Just relax. Give it time to feel good."

He kissed her gently. She bit his lip and pulled his hair, the demon inside demanding more. She wanted to come like this, overstretched by his cock. He pulled out slowly. She could feel him watching her. She didn't care. This was bliss, but not enough.

He forged back in a steady possession. She needed it harder. She needed him harder. She was so close, so close. He worked her clit relentlessly, tugging and pinching, while her inner walls stretched and rippled around every inch of his cock. She tried to twist away from the overwhelming need, but there was nowhere to go.

"More." She needed all of him. Raking her nails down his arms, she begged, "Please."

"Yes." The guttural sound housed all the passion she could see he was withholding.

She did it again. His body shook. She clung. "Please."

"Dammit, Josie."

"More." Clenching around him, milking him, she repeated her demand with her eyes, her body, her soul. "Please, Luke."

She was watching him so intently she saw the moment his walls came down and the man she wanted grabbed her thighs and pushed them apart.

And he took her, this man she wanted, with all the intensity, all the passion he'd been holding back. Inside her rose a storm equal to his. Releasing her legs, he grabbed her hips, tilting them up. She wrapped her legs around his back and met his thrusts with her own, driving him deeper, taking them further to the place where more was reality.

His grip tightened. The intimate pain bound with the pleasure. Her clit throbbed. Her pussy swelled, squeezing him so tightly, she could feel every flex.

"Now, my darlin'. Now."

She didn't have any choice. Slamming deep, he ground against her pussy, rocking her clit against his groin with bruising force. Pleasure, pain, it all came together in a piercing cry as her climax rolled through her.

"Fuck yes. Take it."

Grabbing her breasts, he pumped hard, twisting her nipples as she screamed again, riding her orgasm with his bucking hips, filling her beyond her limits with his cock and then his seed.

She held him as he held her and together they rode out the storm. When it was over and she opened her eyes, he was there, looking very pleased and impossibly smug. "Mine."

Reaching up, she touched the smile tucked into the corner of his mouth. Somehow, there had to be a way.

"Yes."

CHAPTER SEVENTEEN

THERE WAS NOTHING subtle about the knock on the door. Nor Luke's response. He was out of the bed before Josie could work her way up from the blankets.

"Who is it?" he asked from the center of the room before moving to a spot three feet to the right of the door. Predawn gray infiltrated the room in random strips. The faint light glinted off the barrel of the revolver he held at the ready. Looking back at her, he put his finger to his lips before pointing to the floor. Did he want her to hide under the bed? She remembered what he'd told her about spiders. She was not hiding under the bed, but she did sidle to the edge of it. Her heart beat like a drum in her chest.

"It's Ed. Bella's having the baby."

Ed? No! What if he caught her here? Her reputation would be ruined. And then. Oh my God. Bella!

Luke lowered his gun and stepped back. "I'll be right there."

She had a brief moment to admire the set of Luke's shoulders and the tightness of his buttocks before he moved out of the light.

Behind the door, Ed cleared his throat. Luke

looked at her. She looked at him and raised her hands. She had no idea what he wanted.

"Is there something else?" he asked, pulling on his pants.

"Tia thought Josie might like a change of clothes."

Josie's embarrassment, which she'd thought couldn't get any worse, multiplied by ten. They knew? How?

With a shake of his head, Luke walked to the door. By the time his hand hit the handle, Josie had the sheet pulled over her head. The doorknob rattled. She moaned under her breath. This would be the perfect time for the floor to open up and swallow her.

"How's Bella doing?"

"We don't know yet. Doc says it will be a while."

"Tell Tia thanks."

"I will. By the way, she said, 'Congratulations.'"

Josie groaned. Congratulations? Wonderful. Now there was pressure where before there had been none.

The door clicked closed.

From under the covers, she announced, "I am never coming out of this room."

"That's fine by me."

The sheets were tugged out of her hand and pulled down below her navel. The mattress dipped as Luke sat beside her. "Even better if you don't come out of my bed." He leaned over her and propped himself up on his hand. "What do you think?"

He loomed over her like a big cat, a visual feast for her senses with all those sleek muscles exposed. She remembered how the sprinkling of dark hair had tickled her palms when she stroked him. Her fingers curled over the memory. Her "I think it's a possible alternative" was a bit breathless.

"To what?"

"To my dying of shame."

Playing with a lock of her hair, he drew it over her nipple. She shivered at the tickle, the sensitive peak drawing up tight. He cocked a brow at her and smiled that slow lazy smile of his. "Have you done something of which you're ashamed?"

Had she? The softness in his expression mesmerized her. Reminded her. The reality of last night was completely opposite from what she'd been raised to believe. His calloused fingers cupped her breast. She arched into the heat. "Mmm." Debating her feelings a second more, she came to a conclusion. "No."

Leaning in, he kissed her softly, capturing the soft sound. "Good."

She smiled against his lips. "But I have no idea how to brazen out being so…brazen."

"Oh, my darlin', that's the easy part." Brushing her hair away from her face, he cupped her cheek. "All you do is hold my hand."

"And you've got my back?"

"Always."

She believed him. "Thank you."

With a playful smack on her hip, he stood and ordered, "And now, you shameless woman, you need to stop tempting me and get dressed."

Shameless. She liked that. Almost as much as she liked the knowledge she could tempt him. She stretched, watching him watch her, enjoying the feminine power that put that heat in his gaze and that hardness in his pants. He was such a beautiful man. Like a sculpture come to life. Solid and strong with muscular shoulders that flowed to strong arms and a washboard stomach. She liked that he had just enough hair on his chest to accent the muscle beneath. She liked the way that hair skipped his stomach, but picked up below his navel to form a narrow path that disappeared into the open fly of his heavy cotton pants. She liked how he loved for her to touch him. She'd been a little overwhelmed this time, but next time they made love, she wanted to nibble and taste all of him the way he'd tasted her. Next time—

"What are you thinking?" he asked, reaching for his shirt.

"That I'd like to bite your chest."

It just popped out. His eyes narrowed and the space between them filled with heat. He finished shrugging into his shirt. She never wanted to forget how he looked right then. Intensely masculine. Predatory. All man. Her man.

"When this is done, I'm going to hold you to that," he drawled.

"I hope so."

She wouldn't want to chicken out.

He tossed her the bundle of clothes Ed had given him. "Now, stop teasing me and get dressed. I'm about to be an uncle."

LUKE WATCHED JOSIE CLOSELY. She was desperately trying to be nonchalant about sliding out of bed, but the blush covering her from chest to cheek betrayed her insecurity. She didn't have a damn thing to worry about. He wasn't going anywhere. The woman was amazing. She had an intrepid streak that came out at the most surprising times, and an enjoyment for life that she pretended didn't exist. Most women would have been cowed by the tornado. Definitely been done in by the bandits, but Josie just flourished when challenged. He still couldn't believe she'd ridden into that camp on a bomb. They were definitely going to have to talk about her reckless streak. As much as he appreciated her wild side, she couldn't risk herself that way.

As she sat on the bed, sorting out the bundle, Luke acknowledged they had another problem. Along with being reckless, Josie was unconventional, afraid of the commitments most women craved. Society wasn't kind to unconventional women. He'd have to come up with a way for them to work in the bigger world, but Josie didn't need to hear all that right now. Right now she was a woman who'd just crossed the threshold from virgin to lover. He had a few regrets about how that had occurred. But he wouldn't take back one second of it, except for the aftermath. He definitely needed to make up for the aftermath.

Falling asleep immediately thereafter had not been his finest moment. Never mind that he'd slept with her held tight in his arms—a woman deserved cuddling and reassurance. He'd just expected to have more time before the world intruded. Assumption was a dangerous thing, because now Josie'd had the passion without the reassurance and the insecurity that often ensued showed in the way she fumbled with the tie on her pantaloons while covetously eyeing the wash basin. Another regret. He'd meant to be the one to bathe her.

Sitting beside her on the bed, he took the pantaloons from her hand and detangled the string. "Just so you know, I had a different plan for how you would wake up."

"Oh?" She smoothed out her camisole.

"Oh, definitely." He handed her back the pantaloons. "I planned on waking you with kisses from here—" he tapped the top of her head "—to here." He lightly tapped tip of her nose.

Her smile fluttered as he trailed his fingers down the side of her neck. She clutched the pantaloons in a death grip. "You did?"

He nodded. "And then I definitely would have kissed you here and here." He lightly tweaked each nipple.

She gasped. It was his turn to smile. Trailing his fingers downward, skimming her belly, he circled her navel before continuing on to cup her still-damp pussy. She felt small and delicate in his hand. "I planned on lingering a good while here."

And just when she thought she knew what he was about, he retraced his path until he found her heart. Opening his hand there, he finished, "But here was where I wanted to spend the most time."

She blinked. Was that a tear? He didn't want her sad.

"I'm sorry I fell asleep last night before we got to

talk," he continued. "But know this. Last night? That was real. That was us. Pure and simple. That's what I want from now on. Remember that today if things get crazy or you start feeling scared, all right?"

She nodded. "Yes."

"Good."

Getting up, he poured water into the basin. "I'm going to give you some privacy to wash up and get dressed."

He chuckled at the fervency of her thank-you.

"Don't get too used to privacy. You're an exciting, desirable woman, and I'm looking forward to bathing you and dressing you when you're more settled into the thought."

"Oh."

"Is that disappointment or excitement?"

"I think shock."

He shook his head and smiled. "Have I ever mentioned I like your honesty?"

"No, but I had an idea."

"Good." He motioned to the fine wool stockings. He did love a woman's legs in stockings. "Do you need help with those?"

"I may be new to this, but even I know that if you help we're not getting out of here."

She was on to him. "Good call."

With a twirl of her finger, she said, "Weren't you going to give me privacy?"

He turned, staring at the wall.

"No peeking."

He smiled. "I promise."

He might not peek, but he could listen. The splashing of water, the glide of the cloth over smooth sweet flesh. The whisper of clothing being donned. It was a seductive melody he thoroughly enjoyed.

A tap on his shoulder turned him around.

"Could you fasten my dress?"

"With pleasure."

Turning, she lifted her hair. He fastened the buttons with more speed than he wanted to. There was something completely arousing about a woman submissively waiting on her man to make her presentable. He pressed a kiss on the nape of her neck before buttoning the last two. A shiver took her from head to toe. Satisfaction sank deep.

"Just a little something to keep you thinking about me."

"I don't think I need a reminder."

"Maybe I do."

Turning, she smiled up at him. "You don't. That much I learned last night."

"So you were paying attention."

"Absolutely."

"Good."

"Do you have a brush?"

"A comb?"

She shook her head before he could get it. "That's never going to work. I'll make do for now."

Gathering her hair, she twisted it into a bun. "Oh darn, where are my pins?"

"On the floor. I landed on one when I jumped out of bed."

"Ouch."

"Yeah." He handed them to her as he picked them up. She put them in and then all that was left was to open the door and go out into the world. He opened the door. She bit her lip and hesitated.

He held out his hand. "Trust me, Josie."

THE OPTIMISM THAT had thrived when Bella first went into labor was fading fast. The birth was not going well. Josie sat on the settee beside Luke and tried not to panic. The normally peaceful home rang discordantly with stressful voices. Bella's screams and occasionally Dr. Shane's orders easily carried out from the bedroom. Sam's curses were getting more inventive. Tia's and Bettina's voices were much more muted. Josie was glad she wasn't in there.

"I hope like hell Doc knows what he's doing," Luke muttered.

"If he doesn't, Tia does, so between the two of them, they have this handled," Josie countered with more optimism than she felt. Births went wrong all the time.

Bella screamed again. Ed swore. Luke jumped up and strode to the liquor cabinet. He poured an amber liquid into three glasses. "I don't know what Sam will do if Bella doesn't make it."

"We're not talking that way," Ed said. "She'll make it."

"I don't know what either of them will do if the babies don't make it," Josie whispered, letting her own fears into the light.

"They'll get through it," Ed stated firmly. "Whatever happens, they'll get through it."

Luke's "Yeah" lacked conviction.

Josie tried to imagine what she would do if she were Bella and she lost her babies. She couldn't conceive of it, not only losing the babies, but being pregnant in the first place. She'd never planned on carrying life within her. In light of recent events, she might need to reconsider that possibility. She glanced at Luke. Life, she was discovering, was more than the clean, safe plan she'd envisioned.

He shoved a glass into her hand.

"What's this?"

"Whiskey."

Her response was automatic. "I don't drink hard spirits."

"You don't or ladies don't?"

She didn't have an answer. It was another one of those things that just was. "I don't know."

Sitting down beside her, he tapped his glass against hers. "Maybe it's time to find out."

Maybe it was.

"Take it easy on that first sip," Ed warned. "Whiskey's got a kick."

She took a sniff and blinked. It was strong and smoky and mysterious. The kind of drink one of Savage's heroines would favor. "What kind of kick?"

"It burns a little," Luke explained.

She took a bold sip and swallowed fast. She thought they meant like chili peppers, but this burned in a whole different way. She coughed and the fumes stole her breath, causing her to cough again. Luke patted her back until the spasm was over. She finally caught her breath. Wiping her eyes, she croaked, "That more than burns."

"You're supposed to sip it, not throw it back."

"Uh-huh."

"Try it again."

She handed Luke the glass. He pushed it back. "I don't think so."

"You've just got to go slow," Ed said, not even bothering to hide his amusement.

She eyed him suspiciously. "You wouldn't be setting me up for a joke, would you?"

Luke tipped her glass up. "Trust me."

What choice did she have after that? She took another sip, but eased into the swallow. The flavors spread through her mouth. It still burned, but this time it didn't steal her breath, and when it hit her stomach, there was a warm, happy aftermath. "No wonder men drink this stuff. It's warm like a hug from the inside out."

Luke chuckled. "This is finer than what most men drink. This is Sam's private stock."

"We only get to raid it when he's distracted," Ed clarified.

It was a joke. She would have smiled if Bella hadn't screamed again just then.

The next sip she took was bigger. If alcohol could give her an oblivion, she'd like it now. Luke took the glass from her hand.

"Getting flat-out drunk isn't the aim."

"Ha! Men do it every Saturday night."

"Some men," he corrected, but he didn't give her the drink back.

The door to the bedroom opened. Josie had a brief glimpse of Bella sitting up on her big four-poster bed. Her face was pale and shiny, her hair matted to her head with sweat. Tia and Bettina were on the other side of the bed looking grim. She couldn't see the doctor. Sam shut the door behind him before closing his eyes and leaning back against it. For a moment he stood there, looking lost. His lips were white around the edges. Then, opening his eyes, he joined them in the living room.

"Better sit down before you fall down," Luke told him.

Sam sat. Luke shoved Josie's drink into his hand. He held it as if he didn't realize what it was.

"Jesus, Luke, they're going to cut her open."

Oh dear heavens.

Luke said nothing. Ed cursed.

"Doc's done everything he can without surgery," Sam continued hollowly. "It's the only option."

It was Ed who broke the heavy silence. "Drink the whiskey, son. Get your feet back under you."

Sam tossed the drink back like it was nothing.

"I don't know what I'll do if I lose her."

"You won't."

"Or the babies." Sam ran his hand through his blond hair. A long lock fell over his brow, making him look younger. And maybe even a little vulnerable. Human. "I don't know what we're going to do if we lose the babies."

He sat there with his hands between his legs, the cup dangling, forgotten.

"So why aren't you in there?" Luke asked, taking it from his hands and setting it on the table.

"They kicked me out."

"Why?" Ed asked.

Sam looked up blankly. "Doc said I couldn't do anything but get in the way."

Josie blinked at that. How could anyone think, after seeing Sam with his Bella, that she was in any way stronger without him? "He's wrong," she whispered.

All three of them stared at her. "He's wrong," she repeated more strongly. "Bella needs you, Sam. No matter what happens, she needs to know you're there with her."

"She knows that."

Luke poured him another shot. "She's got a point, Sam. Since when did you ever listen to anybody when it came to your Bella?"

"Never."

He handed him the glass. "Then why the hell are you starting now?"

"The hell if I know." He shook his head. "Everyone keeps saying my being here is the right thing to do."

Another scream.

"Josie's right, son," Ed cut in. "Bella needs you."

Sam stood and set the untouched glass aside. His

face was still pale, his lips pressed together, but he didn't have that defeated look anymore. He paused at the door. "Thank you."

Luke's smile was forced. "I'll be expecting a son named after me for this."

"Go to hell," he called over his shoulder before entering the room. The door didn't fully close behind him.

Through the crack, Josie could see Bella lying flat on the big bed, looking so small and defenseless. The doctor placed a small knife beside a collection of scary equipment on the bed stand. Luke came to stand beside her. Everything that was about to happen became very real in that moment. And for once, she didn't want to grab her camera.

Sam never hesitated. On an "I've decided I'm not missing this party," he strolled up to his wife.

Through the crack, Josie caught a glimpse of Bella's utter relief in seeing her Sam.

"You came back."

Sam sat on the side of the bed and stroked Bella's hair off her face. "There hasn't been a day in the last two years, Bella, when you haven't woken up and had me be there. It'll be a cold day in hell before the first time happens on the day my children are born."

Josie reached for Luke's hand. Tears burned her eyes as he took it. He squeezed her fingers.

Please, God, let them all be fine, she prayed.

Sam kissed Bella gently. Her arms wrapped around his neck. "Thank you."

His "I'll be here when you wake up, love," barely

carried. The doctor soaked a rag with the contents of a bottle. Bettina closed the door.

The screaming stopped and the waiting resumed.

IT WAS AMAZING how ten minutes could stretch into an eternity, how silence could weigh like a house on your shoulders, how pacing could do nothing but wear out your nerves. Josie walked over to Luke, and without a word, sat in his lap. His arms came around her immediately.

"I'm scared," she whispered against his chest.

"I know."

Ed looked at them with a cock of his brow, then cleared his throat. "I'm going to step out and tell the men what's going on."

When the front door closed, Josie confessed, "I don't know if I could do what Bella's doing right now. That takes courage."

"You've got courage."

She immediately shook her head. "My courage comes from staying safe. Safe clothes. Safe demeanor. Safe ideas. That—" she waved her hand toward the door "—that takes bravery to a much higher level. I am much more conventional."

"You're one of the most unconventional women I've ever met."

"Only lately."

"Isn't now about all that matters?"

"Not when you're trying to stay safe. Then past, present and future are weapons that can be used against you whenever anyone wants."

"Thinking that way leaves you fighting on all fronts at all times."

She nodded. "It does that." She thought back to her life before Jarl's invitation, the constant worry. The constant stress. The relentless pretense. "More than that, it's absolutely exhausting."

He nodded. "I can see that."

She wondered if he truly could. The sound of metal clanking on glass came through the door. As one they stiffened. His grip tightened on her arm. Her palm pressed against his chest. When no foot-steps approached the door, when the knob didn't turn, she released her breath and slowly relaxed.

Luke's "I've never had safe" broke the silence.

She tilted her head back to see his expression. "Did you want it?"

His muscles shifted as he shrugged. "There was never a good time to ask the question and by the time I thought of it, it no longer mattered. I was Hell's Eight."

"I don't understand."

A tug on her hair tipped her face back. His eyes were dark and serious as they searched hers, his expression intent. He had a tiny scar on his cheek to the left of his nose. How had she not noticed that before?

With a nod of his head he indicated the bedroom. "What's going on in that room, right there with Sam and Bella? That's love. For good, for bad, through the best and the worst, they're there for each other. Always. And stronger for it."

"I know."

This close there was no missing the skepticism in his gaze. "Do you? Because sometimes I get the impression that you think you're the only one who-ever feels alone."

A feather could have knocked her over when she understood what he was implying. "*You've* felt alone?"

"Of course."

How was that possible? He had the Hell's Eight. He had Tia and Ed. He had everything he needed. "I don't understand."

"What's to understand?"

His subsequent frown weighed heavily on her conviction. She had the absurd urge to bolt.

"Family can be there for you most times," Luke continued, "but there are always those moments when you have to stand alone, either because of circumstances or because of choice."

Understanding came in a flash. A "Yes" welled from a place deep inside where conviction struggled for acknowledgment. She'd left her town for the tiny chance she'd find a place in which to be herself out here in the West, following the possibility she'd found between the covers of Dane Savage's novels. And now she was here. Stuck between potential and what she feared. Her options narrowed to fight or run. Similar options to those he must have faced so long ago when orphaned. How had he made the choices as a child that made him the strong man he was today?

She covered that tiny scar with her finger, feeling

the imperfection she could no longer see. He was no more handsome without it. No less handsome with it. She wondered if he'd received it as a boy or a man, so she asked.

His hand came around hers as if searching for the memory through her touch. "Honestly, I don't remember." Another shrug. "I've got a lot of scars."

"I hadn't noticed." And she hadn't. She always saw him in totality, not bits and pieces.

The corner of his mouth crooked up. "Uh-huh."

She was beginning to understand him. That scar was just a piece of his history he'd moved beyond. How did he do that? Snuggling into a more comfortable position, she asked, "So if you can't tell me how you got the scar, can you tell me about how you lost your parents?"

She loved the way he arched his brows at her when he thought she'd taken their conversation off the rails. Their minds definitely worked in different ways, but maybe that wasn't so bad a thing. She was beginning to see that difference, rather than being destructive, could actually provide balance.

His hand dropped from hers and settled on her hip. Did he know he was pulling her closer?

"You serious?"

It was her turn to raise her eyebrows. Bringing her hand down to his chest, she asked, "Do you have something better to do right now?"

"Not particularly."

"Then please?" She stroked his arm through his shirt. The cotton was warm from his skin, a little

rough to her touch. It reminded her of the soft drag
of his calloused finger over her breasts. Awareness
shivered through her. "I want to understand you."

How was a man to deny a woman who requested
that? Luke blew out a breath and drew Josie closer
still. She felt soft in his arms, but not as soft as she
had last night.

"Settle in then."

She made a sound that could have been a chuckle.
"I can't get any closer."

Yes, she could, emotionally at least, but it was up
to him to take her trust from physical to mental and
that was going to take more than sexual prowess.
That was going to take real intimacy. Not to mention
honesty. His conscience twinged. At some point, he
was going to have to tell Josie that he was her be-
loved Dane Savage—and then be in the position of
competing not only with Zach but also competing
with his own damn self—but that could wait. Right
now she just wanted to know about his family. That
he could share, so he told her of his and Ace's friendship, of his parents and the excitement they brought
to his every day with their spirit of adventure. Of
how, when the massacre started, they'd hidden him
and ordered him to always remember how they loved
him, of how his father had told him that they didn't
regret anything. Not leaving the safety of the East
for the danger of the West. Of having him and how
proud they were of him. And how they hoped he'd
carry on that spirit in his life. They'd never let on

that they thought he wouldn't survive. And because of that, he'd never doubted that they would, too.

He told her of how he'd found them in the end and of how, for a long time, he'd felt betrayed that they hadn't survived. He told her of how he'd clung to the bitterness that they didn't regret their life choices, which had ended up making him an orphan.

When she fussed, he hushed her and explained how as he got older he understood they'd died trying to create a future for him, but he knew in his heart, given a chance to do it again, they would have made the same choices. He'd been their world, but they were adventurers and lived their life as such. And now, so did he.

"So no, my darlin', love has always been a wild ride for me, but when I find it, I value it and protect it. I don't hide from it."

"And you enjoy the ride," she said, worrying a spot on her dress, avoiding his gaze.

That could have been a question or a statement. Watching her carefully, he answered, "I enjoy most things in life."

A low murmur of voices came from the next room. Cold fear settled in his gut. Josie leaped to her feet.

The door didn't open. Josie sighed and wrung her hands before spinning back.

She threw her hands wide. "How long does this take?"

He stood, too. "I don't know."

She licked her lips. He knew how she felt. Waiting was hell.

She glanced at the door then at him and hugged herself the way he wanted to hug her. "Have you ever thought about being a father?"

A lot more in the last twelve hours. He glanced at her flat stomach. He hadn't held back when they were together. Even now, Josie could be carrying his child. The smile started deep inside. He definitely wanted their child to have her eyes. "I've always wanted a family."

"Really?"

She didn't need to sound so shocked.

"Just because I've never found someone with whom to build a family doesn't mean I never had the hankering."

"I guess I just never thought of men wanting things like that."

"From what I can tell, you've never thought of men as much of anything other than something that needed to be avoided."

Her chin came up. The woman was bracing for a fight. "You make me sound so cold."

"That's how plans are, cold and calculating. A hedge of a bet."

"And words are walls," she countered immediately.

He nodded, watching the emotions flick across her face: fear, determination, anger. "For you they're more like weapons."

"And for you, they're not?"

"Sometimes."

"I'm talking now because I'm trying to understand you."

She thought this defensive sparring was going to lead to understanding? "We said everything we needed to say last night, my darlin'." If one discounted the words and focused on the emotion. "You just need to think back and listen."

Color flooded Josie's cheeks. She leaned in and hissed sotto voce, "We had sex."

He shrugged. "Maybe you did, but I was talking your ear off."

"Not that I remember."

It amazed him that she couldn't see the reality of what they had. "We're going to have to work on your listening, then."

She bristled. He cut off her retort with a wave of his hand. "At some point, Josie, you're going to have to come to a decision about what you want to do, for good, for bad or whatever. You're going to have to decide to stick with your plan or take a chance and go off course."

"And if I don't?"

From the way her hands balled into fists, she wasn't feeling the same contentment he was in the wake of last night. He was going to have to work on that.

"You're not right about everything," she accused.

"Maybe, but I'm right about this."

Whatever she was about to fire back died when the bedroom door handle rattled. Josie blindly reached out for him. Luke caught her hand, and pulled her close. At least her instincts were sound.

"I've got you."

Her fingers squeezed his.

The door opened. Bettina and the Doc came into the room. Bettina was all smiles. Doc was drying his hands on a towel.

"We have a boy and a girl!" Bettina crowed delightedly.

"And Bella?" Luke asked.

Doc answered. "Surprisingly, the surgery was relatively straightforward. There are a couple of arteries you've got to worry about—"

Who cared about the surgical particulars? "Bella, Doc. How is Bella?"

Doc caught himself. "Oh. Sorry. Bella's a strong woman. She did well. Very well. As long as there aren't complications, she'll be fine. She just needs to stay quiet until she heals."

"She won't have complications," Bettina declared with the ferocity of a mother who'd watched her daughter come out of hell. Luke hadn't known what to think of Bettina when he'd first met her, but the prim woman who'd annoyed him had turned out to be a straight shooter with the determination of a badger. A man had to respect that.

Doc nodded. "From your mouth to God's ears, but right now mother and babies are doing fine, though I think the new father could use a drink."

"We all need a drink," Bettina said. "And for this occasion, only the best will do."

Going over to the cabinet, she pulled out five bottles of Sam's best whiskey. "Call the men and tell them to bring a glass. We shall drink to the newest members of Rancho Montoya."

"And Hell's Eight."

Bettina nodded her head regally. "And Hell's Eight."

Luke shook his head. Damn, Hell's Eight was changing.

CHAPTER EIGHTEEN

SHE'D BEEN SUMMONED. Freshly bathed, her hair no longer feeling or looking like an abandoned rat's nest, a present in hand, Josie hesitated outside Bella's bedroom door. She knew who was in there. And it wasn't the babies that were making her nervous. By now everyone knew that she and Luke had a relationship. That, in the biblical sense, they'd begotten their hearts out. Now there would be consequences. Maybe condemnation. At the very least, expectations. Ugh. She'd rather be nibbled to death by ducks.

Smoothing the brown paper wrapped and tied decoratively around the tintype and taking a fortifying breath, she knocked. It was Tia that invited her in. Opening the door, she pasted a smile on her face and walked into the room.

She didn't know what she expected to see after the harrowing night before, but it certainly wasn't Bella propped up on pillows looking tired but happy, a baby in her arms and a smile on her face. Tia sat in a rocker beside the bed, holding the other baby. Bettina sat beside her, smiling like everyone else.

Bella waved her in. "Come. Come sit here beside me so I can see you. It is hard for me to turn right now."

Josie looked helplessly at Tia, who was crooning to the baby. She couldn't sit on the bed. Bella had just had her stomach cut open.

"It is all right if you sit carefully," Bella encouraged, patting the mattress. "Doctor Shane assures me that I will not pop open like an overripe cantaloupe."

"That is an appalling image, *hija*," Bettina castigated.

Maybe. Maybe not. Josie didn't want to take a chance on being put in a position to judge.

"I'll go get a chair."

"Do not be nervous."

"I'm not nervous."

"You are wrinkling your skirt," Bella pointed out.

Darn it. She was. She released the folds and smoothed them down.

"Come sit."

"How about we compromise and I just stand? You have no idea how awkward I can be and I don't want to be the one who causes you to just—" she motioned with her hand "—burst open."

Bella laughed and then groaned. "I told you, Doc has promised me my insides are well darned like the best socks."

The baby fussed within its bundling. Bella hushed it with sweet sounds.

"I'm not finding that comforting." She looked helplessly at Tia and Bettina.

Tia smiled and rocked the baby she held. "I saw the stitches. They were well set."

"And Tia would know. She's a seamstress," Bettina offered.

"You do know this conversation is macabre, right?"

Bella shrugged. "It is honest."

Josie didn't have anywhere to go with that. "Fine. But I'll still compromise and stand."

"All right." Bella eased the blanket out from under the baby. "Do you want to see my scar?"

Good heavens. "No!"

"I am sad to say, it is truly ugly. It goes from here—" she pointed down low on her abdomen "—to here." She pointed a little bit above her belly button.

"I'm sorry."

"Do not be. Without this operation, I would not have my babies." She kissed the head of the little one she held.

"Will you have to go through it again?"

Bella's smile slipped. "There cannot be more babies."

"I'm so sorry."

Bella shrugged and then winced. "I am happy for what I have. Life is good for me."

There was no doubt Bella was being honest. Her happiness shone. Despite coming out of surgery barren, she was happy. Josie walked around the foot of the bed. "I wish I could do that."

"Do what?"

"Be happy about the here and now without worrying about the future." Josie shook her head. "It's a skill I lack." She thought of what Luke had said about her plans. About last night. "But one I wish I had."

"Ah. You are a worrier like my Sam." Bella shook her head. "Always thinking about what could be rather than enjoying what is."

It was hard to enjoy things in the moment when the future was always looming. "I like Sam."

Bella smiled. "So do I."

Tia snorted. "Too much. That man has a swelled head."

"I feared for you," Josie said. "We all did."

"Me, too, especially when the doctor kicked Sam out." Bella squeezed Josie's hand. "Thank you for sending him back in."

"I didn't do anything."

"You told him I needed him. This he said."

"He was already halfway to the door."

"That I believe. It is only because I was in so much pain that he allowed the doctor to override his common sense. I thank you for giving it back to him."

"In that case, you're welcome."

Tia shook her head and stood. "I don't know why you are so surprised. My boys are men who know how to love strong."

Bella grinned at Josie. "Yet she blames me for Sam's swelled head."

"With reason, too." Tia pushed the blanket off the little one's face. "This *bambina* sleeps." The baby had Bella's hair. It stood out in a dark shock of black, but it looked like she might have Sam's patriarchal nose.

"So does my son."

Tia nodded. "I will put them in their crib so we may talk."

Oh dear heavens, they were going to talk. "I can come back later," she called after Tia. "Bella probably needs to rest."

Tia clucked her tongue as she came back from the adjoining room and gently lifted the baby out of Bella's arms. "You cannot escape so easily, *muchacha*."

More was the pity. "Who said I wanted to escape?" she called after Tia.

Bella whispered in an aside, "You're wrinkling your skirt again."

Darn it! She clenched her free hand into a fist. "I need to break that habit."

Bella groaned as she tried to shift positions. "Do not bother on my account. It makes it easy to understand your moods."

"Wonderful."

Bella groaned again.

"What is it? Can I help you? Is it the incision?"

Bella shook her head. "That does not hurt, but all the other muscles in my body?" She grimaced. "They are screaming protests."

"That's better than the alternative."

"Says the woman who does not hurt."

"True."

"It is the labor that is speaking now," Tia said, coming back into the room.

Bella frowned. "It needs to shut up."

Tia nodded and resumed her seat. There was something inherently regal about the woman that made just sitting seem something more. Josie envied her that.

"It will."

Once she was settled, Tia asked, "So, what troubles you, Josie?"

Josie made sure she wasn't fussing with her clothing. "Nothing. I just came to bring Bella a present for the babies."

Bella's face lit up with anticipation. "Ah. I was hoping that was for me. Is it one of your beautiful pictures?"

Her stomach sank as the moment was here. Had she made the right choice? "Yes."

"I thought they were all destroyed."

"I saved one."

"The best, I'm sure."

Not if she took the emotion out of the choice. "I think so."

"So let us see it."

Very gingerly, Josie sat on the side of the bed and handed Bella the package. The brown paper rustled as she took it.

Bella ripped into it.

Tia snorted at Bella's enthusiasm. "You would think this one was not already spoiled."

"Hush, Tia." Bella laughed. "Presents are good."

Josie smiled at her enthusiasm and the good-natured exchange. "Yes, they are."

She held her breath while Bella tore at the paper. Up until the moment she saw Bella's expression, Josie wasn't sure she'd made the right decision as to which tintype to save. But when Bella froze and teared up, she knew that split-second decision, based completely on emotion, had been the right one.

"It is perfect." Her fingers hovered over the picture. "Very perfect."

"You can touch it."

She did. "This, this is special." She looked up. "You are truly an artist, Josie."

"Thank you."

Tia held out her hand. "May I see?"

"Of course."

Bella passed the picture to Josie, who passed it to Tia. Tia froze when she saw it. "Luke told me of this picture, the one that would give you the standing you needed to make money and have your freedom."

Josie took a breath. She hadn't realized he'd shared that. "Yes."

"This photograph is beautiful. Stunning in all it captures."

She handed it to Bettina, who agreed. "Lovely."

Tia snapped her skirts straight and looked up. "But this is not that photograph."

"No."

Bella perked up. "Oh?"

Tia frowned, and her voice lowered an octave. Her speech slowed to deliberate. "Yet Luke is convinced that is the photograph you saved?"

It was only partially a question.

"I know." When the moment had come and she'd had to choose, her heart had made the choice. The photograph she'd saved was the photograph of all of them together surrounding Bella in her need. Laughing. Living. Loving. Everything that was the epitome of Hell's Eight. Everything that was Luke.

Bella shook her head. "That is not fair, Josie."

Betina tsked and passed the photo to Tia.

Tia stood and handed Josie the photograph back.

"My son loves you, *hija*. When that door opened earlier, whose hand were you holding? When the storm took you, who came after you? Whenever you have needed him, he has been there. Yet when he needs you, you run away. More than that, you deny him the security of knowing your choice."

Bettina shook her head and clucked her tongue in disapproval. "It is a dangerous game, making a man jealous."

"I am not a coward and I'm not trying to make anyone jealous."

"Yet Luke must watch Zach and others pursue you."

"Me?"

"You are not that naive," Tia scoffed.

No, she wasn't. Josie made to return the photograph to Bella. Bella shook her head and quickly pulled her hands back as if to ward off evil. "I cannot take it when it is so cursed."

"Cursed?" Oh dear heavens. "How is it cursed?"

"It hurts Luke. Luke is family." Bella waved her

hand at the photograph. "You cannot give away love when you don't understand it."

That didn't even make sense. "I'm a photographer. I don't have to understand what the camera sees."

"Not understanding is the problem. This you must fix so I can have my gift." Bella sighed and looked longingly at the picture. "I very much want my gift."

Tia stood and took Josie gently by the arm. She was surprisingly strong. In the other room, the babies fussed. Tia lowered her voice as she ushered Josie out the door. "When the time comes that you show this to my son, then we will be very happy to receive this gift. But it is not right that we receive it first. Not right at all."

"You don't understand," Josie protested. "What's between Luke and me is…complicated, but it has nothing to do with the picture."

Opening the bedroom door, Tia urged her through it. "I understand you make it difficult, but that does not make this right. You need to make this right."

"This is why I understand even less," Bella called after them gingerly adjusting her position. "You are both creative. You create pictures. Luke creates books. So much you have in common. How can you stand so much apart?"

"What?" Josie spun around, grabbing the door-jamb, almost dropping the tintype. "Luke writes books?"

Tia muttered something under her breath. Josie got a sinking feeling in her gut.

Bella covered her mouth. "You did not know of his Dane Savage?"

The feeling got bigger. "Luke is Dane Savage?" Josie cut a glance at Tia. Shock, she realized. That feeling was shock. "*The* Dane Savage?"

The older woman shook her head and guided her through the parlor.

"About this you need to talk to your man."

"You could answer my question."

Tia clucked her tongue. "It is not my place to sort out the secrets you two choose to keep, but I will ask you this because I am old and know the danger of pride. Twice, in the short time you have been here, you have spoken of needing to change. Do you feel you are not good enough as you have been made?"

Josie blamed the shock of discovering Luke was Dane Savage for just blurting out the unvarnished truth. "I don't know."

Tia nodded, urging her toward the front door. "This is the same answer Luke gave me when I asked why he hides Dane Savage." Opening the door, Tia pushed her through. Her expression softened as she watched her through the opening. "Perhaps this is the common ground upon which you can build."

With that, Tia closed the door.

LUKE WAS DANE SAVAGE. Josie stood in the yard absorbing that reality. Two hours after the revelation and it was just beginning to sink in. It was no wonder she loved his books so much. They were truly an extension of the man. Bigger than life, principled and written with the passion that was so much a part of everything he did. And he hadn't told her. She remembered a couple times when she'd mentioned the author only to find an awkward pause in the aftermath. Once in particular stood out, when she'd saved him from the bandits. Had he wanted to tell her then? She didn't know. But it hurt that he hadn't trusted her with the information. Just as it was going to hurt him when he found out she hadn't told him her choice. Bella was right. She had to fix this. Butterflies churned in her stomach.

But fixing this meant being ready to confront Luke, and the fact that she was hiding behind the garden shed was not a good sign. It wasn't hard to figure out why. She wasn't afraid of letting him know she knew about his pseudonym. She could think of a hundred reasons why Luke may have needed to keep his anonymity. The problem was she couldn't think of one valid reason to justify why she'd deceived him. She'd lied earlier. She truly was a coward.

The tintype caught on her blouse. Josie moved it away, giving it a glare. She was ridiculously afraid of showing Luke this picture. Always had been. The problem was she wasn't sure why. Was it because she feared his reaction or her own? She hadn't been lying when she said she was much better at hiding. She'd perfected hiding. She peeked around the shed again. Still no sign of him.

"The trick to a good ambush is to make sure you've got adequate cover."

Oh wonderful. Nothing like fate to force her

hand. Josie turned around, clutching the tintype to her chest. "Hello, Zach."

He was leaning against the shed, arms folded across his chest, his black sombrero pulled low on his brow, a small smile tugging at his sensual lips. "It also helps if you blend in. And you, senorita, are a chicken trying to hide in a pigpen."

"You're saying I'm sticking out."

"*Sí.* And the man from whom you hide saw you walking down from the house long ago."

"Really?" She sighed. "Everyone seems to be waiting on me lately."

"Then you must be someone well worth waiting for."

"I hope to be."

His expression softened and he shook his head. "You should talk to your man."

"I'm working up to it."

He motioned with his hand. "Work fast."

She looked over her shoulder. Luke was striding toward them. Her heart did a little flip-flop. Just seeing him boosted her day. And at the same time, this time, filled her with dread. "Darn it."

She was out of time.

She turned back to thank Zach, only to find him already gone. Darn it again. "Oh sure," she muttered to his departing back. "Just desert a lady in her moment of need."

"Who are you talking to?" Luke asked, coming up to her.

"Zach."

"He left."

She couldn't tell his mood from his tone. "I noticed."

He stopped a couple feet away. His hat brim shadowed his eyes, leaving only the firm set of his lips to indicate his mood. They didn't look happy. "So why are you out here?"

"I was looking for you."

"But you found Zach instead?"

"Yes."

There was a certain aggression in his stance that confused her. "And if I hadn't come, how long would you have talked to him?"

Her nerves in tatters, she blurted out the truth. "I don't know."

It was clearly a wrong answer.

Folding his arms across his chest, he growled, "Well, if you can talk to him, you can talk to me."

Was he jealous? She sighed. As if she needed another complication. "That seems to be the common opinion."

"Really?"

She nodded.

His muscles bulged as his fingers flexed. "And you don't agree."

She licked her lips. "I'm very tired of people pushing me where I don't want to go."

"Oh?"

She hugged the tintype tighter. "Yes."

"So why are you here?"

"Tia kicked me out of the house."

"That doesn't sound like Tia."

She shrugged.

"Want to tell me why?"

"No." Not when he was frowning at her.

"All right."

He turned and walked away.

"Aren't you even going to push for a better answer?" she called after him.

"No."

That "No" left a sick feeling in her stomach. Luke never walked away. He always stood and fought. She followed him down to the corrals. She had to skip every few steps to keep up.

"Why not?" she asked a little breathlessly when she reached him. A horse whinnied a greeting.

"It's none of my business."

Josie placed her hand on Luke's arm. He stopped. She hadn't been sure he would, but he stopped. But he didn't turn around. "Please."

He turned and she took a step back. This wasn't the Luke she was used to seeing. This man was cold and distant.

His "What?" was equally as cold.

"Please, talk to me."

Did he really think she could prefer anyone over him?

"So you can amuse yourself between visits with Zach?"

The answer to whether he could seriously think she'd prefer someone over him was clearly yes, and for a moment, the knowledge rocked her world, but when it settled, she could see with freeing clarity.

She'd gotten used to not carrying her weight, she realized. She'd been coasting along like a toboggan on a slow hill, letting time and circumstance dictate more than her own desires. Because that little voice inside declared it safer. She shook her head. That wasn't fair to Luke, who'd always been straightforward. And it wasn't fair to her, who'd always wanted to be more. Tia was right. For this to be fixed, honesty would be needed.

"I know you're Dane Savage."

Darn it. That wasn't at all what she'd intended to say. The churning in her stomach increased.

He froze and then asked on a sigh, "Bella or Tia?"

"Bella. She thought I already knew."

He nodded. There was no softening in his expression. "Anything else?"

"Why didn't you tell me?" she asked. "You let me go on and on…"

"I write books. I am Hell's Eight." His chin set arrogantly. "There's a difference."

"And you don't think I know that?"

"I don't know."

"Why didn't you ask?"

His brow rose. "I just found out you knew."

Darn it. She was making a mess of this.

"You're a wonderful author."

The compliment did nothing to warm his mood. If anything it caused the muscle in his jaw to bunch tighter. "Thank you."

She was losing him. Metal cut into her palm as she debated the best course to take forward. She caught herself as the tin threatened to bend. Wonderful. She'd gone from wrinkling her skirts to almost wrinkling her tintype. A glance at the set of Luke's shoulders told her subtle wasn't going to cut it here. Whatever she did, it had to be bold. Stepping around in front of him, she all but dared him to deny her. It was amazing how distant Luke could seem when he wasn't bending down to meet her. She settled for stroking his chest. "Don't stop making me your business yet."

He caught her wrist and held it away from his chest. "Why?"

She hated those one-word answers almost as much as she hated his stony expression. The man facing her now was a far cry from the lover of last night. The other night, they'd been so close she couldn't tell their heartbeats apart. Now, she'd be hard-pressed to tell he had a heart.

Maybe you did, but I was talking your ear off.

Yes. He had been telling her things, showing her things with his touch, and body. And now it was her turn to reveal truths. "I wanted to show you my picture."

If looks could kill, the tintype would be ash. "The one that's going to get you everything you want."

And she knew the why of his attitude. How could she not? She'd done it so often herself when she was afraid of getting hurt. Withdrawing to a place where she couldn't be touched was a tried and true haven from risk.

"Yes."

"I don't want to see it."

"Tia called it art."

"I'm sure it is."

This time when he looked toward the tintype, there was anger, and oddly enough, longing. She knew all about longing. Suddenly, she wasn't so afraid to show it to him. "Please, Luke?"

He held out his hand and she gave it to him.

"They say in moments of crisis what's important can become very clear." She motioned to the tintype, wishing her words weren't flying so fast they sounded like squirrel chatter. "I didn't have time to save everything. I could only grab what mattered. I thought I knew what I wanted, but then it changed."

He looked at the picture, then at her. Then at the picture again. She couldn't read his expression. She thought she saw comprehension, maybe joy, but then he grabbed her hand, spun on his heel, giving her a fine view of his back. Pulling her along behind him, he headed for his house. It wasn't the reaction she'd been expecting.

She tugged at his hand. "Luke?"

"Keep up."

She muttered, "You wouldn't be saying that if I were wearing a corset."

"That's another reason for not wearing one."

She rolled her eyes. "Now you remember you're always right."

They stopped in front of his room. "Was there a time I forgot?"

"Yes. When you thought I could ever prefer Zach or a pen name to the real thing."

Opening the door, he pushed her in.

"Why is everyone pushing me through doors today?"

"Probably because you bring out the primitive in a person." He set the tintype on a small table.

Now, that had possibilities. Luke going all primitive was very sexy.

The room was dark and cool. She blinked, adjusting her eyes as he shut the door. She barely had time to register that soft click before Luke spun her around and pinned her up against the wall. Chest to chest. Hip to hip.

"You, my darlin', are in serious trouble," he whispered in her ear.

"I am?"

"Yes. I should paddle your butt for letting me assume you kept the other tintype. That you chose a profession without me over a future with me."

"It was a hard choice."

"As hard as giving up Dane Savage?"

She blinked. "Who?"

"Your favorite author."

She frowned up at him. "He doesn't exist."

His fingers made short work of her bun. "Good answer."

"Well," she clarified, "he does in your work, but he's a name, not a person."

Some of the tension left his shoulders. "You really need to learn to quit while you're ahead."

"I'm ahead?" It didn't feel like it.

"Yes." His palm cupped her cheek as her hair fell down her shoulders. "In regard to your profession, it never had to be a choice, me or photography, had you discussed it with me, which is just another reason I should paddle your butt."

She shook her head, freeing the strands. "I thought we were done with the spanking threats."

His hand opened over her collarbone. It could have felt like a threat. It felt more like a welcome home. That sexy deep growl he made in his throat might just have been a promise. "I've got a feeling with a free-thinking woman like you, I'm just getting warmed up."

She gripped his wrist, holding his hand to her. She wanted the welcome and the promise. "I prefer you be sweet."

"Why?"

"It makes me melt inside."

His hands slipped under her skirt and he made that sound again. A very deep, sexy, drawling growl. "Are you telling me it gets you wet?"

"Yes," she gasped as his calloused fingertips grazed up the inside of her thighs. "What are you doing?"

"Seeing for myself how you melt."

"Oh heavens."

"Spread your legs."

As soon as she did, he found the slit in her pantaloons. His fingers slid easily over her slick heat. She winced when he probed deeper, but arched closer, too. The man was always confusing her.

"Sore?"

"Yes."

"I like that."

"That I hurt?"

"No. That you're mine. That excites me."

She drew her leg up his, granting him better access. "It does me, too."

"Good." His lips brushed her ear. "Why didn't you tell me you chose me and love over your independence?"

With his touching her like this she could admit it easily. "You weren't touching me."

Resting his forehead against hers, he shook his head. This close it was hard to focus on one feature but easy to see the whole man. Strong. Solid. Dependable. And as his fingertip teased her pussy, exciting. Very, very exciting.

"That's all it took?"

"Apparently." She slid her hands up his chest, feeling bold and daring and incredibly feminine as she confessed, "When you touch me, I don't see obstacles, just possibilities."

"Good."

"What do you feel when you touch me?"

"Complete."

She reconsidered her position on one-word answers. Not all were bad. Stroking his cheek, she whispered, "That was sweet."

He found a spot that made her shiver. He smiled that predator smile that sapped the strength from her knees. She clutched his shoulders.

He laughed and drawled, "Now, I think that was sweet." A few more strokes and a few more shivers and he asked, "What obstacles?"

"What?"

"What obstacles do you see when I'm not touching you?"

He wanted to have this conversation now? Like this? She bit her lip. With a kiss he defeated the gesture. "Stop worrying and start confessing."

"You might be mad."

"Try me."

She wanted to try him in every way but that one. Slipping her hand down his chest, licking her lips at the tantalizing heat of his skin beneath, she rode the ridges of well-developed muscles to the waistband of his pants. She tucked her fingers beneath. "Can't it wait?"

He stilled his caresses, leaving her hanging with anticipation. "Luke…"

"I'm just helping you think."

"That's not helping."

It truly wasn't. The lack of caress was more stimulating than the actual delivery. Expectation had her excruciatingly aware of what could be to the point he might as well have done it. "I want you," she moaned.

"Good. I want you, too. Now, confess."

There was no hope in it. She licked her lips and tasted him. She didn't want to lose him.

"I'm waiting."

He made it so hard. Closing her eyes, she counted to four and then blurted out, "I may never want to get married."

She felt his shrug. "So, we'll live in sin, just you, me and Rascal. Hell, I might even become notorious for a whole different type of book."

She laughed, took another breath and then confessed, "The thought of children scares me."

"We'll work through it."

She actually believed him.

He had her skirts up around her hips. Cooler air bathed her overheated skin. "I'm still more comfortable in my imaginary box."

"I'll make sure all serious conversations happen when we hug."

The next spurt of laughter caught her by surprise. "How do you always make me laugh?"

"I'm a talented man."

He was. "I'd love it if you'd move your fingers. I'd consider you very talented then."

"Like this?"

"Oh yes." Bliss poured through her. "Just like that."

"I love your honesty in these moments."

She slipped her fingers down the front of his pants. He filled her hand, thick and hard, pulsing with life. Her pussy clenched. "Only in these moments?"

His chuckle choked off to a groan. "Your honesty in others is still in question."

As best she could, she stroked his cock. "You're like a dog with a bone, Bellen."

"And you're trying to evade the issue."

She sighed. "Is it working?"

"No."

This was the hard one. The dream killer. "I don't think I'm the type of person who can settle down in one spot for all time."

His right eyebrow kicked up. "No?"

He didn't believe her. "I'm serious, Luke. I've always been restless about what's out there." She waved her free hand awkwardly, encompassing the world. "I only had books before—"

"My books." He said that with a great deal of satisfaction.

"Yes, yours, but now I've seen how it could be."

"And you want it."

She nodded and released him. Men were funny about their wives, but she couldn't go back to the stifling reality of propriety. Placing her hand over his heart, she took comfort from the steady beat. "I've found I like the thrill of discovery."

"So do I."

She glared at him. "It's partly your fault."

His eyebrows rose. He had no right to cock an eyebrow at her or look so innocent. Especially when he was touching her like that. How could he look so innocent while touching her?

His grip switched to her inner thigh.

"So, I'm to blame for this love of adventure?"

He needn't look so satisfied. "Yes."

"So it's up to me to come up with a solution?"

"It's not fair for you to cause a problem and then just throw away the consequence."

He squeezed her thigh. It was oddly exciting. "I see."

She glared at him. "You need to fix it."

"Of course."

She dug her nails into his chest. "I realize this may be a problem. You've reached a point where you and the Hell's Eight are settling down." Oh dear heavens, now she was wrinkling *his* shirt. "I don't know if I can do that, so…"

"Josie—"

She cut him off, smoothing out the wrinkles. "I know you have to earn money, and maybe…"

A finger over her mouth silenced the flow of words. "Josie?"

"What?"

"Shut up."

She blinked.

"I am not settling down. I'm not going broke no matter what we choose to do. And in case you haven't noticed, I'm agreeing with you."

He was? "You are?"

His thigh eased between hers, spreading her further. "How many times do I have to tell you that I don't say what I don't mean?"

"Probably a lot more. It's an odd concept."

Kissing the side of her neck, he murmured, "I suppose you'll need time to get used to it."

"Yes."

His thumb teased her clit in slow circles. "Like I'll need time to get used to your wild side."

Shivers of pleasure streaked upward and outward, peaking her breasts and stirring sensual memories. Arching up, she circled her hips in counterpoint to his thumb. He pinched and stroked. She bucked and moaned.

"I'm very interested in how wild you can get," he rasped.

She made one last grab for logic. "But we can't always be in bed."

He chuckled. "Good."

Throwing up her hands, she fell back against the wall. "What does that even mean?"

Slipping his hand behind her head, he cradled her skull in his hand. Everything about him intensified. His gaze met hers without flinching. All the emotion she could ever want was there in his expression, all the love she could ever crave was there in his eyes. "It means, Josie Kinder, that I see you. All of you. Your intelligence. Your sense of adventure. Your compassion. Your love. And that creativity that you think no one will approve of? I see that, too. And it excites me."

Wrapping her arms around his neck, she smiled up at him. "And you never say what you don't mean."

"That's right."

With a tug, she pulled those fabulous lips of his within kissing distance. "And you love me."

He didn't hesitate. "Every lush inch. Inside and out."

Catching his lower lip between her teeth she nipped, smiling at his groan. He pressed her closer. It wasn't close enough. With a wiggle she demolished that last inch.

"And you don't want me to change?"

"No."

All the security she'd ever longed for was in that one word.

Everything. He was giving her everything without reservations. She wanted to give it back with the same eloquence and power. "I can be clumsy with words, and I know I often say what I don't mean, but not this time. And not ever with you."

His thumb teased her lower lip. "Good."

Cupping his face in her hands, she whispered with all the emotion inside, "I love you, Luke. I want to be the fantasy you never get over. I want to take your picture every day. Not as a trophy but so I can forever keep the images of how happiness grows, because I promise you, I'm going to make you so happy."

He lifted her up. It was natural for her legs to wrap around his thighs and her arms to tighten around his neck. His cock nudged into the well of her vagina.

"Loving me is enough."

Even more natural to shake her head at such nonsense. "What did you not understand about my need for adventure? I don't want enough. Enough isn't good enough. Not for us. I want the whole picture, complete with flaws. I want the challenge of capturing all the nuances, of perfecting on them. I want the grand adventure that comes with building a lifetime with you. However we want that to be. I want you. I want us." His grip on her thighs tightened. She looked up. He wasn't smiling. Neither was she. Some things went too deep for smiles.

"I want it all, Luke Bellen." She paused and found her happiness, letting it flow as she stroked his cheeks. "With you."

Slowly, his smile came out, like sunshine bathing her in the warm glow of joy. Because he was happy. Very happy. She could see and feel it. And so was she. He lowered her slowly, filling her, spreading her wider, taking possession, going deeper, so deep she couldn't tell where she ended and he began. And there he paused, keeping them balanced on the edge of more. Perfect.

With a sigh, he leaned in. Inside her, his cock flexed. Sensation flared outward. Emotion rode sensation. Powerful and all-consuming. Energizing. He was close. So close only the big picture remained. And it was beautiful. His smile nudged her cheek. His words caressed her skin.

"Would you like to adventure with me, my darlin'? For the rest of your life?"

She didn't have to think about it. She pulled him closer still.

"Yes."

Most definitely yes.

* * * * *

For the perfect blend of sizzling romance with a dose
of suspense, don't miss the next installment in the
Cahill Ranch series by *New York Times* bestselling author

B.J. DANIELS

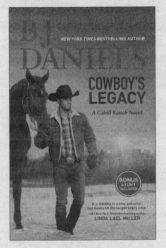

*When Sheriff Flint Cahill's
lover, Maggie, disappears,
he knows his ex-wife is
behind it. But with a winter
storm coming, can he find
her before it's too late?*

Bonus story included!

COWBOY'S
RECKONING

Available November 28!

"Daniels is truly an expert at Western romantic suspense."
—*RT Book Reviews* on *Atonement*

www.BJDaniels.com

www.HQNBooks.com

PHBJD370R

New York Times bestselling author

MAISEY YATES

sparkles in this sweet and sexy holiday tale!

It's Christmas in Copper Ridge, and love is waiting to be unwrapped...

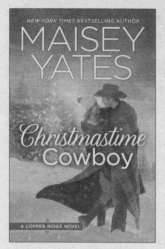

Falling for a bad boy once is forgivable. Twice would just be foolish. When Sabrina Leighton first offered her teenage innocence to gorgeous, tattooed Liam Donnelly, he humiliated her, then left town. The hurt still lingers. But so does that crazy spark. And if they have to work together to set up her family winery's new tasting room by Christmas, why not work him out of her system with a sizzling affair?

Thirteen years ago, Liam's boss at the winery offered him a bribe—leave his teenage daughter alone and get a full ride at college. Convinced he wasn't good enough for Sabrina, Liam took it. Now he's back, as wealthy as sin and with a heart as cold as the Oregon snow. Or so he keeps telling himself. Because the girl he vowed to stay away from has become the only woman he needs, and this Christmas could be just the beginning of a lifetime together...

**Available October 24, 2017
Order your copy today!**

www.HQNBooks.com

PHMY331R

Get 2 Free Books,
Plus 2 Free Gifts -
just for trying the Reader Service!

YES! Please send me 2 FREE novels from the Essential Romance or Essential Suspense Collection and my 2 FREE gifts (gifts are worth about $10 retail). After receiving them, if I don't wish to receive any more books, I can return the shipping statement marked "cancel." If I don't cancel, I will receive 4 brand-new novels every month and be billed just $6.74 each in the U.S. or $7.24 each in Canada. That's a savings of at least 16% off the cover price. It's quite a bargain! Shipping and handling is just 50¢ per book in the U.S. and 75¢ per book in Canada. I understand that accepting the 2 free books and gifts places me under no obligation to buy anything. I can always return a shipment and cancel at any time. The free books and gifts are mine to keep no matter what I decide.

Please check one: ☐ Essential Romance   ☐ Essential Suspense
                         194/394 MDN GLW5   191/391 MDN GLW5

Name _____ (PLEASE PRINT) _____

Address _____ Apt. #

City _____ State/Prov. _____ Zip/Postal Code

Signature (if under 18, a parent or guardian must sign) _____

Mail to the **Reader Service:**
IN U.S.A.: P.O. Box 1341, Buffalo, NY 14240-8531
IN CANADA: P.O. Box 603, Fort Erie, Ontario L2A 5X3

Want to try two free books from another line?
Call 1-800-873-8635 or visit www.ReaderService.com.

*Terms and prices subject to change without notice. Prices do not include applicable taxes. Sales tax applicable in NY. Canadian residents will be charged applicable taxes. Offer not valid in Quebec. This offer is limited to one order per household. Books received may not be as shown. Not valid for current subscribers to the Essential Romance or Essential Suspense Collection. All orders subject to approval. Credit or debit balances in a customer's account(s) may be offset by any other outstanding balance owed by or to the customer. Please allow 4 to 6 weeks for delivery. Offer available while quantities last.

Your Privacy—The Reader Service is committed to protecting your privacy. Our Privacy Policy is available online at www.ReaderService.com or upon request from the Reader Service.

We make a portion of our mailing list available to reputable third parties that offer products we believe may interest you. If you prefer that we not exchange your name with third parties, or if you wish to clarify or modify your communication preferences, please visit us at www.ReaderService.com/consumerschoice or write to us at Reader Service Preference Service, P.O. Box 9062, Buffalo, NY 14240-9062. Include your complete name and address.

STRS17R

Get 2 Free Books,
Plus 2 Free Gifts—
just for trying the
Reader Service!

YES! Please send me 2 FREE Harlequin® Romance LARGER PRINT novels and my 2 FREE gifts (gifts are worth about $10 retail). After receiving them, if I don't wish to receive any more books, I can return the shipping statement marked "cancel." If I don't cancel, I will receive 4 brand-new novels every month and be billed just $5.34 per book in the U.S. or $5.74 per book in Canada. That's a savings of at least 15% off the cover price! It's quite a bargain! Shipping and handling is just 50¢ per book in the U.S. and 75¢ per book in Canada.* I understand that accepting the 2 free books and gifts places me under no obligation to buy anything. I can always return a shipment and cancel at any time. The free books and gifts are mine to keep no matter what I decide.

119/319 HDN GLWP

Name _____ (PLEASE PRINT)

Address _____ Apt. #

City _____ State/Prov. _____ Zip/Postal Code

Signature (if under 18, a parent or guardian must sign) _____

Mail to the **Reader Service:**
IN U.S.A.: P.O. Box 1341, Buffalo, NY 14240-8531
IN CANADA: P.O. Box 603, Fort Erie, Ontario L2A 5X3
Want to try two free books from another line?
Call 1-800-873-8635 or visit www.ReaderService.com.

* Terms and prices subject to change without notice. Prices do not include applicable taxes. Sales tax applicable in N.Y. Canadian residents will be charged applicable taxes. Offer not valid in Quebec. This offer is limited to one order per household. Books received may not be as shown. Not valid for current subscribers to Harlequin Romance Larger-Print books. All orders subject to approval. Credit or debit balances in a customer's account(s) may be offset by any other outstanding balance owed by or to the customer. Please allow 4 to 6 weeks for delivery. Offer available while quantities last.

Your Privacy—The Reader Service is committed to protecting your privacy. Our Privacy Policy is available online at www.ReaderService.com or upon request from the Reader Service.

We make a portion of our mailing list available to reputable third parties that offer products we believe may interest you. If you prefer that we not exchange your name with third parties, or if you wish to clarify or modify your communication preferences, please visit us at www.ReaderService.com/consumerschoice or write to us at Reader Service Preference Service, P.O. Box 9062, Buffalo, NY 14240-9062. Include your complete name and address.

HRLP17R2

Get 2 Free Books,
Plus 2 Free Gifts—

just for trying the Reader Service!

YES! Please send me 2 FREE Harlequin Presents® novels and my 2 FREE gifts (gifts are worth about $10 retail). After receiving them, if I don't wish to receive any more books, I can return the shipping statement marked "cancel." If I don't cancel, I will receive 6 brand-new novels every month and be billed just $4.55 each for the regular-print edition or $5.55 each for the larger-print edition in the U.S., or $5.49 each for the regular-print edition or $5.99 each for the larger-print edition in Canada. That's a saving of at least 11% off the cover price! It's quite a bargain! Shipping and handling is just 50¢ per book in the U.S. and 75¢ per book in Canada.* I understand that accepting the 2 free books and gifts places me under no obligation to buy anything. I can always return a shipment and cancel at any time. The free books and gifts are mine to keep no matter what I decide.

Please check one: ☐ Harlequin Presents® Regular-Print   ☐ Harlequin Presents® Larger-Print
                                    (106/306 HDN GLWL)   (176/376 HDN GLWL)

Name _____ (PLEASE PRINT) _____

Address _____ Apt. # _____

City _____ State/Prov. _____ Zip/Postal Code _____

Signature (if under 18, a parent or guardian must sign)

Mail to the **Reader Service**:
IN U.S.A.: P.O. Box 1341, Buffalo, NY 14240-8531
IN CANADA: P.O. Box 603, Fort Erie, Ontario L2A 5X3

Want to try two free books from another series?
Call 1-800-873-8635 or visit www.ReaderService.com.

* Terms and prices subject to change without notice. Prices do not include applicable taxes. Sales tax applicable in N.Y. Canadian residents will be charged applicable taxes. Offer not valid in Quebec. This offer is limited to one order per household. Books received may not be as shown. Not valid for current subscribers to Harlequin Presents books. All orders subject to approval. Credit or debit balances in a customer's account(s) may be offset by any other outstanding balance owed by or to the customer. Please allow 4 to 6 weeks for delivery. Offer available while quantities last.

Your Privacy—The Reader Service is committed to protecting your privacy. Our Privacy Policy is available online at www.ReaderService.com or upon request from the Reader Service.

We make a portion of our mailing list available to reputable third parties that offer products we believe may interest you. If you prefer that we not exchange your name with third parties, or if you wish to clarify or modify your communication preferences, please visit us at www.ReaderService.com/consumerschoice or write to us at Reader Service Preference Service, P.O. Box 9062, Buffalo, NY 14240-9062. Include your complete name and address.

HP17R2

Get 2 Free Books,

Plus 2 Free Gifts—

just for trying the **Reader Service!**

HARLEQUIN
SPECIAL EDITION

YES! Please send me 2 FREE Harlequin® Special Edition novels and my 2 FREE gifts (gifts are worth about $10 retail). After receiving them, if I don't wish to receive any more books, I can return the shipping statement marked "cancel." If I don't cancel, I will receive 6 brand-new novels every month and be billed just $4.99 per book in the U.S. or $5.74 per book in Canada. That's a savings of at least 12% off the cover price! It's quite a bargain! Shipping and handling is just 50¢ per book in the U.S. and 75¢ per book in Canada.* I understand that accepting the 2 free books and gifts places me under no obligation to buy anything. I can always return a shipment and cancel at any time. The free books and gifts are mine to keep no matter what I decide.

235/335 HDN GLWR

Name _____ (PLEASE PRINT)

Address _____ Apt. #

City _____ State/Province _____ Zip/Postal Code

Signature (if under 18, a parent or guardian must sign)

Mail to the **Reader Service:**
IN U.S.A.: P.O. Box 1341, Buffalo, NY 14240-8531
IN CANADA: P.O. Box 603, Fort Erie, Ontario L2A 5X3

Want to try two free books from another line?
Call 1-800-873-8635 or visit www.ReaderService.com.

*Terms and prices subject to change without notice. Prices do not include applicable taxes. Sales tax applicable in N.Y. Canadian residents will be charged applicable taxes. Offer not valid in Quebec. This offer is limited to one order per household. Books received may not be as shown. Not valid for current subscribers to Harlequin Special Edition books. All orders subject to approval. Credit or debit balances in a customer's account(s) may be offset by any other outstanding balance owed by or to the customer. Please allow 4 to 6 weeks for delivery. Offer available while quantities last.

Your Privacy—The Reader Service is committed to protecting your privacy. Our Privacy Policy is available online at www.ReaderService.com or upon request from the Reader Service.

We make a portion of our mailing list available to reputable third parties that offer products we believe may interest you. If you prefer that we not exchange your name with third parties, or if you wish to clarify or modify your communication preferences, please visit us at www.ReaderService.com/consumerschoice or write to us at Reader Service Preference Service, P.O. Box 9062, Buffalo, NY 14240-9062. Include your complete name and address.

Get 2 Free Books,

HARLEQUIN®

MEDICAL Romance™

Plus 2 Free Gifts—

just for trying the Reader Service!

YES! Please send me 2 FREE Harlequin® Medical Romance™ Larger-Print novels and my 2 FREE mystery gifts (gifts worth about $10 retail). After receiving them, if I don't wish to receive any more books, I can return the shipping statement marked "cancel." If I don't cancel, I will receive 6 brand-new larger-print novels every month and be billed just $5.34 per book in the U.S. or $5.74 per book in Canada. That's a savings of at least 15% off the cover price. It's quite a bargain! Shipping and handling is just 50¢ per book in the U.S. and 75¢ per book in Canada. I understand that accepting the 2 free books and gifts places me under no obligation to buy anything. I can always return a shipment and cancel at any time. The free books and gifts are mine to keep no matter what I decide.

171/371 HDN GLYR

Name _____ (PLEASE PRINT) _____

Address _____ Apt. # _____

City _____ State/Prov _____ Zip/Postal Code _____

Signature (if under 18, a parent or guardian must sign) _____

Mail to the **Reader Service:**
IN U.S.A.: P.O. Box 1341, Buffalo, NY 14240-8531
IN CANADA: P.O. Box 603, Fort Erie, Ontario L2A 5X3

Want to try two free books from another line?
Call 1-800-873-8635 or visit www.ReaderService.com.

*Terms and prices subject to change without notice. Prices do not include applicable taxes. Sales tax applicable in N.Y. Canadian residents will be charged applicable taxes. Offer not valid in Quebec. This offer is limited to one order per household. Books received may not be as shown. Not valid for current subscribers to Harlequin Medical Romance books. All orders subject to approval. Credit or debit balances in a customer's account(s) may be offset by any other outstanding balance owed by or to the customer. Please allow 4 to 6 weeks for delivery. Offer available while quantities last.

Your Privacy—The Reader Service is committed to protecting your privacy. Our Privacy Policy is available online at www.ReaderService.com or upon request from the Reader Service.

We make a portion of our mailing list available to reputable third parties that offer products we believe may interest you. If you prefer that we not exchange your name with third parties, or if you wish to clarify or modify your communication preferences, please visit us at www.ReaderService.com/consumerschoice or write to us at Reader Service Preference Service, P.O. Box 9062, Buffalo, NY 14240-9062. Include your complete name and address.

MEDI7R

Get 2 Free Books,

Plus 2 Free Gifts—

just for trying the Reader Service!

HARLEQUIN *Desire*

THE RANCHER'S CINDERELLA BRIDE
SARA ORWIG

LITTLE SECRET RED HOT SCANDAL
CAT SCHIELD

YES! Please send me 2 FREE Harlequin® Desire novels and my 2 FREE gifts (gifts are worth about $10 retail). After receiving them, if I don't wish to receive any more books, I can return the shipping statement marked "cancel." If I don't cancel, I will receive 6 brand-new novels every month and be billed just $4.55 per book in the U.S. or $5.24 per book in Canada. That's a savings of at least 13% off the cover price! It's quite a bargain! Shipping and handling is just 50¢ per book in the U.S. and 75¢ per book in Canada.* I understand that accepting the 2 free books and gifts places me under no obligation to buy anything. I can always return a shipment and cancel at any time. The free books and gifts are mine to keep no matter what I decide.

225/326 HDN GMRV

Name	(PLEASE PRINT)	

Address		Apt. #

City	State/Prov.	Zip/Postal Code

Signature (if under 18, a parent or guardian must sign)

Mail to the **Reader Service:**
IN U.S.A.: P.O. Box 1341, Buffalo, NY 14240-8531
IN CANADA: P.O. Box 603, Fort Erie, Ontario L2A 5X3

Want to try two free books from another line?
Call 1-800-873-8635 or visit www.ReaderService.com.

*Terms and prices subject to change without notice. Prices do not include applicable taxes. Sales tax applicable in N.Y. Canadian residents will be charged applicable taxes. Offer not valid in Quebec. This offer is limited to one order per household. Books received may not be as shown. Not valid for current subscribers to Harlequin Desire books. All orders subject to approval. Credit or debit balances in a customer's account(s) may be offset by any other outstanding balance owed by or to the customer. Please allow 4 to 6 weeks for delivery. Offer available while quantities last.

Your Privacy—The Reader Service is committed to protecting your privacy. Our Privacy Policy is available online at www.ReaderService.com or upon request from the Reader Service.

We make a portion of our mailing list available to reputable third parties that offer products we believe may interest you. If you prefer that we not exchange your name with third parties, or if you wish to clarify or modify your communication preferences, please visit us at www.ReaderService.com/consumerschoice or write to us at Reader Service Preference Service, P.O. Box 9062, Buffalo, NY 14240-9062. Include your complete name and address.